Shawlworth Hall Estate, on the edge of Bodmin Moor, has been in the Stuart-Palmer family for five centuries. Now, due to death duties and mismanagement, the Hall, the village and six farms attached to it have to be sold.

But the new owner would make those centuries of gentlemen roll in their graves. Leroy Leonard, famed pop star of the early 1970s, with his penchant for hard living and animal activism, doesn't take long to make enemies of the villagers. Nor does it take long for his past to catch up with him.

Then, after months of heated disputes and increasing contempt on all sides, one Friday evening he calls a meeting. With friends and foes in one room, it is bound to get messy, but no one is prepared for what happens next. Leonard is found dead and all those in attendance have a motive – even Detective Inspector George Spring...

ONE TOO MANY

To Janice

Hope you enjoy the book
Howard.

ONE TOO MANY

Howard R Smith

ATHENA PRESS
LONDON

ISBN 10-digit 1 84401 880 6

ISBN 13-digit 978 1 84401 880 2

First Published 2007 by
ATHENA PRESS
Queen's House, 2 Holly Road
Twickenham TW1 4EG
United Kingdom

Printed for Athena Press

Dedicated to my late mother, Roselyn

Chapter One

Leroy Leonard leaned against the boundary wall surrounding the garden. He looked towards the village of Shawlworth and six farms, all of which were obscured by trees, and a lake in the huge frontage. Ten million it had cost to become lord of the manor, but the properties he received in return were well worth it.

He sighed. Sammy Smith, from a north-east grimy pit village, to Leroy Leonard, owner of a £10 million-paid estate in the middle of Cornwall bordering on Bodmin Moor. Thirty-five chart hits, fifteen number ones and umpteen song successes for other artists. Pop star of the late sixties and early seventies. He stood for a while admiring the view and only came back to reality when his wife joined him.

'Lovely or what, bonny lass?'

Catherine was his second wife: tall, blond and beautiful; the type of wife you would expect for a successful pop star. Catherine had once had a successful career modelling and had met him when she appeared on one of his early promotional films. They had been together for ten years, married for eight, with two children: Lee, a boy of six, and Pansy, a younger version of her mother, aged four. They stood together for a while before she replied to his question.

'Yes, I must admit,' she agreed, but deep down she felt that open spaces were best in small doses, like the two weeks she had spent at the beach every summer when she was a child. For the rest of the year, cities, plenty of action, nightlife and fashion shows were what she wanted. She drifted off into a daydream, remembering days of her life as a top model. One week New York, the next Milan, then Paris. Even after ten years dutifully caring for Leroy, she still longed for this lifestyle.

'Ha'way, pet.' It was her husband who brought her back to reality this time. He took her hand and they both walked to the front entrance of Shawlworth Hall.

It was a very imposing building, just as anyone would imagine a house of such size and history to be. Leroy looked at the ivy-clad frontage and once again compared the number of windows in his present home with the one he had grown up in, in the pit village. Looking up once again he enquired, 'How many bedrooms?'

'Twelve in the main house, five in the west wing,' his wife told him for the umpteenth time. 'The east wing doesn't count anymore, seeing as you are having the upstairs gutted and turned into your own recording studios and rehearsal rooms.'

They entered through the large double-glazed wood-framed doors into an imposing entrance hall, which seemed to disappear into darkness beyond a very broad staircase leading to the upper floor. Hand-carved stair rails, lined up on either side in regimented order, guarded a very expensive red carpet that covered each and every stair.

They went into the drawing room and he hopped onto one of the many armchairs dotted about the room. Catherine went to the window and looked out.

'What's for tea, hun?' Leroy asked, his legs stretched out before him.

'Quorn done in Hungarian goulash.' Her reply seemed distant as she looked beyond the large expanse of garden to the imposing Shawlworth Manor House. Small compared to the Hall, it was still a good-sized family house. This was now the home of the Right Honourable Antony Stewart-Palmer, his wife, Lady Vanessa and their daughter, Juliet.

I wonder how they feel, Catherine thought, to have been the proud owners for the last five hundred years of what was now all Leroy's.

When her husband had purchased Shawlworth in its entirety, part of the deal was that the Manor House and two acres of garden would remain in the possession of the Stewart-Palmers. This did not bother Leroy; he just could not understand why anyone would want to stay in the area, looking every day at what they had lost. He knew he wouldn't.

Never having found out much detail about the demise of the Stewart-Palmers, he was not sure what forced the sale, but from snippets of information gleaned from various sources he guessed that Stuart-Palmer's father – now deceased – had let the villagers' farms and local public house pay just peppercorn rents. The result had been that, over the years, obligatory costs on his behalf had continued to rise, while his income had not.

So, after his death, his son Antony was left with insurmountable debts and no one to turn to. His only option was to sell. It had come as a great shock to everyone in the village, but still the biggest shock had come to the Stewart-Palmers.

Chapter Two

That same evening in the Pheasant, the one and only public house in the village, the usual crowd of people had gathered to imbibe the local ale and gossip of the day with the ever-pleasant and rotund host, Albert Bolitho.

Albert had run the local for five years and was at last (in his opinion) being accepted by the local people, now that he was finally being privileged to the juiciest bits of gossip a lot earlier in the evenings, instead of eagerly shouting for 'last orders, please' in the hope that the pumps would flow just that bit longer.

Albert was thirty-eight, married and had worked in engineering from the age of sixteen until he was thirty-two when he had had a very bad accident at work. He had worked in the fitting shop of a large engineering complex that made compressed air equipment further south in Cornwall. One day, when pressure testing an air receiver, there was an explosion. Albert suffered from the loss of an eye and was in hospital for weeks with concussion after he was flung against a wall and received a severe head injury.

Albert was awarded very generous compensation and, not being able to continue in his trade, took the lease on the Pheasant and sunk his capital into that.

He was never going to make a vast fortune but, ticking over in the winter months with the locals and the large summer trade from passing tourists, he was doing all right.

'How long has he been in now?' That question came from John Penrose, the local gamekeeper at Shawlworth.

'*You* should be telling *us*,' retorted Albert. 'You work for the new owner.'

John looked intently at the half-filled pint glass, shuffled on the bar stool and said, 'True.'

'Well?' queried Albert, pulling another pint for a tall well-dressed gentleman who had just walked in the door.

Picking up the pint, he said, 'Cheers.'

Albert held out his hand. '£1.25 please.'

The gentleman drank long and deep. A small exhalation of air from his throat gave an interpretation of 'I needed that', before he placed his hand in his pocket and gave Albert the required monetary reward.

'Well?' repeated Albert, placing the money in the till and wondering if John was trying to eschew the question. Looking straight at John, he waited.

'True,' he reiterated, 'but I've never seen him.'

'You mean you work for someone you've never seen and you don't know how long for?' said Albert.

'Yea, that's about the size of it,' said John, having another shuffle on the bar stool.

'But what about your wages?' enquired the gentleman.

'When 'is Lordship sold up, he comes and sees me, saying the estate 'as been sold, it now has a new owner and paid me up to the end of the month. That was about three weeks ago, and I ain't seen anyone since.'

'So what are you doing?' Once again the question came from Albert, who by now was wiping down the bar.

'Just me normal job until I'm told hotherwise, but now tis near the end of the month and hoo pays me?'

'Go to the Hall.' This time the answer came from Reverend Peterson.

The Reverend always had one port and one pint of light ale. Sitting by the log fire, he hardly ever spoke; not that he was being unsociable but he loved to sit in the early evening with his flock, as he put it, listening for gossip or news of anyone needing his spiritual guidance.

The gentleman removed his coat, hung it on the back door, and returned to the bar. He was Detective Inspector Spring of the CID, based in Bodmin and residing in Shawlworth. The Detective Inspector and John Penrose were also, apart from living in the same village from 12 August onwards, working (or had been) very closely.

John made sure that everything was in order for the shoots, but the Detective Inspector organised them for the lords of the manor, making reservations and bookings, giving out peg numbers and, on the day, making sure everyone obeyed the rules – no low shooting, etc. – and that all weapons were up to standard.

It was very difficult at times to combine the two and obviously his police work came first, but the shoots were still a nice little earner – a very nice little earner. Up to now he had been very lucky that the two did not clash.

Everyone continued to stare at Reverend Peterson.

'Go up to the Hall?' said John.

'Go up to the Hall,' said the vicar.

'Go up to the Hall?' repeated John.

'Oh, for crying out loud!' This time it was Dr James. 'I think that's what he means, John.'

'But, Doc, I've never been up to the Hall all the time I've worked there.'

Dr James was at the end of the bar with his usual malt. He had been the local GP for the last twenty years. A man in his fifties, he had endeared himself to one and all. Although he had entered as a 'foreigner' from the North all those years ago, he had blended in a lot quicker than most.

He was a distinguished man: very short – five feet four inches tall – with grey hair, but he was tall among men, as everyone looked up to him in both medical and personal problems, one often encroaching on the other.

'Yes, but you are going to have to know where you stand,' he retorted.

'Suppose so,' John submitted and that was that, or so they thought.

'He's been there nearly three weeks.' This time it was a man who was a stranger to everyone present, but who had been once before to the Pheasant. He continued, 'There's him, his wife and two children.' By now the stranger had everybody's attention and none more so than the vicar's.

A hushed silence hung heavy; no one spoke. Only the hum of the beer pumps and the crackle of the log fire dared break the silence that was in evidence. Everyone looked at the stranger sitting on the opposite side of the fire to the vicar.

While the others were preoccupied with this news, Detective Inspector Spring, having been trained to observe the ways and mannerisms of people, paid more attention to the man.

He was in his late forties or early fifties and no stranger to some form of drugs by the look of his thin, drawn face and dark circles around empty pale blue eyes. His hand shook with nicotine-stained fingers, and Spring's police instinct told him 'grass smoker'. As he had on a short-sleeved pale blue shirt and no jacket, the Detective Inspector could see his bare arms, but there was no sign of a needle.

The vicar finally broke the silence with the question everyone was thinking. 'You are?'

'Farmer. Andrew Farmer.'

The silence flooded back, but it screamed at him, 'How do you know?'

Picking up on this silence, he continued, 'I'm the new gardener at Shawlworth Hall.'

They looked at one another. Who would ask first?

Albert, in the unwritten role of chairman, spoke. 'Well, I suppose the first thing we'd like to know is, who is he?'

Andrew not only looked old but felt old. He hunched his shoulders, drank from his half glass, then wiped his mouth with the back of his hand.

'Pop singer, heyday was late sixties, early seventies. Lots of hits, wrote many scores for other artists, quite a few number ones, thirty or so in the charts – made a bundle.'

Must have, thought Detective Inspector Spring, to have bought this lot.

'Will we have heard of him?' questioned Dr James.

'I don't know,' retorted Andrew. 'Will you?'

'Well, I might,' spat Dr James, somewhat agitated, 'if you told me his name.'

Detective Inspector Spring raised ever-so-slightly a bushy left eyebrow. Now why should this chap answer in the negative with sarcasm? His policeman's mind was working again.

'Anyway,' continued the doctor, moving away from the bar, 'I must go to the gents.' With that he left. He returned to the bar some ten minutes later. Albert was waiting on the other side by his empty glass. The doctor gave him a nod of approval and Albert did his duty.

'We know something you don't know,' sang John Penrose, mockingly.

'Don't be childish,' admonished the doctor.

John sank back into silence.

'I take it it's the name of our new metaphorical patriarch.' The doctor smiled at John and picked up his glass.

'Big-headed git,' whispered John into his glass.

'So who is the great monetary "pop" figure who has blessed us with his presence?' The doctor continued in the same vein as before his temporary absence.

Once again Albert became the unwritten spokesman. 'Leroy Leonard.'

The doctor paled, swayed ever-so-slightly, steadied himself with his left hand on the bar, coughed and mumbled, 'I'm sorry, I must go. I've just remembered I have a sick patient to see.' Without another word, he very quickly left.

Once again the Detective Inspector noticed something out of the ordinary; his gimlet eye missed nothing.

Chapter Three

The following afternoon, Reverend Peterson was doing his duty and calling on his flock. Once again, it was a bright crisp day with plenty of sun. Well wrapped up, he was enjoying life. Having walked a considerable distance while deep in thought, he looked around to get his bearings. A surprised look came over his face as he realised he had walked a lot further than he had intended.

How did I get here? he mused; the 'third eye' has been active today. Never mind where I am. Sunday's sermon, yes that's it, Sunday's sermon.

When out and about on his parochial duties, he often planned his Sunday sermon, but somehow today was different.

Why was that name coming and going in his thoughts? He was not a pop fan, never listened to it on the wireless and certainly never watched it on the television. He sighed. No matter, no matter.

'Good day, Reverend.'

He looked; a smile came over his face as he found himself at the gate of the two Miss Cawthornes. 'Dear Jane, dear Ruby, how are you both today?'

'All the better for seeing you, Reverend,' they answered in unison.

They seemed to do that quite a lot. It annoyed some people, but definitely not him. Identical twins, they had the same hair, same clothes, same spectacles… They were sixty-seven years old – and very sprightly for their age – and they had never married.

'Will you join us for tea?' This time it was a singular question.

Oh, God. The vicar's mind was working overtime. Who said it?

Looking at the speaker, he noticed no mole on the left cheek, so it had to be Jane. This was how he told the difference. Not many people could and when the sisters were out people would duck and dive out of the way, not because they were not well-liked – they were – it was just that unless you knew about the mole, telling them apart was nigh on impossible. 'Jane, that would be lovely, dear.'

She beamed at him because he always used their names and never got it wrong. Ruby also gave an approving smile.

Seated in the small but cosy living room, the three dutifully waited until the kettle sang. The tea was made in the best floral pot: a ceremonious tray, adorned with cups, milk jug, sugar bowl and spoon, was carried through from the kitchen and placed upon the table by the homemade cake and scones. It was given a satisfactory nod from the sisters and now they were ready. Firstly, Reverend Peterson received his, with no questions asked about how many sugars or milk, as this was a weekly occurrence that both sisters looked forward to. This week he was early, but as they always had things ready in plenty of time, this was not a problem.

Looking around the room, it never ceased to amaze him how many certificates and medals hung in abundance.

Who would have thought that two such refined and demur ladies were, when younger, the two top female rifle and handgun shots in the country? The rewards spanned from county level through to Bisley. In competitions they had also been known to leave top men in their wake, but pride of place went to the pair's handgun silver medal.

They saw the Reverend looking intently. Again they smiled and at once their minds went back to the good old days.

The first cup of tea was enjoyed by all, a second was poured and then it was down to the serious business of exchanging happenings and news. The vicar commenced.

'Well, dear ladies, last night, whilst partaking of refreshment in the local hostelry, we found out at last who our new landlord is.'

'Oh! Please do tell.' Once again they spoke in unison, both clasping their hands together in their laps. 'From the beginning. From the beginning.'

Getting himself comfortable for a fairly long stay, Reverend Peterson cleared his throat and began.

'There was John Penrose, Dr James, Detective Inspector Spring, Albert Bolitho (obviously) and myself, a few more of the regulars in the lounge bar and the usual younger patronage engrossed in the competition of darts and dominoes.' Having set the scene he continued.

'John enquired of us how long the new owner had been in residence. Albert said, "You should be telling us as you worked for him." John agreed, but according to him when the Stewart-Palmers vacated the estate he paid John up to the end of the month. As that was three weeks ago and it was now getting near the end of the month, how was he getting paid in the future?'

'Oh dear.'

'Shush, dear.'

The Reverend did not see who spoke first or answered, as he had his eyes closed.

'Anyway,' he continued, once again in full flow, 'I suggested he went to the Hall.' Amid approving nods from the ladies opposite, he ploughed on. 'It was at this point that Detective Inspector Spring hung his coat on the back of the door – or was it – no matter. This gentleman sitting opposite me, who I had seen once before in the lounge bar, said that he'd been there about three weeks. Well, as you can imagine, everyone looked and the next question was who was he, the next what he did and so on.

'Eventually it became clear that he is married to his second wife, two children, in his early forties and a huge rock and roll star of the late sixties, early seventies who is worth an absolute fortune.'

'Well, he would have to be, wouldn't he, to buy all this lot.' This time the Reverend was ready; no mole.

'Please be quiet, Jane dear,' admonished Ruby. 'Kindly go on, Reverend.'

'Where was I? Oh yes, the gentleman in question turned out to be Andrew Farmer, his new gardener. Dr James left to go to the, err, the gents toilet and, upon returning, discovered, as we had already, the name of the new owner.'

He paused and the ladies' eyes widened. '*Come on, come on, please.*' The waiting was killing them.

'Leroy Leonard. All of a sudden, Dr James said he had to leave and was gone out of the door like a cork from a champagne bottle. Speaking of which, dear ladies, I must depart myself.'

Looking at the clock and seeing it was 4.30 p.m. he realised himself that he must have been early. Not to worry. I don't want to outstay my welcome, he thought.

'Please stay, Reverend.' Once again two were sounding like one.

Why does that name bother me? Once again he found himself drifting away.

'Reverend.'

'I do beg your pardon.' Apologetically, he took their hands in his.

'Please stay.'

'I'm sorry, but I must go.' He left more troubled than he could explain.

'He seemed miles away,' said Jane.

'He did, didn't he,' agreed Ruby.

They set about clearing the table, carrying the crockery through to the kitchen and placing it in the sink. Whilst waiting once again for the kettle to boil, they looked out of the window. The evening shadows were starting to form but they could still see enough to appreciate the view.

The window looked out over a huge expanse of ground that formed a natural amphitheatre. In the distance, the Manor House stood to the left and, further into the distance, the outline of the woods hid the Hall from view. The kettle sang.

Chapter Four

Three months had come and gone. It was now a picture postcard summer, very hot weather, clear blue skies and thousands of tourists.

The village had settled back into its own routine, while Albert in the Pheasant had been on to the brewery a lot more times this year than last for supplies, due to a large increase in his tourist trade.

John was getting his wages on a regular basis; a man who he now knew so well as to call Andy brought them each week as regular as clockwork. He made sure that he was in the same place every Thursday, so Andy had no trouble finding him on the estate. He was always by the game bird runs, which he had looked after until even he admitted to himself that he just knew this was going to be the best shoot in many a long year. A good shoot also meant extra in the pocket because, if George Spring did well, so did he. Good old George always saw him right.

Detective Inspector Spring had taken over years ago when Antony said he couldn't run the shoot and take part as well. So, as the estate had no manager to speak of, George had volunteered his services on the clear understanding that it would not clash with his police work.

By now he had made contingency plans with John so that, if he was called away at the last minute, things could still run smoothly. But George always liked to be there; he arranged his annual leave so that he could. Open air, good company, a successful shoot; a perfect day away from police work. He was sure that's what kept him sane.

Andy was, of course, Andrew Farmer, the gardener, and today he was expected, so John was by the pens.

John heard tree branches being moved and twigs snapping underfoot. He pulled out his pocket watch, looked and smiled. Good old Andy, you could set your watch by him. Sure enough,

Andy came through the hedge – a shortcut he had found to get to John.

He handed John his wages and got him to sign the book. Then, once the formalities were over, he sank down onto a log, wiped his forehead and complained to John that it was far too hot.

'Get away with ee,' mocked John, ''tis boutiful.'

'It's all very well for you in the shade of the woods,' moaned Andy.

'Tellee what. Why don't you come down for a pint tonight with us. Wadee say?'

'Thanks all the same, I couldn't if I wanted to.'

'Why not?'

Once again Andy wiped his forehead. 'You know,' he said, 'that the boss went away some weeks ago while the east wing was being converted into his recording studio. I told you all this.'

'Yes,' nodded John.

'Well, it's finished and he's back tonight.'

Andy stood up, stretched, bid John farewell, thanked him for his offer of a pint and left.

Bit more news tonight, mused John; all the conversations lately had been about tourists. Everyone was enjoying the summer in Shawlworth – well, almost everyone. The vicar was still having trouble with Leroy Leonard's name and the doctor had gone very quiet indeed.

That night in the lounge bar, it was almost impossible to move. The bar, beer garden, children's play area and outside square frontage were also full of smiling people from various parts of the country and even some from abroad. With glasses in hand, toasting each other, Albert felt a little guilty that he was making so much at the expense of his regulars. But business was business. To compensate for this, he always tried to keep the corner nearest to the bar free for them. Most times he succeeded but tonight he was really pushing his luck to do so. The Reverend was there, as was John; Detective Inspector Spring had just arrived so if Dr James hurried it would be OK.

The doctor didn't show, so he didn't find out that the owner was back. One thing that nobody knew was that, although it was summer, storm clouds were gathering on the horizon.

Chapter Five

The last few weeks had been real heaven for Catherine Leonard. Now back in London, Leroy was away at the studios, discussing his new-found success since one of his old songs had been re-released and was at that very moment at number twenty-five in the charts. His record company and producer wanted to know if he had any songs they could release.

They had only been in Shawlworth for about three weeks, just getting settled in, when the phone rang. As Leroy was the nearest, he picked up the receiver, held it to the side of his head and yawned, 'Hello.'

'Leroy?'

'Yea, who's this?'

'Don't piss about, Leroy.'

'Stu, is that you?'

'Who else, my son, who else.'

Stuart Iveson was at his desk in his London office, the top A and R man for Singles, one of the biggest record companies on the scene. 'Leroy, my son, some good news for you.' Puffing on a large cigar, he yelped and began to rub his eye as it was stung with the smoke.

'You OK, Stu?' enquired Leroy.

'Sure! Sure! Listen, you know that record we re-released? Guess what.'

'It hasn't. Oh God, say it has.' Leroy's heart began to pound in the expectation that Stu was going to tell him that it had made the charts.

'It's made the charts,' Stu shouted down the phone.

'Yes, Yes!' Leroy dropped the phone and ran round in circles, punching the air.

Catherine looked at him and sighed. The last time she had seen him do that, his beloved Magpies had won their semi-final FA Cup match.

'We're in the charts, hun,' he sang to his wife.

She nodded towards the phone.

'Oh shit,' he said and dived for the phone. Stu sat patiently waiting on the line, still rubbing his eye.

'Stu, Stu, are you there?' questioned Leroy. 'Sorry about that, bonny lad.'

'Leroy, now just listen. Have you any previously unrecorded material?' asked Stuart. 'We want to put a new album out.'

'It just so happens I have. In the move, I came across some old scores that would do just great. All of it would be recognised as our stuff by all our old and now new fans,' Leroy said proudly.

'Great, baby, great. What I want you to do is get your arse back to civilisation. We can go over all the details, then get contracts drawn up and let's all make loads of moneeeeeey.'

'When do you want me? Tomorrow? Saturday? When?'

'You know it's going to take a few weeks to set up, don't you, so come Thursday and we'll take it from there. OK?' Stu was still rubbing his eye.

'See you Thursday,' chortled Leroy, as he replaced the receiver and turned to Catherine.

'What do you think?' he now questioned his wife.

'I think I'll look forward to a few weeks in London,' she replied.

Leroy frowned.

'What about the record?' Another question, but this time with no levity.

'Oh, the record.' Before she could go any further, Leroy was very close to her face and now angry.

'Listen, you stupid thick-headed cow, all this is due to me and all you can think about is a few weeks in London. If it wasn't for my music, there would be none of this.' Leroy waved his arm in a circle. 'No fancy clothes, no horses in the stables, no flash cars. So get your act together or you'll be like the other whore I married: out on your ear.'

He could see tears welling up in her eyes. 'Oh great, here come the waterworks. It won't work, bitch, you make me want to puke. Going to piss off back to mammy, are we? Tell us when, I'll help you pack your bags,' he taunted.

One day I will, you piece of north-east shit, she vowed under her breath, but not before I've killed you first.

That Thursday they were up early. The children were excited and the family was ready to drive to London. The atmosphere was a lot more convivial, but he had still not forgiven her for, as he put it, not being thankful for all she had and all she owed to him. They all got into the car just as Andrew Farmer came out of the summer house.

'Andy.'

'Yes, Mr Leonard,' he said in a subservient manner, which he hated.

'We're off to London for a few weeks. I want you to keep an eye on the builders, house, grounds, etc., until we return. Here's a cheque to cash at the bank for your wages and anything else you need, but I want receipts for everything, OK?'

'What about John Penrose?' enquired Andrew.

'Who the fu—' He stopped himself just in time, remembering the children in the back of the car.

'Your gamekeeper.'

'My what?'

'Your gamekeeper for the estate,' he replied.

'What do I want with a soddin' gamekeeper?' Leroy was getting agitated again. 'We'll sort it out when I come back. Find out what he earns, give it to him out of that and I'll sort it all out with the accountant when I come back.'

He handed over a piece of paper. 'That has the telephone number of where I can be reached in London, but only use it in a real emergency.'

Don't worry, the whole house could collapse with the builders in and I wouldn't phone you, Andrew thought to himself, but it came out of his mouth as, 'Very good, Mr Leonard.'

They were gone.

The journey to the capital proved uneventful and they arrived at their destination tired, with tempers fraying once again. The children, whingeing and hot, were hungry and needed the toilet, Catherine was sweating and trying to console them.

Leroy had been giving a lot of thought, not to his record and forthcoming album, but a gamekeeper. Me with a gamekeeper, he thought, having made up his mind that a gamekeeper was the last thing he wanted. As far as Leroy was concerned, a gamekeeper was not a person, married with children, like him. He was someone who shot foxes, birds and other animals classed as vermin. No, he was out with a capital O.

'Out you get. Come on, Lee, Pansy, out,' ordered their mother.

'Mammy, please,' cried Lee.

'Lee, get out or I'll kick your arse,' his father ordered and was in no mood for any arguments.

How refined, mused Catherine. 'Come on, darling, *please*,' she pleaded.

The children alighted from the car and stood on the pavement. They were outside a row of rather impressive houses, where trees lined either side of the road from one end to the other. They looked across the pavement, side-stepping the trees into a small front garden, and then to a communal front door for both the downstairs and upstairs.

They rang the upstairs bell to attract the attention of Mrs Mason, the widow who occupied the flat. Mrs Mason was aware of their impending arrival, but not of the exact time.

She had lived in the top flat a lot longer than the Leonards who had bought and lived in the ground floor flat. She and her late husband had lived there for many happy years, until he lost his battle with cancer.

Leroy rang the bell again. 'Come on, you old harridan,' he shouted.

'Shut up, Leroy.' His wife looked around, totally embarrassed.

'What's a harridan?' enquired Pansy.

'Shush, dear.' Catherine patted her daughter's head.

Unbeknown to them, the tall ladylike figure of Mrs Mason, in a black dress with hair that had clearly been professionally styled, was only the thickness of the door away. She treated the remark with the contempt it deserved. To her he was nothing but a coxcomb who would cozen his way to getting what he wanted. She opened the door.

'Hello, dear,' she said, looking at Catherine. Next came Lee and Pansy. 'And how are my favourite young man and lady?'

'Well, thank you, Mrs Mason,' Lee answered for both of them.

Leroy was totally ignored but that suited him.

'I've done as you requested, Catherine, opened the windows and put the hot water immersion on.'

'Well, take it off, it'll burn your back,' muttered Leroy.

'I beg your pardon?' It was a hard cold stare she gave Leroy.

'Nothing! Nothing!' he said, turning away.

'Thank you, Mrs Mason. It's good to see you again. It seems like years instead of a couple of months,' smiled Catherine.

Turning once again to Catherine, she asked, 'How is your new home? As picturesque and grand as you thought?'

'Oh yes,' agreed Catherine. 'But I still love this place, even though it would fit into the Hall about five times over.' She saw the irritated look on Leroy's face and took that as a cue to take her leave. She would catch up on the news later.

'Bye bye, dear. Oh, I put a few groceries on the table. I thought they would be of help.'

'Oh, Mrs Mason, you are an angel. I forgot all about that.' She gave her a thank you kiss on the cheek and followed Leroy, Lee and Pansy into the flat.

On closing the door, she saw Leroy in his favourite prone position.

'She heard you, you know.' Catherine looked at her husband accusingly.

'What do you mean?' He looked at her with a blank stare on his face.

'Harridan and that bit about putting the immersion heater on. "Well, take it off, it'll burn your back."'

'It's a joke.' Leroy tried to defend himself.

'*You* are,' she retorted.

'Look, don't start, and put the kettle on. I'm gagging.'

'Will I not burn myself?' she said.

'How?' Another blank stare.

'If I put the kettle on.'

'Oh, very funny,' he mocked.

Catherine left it at that. She was in no mood for another set-to with him. She switched the kettle on to boil and shouted through,

'It's on, I'm going for a shower.' Not waiting for a reply, she went out of the kitchen and along the hall to the bathroom. She went past the door to the bathroom into the children's bedroom; they were playing on the floor by the bunk beds.

That's how this episode had all started – bunk beds. Catherine had asked Leroy one day if he didn't think that the children were getting too old to be sharing a bedroom and, now his travelling days were over, that they needed a bigger place.

He totally agreed, to her surprise. 'Leave it to me and I'll fix everything,' he had said.

So that's how Shawlworth came about – bunk beds.

'Be good, children. I'm going in the shower and then it's your turn, OK?'

'OK, Mummy,' Lee said, again for both of them.

Catherine stood in the shower, the water cascading all over her body and the cracked tile. She looked at the tile; she was home again, but for how long?

Chapter Six

All too soon the days of seeing old friends, visiting old haunts, and seeing catwalks she had once graced had come to an end. How many job offers had she had? Ten, twenty, even after all this time and with two children. According to many in the business she still had what it takes.

'I'll give you an open contract.'

'I'll give you any salary, name it, it's yours.'

'Name your own price.'

The more offers she received, the more she hated the name of Leroy Leonard; if it wasn't for the children she would be gone tomorrow. This question had arisen once before, but she had been told that there was no way she would get the kids. Oh yes, she could fight him in court. But money talks and he had a lot more than her. He would get the best lawyers and fight her all the way and if, as far as Leroy was concerned, she managed the impossible, how could she look after two children with two broken legs and arms? That hadn't been a threat, but a 24 carat gold promise.

Mrs Mason had been more than kind, looking after the children when she wished. She couldn't ask *him*, and he had important work to see to. Anyway, it was her job to look after the kids.

On Thursday lunchtime they said their goodbyes to Mrs Mason, piled in the car and headed south-west.

It was a silent journey.

They drove into Shawlworth Hall at 4.30 p.m. Catherine looked at her watch. Leroy got out of the car; the breeze felt good but cold on the back of his sweat-soaked shirt. He stretched, looked around and, seeing Andrew Farmer, remembered about the gamekeeper and decided now was the time to start using his plenary power around the estate.

He whistled and waved Andrew over. 'Tomorrow I want you to take me to see this gamekeeper guy and give me a tour of the estate. Get all my receipts?'

'Yes, Mr Leonard,' sweated Andrew.

'You'd better,' he said, 'or I'll stop it out of your pay.'

You would and all, wouldn't you, you tight-fisted bastard, Andrew thought. I mean you only have about thirty million. Once again it came out as, 'I have, Mr Leonard.'

He gave Andrew a nod of dismissal and headed into the Hall.

'Nice to see you again, Andy. Isn't it warm,' Catherine spoke in passing.

Andrew's eyes followed her all the way to the door. He shook his head as if to clear it and asked himself what a woman like that saw in a louse like him. As he walked round the back of the east wing, the builders were just putting the last of the equipment into the van and were just about to leave when the foreman saw him.

Walking over, he said, 'All that extra sound-proofing he wanted is going to cost him dearly.'

Not as dearly as what some people would do to him if they got their hands on him, thought Andrew, but he left without a word, leaving the poor chap scratching his head.

Andrew wished now that he had taken up John on his offer of a pint that evening, as he could do with it. It would have got him away from Shawlworth, or the Hall at least. Andrew had been given the gateman's cottage at the main entrance of the drive. It had one bedroom, one tiny kitchen, one bathroom and one living room cum dining room, but it served his needs. He unlocked the door. It was lovely and cool in there and as he kicked off his boots the air felt great as it circulated his stockinged feet. Realising how badly they stank, he quickly had the socks off, wiggled his toes and went straight into the bathroom.

Don't know why they call it a bathroom, he thought. There's no bath. Just a toilet, shower and hand basin.

He turned on the shower, stretching out his left hand to close the door, and disrobed. He stood in the shower for much longer than he had first intended, but it felt so good. But it was electric and, of course, he had to pay for it.

Finally he came out, dried himself off, picked up his clothes and walked into the bedroom naked as the day he was born.

So what? I've got no one to be modest for.

Andrew whistled as he sorted out his clothes and started dressing.

'Isn't it funny how men always whistle the same song,' he said out loud.

God, he realised, I'm talking to myself now. First signs. Anyway, as long as I don't answer myself. He went from there into the kitchen and switched on the kettle.

'Now what's for tea?' I've done it again. Looking in the cupboard, there were tins but nothing he fancied.

What now? That's it, down to the village, go in the Pheasant, have a pint or two, see John, tell him our lord and master wants to see him, arrange a place and time for tomorrow, out to the mobile fish and chip van and then back for a spot of telly.

How could he stand all this excitement? He looked at his watch: 5.20 p.m.

Now what do I fancy from the fish and chip van? Decisions, decisions.

The hissing of steam and the click of the kettle switch brought him out of his thoughts, but he had just decided on fish and chips instead of patty and chips. He made a cup of coffee and walked into the living room, stopping to check if there had been any post.

There *is* someone who likes me? he mused, until he picked it up and saw it was a circular for 'Are you over fifty and insured?' He threw it down, sat in his chair and ruminated whilst the coffee cooled down. Having then slurped the last dregs, he again looked at his watch. It was five forty-five. Time to refine his plans.

Leave at six, get to the Pheasant by twenty past, nice walk, two pints; seven fifteen, mobile van; seven thirty, home for quarter/ten to eight; put on plate, salt, pepper, tea; settle for eight o'clock programme.

He went into the kitchen, rinsed out his cup – the kettle was still full enough – prepared a plate, cup and saucer, knife and fork, salt and pepper, tomato ketchup and a slice of bread and butter, covered with another plate.

At exactly six o'clock, he closed the door, locked it and set off for the village.

Behind the bar, Albert looked at the clock, bowed his head in defeat, turned to his wife and said, 'Quarter to six.'

It felt as if he had put in a full shift. They had been open since four thirty and already it was full, mainly of tourists.

She laughed. 'What's that got to do with the price of fish?'

He smiled back and mouthed, 'I love you.' She blew him a kiss and again everything was right with the world.

John Penrose had just come in with the Reverend. 'Evening, gents,' said Albert. 'Usual?'

Albert always took on extra bar staff in the summer to see to the tourists, so he could give his undivided attention to his regulars as and when required, and try to save the corner, of course.

'Yes please, Albert,' they both said.

'One port and pint for you, Vicar, and a pint for you, John. I've turned the coolers down a bit, hope it's not too cold.' A look of concern came over his face.

'I'll soon tell ee,' said John, raising his glass. Drinking long and deep, he put it back down.

'Albert, handsome just handsome.'

The only other person in was Dr James.

'Evening, Dr James.' Firstly Reverend Peterson, then John, cordially greeted the local practitioner.

'Don't suppose you've seen George Spring yet?' requested John to Albert.

'Not yet,' he replied. 'Nothing wrong?'

'No! No!' said John. 'It's nigh on short of two weeks to the opening shoot and I just wanted to confirm one or two things with him.'

The door opened and Andrew Farmer walked in; it was exactly six twenty.

'Hello, Andy.' John looked surprised. Andrew had been into the Pheasant a few times now, so was rewarded a greeting from the barman and the others. 'Thought you weren't going to come this evening,' he continued.

'I wasn't,' replied Andrew.

'Pint was it, Andrew?' Once again Albert was doing his duty.

'I'll get that,' said the doctor. People had noticed that he was back to his normal self again after a period of looking downcast and, some said, even worried. The Reverend had managed to forget his nagging problem too.

'Thank you, Doctor,' smiled Andrew, and carried on with his story. 'As I told you, John, he's back today. Anyway, he arrived about a couple of hours ago, saying he wanted to see you tomorrow morning. So, as I didn't know where you would be, I thought I would come down and arrange a time and place with you.'

'See me what for?' John looked puzzled.

'I don't really know,' said Andrew, 'unless it's to know who he has got working for him.'

'Oh yea, that's probably it,' replied John, but he wasn't convinced.

'So how about in our usual place at ten o'clock break time, then he can't accuse you of slacking off?'

'That suits me fine,' said John, none the happier.

'Andrew, may I have a word in private?' Dr James once again looked worried but did his best not to show it.

'Sure, Doc,' agreed Andrew.

The doctor took Andrew's elbow and guided him to the corridor adjoining the bar, where the toilets were.

'Andrew, this is a bit awkward really.' Dr James was being rather evasive, first checking that no one was within earshot and then speaking only in a loud whisper.

'Fire away, Doc.' Andrew spoke normally.

'No! No!' The doctor was waving his hands up and down, palms down. 'Please, keep you voice down.'

'Sorry,' said Andrew. 'Ahh! Doc, it's not about my habit, is it?'

'Habit, what habit?' The doctor was momentarily sidetracked.

'Grass? Smoke? Wacky baccy?'

'Oh no! You will be fully aware of the dangers without me telling you. No, your boss, am I right in thinking he's called Leroy Leonard, from the north-east of England, in his early forties, used to be in a group called Rock Express in the late sixties, early seventies?' He added silently, Please, God, let the answer be no.

'That's my boy,' Andrew replied sarcastically. 'How—'

Before he could ask any more of the question, the doctor charged away down the corridor and disappeared into the bar.

How did he know about Rock Express? thought Andrew. He stood for a while and then returned to the lounge bar, as he was getting funny looks standing outside the gents' loo by himself.

When he got back to the bar, Detective Inspector Spring had arrived and was in conversation with John, the Reverend and Albert.

Albert was the first to question Andrew on the whereabouts of Dr James.

'It's rather strange really. We went into the corridor, he looked around, made sure we were alone, whispered for me to keep my voice down. I jumped to conclusions what he wanted to ask me, but I was wrong.' He paused.

By this time, John and Detective Inspector Spring had joined Andrew and the Reverend at the bar with Albert. 'What was that?' Detective Inspector Spring had his copper's hat on again.

'Eh? Oh, er, nothing really. So he started asking me... asking me about Leroy Leonard, if he was from the north-east, pop singer, very big in the sixties and seventies. As soon as I confirmed it, he was away down the corridor into the bar and disappeared like a scalded cat.'

Very strange, everyone agreed, except the Reverend. Once again he stood with a puzzled look on his face.

Andrew asked for a refill. He looked at the clock: 6.50 p.m. Still in time, he said to himself.

For the remaining time Andrew had allotted himself, the conversation was of a general nature – small talk really – but they found it difficult to include the Reverend. From the look on his face, you did not have to be a trained police officer to know that the body was present but the mind elsewhere.

At 7.20 p.m. Andrew finished his pint, bid everyone a good and pleasant evening with the addition to John of 'Don't forget tomorrow, ten o'clock, usual place' and eased his way through the throng to the open air and the welcome fresh summer breeze. If he had turned before he left the lounge bar, he would have seen Albert once again performing his duty, George Spring questioning John and Leonard's assignation, John giving it plenty of thought and trying to formulate some beneficial conclusion, and the Reverend Peterson wondering why the name of Leroy

Leonard should once again trouble him so much. But, as he did not turn, he saw none of this.

Outside, there was a small queue at the mobile fish and chip van, so Andrew took his place. Whilst waiting, he caught sight of a group of young teenagers, causing, in the eyes of the village bobby, Police Constable Trevithick, a minor disturbance. If they did not behave, as he knew them all by sight and name, reports would be sent to their parents with a warning that, if there was ever a repetition of this behaviour, sterner measures would be taken.

After receiving verbal confirmation of their future actions that was of a satisfactory nature to the custodian of the law, they went upon their way and he upon his.

As he happened to pass the fish and chip van, he saw Andrew looking, smiled, winked and said, 'Little buggers.'

Now it was Andrew's turn. He duly placed his order, asked if it could be well wrapped as he was walking home, paid the required emolument, thanked them and headed for the gate-house. It was 7.35 p.m. Certain now that he would meet his allotted deadline, he was satisfied with himself at the disciplinary task he had set, and relished the reward of a plate of fish and chips, salt and pepper, tea, bread and butter and his beloved tomato sauce.

Chapter Seven

Friday morning dawned bright and sunny, accompanied by the dawn's early call of birds, the odd dog barking and people going about their daily duties.

Antony Stuart-Palmer awoke and checked the time: eight o'clock. He felt for his wife Vanessa and as she was not there, rolled over in bed. She was by the window.

'Oh! Darling, come back to bed, please,' he pleaded with his wife.

'No, it's time to get up anyway, sleepy head,' she said.

'You were looking across again, weren't you?' He didn't need an answer. 'Darling, you must accept things as they are. Staring at the Hall is not going to get it back – it's gone, finished, over. The longer you keep this up, the harder it's going to get and you are only going to make yourself ill. Shall we move away? You only have to say the word and we're gone. With the profit we made on the sale of the Hall and estate – although small – and the sale of this place, we should be able to find something really nice, to our mutual satisfaction. What do you say?'

She looked at her husband, tried to hold back the tears, but failed. He jumped out of bed, held her and tried to ease the pain.

'This estate has been in your family for hundreds of years. It is so beautiful in summer and winter and now it's gone. It's not fair,' she cried, with intermittent sobs.

The weeks that had passed had not eased his wife's pain at the loss of the estate. He had hoped that time would be a great healer.

'Should we move away?' he repeated.

'Oh no! I couldn't bear to be away from here. This is better than nothing at all. Sorry, darling, I'm being a silly fool. I'll try harder, I promise.' She wiped away the tears with her finger, kissed her husband and went into her dressing room. Actually it was more an offshoot to the bedroom, but a new lifestyle takes some adjusting to.

'Juliet's already left,' she called to Antony. 'She's taken Gladiator for an early morning ride. Just gone, held up both hands, fingers apart, so I assume she'll be back by ten.'

'Then come back to bed,' he called back.

'Sorry, darling, I'm up now,' she said apologetically.

He sighed, knowing that he might as well get dressed too. Antony was ready before his wife, after cleaning his teeth, shaving and dressing in a casual summer style consisting of thin fawn slacks, yellow short-sleeved shirt and brown casual shoes with fawn socks. 'See you downstairs,' he called loudly.

'OK, darling,' she replied.

In the kitchen, Mrs Pengelly, the cook, who lived in the village, was preparing the morning breakfast and singing softly to herself. As she was not what you might call a professional, she was rather hesitant at first to accept the offer. But as they understood that, and considering what they were prepared to offer, she had said yes.

She had come highly recommended as a good cook and had proved it over the weeks she had been employed. She was now in a working relationship that suited both parties. It was a good arrangement, hence the happiness in her work.

The only vestige of the former occupants left in the Shawlworth estate other than the Stuart-Palmers was Fielding, the butler. He lived in a small but cosy flat over the garage block and was also very happy, although nowhere near as happy as when they were all at the Hall in its heyday: Master Antony, as he was then, getting up to all sorts of mischief with the servants, and then the gardeners, then the grooms – everyone. Lavish parties, the shoots, the hunts and the hunt balls. Those were the good days.

He had started as a young boy and worked his way up and, although circumstances had totally changed, he still had his Master Antony.

He entered the morning room, but not until he had given the door a polite knock and heard, 'Come in.'

'Good morning, Sir. Your post and papers.' He placed them on the small antique table by the chair in which the Right Honourable Antony Stuart-Palmer was now seated.

'How are you this morning, Fielding?' he questioned.

'Very well, thank you, Sir.' He gave his customary reply.

'Fielding.'

'Sir.'

'Miss Juliet has taken Gladiator out for exercise. Could you please relay this to Mrs Pengelly and ask her just to make it a light breakfast – orange juice, coffee, toast, marmalade, that sort of thing, there's a good fellow.'

'If I may, Sir,' he paused, 'I have already spoken to Mrs Pengelly on that very subject, as I spoke to Miss Juliet before she went out. She told me of her intentions and said she would return by ten, so could she please just have a light breakfast.'

'Well done, Fielding. I don't know what we would do without you.' He looked at his trusty servant and smiled.

Fielding left. Placing his reading spectacles in position, he picked up the mail, glanced at each and every letter, found nothing that he regarded as of any importance and so went to his paper, the *Guardian*.

He read his paper until his wife joined him, when he folded it, smiled at her and said, 'How do you feel now, darling?'

'OK. Don't take any notice. As I said, I am just an old fool,' she replied.

'But I said if you want to…'

'Please, dear.' She held up her hand. 'Can we please change the subject.'

'Fielding spoke to Juliet before she went out and said about a light breakfast, so he sorted it with Mrs Pengelly.'

'He's a treasure,' she said, walking to her writing desk.

'Much on today?' he asked.

'No, not really. A meeting of the women's committee of the hunt ball,' she replied. The hunt ball! She panicked and spun in her chair.

'The hunt ball?' Antony looked at her and saw tears welling up again.

'The hunt ball, the hunt ball!' She was now nearly hysterical.

'Calm down, calm down.' He placed his arm around her shoulder. 'Now what about the hunt ball?'

'Where's it going to be held?' she pleaded.

He tried to think fast.

'Well, that Leonard fellow may allow it at the Hall.'

'But you don't know.'

'No, I know I don't, but he might and if not, well, there's, there's the village hall.'

'The village hall! You cannot be serious, Antony. After centuries at Shawlworth Hall, we can't hold the hunt ball in the village hall. No, you will just have to go and see this, this, Leonard chap, explain the situation to him and demand the ballroom at the Hall.'

'Couldn't someone else hold the ball?' he asked hesitatingly.

'Antony, if you are not going to treat this seriously,' she retorted.

'But I am, darling,' he tried to convince her.

'The hunt balls have always been at Shawlworth and Shawlworth it will be.'

He could tell by the finality in her voice that as far as she was concerned, the matter was closed. He wasn't so sure. From the few dealings he had had with Leonard over the sale, albeit in a solicitor's office, there was something about the man he just did not like. 'Let's have breakfast,' he suggested. 'You can think better on a full stomach.'

They went into the dining room, where Fielding was patiently waiting.

'I'll bring the tea and coffee, Sir. Good morning, your Ladyship.'

'Good morning, Fielding.' It was not her usual tone to the beloved servant.

'Come on, darling, it's not his fault,' Antony said. 'Is it?'

'No, you're right, I'll apologise to him when he comes back.'

Upon Fielding's return, she said guiltily, 'I'm sorry, Fielding.'

'My Lady?'

'I'm sorry for the way I spoke. Please accept my apology. Yes, it *is* a good morning.'

'Thank you, my Lady.' He bowed slightly. 'Will that be all, Sir?'

'Thank you, Fielding.'

Once Fielding had departed, they set about having breakfast, but no culinary enjoyment came from it, for he was as concerned for her as she was about this wretched hunt ball. They had just finished breakfast and rung for Fielding when they heard the slamming of a door. The breakfast had turned out a leisurely affair as both had been deep in thought.

'That must be Juliet,' Vanessa said, turning to the door and waiting for the young twenty-two year old, auburn-haired, beautiful, vivacious young lady to come bounding in and greet them with 'Good morning, Mother.' Kiss. 'Good morning, Father.'

But it did not happen. Another door slammed. The door did open, but it was Fielding.

'You rang, Sir?'

'Yes, Fielding. Was that Miss Juliet who came in then?' he enquired.

'Indeed, Sir. She ran past me, and headed down straight into the drawing room. Is anything amiss, Sir?'

'I don't know, Fielding,' he replied, 'but I intend to find out.'

Both he and Vanessa headed for the drawing room. Upon entering, they found their only daughter lying on the settee face down, but they could tell she had been crying.

'Whatever is the matter, darling?' Her mother had reached her first.

'Oh, Mummy,' she cried, flinging her arms around her mother's neck.

Her father waited patiently.

'Darling, is it Gladiator? Is he hurt?'

She shook her head.

'Have you had a fall?'

Again she shook her head.

'Then will you please tell me what the problem is,' her mother urged.

'Well, I took Gladiator out for his exercise. We went across the moors, I gave him a break, walked him for a while, then started back. It was about nine fifteen by then and I decided to come back skirting the village, have a look at the Hall and then come through the woods, to return home that way. By the time I got to the woods it was nine forty. I had just entered them when I saw two men in front of me.'

Both parents looked at each other and, with a horrible feeling in their stomachs, allowed their daughter to continue.

'When they heard Gladiator they turned and watched me approach them. I did not want to have anything to do with them, so I broke Gladiator into a trot to go straight past, but they just stood blocking the path. I had no alternative but to pull him up. "May I please go past?" I asked of them, but received no reply. They just stood smoking that horrible stuff.'

'What horrible stuff?' Her mother could keep silent no longer.

'Weed, Mummy. Pot.'

'How do you know it was that?' her mother said, surprised.

'Oh, Mummy, I haven't...' Juliet quickly replied. 'So they just stood there smoking,' she continued. 'By this time I must admit I was getting a little scared, but I wasn't going to let that smarmy pig see that. The one at the side never spoke, but the other one – the smarmy one – said to me that he liked what he saw as I came trotting towards them; especially the way my breasts bounced up and down. Only he said T-I-T-S and that he could think of a much better way to make them bounce.'

Her father ran his fingers through his hair.

'I again asked him to step to one side but again he refused. The other man could see I was getting scared and was really embarrassed by the whole thing. He then asked me if I wore a bra to make them bounce like that. I did not reply but raised my crop to hit him. He said, "Don't even think about it or I'll have you off that horse, wrap that crop around your neck and really make you bounce." The other man at this point stepped over, pulled his arm and said, "Come on, we're going to be late." The other man looked at me, laughed and moved over.'

'Was that it?' said her father.

'Yes,' she replied.

'Right, give me a description, I'll get straight on to Police Constable Trevithick. You can tell me what they looked like, clothes, etc., and I'll relay it to Trevithick.'

'Just one thing he said,' she remembered.

'What?'

'Well, as I rode off, he said get out of his woods and don't come back unless I wanted seeing to.'

'He said *my* woods? You're sure he said *my* woods? Did he have iron grey hair in a bit of a ponytail?' he asked.

'Why yes, do you know him?' His daughter looked perplexed.

He didn't answer her. Instead he picked up the phone and dialled a number.

Catherine Leonard was going about some of her daily duties, one of which was to try and keep the children amused. She wasn't succeeding.

The phone rang.

She walked over to it, lifted the receiver and said, 'Shawlworth Hall, Catherine Leonard speaking.'

'Mrs Leonard, how do you do. My name is Stuart-Palmer, Antony Stuart-Palmer. May I speak with your husband.'

'I'm sorry,' she said, not knowing whether to say Sir, your Lordship, my lord… How *do* you address a right honourable? So she just carried on. 'He's out on estate business and I have no idea when he will be back.'

'Will you please tell him I shall call on him at eight thirty this evening? Goodbye.'

The phone went dead.

She replaced the receiver and returned to the children.

Antony Stuart-Palmer stood looking at the phone.

'Was that him, Father?' Juliet was now a lot calmer.

'Oh yes, darling. That was him all right.'

Her mother took her up to her room, made her lie down, promised her some tea and said she must have a sleep. Juliet did not argue.

Chapter Eight

Andrew Farmer lay in bed, hand behind his head. He was not looking forward to today – he didn't know why, he just knew. The feeling of foreboding he had about today would just not go away.

He looked at the clock – it was eight o'clock. Throwing back the duvet, he got out of bed with the greatest reluctance.

All he wore was a pair of boxer shorts, but he had still felt the heat of the night.

Yawning, he went into the bathroom, urinated, cleaned his teeth and showered. After drying himself, he went back to the bedroom as he was, having no one to be modest for.

He dressed, looked in the mirror – no, his hair did not need combing – and he walked towards the kitchen.

During the night he had hoped that some kind fairy had come in to clean the kitchen and wash up all the crockery. Outside the kitchen door he closed his eyes, made a wish and went in.

He opened his eyes.

Damn! No fairy had been. There was a cup, a plate and a knife and fork, just as he had left them. He looked with disgust at the congealed grease and dried tomato sauce. Turning his back, he switched on the kettle – still enough water in – got a mug out of the cupboard, spooned in coffee, milk and sugar and waited. Having finished his coffee, he realised it was time to go and face whatever the day had in store for him and others.

Arriving at the door of the Hall just before nine, he rang the bell.

Catherine came.

'Hello, Andrew. He won't be long, just powdering his nose.'

'No problem, Mrs Leonard, I'll just wait here,' said Andrew.

'Fancy a coffee?' she asked.

'Just had one, thanks,' he replied.

'Well, as I say, he won't be long.'

It was nine fifteen when he finally showed and they left.

They only got as far as the stable block. Leroy turned into one of the empty stalls, sat down and ordered Andrew to do the same.

Leroy pulled a green 2 oz tobacco tin from his coat pocket, prised off the lid and offered one of the contents to Andrew.

'Here?' Andrew said, looking around.

'Good a place as any,' shrugged Leroy.

Andrew took one and waited for Leroy, then they both lit up. There they sat, inhaling the smoke deeply and hissing through their teeth as they did so.

They sat for a while, before rising and heading for the door, making sure no physical evidence of their presence remained. They walked through one of the lower pastures and onto the path through the woods. Andrew looked at his watch: 9.35 a.m. Plenty of time, he thought, if we go my way to meet John.

They ambled along as the smoke from their 'specials' began to take effect.

'Let's have another,' said Leroy.

Andrew, to his shame, didn't argue. Once again the tin was opened, one each removed and lit, and that's when they heard the horse. They turned around and saw this beautiful girl riding towards them – she looked great astride the horse in her long boots, fawn jodhpurs, and white wool roll-neck jumper that clung to her upper body like glue. A safety helmet and crop completed her outfit.

The horse trotted towards them.

'Will you get a load of that.' Leroy's eyes lit up.

'Leave it.' Andrew was cautious.

'Bollocks' was the response.

After a while Andrew felt that things were getting out of hand, so he stepped over, grabbed Leroy's arm and said, 'Come on, we're going to be late.'

Leroy moved over, still smiling; the girl took no further telling and moved off. Leroy pulled away from Andrew and shouted after her to stay out of his woods unless she wanted seeing to. He turned to Andrew. 'Know what I mean, kid?' winked Leroy.

Andrew knew exactly what he meant; the girl had now disappeared.

'Her loss,' said Leroy, taking another long draw on the 'special'. Andrew was sure that Leroy believed what he had just said.

When they arrived at the appointed meeting place, John was there; hearing them he looked up.

Andrew broke the ice. 'John, this is Mr Leonard, the new owner of the Shawlworth estate. Mr Leonard, John.'

'How do you do, Sir.' John, holding out his hand, waited for a response. None came.

'How do I do what?' laughed Leroy.

God, why did we have to smoke them things, thought Andrew.

'Sorry, Sir?' John was thrown.

'Nothing! Nothing! Down to business. I believe you are the estate gamekeeper. What do you do?'

John looked at Andrew and he mouthed behind Leroy's back, 'Tell him.'

'Well, Sir, I rear the birds for the shoot, look after the deer, look out for poachers, keep down the rabbits and other vermin.'

'Like?' Leroy's head was on one side and he was far from steady on his feet.

Once again John looked at Andrew. 'Go on,' Andrew mouthed.

'Like foxes, badgers and the like,' John mumbled.

'Like foxes, badgers and the like,' repeated Leroy. 'Well, what if I told you I like foxes and badgers, eh!'

'Yes, Sir.' John could not think of anything else to say.

'What are these?' he said, looking at the runs.

'For the birds, Sir. We bring them on in here to keep them safe from the foxes and when ready we turn 'em out in the moor for the shoot.'

'So let me get this right; you lovingly rear these birds, then turn them out on the moor just so some rich, boss-eyed, buck-toothed arsehole can blast them with a shotgun?'

No reply.

'I asked you a question,' Leroy snarled at John.

'Yes, Sir,' John agreed.

'Yes, Sir,' nodded Leroy.

The 'specials' were taking their toll.

Andrew shrugged his shoulders at John.

They were now back to foxes and badgers.

'Not so many badgers as foxes.' John tried to ease the tension that was building.

There was a long pregnant silence, finally broken by Leroy. Turning to Andrew he said, 'When's he paid till?'

'A week today,' replied Andrew.

Still looking at Andrew, Leroy continued, 'Where's my receipts I told you to keep.'

'I've got them, Mr Leonard; I told you I had them.'

'I want them,' he said warningly.

He turned back to John. 'Right, bonny lad, this is the score from now on. Firstly you dismantle these pens PDQ, you let the birds go – there are to be no more animals to be killed on this estate. Secondly, if there are any traps or nets, they are all to be removed and no more of the deer to be killed. Understand!'

John could not believe what he had heard.

'But, Sir,' he gasped, 'what about the shoots? The Shawlworth shoots are talked about all over the country, not just here. They come from far and wide to take part. They start shortly, everything is arranged.'

'Watch my lips,' said Leroy. 'There-are-no-more-shoots-cancel-them-give-them-their-money-back. Are these shoots your number one concern?'

'Of course, Mr Leonard.'

'Well, think about this then. There is no game or fowl for shooting on my land, so no game means no gamekeeper.' He held his hands palm up and shrugged. 'Be at the Hall next Friday at 7.30 p.m. and, depending on how my orders are carried out, we'll see whether you have a job or not. And one other thing, no job no home.' Once again he turned to Andrew. 'Let's go,' he said and off he went.

'I'll come down to the Pheasant tonight, John. Be there,' whispered Andrew hurriedly.

'OK.' It was an automatic answer.

'Are you coming or what?' Leroy shouted over his shoulder. Andrew sprinted and caught up with him and they walked along in silence. They covered a lot of ground of no interest to Leroy, until he came to the back of the two Miss Cawthornes' cottage. He saw the natural amphitheatre.

'Oh yes! Ideal for open-air pop concerts or what?'

'Are you sure about that?' questioned Andrew.

'Look at it, dickhead, it couldn't be more perfect. Right, we'll have to find out about the local by-laws. Rubbing his hands together, he could already see thousands of people, a huge stage, top-class groups – but guess who topped the bill.

'Whose is that cottage?' he enquired of Andrew.

'I don't know. I've seen two middle-aged ladies going in, identical in every way, but I don't know their name.'

'I hope they're deaf,' said Leroy.

'That's not a very nice thing to say,' reprimanded Andrew.

'Well, you know what I mean,' replied Leroy. 'The decibels will be off the counter when I get this lot set up. What time is it?' he queried.

'Ten past eleven,' said Andrew.

'Let's go a visitin'.' Leroy was still under the influence.

They made their way over to the back of the cottage.

'Should we not go to the front?' said Andrew.

'Bollocks.'

Ruby and Jane were in the kitchen and saw the two men coming across to the cottage from the back, which was highly unusual.

'Strange, dear.'

'Very strange, dear.'

They continued to look at the two men.

Hopping over the back fence, the one with the ponytail knocked on the kitchen door. Miss Ruby Cawthorne opened it.

'May I ask why you are coming to our home this way? Normal people use the front door,' she scowled at him.

'Who says I'm normal?' he replied.

'Please state your business and then leave my premises.' Miss Cawthorne was equal to him, or so she thought.

'May I correct you, dear lady.' Leroy had suddenly become very polite.

'Oh, in what way?' They were now verbally fencing.

'In answer to your two-part question, firstly, I will state my business and secondly, these premises are mine, not yours. You only lease the cottage from me.'

The penny dropped.

'Very well, Mr, er, please state your business,' said Ruby.

'Leroy Leonard,' he replied.

'Please state your business, Mr Leonard,' Miss Cawthorne again requested.

'Come to the Hall next Friday at seven thirty in the evening.'

'Why ever should I do that?' Miss Cawthorne said, wonderingly.

'Because by then I will be in a better position to answer any questions you have about my plans.'

'I can assure you that your plans are no concern of mine. I have no interest in them in any way, shape or form. I bid you good day,' she said.

'Hold fire, don't get excited. Let me explain. You live here, there's a natural amphitheatre, ideal for my pop concerts.'

'Your what! My dear sir, are you mad?' Miss Cawthorne swayed back. 'Pop concerts, here in Shawlworth? You *are* mad! I have never heard of anything so ridiculous in all my life.' She was joined by her sister. Leroy thought he was seeing double.

That baccy was stronger than I thought.

'Don't forget, ladies, seven thirty next Friday night. I'll also tell you how much rent you have to pay.'

'Come away, Ruby dear. It's obvious the man is deranged.' Jane, overhearing the conversation taking place, came to her sister's side.

The door was closed and the bolt shot home. Leroy stood shaking his head.

'Pity, a great pity,' he sighed.

Is he at last showing compassion to a fellow human being? wondered Andrew.

'They're not deaf.' Once again Leroy laughed. Andrew did not reply.

'What time is it?' he again asked of Andrew.

He didn't have to answer, as the church clock began to strike twelve.

'Right, I have work to do in my studio for tomorrow. I've got a top sound engineer and four session musicians coming down. Hey, still in the charts, eh! Good, eh! Listen,' he continued, 'they are arriving at about lunchtime. As soon as they come, show them up to the Hall. I'm cutting a new album. I found some stuff when we moved; go down great.'

'Yes, I know you are still in the charts,' he stammered. 'And a new album too, very good.'

'You OK? You've suddenly gone very white,' he said.

'Fine, fine. It must have been them "specials". Look, if it's OK by you I'll go for lunch now.' Andrew looked away.

'Sure, sure. Look, if you don't feel well, take the rest of the day off, OK, and I'll see you later,' said Leroy. 'I'll find my own way back. Can't really get lost in my own back garden, can I.'

He walked away, leaving Andrew staring at his back; Andrew went off at a tangent and headed for his own little sanctuary.

Catherine heard the front door. It must be him, she thought. It was twelve thirty.

'Leroy, want any lunch?'

'Depends on what is on offer,' he shouted.

'You can starve first,' she replied.

'I love you too, dear,' laughed Leroy.

'You had a phone call earlier on.'

He popped his head around the door. 'Who?'

'The Right Honourable Antony Stuart-Palmer.'

'What did that poxy git want?'

'Leroy, the children,' she said, looking at Lee and Pansy.

'Sorreee.'

'He didn't say, just asked for you and when I told him you were out on estate business he said would I tell you he would call at eight thirty this evening.'

'He's welcome to come. Doesn't mean I've got to see him.' And with that he was gone.

Chapter Nine

It was early Friday evening. With the weekend off work for most villagers, there should have been many smiling faces and justly so, but in the corner of the Pheasant lounge bar a huddled group stood in whispered conversation. It started with smiling faces, three, non-smilers two. It rapidly went to five–nil for the non-smilers.

The only parts of the day's events John Penrose left out were the 'specials' and the confrontation with the young lady on the horse. The rest was told in graphic detail.

'So let's get this right.' Detective Inspector Spring held up both hands, spread the fingers on his left and started to point with the forefinger of his right. He spoke very slowly to allow John's news to sink in to each member of the group. From left to right of the customer side of the bar were John Penrose, Reverend Peterson, Dr James and Detective Inspector Spring, with Albert Bolitho making up the number from the other side of the bar. Apart from John, who had had an extra eight hours to think about things, the other four thought first that it was a joke and in very bad taste to boot. When convinced he was not joking, it was still very hard to believe.

'One,' began Detective Inspector Spring, 'no more shoots, and all pens to be dismantled, birds to be set free. Two, no more shooting of foxes, rabbits, etc. Three, no traps or nets of any description. Four, anyone, *anyone* caught will be prosecuted to the full level of the law. Five, no trespassing on his land.'

'That's it,' confirmed John.

'You yourself, how do you figure in this?' Albert spoke on everyone's behalf.

'Simple: no game, no gamekeeper. If I carry out his instructions to the letter, and to his full satisfaction, I have to see him next Friday at seven thirty to find out if I still have a job. But he also said no job, no cottage, it's up to me.'

'Did you not tell him that the first shoot is already planned and settled, monies paid – the lot?' Detective Inspector Spring looked worried.

'Course I did. All he said was tough, give them their money back, as there are definitely to be no shoots on his land. But that's only part of it.'

'How do you mean? Surely there cannot be any more?' This time it was the Reverend's turn.

'Wanna bet?'

'God, it's getting worse all the time,' said Albert.

Dr James was not hearing much of this. He never spoke but, from personal experience, ever since his conversation with Andrew Farmer in the corridor, he knew the sort of man they were dealing with: scum, filth, and subhuman filth at that.

'What do you think, Doc?' Albert looked at Dr James.

'Sorry?'

'John's news. What do you think?'

The doctor put down his glass; his diminutive stature rose.

'Scum, subhuman filth. If I had a gun, I would shoot him in a place in his anatomy where it would take him hours to die, writhing in agony.'

'That's a bit strong, Dr James.' The Reverend Peterson shook his head.

'Who do you mean?' said John. 'For a moment I thought you meant me.'

'No, no, please, John. I mean that piece of human filth at Shawlworth Hall.' He could not even say his name. 'He's an animal, scum, vermin…' The doctor's voice began to rise. 'He's, he's, he's putrefaction personified.'

'Doc, Doc, calm down,' said Detective Inspector Spring.

Once again the doctor ran from the public house.

'Well, what do you make of that?' Albert was aghast. No one said anything, so John went on with his next piece of news.

'When Andrew and Leonard left me, like you lot, I just couldn't believe it. I thought, has this just happened or am I dreaming it? Andrew whispered to me, "Be in the Pheasant tonight." I thought he might have showed by now. So the rest of the day has been like a daze. I tried to explain to him about the tradition and success of the Shawlworth Hall shoots, but he just didn't want to know. It was his now – no one else's, his – and if they did not like it, tough. Great for Christmas and no job.'

'Have you told your wife, John?' enquired the vicar.

'Course, and before anyone asks; how do you *think* she feels? Possibly no job, no home. We've lived 'ere all our lives. Where would we go or live?' John was frightening himself now, so he shut up.

The clock said seven.

Detective Inspector Spring thumped his glass down hard. 'Won't listen? By God, he'll listen to me.' He headed for the door.

'Where you off now, George?' asked Albert. 'You haven't finished your drink.'

'Where do you think?' he said. 'Shawlworth Hall now and he'll listen.'

'If you see Andrew, tell him I'll wait here for him.'

'I want you to all wait until I get back. I shouldn't be more than a couple of hours at the most. Oh, is that OK with you, Reverend?' he asked, as he knew the Reverend liked to be away.

'Under the circumstances, yes, dear boy.'

'If I see Andrew, I'll tell him OK, John.'

'Cheers,' was the reply.

Detective Inspector Spring was gone.

'Well, there's not a lot we can do now until he comes back,' said John.

'I'll go and see poor old Mrs Verron and spend some time with her, but I will be back for nine,' promised the Reverend.

'Well, that leaves thee and me, JP.' Albert tried to cheer John up a bit. 'Hang on, I'll only be a minute.' A thought had just come into Albert's head. He left John at the bar and walked over to his wife. They were engrossed in conversation for two minutes, before Albert returned to John at the bar.

'That's all settled.' Albert looked pleased. 'Tomorrow night I've got Tommy Curnow standing in for me, so as I can take Trish to Carn Brea Castle for a meal. Why don't you and Linda come with us? My guest. It'll make a break from all this.'

'Thanks very much. I'll ask Linda and let you know tomorrow. Very good of you both.'

'No problem,' smiled Albert.

'Carn Brea Castle, where's that?' plied John.

'Near where I come from.' Albert began to explain. 'Camborne, out the village, pick up the southbound A30, keep on that road until you nearly get to Redruth. Then you hit the new bypass, well… don't take the new bypass, keep to the old A30.' Albert came up for air.

Wish now I'd never asked, John said to himself.

'Go through Redruth, follow the old road, past the old Barncoose hospital on your left, Rounding Walls, through Illogan, past the old beam engine on your left, the old Flamingo Ballroom on your right, into Pool. That's now a superstore.'

'What is?'

'The old Flamingo Ballroom.'

'Oh!'

'Once you go down the bank in Pool you come to crossroads. Turn left.'

'God, if you're not hungry when you set off, you will be by the time you get there,' mused John.

'Anyway, turn left, go past the Sir Humphrey Davy Stone plaque on your left – he invented the miner's safety lamp, you know – keep going, go past the old John Heathcote factory, Carn Brea Station on your left, follow the road sharp right, up, sharp left over the main railway line down to the T-junction. If you turn right that takes you to Brea village. You turn left, follow the road round to the right, up the bank, through Carnkie village, left at the top along the road, and there you are, Carn Brea Castle.' Albert was pleased with his route, which is more than could be said for John.

Detective Inspector Spring was not a happy man. The closer he got to Shawlworth Hall, the angrier he got. Five generations of Shawlworth shoots out the window. His shoots, famed all over by the shooting fraternity, gone. Not if I can help it, he thought.

His pace quickened as the gates of the Hall came into view. Andrew Farmer sat outside his cottage, strumming his acoustic guitar. The wind being in the right direction, George Spring heard it while some distance away. By the time he got to Andrew, he realised that the same tune was being played over and over again.

'Andrew, how are you?' George greeted him as he came through the small gate at the side.

'So, so.'

'I've heard about it in the Pheasant off John. That's why I'm here.'

'You haven't heard the half.' Andrew stopped playing. 'It gets better.'

Detective Inspector Spring was once again more worried than angry. 'Better? Look, I've come to sort him out. John's waiting for you in the Pheasant. Why don't you pop down and have a jar. I'm coming back to the Pheasant as soon as I can.'

'Yea, OK. I forgot about John, but I will go down. Tell you the rest of the news when you get back.'

'See you later, then,' George said, walking towards the Hall.

'Mr Spring?'

George turned.

'Good luck. You're going to need it.'

'Thanks, Andy.' Instead of walking on, he came back. 'Look, Andy, you know I'm a copper and I can smell what you have been doing apart from *that*.' He pointed to a cigarette end lying at his feet. 'So please be careful in future. Be more discreet, because if I catch you again I will nick you.'

'Sorry, Mr Spring.'

'OK, Andy. Remember, inside your own four walls.'

'Good luck,' repeated Andrew.

'No sweat,' smiled George, and this time he did walk up to the Hall.

Leroy Leonard was in his favourite position, sprawled out in an armchair.

'Tomorrow, about lunchtime, I've got session musicians arriving and a sound engineer. They'll need some lunch and they will be here for two and a half to three days. Of course they'll be staying at the Hall, you silly mare. Where else are they going to stay?'

'Ask a civil question,' breathed Catherine.

Before the conversation got any further, the front door bell rang.

Leroy looked at his watch. It read 7.30 p.m.

'Can't be Lord Haw Haw, he isn't due until eight thirty.'

The bell rang again.

'Answer it then,' he ordered Catherine.

'What's the matter with you? Are you paralysed?'

He lifted himself out of the chair, scowled at her and headed for the door. Good job I'm in a good mood, he was thinking to himself.

He opened the door; he had already seen the man standing there through the glass panel, but did not recognise him.

'Yep.'

'DI Spring.'

'No, I'm Leroy Leonard.'

'Detective Inspector Spring, smart-arse.' He could have done without this start.

'Catherine,' he shouted, 'it's the police. You haven't been overcharging the bishop at the massage parlour again, have you? I always said you gave good value for money.'

'It's you, Sir, I wanted to see.'

'Me?'

'You.'

'You had better come in then.'

'Thank you, Sir.'

'The name's Leroy.'

'Very well. Mr Leonard.'

They went into a room full of boxes, with tapes, music, speakers, amps, microphone stands and everything connected with the music business.

'Rubbish, all getting slung.'

'There still has to be some money's worth there, surely,' said Spring.

'Who's counting? How can I help?'

'John Penrose.'

'John Penrose, John Penrose… Oh, the gamekeeper chap. Has something happened to him?'

'No, nothing like that, Mr Leonard.'

'Look, Inspector, I don't want to be rude, but I have an appointment shortly, so if you could get to the point – please.'

'Certainly, Mr Leonard. The game bird shoots that start on August 12th.'

'What's that got to do with the police?'

'Nothing really.'

'Look, Inspector, you've completely lost me. Could you please get to the point.'

'For several years now, I have organised the shoots for the Shawlworth estate. Tonight in the Pheasant, John tells me you informed him this morning that there were to be no more shoots on Shawlworth land. This has been a tradition for—'

'Yes, yes, I know all that. He told me this morning.' Leroy was starting to get annoyed. 'Look, my land.'

'Yes, Mr Leonard.'

'So I can do as I please on my own land, yes?'

'Yes.'

'So what is your problem?'

'The problem is that the first shoot has been organised, fees paid and everything signed, sealed and left for us to deliver.'

'Not my problem.'

'Would you not allow us to hold the shoot for this season and then stop? You only took over about six weeks ago, were here for three, and then gone until last evening.'

'I'm not stopping you from holding your damn shoot. What I said was you were not holding it on my property.'

'But there is nowhere else.'

'As I said, not my problem.'

Detective Inspector Spring, for the first time in many a blue moon, was losing. This was not a good guy, bad guy situation.

'What if we were to pay?'

'You *are* joking.'

'No.'

'Look, I've not long paid nigh on ten million quid for this place. Not peanuts, but it hasn't broken me by any means. So do I need what… one hundred, two hundred? Behave yourself.'

'May I ask a personal question?'

'Go ahead. Doesn't mean to say you'll get an answer.'

'Why are you so against the sport?'

'Sport? Sport? You call that sport? Blokes beating the ground, shouting, whistling, frightening the crap out of some poor little bird to make it fly and then some git stood there with a gun ready to blast it out the sky. Look, sod off. NO! NO! I'll tell you why,' he stormed. 'I was a raggy-arsed kid from a north-east pit village, grimy terraced houses, out the front door straight onto the pavement and a lovely view from the back. We used to stand for hours watching the sun go down over the slag heaps. Wake on a morning and hear the birds coughing. My grandfather vowed that, unlike him, my father would never go down the pit, and he never did.

'The only other job my dad could get was working in an abattoir. As a kid, me and my brother never said, "What's it like working there, Da?" What did I do, though, when I left school? Got a job with my dad.

'I'll never forget my first day and the carnage I saw, ankle-deep in blood – a smell that's impossible to describe – and the cries of animals everywhere. Animals being strung up, blokes waiting, my dad included, for their animal to come along. Thump! In goes the knife, rip down, out spills the guts, my dad wipes away the gore and waits for the next one. That's the first time, Mr Spring, I cried for my dad. Hides being ripped off carcasses. Do you want me to go on? Young lads like myself washing the shit off tripe.'

'I think I get the picture.' Detective Inspector Spring knew he was up against it. He was used to trussing up a case; now he was being trussed up.

'I vowed from that day that not one piece of meat would cross my lips, and it never has. I stuck the job for one day, then left and got a job with a building firm. So whether you like it or not, there'll be no shoots or killing of animals in any way, shape or form on my land. Got it?'

'You are bringing about the end of an era.'

'I've spoilt your nice little earner, but the answer is no, no, no.'

Detective Inspector Spring was in trouble.

'By-laws.'

'Sorry?'

'How well up are you on local by-laws?'

'Depends on what it concerns.'

'Noise.'

'Could you please explain?'

'Out and about today with Farmer, we came across a part of my land that would be absolutely great for open-air pop concerts.'

'You're mad.'

'That's the second time today I've been told that. Two old biddies who looked exactly alike also said it.'

'You mean the Cawthorne sisters? How does that affect them?'

'It's round the back of their cottage.'

'But you cannot do it, not in Shawlworth. Thousands of teenagers running riot.'

'My lawyer thinks I can.'

'I'll fight you all the way over this.' Detective Inspector Spring was now getting angry. 'You haven't been here five minutes and already you've put a man out of a job, stopped decades of tradition, and now, if you get the go ahead, you are going to stage open-air concerts.'

'Who said coppers were thick?' Leroy replied.

'Don't get smart.' Detective Inspector Spring was now like a wounded tiger. He wanted to lash out, both verbally and physically.

'Times change, Mr Spring. March with them.'

'We are a quiet backwater village and that's how we want it to stay.'

'As I said, times change.'

'I'll fight you and so will the rest of the village.'

'May the best man win.'

Detective Inspector Spring was now livid. 'One step out of line, Leonard, one step. I don't care how much money you have, I'll get you. I'll have you in the nick in Bodmin so fast your feet won't touch the ground.'

'Are you threatening me?'

The doorbell rang.

Chapter Ten

'How did your meeting go, darling?' Antony asked of his wife.

Evening meal at the Manor House was finished and the Stuart-Palmers were winding down after the day's events. Firstly the morning and the trauma of Juliet, and Vanessa's meeting in the afternoon to discuss the future of the hunt. The latter was not of such great importance as his daughter's welfare, but as he knew the outcome of this morning, that is why the question was asked.

'Antony, it was a disaster. No blame was laid at our door, but a few "ifs" were put forward. If we hadn't sold the Hall, if better provision had been made. I told them we had no choice but to sell. Oh, they were understanding, but where was the hunt ball going to be and, as I was organiser, it was up to me to organise it.'

'Not the best of days,' bemoaned Antony.

'It looks as if this year is going to be as bad as last year.' Once again Vanessa started to cry.

Being a 'gentleman' and knowing what had transpired that morning to his daughter, he decided that, once he had seen Leonard, he would inform the police. But not before he had taught him a lesson he would never forget. He was no aristocratic fop.

'I'm going to see that animal. Will you be OK until I get back?'

'Please Antony, don't cause any bother. Leave it to the police; go and see George Spring.'

He did not answer because he knew he could not promise to keep his hands off Leonard.

'Antony. Promise.'

Again he did not answer, just left the room and went for his coat; it looked like rain for the first time in many a long day. Hate was something he could not remember feeling with this intensity before. This was a deep burning hate; if he got his hands on the scum he probably wouldn't stop.

Walk slowly; calm down. Antony set about disciplining himself as he headed for Shawlworth Hall for the sake of Vanessa and Juliet. For the first time, his face broke into a slight smile as he thought, I wonder, once I have finished with him, if I should ask if we could have the hunt ball at the Hall, of course not forgetting to say please.

The closer he got to the Hall the calmer he got and by the time he pressed the doorbell he was totally calm.

The door opened.

Once again Catherine was not sure how to address him. This time it seemed worse, face-to-face rather than over a telephone.

'Please come in. I'll tell my husband you are here.'

'Thank you. I take it you are Catherine Leonard. Antony Stuart-Palmer.' He held out his hand. She took it and shook it warmly.

Charming, absolutely charming, he thought.

'Please wait here,' she summoned. 'My husband has someone with him, but I am sure he'll see you.'

She turned her back and walked to a door, knocked and went in.

'What?' Leroy was not a happy man.

'Antony Stuart-Palmer to see you,' she said. 'You knew he was coming.'

'Show the twit in.'

Detective Inspector Spring raised his eyebrow. 'Do you wish me to leave?' he offered.

'Please yourself, but I shouldn't be long with this pillock.'

Antony Stuart-Palmer entered. 'Mr Leonard, George, how nice to see you.'

'Antony, nice to see you too.' Turning to Leroy Leonard, he said, 'I'll go.'

'No, please stay. It might be for the best.' Antony caught George in mid-stride.

'That OK with you?' he asked of Leroy.

'Make yourself at home,' he gestured.

'Mr Leonard, I won't beat about the bush. Were you on the woodland path this morning with a companion around nine forty?'

'What's this, question time?'

'Please, Mr Leonard. This is very serious.'

'OK, so I was on the path with Andrew Farmer, my gardener; so what?'

'I thought so. And did you meet a girl on a horse?'

'Look, it's my land and what I do on my land is no concern of yours.'

'Did you meet a girl on a horse?' Antony repeated the question.

'As a matter of fact I did. Fine young lady.'

Detective Inspector Spring began to feel uneasy. The conversation was leading up to something and Antony was getting more and more angry.

'That young lady was my daughter,' spat Antony.

'Oh.' Leroy paled somewhat.

'If you ever say anything like you said to her again, or lay a finger on her, so help me God, I'll kill you.'

'Careful what you say, Antony.' Detective Inspector Spring cast a friendly warning.

'George, he passed a lurid remark about her chest and virtually asked her for sexual intercourse, only not so politely.'

'Antony, do you wish, before we go any further, to lodge a formal complaint? If so, I will caution Mr Leroy.'

'Hey, come on, it was only a bit of fun.'

'I would not call sexual harassment harmless fun.' George Spring was now winning.

'If you hadn't been here, George, I was going to knock his head off.'

'Not worth it on scum like him to get charged yourself,' answered the Inspector.

'Oh great, welcome to my home,' said Leroy, but he was sweating.

'Well, as I said, do you want to lay charges against him?'

'No, no, not this time. But once more and I'll swing for this low life.'

'Just tell her to keep off my land and there's no problem.'

'Don't worry, she will. And by the way, George, he was smoking drugs,' said Antony, before he turned and left.

'He should have laid charges, you filth.'

'Don't matter how nice you are to me, you're still not getting your shoots. Now if that's all.' He walked to the door. 'Are you going anywhere near the Pheasant?' enquired Leroy.

'As a matter of fact I am. Why?'

'Tell the landlord I'll be down to see him at ten o'clock in the morning.'

Leroy pulled open the door; his wife was standing outside.

'Goodbye, Inspector. I'm, I'm sorry.' She held her head in a downcast manner.

'For what, dear lady?' He placed his hand on her shoulder. 'We cannot be blamed for falling in love.'

'Piss off.' Leroy was back to his normal self. 'Be here next Friday at seven thirty. There's a good cop.'

'Why?'

'Because all you in the village have got away lightly with rent up to now, so I can give you a nice new rent card. Bye.' He walked away.

In the lounge bar, Andrew Farmer had joined Albert, John and Reverend Peterson. The conversation was only about one subject and when Andrew filled them in about Juliet, and Jane and Ruby Cawthorne, the anger was at a very high pitch. The door opened and Dr James walked back in.

'OK, Dr James?' Albert looked worried.

'Fine! Fine! Thank you, Albert.' The doctor looked embarrassed.

'Doctor, how did—' started Andrew.

'Please, no more questions regarding Leroy Leonard. There is something I have to do first, but after that all your questions will be answered about that piece of filth. Just give me time.'

No more direct questions were put to Dr James, but the conversation about Leroy still prevailed, until George Spring returned.

'Well?' It was John who spoke, but everyone wanted an answer.

'Not good, not good at all. I nearly ended up arresting him.'

'Why?' asked John.

'As you all know, my main reason for going was to explain the situation about the shoots. I was also going to ask, on behalf of John, how safe his job was.'

'Thank you, George, I appreciate that.' John reached out and patted George's arm.

'The bottom line is that the shoots are definitely out. When I asked him why, he said it went back to the first job he had had working in an abattoir with his father. He never forgot the carnage he saw and has never eaten meat since, and as a direct comparison with the shoots, how could anyone in their right mind call it sport when a group of men beat the ground with sticks just to make birds fly and then others wait with guns to blast them out of the sky?'

Albert secretly thought he had a good point.

'He then went on to say about the pop concerts at the back of the Cawthorne sisters' cottage and that's when I, to my shame, blew it. I threatened that, even if he blew his nose the wrong way, I'd have him in the nick so fast his feet wouldn't touch the ground. That's when the doorbell rang and who should come in but Antony Stuart-Palmer. From there it was all downhill. What Antony had to say you wouldn't believe.'

'We would,' said Reverend Peterson. 'Andrew told us.'

'Oh yes, you were there.'

'To my shame,' admitted Andrew.

'Antony threatened him. I thought he was going to kill him. Anyway, how did you know it was Juliet?' Detective Inspector Spring looked at Andrew.

'I didn't know who she was at the time. I just found out when I was telling them,' he said, looking round at the assembled group.

'I asked Antony if he wanted to press charges for sexual harassment,' said Detective Inspector Spring. 'He said no, but if ever there was a next time he – Antony – would swing for the lowlife that Leonard was. Just before he left, he said Leonard was smoking drugs.' He looked at Andrew but never mentioned his name.

Andrew turned bright red.

'His final words were for you, Albert.'

'Me, what have I done?'

Albert's face changed. Now he looked worried.

'Didn't say. All he said was, if I was coming anywhere near to the Pheasant, could I tell you that he was coming here at ten o'clock in the morning. Oh, and I have to be at the Hall next Friday night at seven thirty.'

'I wonder what he wants with me?' sighed Albert. 'If your experiences with him are anything to go by it's not good. Shit! Oh, sorry, Reverend.' Albert looked apologetically at the Reverend.

'Not at all, dear boy,' he said.

For the last hour, the not-so-happy band tried to make light of things.

'Reverend, you'll never find your way home from here this time of night,' said Dr James.

'I do believe you are right, Doctor,' he replied. In his mind he asked himself, Why, oh why, Leroy Leonard? His self-examination was intensifying.

John Penrose felt deflated, beaten.

Dr James knew whom he was dealing with and knew what he had to do.

Albert was putting on a brave face for his customers, but was a worried man.

Andrew also hated the personage of Leroy Leonard.

Detective Inspector Spring was angry with Leonard and himself.

In the lounge bar that evening, the presence of Leroy Leonard hung like an omnipresent cloud.

The Right Honourable Antony Stuart-Palmer left Shawlworth Hall a very angry man; angry with that lowlife Leonard, but also with himself. "By the way he smoked drugs." He couldn't believe he had said that to George in the manner he did. He had gone to Shawlworth Hall with the sole purpose of knocking Leonard's head off; the last person he had expected to see there was George Spring. Good job really, under the circumstances. To say that, though, sounded very childish.

He walked home rather quickly, as he didn't know if it was going to rain or not, and anyway he had to vent his anger some way, so setting himself a punishing walk was as good a way as any.

By the time he arrived home, he had calmed down somewhat.

'How did it go, darling?' Vanessa looked anxious.

'George Spring was there.'

'What was George doing there?'

'Now you come to mention it, I don't really know.'

'So what happened?'

'I told him to stay away from Juliet, he told me to keep her off his property and I replied that that was fine by me. Basically that was it, then I left.'

'I don't suppose you mentioned about the hunt balls?'

'Darling, I cannot believe that you have just asked me that. How in heaven's name, after what has gone on between us and him, can I ask, "Oh, by the way, can we still hold the hunt balls here?" I was only concerned about Juliet.'

'So am I, Antony, but the hunt balls—'

'Vanessa, I am sick and tired of hunt balls. Our daughter had to suffer harassment of the worst kind and all you can concern yourself with is these blasted hunt balls. It's time you got your priorities right.'

'How dare you! How dare you even think such a thing. That I would put the hunt balls before my own daughter.'

'Look, I'm sorry. Please don't let us fall out over him. You'll just have to find a different venue. I'm sorry but you will.'

'I could kill him for being the arrogant pig he is.'

'Join the queue.'

'What do you mean by that?'

'Nothing, darling, nothing,' he replied.

'George, can I have a word, please?' said Albert. He had called last orders ten minutes ago and people were drifting away, but not fast enough. 'Ladies and gentlemen, please, I have my licence to think about. Will you please drink up and go. Thank you.'

'Anything special, Albert?'

'Please, George. Wait, eh, as a favour.'

It took a further five minutes to finally clear the lounge bar and Albert got a confirmation from his wife that the bar was empty. She added, 'Goodnight, George – I'm going up, luv.'

'OK, petal, won't be long. Just a quick word with George.'

'I know your quick words,' she laughed.

'Goodnight,' said Detective Inspector Spring.

Albert shot the bolt home in the door and returned to the bar.

'Drink?'

'Go on then, just a half.'

'Naw, have a short.'

'OK. Rum and black, thanks.'

'Cheers.'

Albert supplied the drink and leaned on the bar.

'Now, how can I help?'

'Well, after what we were told about the shoots—' said Albert.

'There are no shoots and that's it.' The rum tasted good.

'What are you going to do?' Albert looked concerned.

'What can I do? I am just going to have to write to everyone, explain the situation and give them their money back. I could kill that man.'

'I might be saying that after tomorrow morning.' Albert hadn't forgotten; he now reached out to the optic. 'No, after you and John had told us what happened, of course I gave it thought – a lot of thought – about how it will affect the village. But as I was rummaging in the drawer earlier on for a pen and paper, to show John how to get to Carn Brea Castle, I saw an old programme for the hunt ball.'

'Go on,' said George.

'Well, it came to me about half an hour ago: if he's not going to allow shoots, he's certainly not going to allow horses and hounds galloping all over plus the danger of a pack of hounds catching a fox, is he!'

'Oh my God, the hunt.' George felt sick. If the shoots were important they paled into insignificance compared to the hunt.

Shawlworth Hunt is the Mecca of the hunting season, he thought, and the balls! The balls! Where are the balls going to be held?

'So when you mentioned Antony Stuart-Palmer was at the Hall, association of thought…'

George felt his throat go dry.

This cannot be happening, think, nothing was mentioned about the hunt tonight at Shawlworth. Antony doesn't know.

'Albert, can I use your phone please?'

'Sure.'

'Thanks.' George's nervous finger dialled the Manor House.

'Antony Stuart-Palmer speaking. Who is that?'

'Antony, it's George Spring.'

'George, if you've just rung to ask if everything is OK, could it have not waited until morning?'

'I'm sorry,' said George, 'but it's more serious than that.'

'It's George Spring, dear. Says it's serious.'

George heard Antony talking to Vanessa.

'What's that animal done now?' spat Antony.

'Why I have phoned is,' began George, 'did you know that Leonard has stopped all shooting and killing of animals on his land?'

'He's what?'

'There are to be no more game shoots on his land.'

'But he cannot do that,' shouted Antony.

'He can, I'm afraid.'

'Darling, wait please.' George heard Antony talking to Vanessa again.

'It's been tradition at Shawlworth for generations. He can't do it.' Antony was really shouting now.

'So has hunting,' said George.

The penny dropped.

'Darling, are you all right? George, George, what's happened?' It was Vanessa.

'Is he OK?'

'Yes I'm fine.' Antony was back. 'Has, has, he told you?'

'Not about the hunt, but about the shoots. How I found out was when John Penrose told us and I went up to see him. That's when I bumped into you.'

'Well, thanks for letting me know. I suppose I shall have to see him again.'

'Sorry about the news,' said George, after further disclosures.

'Not your fault, George. Goodnight.'

Antony replaced the phone in the receiver.

'Will you please tell me what is going on,' begged his wife.

'I think you had better sit down,' he said gently, guiding her to a chair.

'For God's sake,' again she begged for an answer.

'As you know, that was George Spring. He has just told me that today John Penrose, and then this evening George, was told by Leroy Leonard that there was to be no more shooting or killing of animals on his property. That's where he met Juliet this morning – on his way to tell John that he wanted all pens dismantling, all traps and nets removed and no more killing of animals. If he didn't do it, he would be out of a job, so no job, no home.'

'The man's insane, totally insane.' Vanessa could not believe it. 'He just cannot do this. We must stop him at all costs.'

'How, darling?'

'I don't know, but we will. He cannot just come here and wipe away centuries of tradition. It's part of our lives, part of our history. No, he just cannot do it.'

'Darling, listen,' Antony interrupted.

'No, I will not. We must stop him.'

'Vanessa, for once please listen.'

'Go on then. What's more important than this?'

'The hunt, my darling.'

'What are you talking about the hunt for? We are talking about the shoots.'

'Oh please, darling. No shoots, no nets, no traps, no killing of animals in any shape or form.'

'You, you cannot mean…'

He nodded.

'No, that's too ridiculous even to think about.' She shook her head.

'Darling, yes. Do you think for one minute he's going to allow horses and hounds all over his property to catch a fox?'

'Antony, please.' Once again Vanessa was crying. 'Oh please, Antony, do something. To lose the hunt ball, now the hunt, and the shoots. Oh no! No! I'll kill him first.'

'Relax, darling, please. If there is anything that we can do, I don't know what it is.'

'But all those hounds, they'll have to be destroyed.'

'Darling, I'll do everything in my power to stop him. I promise,' vowed Antony.

Chapter Eleven

Albert Bolitho had a very restless night. He went through the motions of going to bed, but knew he would not be able to sleep.

'What did George want, love?' Trish asked as soon as Albert came up.

'To tell me that Leroy Leonard was coming here at ten o'clock in the morning.'

'What's he want coming here?' His wife lay in bed reading a book by one of her favourite authors.

'Search me,' Albert pondered.

Ever since George had told him, he felt the sword of Damocles over his head. Following his accident, Albert was prone to violent headaches when stressed out. His head was throbbing now; one of the worst he had ever experienced.

'Bad head again, pet?'

'You'd better believe it,' he replied.

'There's some of your pills in the drawer there,' she said, pointing. 'At least you've got tomorrow off.'

'Eh?'

'Tommy Curnow, Carn Brea Castle… remember?'

'Oh yes, sorry, Trish.'

Albert took a pill.

'The shit is really hitting the fan,' he said.

'How's that? What's happened?'

'Wait till I get ready for bed and I'll tell you all about it.'

Trish went back to her book and read about six pages before Albert joined her in bed. 'Spill the beans,' she said, slamming closed her book.

'Just a minute, Trish.' His head was bursting. 'Put the light out, please.'

Darkness enveloped the room and eased Albert's head.

'I'll start at the beginning,' he said, adding, 'I know you have gleaned bits here and there but I'll go through the lot.'

For the next half-hour, Trish heard about Juliet Stuart-Palmer's encounter with Leonard and the part Andrew had played. Then she heard about the meeting with John Penrose and what he had been told; then the meeting with Ruby and Jane Cawthorne later in the afternoon; how Detective Inspector Spring had gone to the Hall when he found out about the fracas; the arrival of Antony Stuart-Palmer and all that had transpired; the strange behaviour of Dr James over a period of time and what he knew about Leroy Leonard but refused to say. Finally, he told her how George had phoned Antony Stuart-Palmer about their feelings on the hunt.

'And that, my love, is about it,' Albert concluded. 'Oh, I nearly forgot. Both Dr James and George threatened him. Dr James wanted to kill him in a slow painful manner. He shocked everyone with that.'

'How does he know about Leroy Leonard?' Trish looked puzzled.

'I haven't a clue. He refused to say. All we know is he called Andrew into the corridor by the gents, told Andrew to keep his voice down and then asked him if his boss was called Leroy Leonard, from a group called Rock Express, and did he come from the north-east of England. When Andrew said yes to all three questions, Dr James, not for the first time, made off like a scalded cat, through the bar.'

'Very strange,' exclaimed Trish.

'I'll tell you something else that is odd as well.' Albert's head felt a lot better. 'About Reverend Peterson.'

'Reverend Peterson?' replied Trish.

'Every time that you mention Leroy Leonard's name, Reverend Peterson can be talking away and, as soon as he hears it he seems to drift off as if he's on another planet. I don't know if anyone else has noticed,' he said.

Someone had: Detective Inspector Spring. He had formulated quite a lot by now. What did Dr James know? Why was Reverend Peterson so worried? He knew why John was worried, why he himself was worried, and he also knew Albert was worried. And as for the poor Cawthorne sisters… He knew why Antony hated him so much and if there was any truth in the adage that looks can kill, with the looks he saw Catherine give Leroy he should be well and truly dead by now.

Trish was now worried because she concluded that, although she had never met Leroy Leonard, she did not like him. She knew the others, knew they would not lie. So why did he want to see Albert?

'Albert.'

'Hmmm.'

'You asleep?'

'Nearly.'

'Listen.'

'OK!'

'This Leroy Leonard. He cannot chuck us out of the pub, can he?' Trish was worried.

'No, we have a lease on this place for as long as we want,' he said.

'We must have a fixed term though.'

'Trish, we have a ninety-nine-year lease, so don't worry.' He squeezed her hand, 'There's no way he can get us out of this place. Do you think I would have sunk all our money in this place if I wasn't sure?'

'Phone the solicitor please, for my sake.'

'OK, I'll phone him first thing Monday morning.'

'So what does he want to see you for, then?' she asked.

'I don't know.' Albert was also worried, but tried not to show it. 'Perhaps he just wants to have a look round, see what he owns.'

'He doesn't own me.' Trish was indignant.

'I know that, love,' he laughed.

'It's not funny, Albert.'

He knew only too well it was not funny.

'Do you still want to go to the castle?' she asked.

'What castle?'

'Carn Brea.'

'Of course, we're taking John and Linda.'

'Oh yes, I forgot about them.'

'He's not spoiling our evening.'

'It won't be the same though, will it, what with poor John and Linda and possibly us in for some bad news.'

'Look, let's cross that bridge when we come to it.' Albert tried to comfort her, but who would comfort him?

Albert awoke next morning; his head was thumping once again. Still half-asleep as he thought through that day's schedule, he began to remember what had been worrying him. Oh yes, Saturday, Leroy Leonard, ten o'clock. He looked at the bedside radio alarm – the red figures of 7.27 glared back at him.

It had been one of those nights where, the harder he tried to sleep the worse it was. When he eventually went into a restless sleep, the last time he could remember looking at the clock it read 2.53 and the red dot was lit to signify a.m. 'Oh God,' he groaned. 'Four and a half hours kip.'

Trish stirred.

'You go back to sleep, love. I'll see to things this morning. Have a lie in.'

'No fear,' she said. 'That pub is going to gleam when he comes this morning.' She was out of bed before Albert.

'Oh God,' he moaned again.

Trish went to the bathroom. Another pill, thought Albert, and then ten minutes extra in bed.

He must have dozed off again, for the next thing he knew Trish was saying, 'I'll go and do some breakfast.'

'What time is it?' Albert rubbed his eyes.

'Seven fifty-five,' she replied.

Albert reluctantly climbed out of bed, stretched, yawned and headed for the bathroom. Head not too bad now, he thought.

Trish busied herself in the kitchen preparing breakfast whilst waiting for Albert: fresh orange juice, toast, tea and two eggs boiled for exactly six minutes.

'Breakfast ready,' she shouted.

'About five minutes,' he replied.

She placed the eggs in the boiling water. They had a hurried breakfast that morning and went straight into the public bar.

'Morning, Jenny.' Trish and Albert greeted the cleaner. Jenny had worked for them for the last four years, so she now had her own key for the back door.

'Morning, Mrs Bolitho, morning, Albert.'

Trish had said many times, 'It's Trish, not Mrs Bolitho,' but she always said the same, so Trish had given up some time ago.

'Pick up the morning paper, Jen?' Albert asked.

'Sure did, in the bar.'

'Good girl.'

'We haven't time for papers, Albert, I want this place spick and span before ten o'clock.' Trish was already polishing the bar.

'Something special on?' Jenny was curious.

'The new owner is coming at ten,' Albert said.

Jenny wanted to ask what he was coming for, but knew it was none of her business.

'Heard some rumours about him.' Jenny had news of her own so looked pleased.

'Oh? What's that then, Jenny?' Trish spoke.

'Jane and Ruby Cawthorne were sayin' he's mad. They were tellin' Joan Blake in the village shop how they had to go to the Hall next Friday night to find out more about open-air pop concerts and how much rent they were going to have to pay. Joan just listened, but thought they must have got their wires crossed somewhere, because no one else had heard of rent payments or pop concerts in the open air. Never.' Jenny was now in full flow. 'Joan prides herself on being the gossip hub of the village. If anyone would hear, she would hear first.

'Well, Joan said to me she hadn't heard anything, so the poor old dears must be mistaken. Anyway, when I came out of the shop I bumps into Mrs Pengelly, his Lordship's cook, on her way up to the Manor House and she says that there had been some bother with Miss Juliet and that there new owner of the Hall, Leroy Leonard. She did not know what but from what she could gather it was something he said to her while she was out ridin' her 'orse Gladiator.'

'I wouldn't listen to gossip, Jenny.' Trish tried to make light of it but she knew enough to know that Jenny was not far from the truth.

'What time's Tommy Curnow coming?' She changed the subject.

'Should be here for ten thirty,' Albert answered. 'We should be finished with Leonard by then.'

'Oh good.'

If there was bother, Trish didn't want Tommy involved.

'Fancy a coffee, Jenny?' Albert asked, knowing that Jenny had been hard at it since about seven thirty.

'Oh that would be lovely, thanks, Albert.'

'You, love?'

'No thanks. I want this place finished,' she replied, not even looking up from her task.

'Come on, ten minutes is not going to make much difference.' Albert tried to get her to slow down a bit.

'Go on then. You make it and me and Jenny will carry on here.'

'One sugar, Jenny?'

'One sugar,' she confirmed.

'Won't be long, don't work too hard,' Albert said and was gone. The two ladies carried on making the place shine for Leroy Leonard.

Albert returned with three mugs emitting a coffee aroma and steam.

'Green yours, Trish, blue yours, Jen,' he pointed. They sat down and drank their coffee, mostly in silence.

'Won't be long now.' Trish looked at the clock – it was 9.29 a.m.

Albert hoped everything would go well; he did not want things to take a polemic twist. 'Don't worry, everything will be just fine.' He smiled at his wife.

They finished their coffee and went into the lounge bar, having satisfied themselves that the bar was up to standard.

They worked hard in the already climbing temperature and finished just as the lounge bar clock reached ten. At that moment there was a knock on the lounge door.

'Thanks, Jenny, you can go now,' Albert said as he opened the door.

Trish tied her hair, smoothed her dress down and tried to look relaxed.

Albert opened the door to a man with a ponytail in his hair, T-shirt, jeans and a pair of Jesus sandals.

'I'm Leroy Leonard, Spring tell you I was coming?'

'He did, Mr Leonard.'

Albert stood to one side and allowed Leroy to pass.

'This is my wife,' he said, raising his arm to a thirty degree angle, palm up. 'Trish, Mr Leonard.'

'Pleased to meet you,' she said, extending her hand. He gripped it and took his time to let go. Trish pulled away and automatically wiped her hand down her skirt.

'Nice place,' said Leroy. 'Get many people in?'

'Bursting at the seams in summer,' Albert said, 'and a local regular trade in the winter period.'

'What sort of things do you have?' Leroy looked around again.

'How do you mean?' Albert looked a little puzzled.

'Darts, dominoes, I suppose.'

'Yes,' said Albert cautiously.

'Ever thought about karaoke, talent competitions, things like that?'

'No, never.'

'I think you should,' said Leroy.

'What are you getting at, Mr Leonard?' Albert was fencing with Leonard.

'I want a venue for talent competitions, local rock bands, singers, etc.'

'Not in here, you don't.' Albert started to get angry.

'Are you aware this is my pub?' said Leonard.

'Are you aware I have a lease agreed and it's watertight for five years now.'

'Oh yes, Bolitho, I've done my homework. That's a pity, a great pity.' Leonard looked pleased. 'Could you please come to the Hall next Friday at seven thirty. Goodbye, Mrs Bolitho.'

'What for?' asked Albert.

'I should have your rent worked out by then.'

'How do you mean?'

'You read your agreement, pal,' Leonard hissed, 'and you will find a nice little clause there which states you agree to pay a fair rent plus a five per cent increase every year. What do you pay at the moment?'

'Well, hundred a month.' Albert swallowed hard.

'One hundred a month? Peanuts,' smirked Leonard. 'One hundred a week is nearer the mark.'

'You can't do that,' gasped Albert.

'Read our agreement. All it says is a fair rent – no figures.'

'I know, but your predecessor said that he was happy with that. We shook hands on it in front of our two solicitors.'

'Not with me you didn't.' Leonard was crowing.

'But one hundred a week,' Albert pleaded.

'I never said one hundred a week now,' explained Leonard. 'That was then. I want about one hundred and forty-eight a week now.'

'You've got to be joking.' Albert looked disgusted.

'Talent competitions.'

'Never.'

'See you Friday then.'

'You bastard!' Albert totally lost it and went for Leroy.

'No!' Trish jumped up and grabbed Albert's arm.

'Lay one finger on me, you idiot, and I'll make it two hundred a week. You think it over and come to the Hall next Friday. Bye.' He quickly left.

'Did you hear that? Did you hear?' Albert was stuttering.

'I heard. Can he do that?' Trish was nearly in tears.

'I'll have a word with the solicitor on Monday morning.' Albert was stunned.

'We cannot afford that,' Trish said.

'I know that, but we have a signed agreement,' said Albert.

'So what do we do?' Trish looked at him for an answer.

'Well, we either pay or let him have his way on the karaoke and talent competitions.'

'But we'll lose all our regular customers. The place will be full of youngsters; more than likely drugs, fights and no end of trouble,' Trish said.

'The trouble that man has caused, I could kill him myself.' Albert meant what he had just said.

The phone rang.

Albert picked it up and said, 'Hello.'

'Oh hello, John,' he said after a pause. He listened and then placed his hand over the mouthpiece. 'It's John about tonight.'

'You're going to have to tell him no. I can't go like this.' Trish began to cry.

'John, mate, can you come over at lunchtime?'

Pause.

'Yes, he's been.'

Pause.

'Oh yes, some really great news.'

Pause.

'You can? Good. See you then.'

Pause.

'No, mate, I'm afraid tonight is off. See you later, bye.' Albert replaced the receiver, saw Trish crying and went to comfort her.

'Look, love, wait till Monday and see what Mr Tilling, the solicitor, has to say.'

The lounge door opened and in walked Tommy Curnow. It was 10.35 a.m.

'Morning Alb—' He got that far, then stopped when he saw Trish. 'What's the matter?' he continued.

'Oh, we have just had the new owner down here and he has told us that unless we play ball with him he's going to put our lease fee up by five hundred per cent. He said he can,' said Albert. Trish had nearly stopped crying; more of a sucking in of air every now and again.

'No way. I'm no lawyer,' said Tommy emphatically, 'but no way can anyone just increase anyone's rent by five hundred per cent.'

'But he insists he can,' reiterated Albert.

'See your lawyer.' Tommy was adamant.

'I'm phoning my solicitor first thing Monday morning.' Albert looked at Trish and saw she was much calmer.

'Look, we open at eleven; it's now about quarter to. You take Trish through the back and I'll get ready for opening. The staff should be here soon. Go before they come. Shoo!' Tommy took charge.

'Tommy, John Penrose is calling in. As soon as he comes send him through, will you please.'

'Will do.'

Albert led Trish away.

'Now there's a turn up for the books,' Tommy said thoughtfully, busying himself behind the bar. 'A rum do indeed.'

'Morning, Tommy.' Two girls walked in, dressed in T-shirt and jeans.

'Morning, Mandy! Morning, Sue!'

It was time to open up.

Away from the public eye, Albert sat Trish down, went to the sink, filled the kettle and prepared two mugs again for coffee.

'Albert, what are we going to do?'

He wanted to say, 'Don't worry, that slime ball cannot do that. We just go on as we are. Forget about turning this place into a haven for young people and drugs.' But he couldn't. 'I'll phone on Monday and get things sorted out, promise.' Albert tried to reassure his wife.

'He may still be there,' Linda looked at John.

'He might be gone by now.' John was persistent. Mainly to find out if there was any news, he rang the Pheasant.

'Hello?' He recognised Albert's voice on the other end of the phone.

'Albert, it's John about tonight.'

'Oh hello, John.'

John heard a hand being placed over the mouthpiece.

'John, mate, can you come over at lunchtime?'

'Has that scum been?'

'Yes, he's been.'

'Good news?'

'Oh yes, some really great news.'

'Yea, I'll come over at lunchtime.'

'You can? Good. See you then.'

'About tonight, so I can tell Linda.'

'No, mate, I'm afraid tonight is off. See you later, bye.'

John replaced the receiver. It did not take a genius to know the news was far from good.

'I'm pleased somebody had some good news,' said Linda.

'Hmmm?'

'Trish and Albert. Good news.'

'Don't you believe it.'

'But I heard you say—'

'Albert was being facetious.'

'How do you mean?'

'He's had bad news. I heard Trish crying in the background. Tonight's off and he wants me to go over at lunchtime. Does that add up to good news to you.'

'Oh God, not more.' Linda knew all about the recent events. John was keeping her fully up to date.

'Looks like it,' said John. 'They're going to find that man dead before long.'

'How do you know that?'

'You'll see. You'll see.' John did not expand any further.

Chapter Twelve

'We shall have to leave, dear.'

'Jane, how could you think of such a thing?' Ruby Cawthorne looked at her sister.

'I know, dear. We love this place, you don't have to tell me. But how can we stay here if that man goes ahead with open-air pop concerts out our back and on our stipend? How can we pay more rent than we already do?'

'I've told you, dear, the man is mad.'

'He didn't look mad,' replied Jane.

'No sane person could come out with ideas like that, you believe me.' Ruby was adamant.

'But what if he does go ahead?'

'Look, dear, you know when we called into the shop and told Joan?'

'Yes, I should,' said Jane. 'It was only late yesterday afternoon.'

'And what did she say?' plied Ruby.

'How do you mean, dear?'

'Look, when we told her she said that she had heard nothing. And she prides herself on knowing everything that goes on in the village.'

'True,' answered Jane.

'Well then, the man's mad.' Ruby had convinced herself, although it still proved illogical to Jane.

The Cawthorne sisters had spent most of Friday afternoon and evening discussing the meeting with Leroy Leonard and now, at ten fifteen on Saturday morning, they were still making it the main topic of conversation.

There was a knock at the door.

'Now who can that be?'

'Well, if we don't open it, we shan't find out.'

They headed for the door and opened it.

'Reverend Peterson, how very nice to see you.'

As always, the first thing he did was look for the mole.

'Ladies, may I come in?' He looked grave.

'Please do, please do. Is anything wrong?' Ruby spoke.

'I sincerely hope not, but, if I may come inside.'

They went into the living room and sat down.

'It's very difficult to know where to begin.' Reverend Peterson almost wished now that he hadn't bothered the ladies.

'I think the best thing to do,' said Reverend Peterson, 'is start with Friday morning.'

It was his turn now to tell the two demure ladies before him all that had happened over the last twenty-four hours or so.

'There you have it, dear ladies. So once I found out about you both, I felt it my duty to come and see if you were both OK.'

'Very kind of you, Reverend, very kind indeed.' Jane thanked him for them both.

'Dear ladies, do you have any questions?'

'You'll have no idea then what he wants with Mr Bolitho and his dear wife, Trish.' It was Ruby's turn.

'None, dear lady. That's my next port of call: to find out how Albert and his wife have fared.'

'So, poor John out of a job, that poor, poor girl Juliet, the shoots stopped, us, and now possibly Albert, for whatever reason.' Jane took her turn.

'See, I told you the man was mad.' Ruby looked smug.

'Don't you see, dear? If he is going to do all this it only makes the possibility of the concerts that much greater.'

'Oh dear.' Ruby felt deflated.

'Don't worry, dear ladies, I'm sure that if we all stick together we will defeat him.'

'He wants us to go to the Hall next Friday at seven thirty, you know.' Jane again spoke.

'To the Hall? May I be permitted to ask why?'

'Rent increase,' said Jane.

'Rent increase?' said Reverend Peterson. 'You jest.'

'We don't; rent increase,' both ladies answered.

'Unbelievable.' All Reverend Peterson could do was shake his head. 'So that's John, Detective Inspector Spring and your good selves, summoned to appear at the same time. Very strange.'

'What do you advise us to do, Reverend?' They both looked for help.

'Firstly, do not worry. Secondly, I'll find out all the information I can and keep you up to date.'

'Thank you, dear Reverend.' Jane and Ruby Cawthorne felt a little easier.

'I must go, but, as I say, don't worry. Above everything else, don't worry, promise me.'

'We promise.'

'Good.'

Reverend Peterson bid his farewells to the ladies, far from happy himself as he headed for the Pheasant. How could he tell them not to worry when just at the mention of the name of Leroy Leonard, he himself started wondering and worrying?

Catherine Leonard had been busy for most of the morning. She had had to make an early start, getting the rooms prepared for Leroy's session musicians and with the children to see to. With it being such a big house, she had asked Leroy for a nanny for the children, but the reply she got was, 'You've got two arms and legs – use them.' Whatever had she seen in that misanthrope?

The early start she made was far from cordial with her husband. By the time she saw him, after leaving him still asleep in bed, she had prepared one bedroom and started another.

'My breakfast ready?' Leroy shouted, although his tone was very stolid.

'What do you think I am, superwoman? You want these rooms ready for your musicians, don't you? Get your own.'

'Talk about keeping a dog and barking yourself.' Leroy was peeved.

'What time is it then?'

'Look at your watch.'

'Clever shit,' he said, but he did and saw it was nine fifteen.

'I'll skip breakfast. I'm going for a spin in the car, then calling in the Pheasant in the village.'

'Mind you don't ruffle your ponytail.'

'What?'

'Nothing.'

'Don't forget, they'll want some lunch.'

'Don't forget, they'll want some lunch,' Catherine mimicked.

'Bye then.'

'Bye,' she replied. 'Good riddance.'

'What?'

'Nothing.'

Not long after Leroy left she heard Lee and Pansy shouting for her.

God, what does he want a house this big for? she thought. You have to walk half a mile to find the children. 'Coming, darling,' she shouted.

She dressed the children, took them downstairs and gave them breakfast.

'Daddy has guests coming today, so don't upset him, OK?' She looked at the children.

'No, Mammy,' said Lee.

'Yes, Mammy, I mean no, Mammy,' said Pansy.

'That's good children, now go and play while I finish the bedrooms.'

She busied herself for the rest of the morning until Leroy returned. She could see by the look on his face that the morning had not been good. 'Who have you upset this time?'

'The landlord of the Pheasant.'

'How?'

'The stupid git is so behind the times, it's unbelievable.'

'Have you never thought that that's the way they like their lifestyle?'

'Oh go on, take their side.'

That was the signal for Catherine to shut up and carry on with what she was doing.

'I'm going along to the studio to get the music prepared for the lads coming. Don't forget lunch.'

She turned to protest, but he was gone. She finished the rooms, called to see if the children were OK and went down to the kitchen.

Sandwiches – that's all they are getting. If he wants a cooked meal for them, let the useless pig come and cook it for them himself, Catherine mused. She busied herself once again, getting bread, butter and filling for the sandwiches. As it happened, it was cheese and pickle, as Leroy would not have meat in the house.

She made up a good platter of comestibles, covered them in cling film, placed a bowl of fruit by the side and, in the fridge, two dozen cans of lager. 'That's that,' she said, before going to get the children and, as it was a nice day, decided to take them for a walk on the moor. Firstly she went and told Leroy in the east wing what her intentions were. He was not interested what she did, as long as lunch was made. He was not pleased with sandwiches and beer. She left him; she was too hot to argue.

'Come on, we'll go for a walk on the moor,' she said to Lee and Pansy.

'Yes please. Can we look for butterflies, Mummy, please. Can we?' Pansy was really excited.

'Of course, darling.'

'Goody, goody.' Pansy clapped her hands and jumped up and down.

Lee was more subdued than his sister, but still welcomed the chance to get out of the house. They went through the Hall's upper level to descend by the back staircase, out through the back door and into the fresh air. The glare of the sun made them squint for a while but, once their eyes adjusted, they enjoyed a pleasurable time away from the Hall.

Reverend Peterson entered the Pheasant and headed for his usual post at the bar.

'Hello, Tommy, nice to see you. How are you?' Reverend Peterson cordially welcomed Albert's stand-in.

'Very well, thank you, Reverend. Usual is it?'

'Just a pint of shandy, please.'

'Coming up,' said Tommy.

Dr James was there and so was Detective Inspector Spring.

'Is Albert available please, Tom?' enquired Dr James.

'I'm, er, afraid he's a bit indisposed at the moment, Doctor. Sorry.'

'Anything wrong?' Detective Inspector Spring interjected.

'I don't really know,' he lied.

'Oh.'

Reverend Peterson, Dr James and Detective Inspector Spring knew about the visit of Leroy Leonard. And if *he* had been, they guessed that the news was not good.

'Don't suppose you know if a chap called Leonard has been, do you?' Detective Inspector Spring addressed Tommy.

'I do believe he has,' nodded Tommy.

The three patrons cast a knowing glance at each other. They left it there and continued to enjoy the drinks before them. Shortly after this, John Penrose walked in.

'Hi, everyone,' he looked around.

'Hi, John,' everyone chorused.

'Just go through, John, Albert's waiting for you.' Tommy lifted the hinged part of the bar and opened the half-door, allowing John to pass.

'Cheers,' he replied.

He knocked on the door and waited until he heard, 'Come in.'

John entered the room, not really knowing what to expect. He got confirmation that Trish had been crying.

'John, sit down.' Albert pointed to a chair.

'Albert, I hope you don't think I'm being forward, but I can tell the news is not good. Out in the bar is Dr James, Detective Inspector Spring and Reverend Peterson. You know their concern is genuine. Why not ask them in, as we all wish to help.'

'You have enough problems of your own, John,' said Trish, touched by his concern.

'Look, we all stick together, right?' John said. 'United we stand, divided we fall.'

Albert left the room and returned a couple of minutes later with the concerned trio following him.

'Find a seat everyone,' Albert gestured. They all sat.

Albert took a deep breath and started. 'As you can guess, our friend has been. He was pleasant to start with, asking about the pub and what form the entertainment took. So I told him darts, dominoes, that sort of thing. His reply was that he wanted to run talent competitions, local rock groups, karaoke, singing competitions, etc. I told him no way, I had a watertight lease agreed five years ago. He said that's true but he had done his homework, so I asked him in what way. He said it was true about the lease, but what about rent? He asked me how much I paid; I said the amount that was agreed. He said not with me you don't and unless I cooperated with him, he was going to increase my rent by five hundred per cent.'

'Can he do that?' Reverend Peterson looked shocked.

'As there was no figure in the original lease drawn up between us and the owners, as it was just a gentleman's agreement in front of our solicitors, he maintains a fair rent for this place is £148 per week.'

'That man is capable of anything,' interjected Dr James. 'He causes dissonance everywhere he goes.'

'So there you have it, gentlemen. I must admit I went for him, but Trish stopped me. I'm going to phone my solicitor first thing Monday morning and see what he has to say. Leonard's parting words were to be at the Hall next Friday at seven thirty with my answer.'

'Well, that make's five up to now,' said George Spring.

'Five?' said Dr James.

'Yes, summoned to the Hall next Friday night at seven thirty.'

'I wonder if it will be our turn next,' said Reverend Peterson, looking at Dr James.

Dr James knew exactly what he would like to do to Leroy Leonard the next time he saw him. Should I tell them what I know? he wondered. The pain and sorrow he caused my family? How that piece of filth murdered my sister? He decided against it. He would sort out Leonard on his own when the time was right.

'Would you all like coffee?' Trish asked.

They all agreed.

'John, you can see about tonight, can't you?' Albert was hoping for the right response.

'Sure, sure, don't worry. I told Linda that something must be up; she understands.'

Albert had the response that he had hoped for.

Coffee was served and nobody really knew what to say.

'Day off today?' Detective Inspector Spring broke the heavy silence.

'Yes, we were going to Carn Brea Castle for a meal with John and Linda but—' Albert stopped.

'Tell me about it,' Detective Inspector Spring shrugged his shoulders.

Once again the silence hung heavy.

'Thanks for the coffee, Trish, but I think it's best if we went.' Dr James spoke what everyone was thinking.

'Really good of you all to come.' Albert was grateful, but a very worried man.

They all departed and went their separate ways.

Chapter Thirteen

Andrew Farmer was kicking his heels. That Saturday morning he had planned to go down to the Pheasant at lunchtime, have a pint or two and also find out what had happened between Albert and Leroy.

He breakfasted early – or at least early for him on a Saturday – wandered around, read a magazine and was getting progressively bored. That was when he heard the sound of a high-powered car engine and the screech of brakes. He didn't need to look to know who it was.

What does he want now? he said to himself.

There was no knock. The door burst open and Leroy walked in. 'Andy my son, I'm going out for a while. If the musicians arrive before I get back, take them up to the studio. I've left the side door to the east wing open. They shouldn't; I should be back in time, but just in case. By the way, the drive borders are a bit tatty – smarten them up. That's what I pay you for.'

'First thing Monday.'

'What's wrong with today?'

'You don't pay me for today.'

'Don't get clever, Andy, just do the borders.'

'As I said, Monday.'

'I'm not going to argue with you. Just do the borders or take a hike.'

'Do I take a hike before or after the musicians arrive?' Andrew threw caution to the wind. He didn't care anymore now.

Leroy glared at him, said nothing and left. Andrew breathed hard. Why do I put up with this shit? he pondered.

He went outside, round the back of the cottage, to a large shed. He unlocked the door, pulled out a wheelbarrow, a hoe and a rake, then relocked the door. It often amazed him how large a space there was behind his cottage that could not be seen from the front.

I suppose it was originally planned that way so years ago things could not be seen to offend the gaze of the gentry, he surmised. God, I must be mad doing this on my day off, waiting for his musicians, tidying the borders. He was only doing it because he was bored, he tried to convince himself. Where would I go? What would I do if I didn't? Go down to the village, watch telly, sleep, go for a walk? Now, if I had the use of one of his cars; the tight git has three parked up, but no such luck.

He pushed the wheelbarrow round to the front and headed up the drive, stopping so far along. The drive must be nearly a thousand yards long, he thought, as he looked back at the cottage nestled on the right immediately inside the gates. His eyes followed the drive curving up and to the left until it reached the Hall.

The area on the cottage side got naturally wider as it progressed up to the Hall, and was interspersed with trees, bushes and flowerbeds. On the left was a huge expanse of land with trees, flower gardens and sectional hedges, and in the middle a Japanese-style lake with an ornamental fountain in the middle. From the front of the Hall, the drive opened up to a large gravelled area, a wall along the boundary of the garden and then the beautiful grounds and lake giving a panoramic view before them. Whoever had planned the grounds years ago certainly was a master of their craft. Andrew decided to do the border on his side, start at the top and work down. That way, any refuse he picked up on the way could go onto the refuse heap by the shed to break down.

If he wants me to start the vegetable garden, he'd better get me some help. Andrew was by the east wing and now had a view to the rear, as well as the front. When he saw the vastness of the front and the rear, he knew he needed help. The back on the east side was just open grassland, fenced for the horses; the stable block was halfway down against the boundary; the middle was one huge lawn area that gave views and access to the moors and the woods; and on the west side was the walled vegetable garden and the garage block. The wide gravelled area circumnavigated the Hall.

Andrew made a start on the border and worked without a

break for some considerable time. It was another very hot day and Andrew welcomed the shade of the trees from time to time.

Head bowed, Andrew was working his way steadily down the border. When he heard Leroy coming back up the drive, he looked at his watch – it was ten thirty. Leroy did not stop; he just drove straight past and put up an acknowledging thumb.

Andrew pretended not to see, but carried on working for another half an hour, stopped, wiped his forehead with the back of his hand, plucked at his shirt, which was sticking to him, and regretted not having a can of Coke or something suitable. He viewed his work and saw he had cleaned about one third of the border. He made a quick calculation that, if he worked at it, he could have the border finished by twelve thirty. If those blokes are here by then, I could be showered and down to the Pheasant by one to one fifteen at the latest. Once again, Andrew set himself an itinerary.

He carried on raking, hoeing and picking out tufts of grass. He stretched his back a few times, then more weeds and more grass until his barrow was full and he found himself back at his cottage. It was twelve twenty-five. Good, he thought, it's working again, my plan. He took the loaded barrow round the back, emptied it, unlocked the shed, put away the barrow, rake and hoe and returned to the front of the cottage. He walked through the gates, looked left, looked right – no sign of any musicians. 'Damn,' he said.

He closed the gates, got a notice which read 'WILL VISITORS PLEASE SOUND HORN', went into the cottage and ran the gauntlet of having a quick shower and change of clothing before anyone arrived. He made it without any interruption.

'Damn,' he reiterated. Twelve fifty-five by his watch. 'Come on, come on.' But no one did. Andrew's plans this time were going right out the window.

He sat in his favourite chair and sulked. He felt his eyes getting heavy, but he did not protest – only made himself more comfortable in the chair and into slumber.

The sound of a horn caused him to start. He opened his eyes, got his bearings and looked at his watch. It said two fifteen.

The horn sounded again.

'All right, all right, I'm coming.'

He eased himself out of the chair, quickly went outside and opened the gates for a blue transit van. It came level with Andrew.

'This Shawlworth Hall?'

'It is.'

'Thank God for that. What a sod of a place to find. It's took us nearly as long to find this as it did to get from London.'

Inside the van were three in the front and two in the back. All windows that could open were open. 'It's like a friggin' oven in here,' said a long-haired chap sitting in the middle in the front dual seat.

'You should try being back here,' a voice drifted forward.

'If you follow the drive to the top and just park on the right, I'll be there in two minutes.' It was five minutes before Andrew got there. Even then he was walking fast, and breaking into a trot every now and again.

The five musicians were standing outside the van, some stretching their legs, one stamping his foot and wailing that 'his pissin' leg' had gone to sleep.

'Follow me, please,' he said and headed for the east wing door. The door opened and Andrew led the way. He went down the corridor and up a flight of stairs. Hearing them tramping up behind him, at the top he turned and entered through a door.

Once inside, the musicians were impressed with what they saw.

'Very impressive,' one said.

'Mr Leonard, your musicians.' Andrew made the introductions.

'Right, off you go, Andy.' Leroy waved his hand. 'Andy, go through the house, find Cath and tell her to bring up the sandwiches and beer.' He turned to the musicians. 'Right, lads, I'm Leroy and you are…?'

'I'm Robbie, drummer.'

Handshake.

'I'm Satch, base guitar.'

Handshake.

'Nigel, rhythm guitar.'

Handshake.

'Sol, lead guitar.'

Handshake.

'Harv, sound engineer.' He walked over to the mixing desk. 'This is one hell of a set-up.' He stood running his hands and eyes over the equipment. It was all the latest technology, but Harv was familiar with it.

'Fully soundproofed, too.' Leroy was proud of the set-up.

'Right, we'll go and get our gear and make a start.'

Andrew walked through the house and could find no sign of Catherine. He finished up in the kitchen, seeing the sandwiches and finding the drinks in the fridge, so he gathered them up and carried them back to the studio.

When he entered the studio, the musicians were back with their gear and were busy setting up.

'No sign of Catherine anywhere,' he said.

'Oh yea, she's taken the kids for a walk on the moor. I forgot. Just put them there on that bench and then you can go.'

Yes Sir, no Sir, kiss my arse, Sir, Andrew thought to himself.

'Right, lads, twelve songs to get down for this new CD. I've worked out that if we do two today, four tomorrow, four Monday and two Tuesday, you can be away by Tuesday teatime. Harv, you can stay and get the train home, say Thursday or Friday, 'cause if we get the instrumentals down by Tuesday we can then do the vocals. OK, lads?'

It was agreed.

'Right, everyone set, guitars tuned, drum kit miked up, let's just jam until Harv gets the levels right.'

By three thirty they were ready for their first practice. Catherine was still on the moor with the children. They were having a good time chasing butterflies; they saw rabbits and a few game birds. Although Catherine preferred city life, she had to admit to herself that the scenery was beautiful and it was a lot healthier for the children.

'Look at this, Mummy,' Lee shouted.

'What, darling?'

'This,' he pointed.

It was a hole in the side of a small bank that ran down to a flat area of lush green grass, interspersed with gorse bushes covered in a myriad of yellow flowers.

'That's a rabbit hole,' she said.

'Is there any rabbits in it, Mummy?' Lee questioned his mother.

'I don't know, darling,' she replied.

Her answer serviced his curiosity and he ran off to join his sister at the bottom of the bank. 'Careful, Lee, Pansy, watch out for holes and things.'

'We will, Mummy,' Pansy spoke.

They wandered around in a semicircle for some time; the children picked a few daises and buttercups for their daddy.

Catherine quickly glanced at her watch, saw it was approaching four o'clock and decided it was time to go home.

'Pansy, Lee, come on, time to go home.'

'Oh, Mummy, just a little longer,' they choroused.

'No. Now please.'

'Never satisfied are they?' The voice came from behind.

'Oh!' She spun round, hand on her chest, and saw that it was Antony Stuart-Palmer. She smiled. 'You frightened the life out of me.'

'I'm sorry, Mrs Leonard.'

'Catherine, please.'

'Then I am Antony.'

'Hello, Antony.'

'I saw you walking on the moor's edge. I was on my way over to see your husband. Is that possible?' he enquired.

'I'm sorry, Antony, but by now he will have musicians with him in his studio and I don't think he would appreciate it if I disturbed him. He's recording a new album.'

'Oh, I see. Well, could you get him to ring me as soon as he possibly can, Catherine?' He smiled at her; he found her to be of a pleasant disposition as well as being beautiful.

'Of course I will,' she replied, 'but I, I, am afraid I don't know when that will be, you see…'

Antony put up his hand. 'I understand perfectly,' he said, knowing what he was dealing with in Leroy Leonard.

'Could I tell him what it is about?' she said, looking at Antony.

'Fox hunting.'

'Fox hunting, oh dear.'

'I know. I have heard through the local grapevine that he had banned the shoots and I was wondering about the fox hunting and the ball.'

'I'll get him to phone you as soon as I possibly can,' she said, knowing full well what the answer would be. But how well it would be put, if any diplomacy would be used by her husband or not – more likely not. She again called the children, bid Antony farewell and headed back to the Hall.

Antony Stuart-Palmer watched her for a while, turned and headed back to the Manor House.

Catherine with the children arrived back at the Hall and went straight into the kitchen.

'Mummy?' said Lee.

'Yes, darling.'

'Well, you know you and Daddy have horses? When are we getting our ponies?'

'I'll ask Daddy, Lee, OK, when he has finished in the studio.'

'When's that, Mummy?'

'I don't know, darling. Probably about Wednesday.'

Lee had a quick count from Saturday to Wednesday. 'But Mummy, that's ages away.'

'You know Daddy is busy, so I'm afraid that you will just have to wait.'

'Augh.'

'Lee, now that's enough. What would you like for tea Pansy?'

'Sagette,' replied Pansy.

'Spaghetti please,' said her mother.

'Sagette please,' repeated Pansy.

'Lee?'

'I'll have the same but on toast please.'

'OK, spaghetti on toast it is.'

All the time Catherine was thinking, What can I give that lot upstairs? What can I cook when I don't know what time they will finish.

She busied herself with toast and spaghetti, deep in thought. Oh God, Antony Stuart-Palmer. The toast popping up brought her back to her immediate task. She buttered it, spooned on the spaghetti, told Lee and Pansy to sit at the table and placed a plate each in front of them.

'Milk or pop?' she said.

'Milk please.'

'Milk please.'

She poured two glasses of milk.

'Now listen, I want no playing or fighting, just eat your teas. I am going to quickly go and see Daddy and I will be straight back.'

'Cut my toast please, Mummy,' Pansy said, looking at her mother. Catherine did as she was asked.

'Now remember, no fighting or playing, you stay here until I return.'

'Yes, Mummy.'

'Yes, Mummy.'

Catherine gave them a warning look and left the kitchen. She made her way to the main hall, up the stairs, turned right down the corridor and past the main bedrooms and bathrooms. At the far end was a door that she headed for.

God, give me the flat in London, she thought. I've never seen or been in such a large place before. She had already convinced herself that she would never get used to a place so big; it was spooky, she always felt that someone was watching her or something was behind her.

She hurried for the door. Passing through it, she was now in the east wing, and straight ahead were the stairs. Going down, she turned to her right and went into the first door she came to.

It was the first time Catherine had been into the studio and the noise was deafening.

'Leroy.'

Leroy was by the mixing desk. 'Leroy!' This time Catherine shouted, but there was still no response. She went over and tapped him on the shoulder. He spun round.

'What the hell do you want?' he said.

She pointed outside and headed for the door; he followed.

'This had better be good,' he said once they were outside.

'When I was out on the moor I bumped into Antony Stuart-Palmer and he said could you phone him as soon as possible. I told him you were busy in your studio, but I also wanted to know how long you were going to be in here so as I could have a meal ready for you and your friends.'

'I don't believe this, you've called me out because of that poof and a meal? What did he want?'

'To know basically about the fox hunt – if you will still allow it, and the hunt ball held every year at the Hall.'

Leroy smiled. 'Tell him and his lady whatever-her-name-is that they stand no chance of a hunt ball here and any hunt on this land and I'll blast them to kingdom come. Tell him to be here next Friday with that wife of his at seven thirty. We'll be here until about nine tonight. Now piss off.'

Leroy went back into the studio, Catherine to the children.

Chapter Fourteen

Linda was waiting for John when he arrived home.

'Well, what happened?'

'More bad news,' John said.

'Oh come on, John. Do I have to squeeze it out of you?'

'I went in,' John began. 'The Pheasant, that is. Saw Tommy Curnow who showed me through to the back, said hello to the doc, the Rev and George. When I got into the back, Albert and Trish were there. I could see straight away Trish had been crying, so I says to Albert that I can see it's bad news and, as the doc and them were in the bar, ows about hasking them in. Albert thought that a good idea so in they comes. Albert tells us that *he'd* been and said 'olding rock bands an' singers in the pub is what he wanted Albert to do. Straight away Albert he says no way. Mr high and mighty says, OK then, come up to the Hall Friday night with your answer but if you don't agree I'm hincreasin your rent by five hundred per cent.'

'He can't do that,' gasped Linda.

'Says he can.'

'Poor Trish and Albert. What are they goin' to do?'

'Dunno,' said John. 'We has enough to worry ourselves about.'

Linda could not argue that point with John.

'He's causin' some bother, that man.' John looked at Linda.

'He's in the drivin' seat.' Linda hated to admit that.

'Perhaps not for long.'

'What do you mean by that?'

'Nothin', nothin'.'

John said no more about things concerning Leroy Leonard, just that he was going for a walk.

'OK, luv, should I come with you?'

'If you don't mind, I'll go alone. Give me time to have a good think. You don't mind, do you?'

'No, you go. Tell you what, fancy one of my pasties for tea?'

'That'll be great,' said John, before he blew his wife a kiss and went out. He covered some of his favourite haunts, even stretching back to his childhood. Between the moor edge and the village was a favourite place for all village children – Miller's Pond. John didn't know how it got its name, but that was what it had always been called. He found some flat pebbles and made them skim across the water, turning to the way he had originally come. John retraced his steps so far and headed for the old gamekeeper's cottage, which nestled on the edge of a copse not far from Miller's Pond. Years ago this would have been very handy for most parts of the estate, where most of the work of a gamekeeper would have been done. A small stream ran to the side of the cottage, which some people said was fed from Miller's Pond and ran on to the River Camel. But where the water in Miller's Pond came from, no one knew, although one or two people speculated that it came from underground and was then forced up from Colliford Reservoir to the north-east. But no one was ever able to prove it.

The cottage, considering it had stood empty for some years, was still in a remarkably good state of repair. It was a structure of granite blocks and a thatched roof that had withstood the ravages of time and weather. The paintwork was flaking but the woodwork was still sound and the glass unbroken in the windows. It had three rooms and a door from the outside opened into a room that was both a living and dining room. The room had rustic beams and a big open fireplace – no Cornish range as one would have expected. Either side of the fireplace was a door: one into a small bedroom, the other into a small kitchen. There was no sanitation; that is to say there was a lean-to on the side of the cottage, housing a wooden plank from wall to wall with a hole in it and a bucket underneath. It had no water coming from the stream and no electricity, but it was as dry as a bone.

John kept a camping stove in there, so that, if he was ever out, he could pop in and make a cup of tea. He had whiled many an afternoon in there over the years, instead of checking the moors as he had put on his weekly time sheet. John had the key in his pocket, so he unlocked the door and pushed it open. Every time, the hinges creaked in protest; John had been promising for months and months to oil them, but had never got round to it.

Will this be the last time I hear them hinges? he thought. John found himself getting a little maudlin, so he quickly snapped out of it and went into the little kitchen. Cups, teapot, tea bags, powdered milk, kettle, matches – full complement. Why not.

He lit the camping stove, shook the kettle to check for water and placed it in the flame. The outside door opened. God, who's that? John thought and looked around for a weapon.

'John, you there?' It was Antony Stuart-Palmer. 'So this is where you hide out. I often wondered,' he smiled and winked at John.

'You knew, Sir?'

'Course I did.'

'You never said, Sir.'

'Why should I? You always carried out your duties to my satisfaction, and my father's.'

'Thank you, Sir.' John felt humbled.

'I saw you from over the moor and thought it was a good opportunity for a chat.'

'Chat, Sir Antony?'

'Oh, don't worry, John. Remember, I am no longer your employer.'

John relaxed.

'Cup of tea, Sir?'

'That would be nice, thank you, John.'

'It's only powdered milk and no sugar I'm afraid, Sir.'

'That will be fine. Don't worry, John.'

John felt uneasy at being in the company of his former employer and a member of nobility to boot. Antony had picked up on this and once again tried to put him at his ease.

'All I wish to discuss with you is that which concerns the new owner.'

John poured the hot water into the teapot. 'Oh I see, Sir.'

'No doubt you have heard about Miss Juliet.'

'I did, Sir, and could kill the animal for that, Sir. She's a lovely girl and doesn't deserve treatment like that.'

'Thank you, John, for saying that. I see he has stopped all shoots and it looks as if he is going to stop the hunts as well.'

'Merciful heaven, he hasn't told you that, has he?' George had not told him about last night's telephone call to Antony Stuart-Palmer.

'No, no, I got a phone call last evening from George saying that if he has stopped all shoots and killing of animals by gun, trap, etc., he won't allow hunts, so that is where I was going when I saw you. To ask him outright. Although our meeting of last evening was far from cordial.'

'He cannot stop the Shawlworth Hunt, surely, Sir. Can he?'

'"No, I cannot stop the hunt," I can imagine him saying, "as long as it doesn't come over my land".'

'But, Sir.' John did not know what to say.

'I know, John, I know,' said Antony.

'You 'eard what he done to Albert, Sir?'

'Albert in the Pheasant?'

'Yea, Sir.' John seemed to lapse into a pronounced dialect when angry.

'What now, John?'

'Well, Sir, ee went to the Pheasant this mornin' and told Albert ee wanted to 'old rock bands in the Pheasant, talent competitions, and singers an awl that.'

'Rock bands in the Pheasant? Is the man mad? Albert, what did he say?'

'Ee tells 'im that ee 'as a watertight lease and no, he could not 'old rock bands in the Pheasant.'

'Good for Albert.'

'Aye, but what does ee say to Albert? Read your lease. Fair rent with a five per cent increase every year. As no figures are mentioned, or something like that, in the lease, he's going to hincrease Albert's rent by five hundred per cent.'

'He's *what*?'

'That's it, Sir.'

'The man is a maniac. Just because of rock bands in the Pheasant.'

'Do you know about the Miss Cawthornes, Sir?'

'You've lost me, John.'

'Well, you know he wants to put rock bands in the Pheasant? That be only half of it.'

'You've still lost me, I'm afraid.'

'You knows that big dip in the ground out the back of their place over yonder.'

'What people call the amphitheatre? Yes.' Antony was still puzzled.

'Well, he is going to have open-air pop concerts with big-named bands on the bill.'

'John, please, please tell me you're joking.'

'I be not, Sir Antony.'

Antony Stuart-Palmer looked at John, drank some tea, and said, 'I'm sorry, John. I'm not calling you a liar, but I just cannot believe that, for that is unbelievable.'

''Tis the truth, Sir, I promise ee.'

'Do the Miss Cawthornes know?'

'Yes, Sir. He went and told them himself and told them he's putten up everybody's rent as well. He says for them to be at the Hall Friday seven thirty, so that's the sisters, Albert, George Spring, and me up to now who has to be there.'

'Very strange. I wonder why altogether? But then some people let power go to their heads and the more the merrier, I suppose, for him.'

'Dunno, Sir'.

'Well, thanks for the tea, John. I must be going now. Things have a way of sorting themselves out, they always do. Goodbye, John.' Antony Stuart-Palmer left.

John cleaned up the cups, made sure the stove was shut off and left himself. Making sure he locked the door, he headed home, looking forward to one of Linda's pasties.

'Hello, darling.' Vanessa greeted her husband. She had been looking out for him for some time. It was now five o'clock – she had expected him home long before now. 'You have been ages.'

'Sorry, darling.' Antony kissed his wife on the cheek but he was deep in thought.

'Daddy?' Juliet spoke.

'Hmmm.'

'Daddy, please, you're miles away.'

Juliet was looking at her father. Her eyes had their usual sparkle and seemed composed after the tribulations of yesterday morning.

'Sorry, darling.' He hugged his daughter. 'Fire away.'

'Where have you been? Mummy has been to the window at least six times looking for you.'

'Well, what did *he* have to say this time?' Vanessa asked.

'I never got to the Hall,' Antony said, looking a little sheepish.

'Never got to the Hall? Then where have you been all this time?' Vanessa's voice was going up again.

'Mummy, calm down.' Juliet found herself in the role of mediator. 'Let Daddy speak.'

'Thank you, Juliet,' he said and bowed. 'I was walking to the Hall when I saw John.'

'John?' his wife interjected.

'Mummy,' Juliet admonished her.

'John Penrose the gamekeeper. He was over by the small copse at the cottage, so I went over for a chat but stopped longer than I had intended. John made some tea, so we had that. But John's news about *him*, you would never believe in a million years.'

'Antony, please. The hunt, the hunt.'

'I'm coming to that. Firstly John. You want to know where I have been, so I am telling you. Where was I? *Now* look.' His train of thought had gone.

'You were having tea with John.' Juliet looked accusingly at her mother. 'Who's him, Daddy?'

'That piece of scum, Leonard. Tea with John. Yes well, what happened yesterday morning to Juliet and in the evening was not even a quarter of the story.' Antony then went on to tell his wife and daughter about the pop concerts, open-air concerts and all the rest of the news.

Vanessa stared; Juliet stood open-mouthed throughout the story Antony had to tell about Leroy Leonard.

'Is that it, Daddy?' Juliet was first to speak.

'Not quite,' he continued. 'When I left John, I headed once again for the Hall and as I got nearer I saw Catherine Leonard with her children. When I spoke, she nearly jumped out of her skin, as she had her back to me. We made light conversation and then I asked her if her husband was available to see me. She said no, he had musicians arriving as he was cutting a new album or something. So I said could she please get him to ring me as soon as possible. Catherine asked me if I could tell her what it was about, so I told her about the hunts and the ball. She promised she would tell him and get him to phone.'

'That's it?' said Vanessa.

'That's it,' reiterated Antony.

'So we are still no further forward?' Vanessa sounded irritated.

'You can hardly blame Daddy, can you.' Juliet once again stuck up for her father.

'I'm not blaming your father, dear, but it is the hunt we are talking about here.'

'Please, Vanessa, don't let's go into all this again,' begged Antony.

Vanessa opened her mouth but nothing came out.

'Really you know, perhaps it's just what this place needs.'

Both parents looked at their daughter.

'Explain please.' Juliet's father spoke in a very cautious tone.

'Well, open-air concerts.'

'Juliet, have you taken leave of your senses?' Her father could not believe he was hearing this.

'Look at the money it would bring to the area,' Juliet replied, trying to validate the point she was making.

'Utter rubbish. Who would benefit? The pub? I think not. The shop? No way. So who?' Antony looked at her with disdain.

'Well, answer,' said her mother.

'Well, well, I don't know, T-shirt sellers and things.'

'T-shirt sellers? The only one to make anything out of this is that piece of offal over there and I am more than surprised at you sticking up for him after what he has done to the community and especially to you.'

'Daddy, all I was saying was—'

Juliet was cut short.

'I think that you have said enough, Juliet.' Her father wanted to hear no more on the subject.

'But Daddy—'

'Enough.'

Juliet turned and flounced out, saying, 'You get treated like a child here.'

Antony went to go after her, but Vanessa grabbed his arm.

'Let her go, darling. Let her cool down a bit. She has had a nasty shock.'

'Vanessa, I know that, but to stick up for him.'

'Please, dear, don't let us argue.'

'OK,' he said and kissed his wife.

After a brief period of silence, Antony spoke. 'Come on, you're dying to get it off your chest.'

'I don't know what you mean,' she said.

'Come on, darling, the hunt.'

'*You* mentioned the hunt, not me.'

'I know, but that *is* what you're thinking about, isn't it? Be honest.'

'Yes, you're right. What are we going to do about the hunt?'

'Until he phones me back, I don't know.'

'We all know what his answer will be.'

'Of course we do.'

'Well then.'

'Well what?'

'What are we going to do about it?'

'I don't know.'

Vanessa knew her husband was right, but the hunt and ball were mainly her organisational territory and she was at a dead end.

The telephone rang. Antony Stuart-Palmer picked up the phone and spoke his name.

'Antony, it's Catherine.'

'Hello, Catherine, nice to hear from you so soon.'

'Antony, I've spoken to Leroy. I gave him a brief indication as to your requirements. He said that he was very busy and would be for the next few days, and could you and your wife please come to the Hall at seven thirty next Friday. But I hasten to add, Antony, I am almost one hundred per cent certain that the answer to both requests is no. Antony, I'm very sorry.'

'I thought that would be the reply. Please don't blame yourself and yes, we will join the others on Friday.'

'The others?'

'Yes, those required to attend the Hall next Friday at seven thirty.'

'I'm sorry, Antony, I don't know anything about that. Do you know who the other people are?'

'There's the Cawthorne sisters, John Penrose, Albert Bolitho, Detective Inspector Spring, Vanessa and myself up to now.'

'Thank you, Antony, but I'm still none the wiser. I only know of Detective Inspector Spring who was here last evening, yourself and of course, although we have never met, your wife Vanessa. Who are the others?' Catherine felt like an interlocutor.

'John Penrose, gamekeeper, Albert Bolitho, licensee of the Pheasant; and the Cawthornes are delightful identical twin sisters in their sixties who live in the village,' he replied.

'Well, thank you once again, Antony, and once again I'm sorry. Please give my regards to your wife.'

'Thank you, Catherine, I will.'

'Goodbye then.'

'Goodbye, Catherine.' Antony replaced the receiver.

'Bad news?' said Vanessa.

'The worst possible for you,' he replied. 'Catherine has spoken to her husband, but the bottom line is *no* to hunts and ball. Of course, she put it politely but I can guess what he said with his foul mouth.'

'Is he that bad?' Vanessa was clutching at straws.

'Oh come on, darling, look what he said to Juliet.' Vanessa fell silent. 'Come on, darling. They say it's darkest before the dawn – and it's pitch black at the moment.' Antony sat on the arm of his wife's chair and placed his arm around her shoulder.

'Could we lease that land from him? The hunt will pay.' Vanessa was again hopeful.

'Come on, darling. He needs the money we can offer like a hole in the head.'

Vanessa again fell silent.

Juliet came back into the room, sat in a chair and said sorry.

'That's OK, darling. Please listen, I have some news for you.'

'For me, Daddy? Who from?'

'Mr Leonard.'

'What news has he for me? I only met him for the first time yesterday, and then he was rude.'

Antony cleared his throat; Vanessa sat up and took a keen interest.

'It's Gladiator.'

'Gladiator?' Juliet dived out of the chair and stood in front of her father, a scared look on her face.

'Calm down, darling, Gladiator is fine. It's just that, er, you are not allowed to ride him anymore on Shawlworth land.'

'Daddy, you're joking. Gladiator loves those moors as much as I do. He loves his gallops.'

'I'm sorry, darling, but he said in future you were to stop riding your horse on his land.'

Tears flowed down Juliet's cheeks; she fell into her mother's arms.

'Oh, Mummy, where am I going to go with Gladiator now? We are virtually surrounded by Shawlworth land.'

The last time Juliet was sobbing in her mother's arms that copiously, she had been just a child. Vanessa wept too.

'You'll have to go over Helland and Helland Bridge way.' Antony tried to strike a compromise.

'How do I get over there? You tell me,' she shouted.

'Through the village and take the B3266 road.'

'Daddy, Gladiator is a horse not a car.'

'Juliet, I am only trying to help.' Her father's heart was aching for his daughter.

'He should be put down. Leonard, I mean.' Vanessa had stopped crying and spoke with venom. Juliet finally stopped crying.

'Have a sherry dear, I am,' said her mother. 'Whiskey?' She looked at Antony.

'Yes please. Why not make it a large one,' he replied.

'This is just getting worse and worse,' said Vanessa. She poured the drinks and handed one to Juliet, the other to Antony.

'Please, darling, this is getting us nowhere.' Antony could not take much more.

'Why does he want us at the Hall next Friday at seven thirty?' Vanessa asked.

'I really don't know, but you heard me say to Catherine, he wants other people there at the same time.'

'Do you know what they are wanted for, Daddy?' It was Juliet's turn to ask a question.

'John Penrose, to find out if he still has a job or not; Albert

Bolitho, to find out how much rent he has to pay if he doesn't agree to the concerts; the Cawthorne sisters, if they don't agree, how much rent they have to pay; George for his rent increase; and your mother and I, well I am really not too sure. He cannot put our rent up; possibly just to gloat over saying no to the hunt and hunt ball. Another please,' said Antony, holding out his glass to his wife.

'You'll get drunk,' Vanessa warned.

'Can you think of anything better at this moment in time? Tomorrow I'll wake up with a thick head, but for now it will be great.'

'I think I'll join you, Daddy.'

'Me too.' Vanessa did not want to be left out. The evening wore on and they kept to their promise. The next morning they all woke with thick heads.

Chapter Fifteen

Catherine replaced the receiver. She felt awful, but tried to put things from her mind. Since leaving Leroy, she returned to the children. They had obeyed her wishes and stayed where they were.

'That's good children,' she said. 'Now, have you had sufficient?'

'Yes thank you, Mummy,' they both agreed.

'Good, so let's have these dishes done, and then we will have an hour's playtime before you go to bed.'

'Will Daddy be playing games with us?' Lee asked hopefully.

'I'm afraid he will be too busy, darling. Perhaps next time.'

'He's always too busy,' sulked Lee.

'Don't be cheeky, darling,' Catherine admonished her son, but she knew he was right.

The door burst open and Leroy came flying through.

'Goin' to make a phone call,' he said.

'Daddy, will you play with us, please.'

'Too busy, son.'

'Please, Daddy.'

'Lee, I said I was too busy. Now shut up or go to bed.'

Tears welled in Lee's eyes.

'You can tell you are your mother's son.'

Catherine spun round from the sink.

'What do you mean by that remark?'

'Blubbin' like a baby.'

'You are a pig,' she said with contempt. 'A first-class shit.'

He blew her a kiss and went to the phone and dialled a number.

He waited for a while and then said, 'That you, Fredricks? I want to see you. No, not now, you pillock. Monday morning.' There was another silence. 'Look, I know you are a lawyer; you're *my* lawyer and have made a fortune out of me, you bent bastard.'

More silence.

'Look, just meet me in your office on Monday morning at ten o'clock.

Again Leroy listened.

'I don't give a shit. Who's more important? Him or me? Who pays you the most?'

Pause.

'Thank you. Monday, ten o'clock.' Leroy slammed down the phone.

'It's a Saturday night, I'm a lawyer, please moderate your language,' mimicked Leroy. 'Stuck up arsehole.'

Leroy turned to his son. 'I promise I'll play with you tomorrow, son,' he said, ruffling his son's hair.

'Daddy, can Pansy and me have a pony each, please?' Lee looked up to his father.

Leroy smiled. 'Course you can, son, and you, Pansy. What colour would you like?'

'Black and white please, Daddy,' Lee jumped up and down, smiling and clapping his hands.

'I don't know, Daddy,' said Pansy.'

Leroy picked her up and kissed her fondly on the cheek.

'Wait till you see one you really like and then choose, eh.'

'Yes, Daddy.' Her big blue eyes shone.

'Mummy, Daddy is going to get us a pony each.' She ran to her mother.

Catherine hugged her. 'Yes, darling.' Why can't he be like this all the time? she thought.

Leroy went back to his music.

Lee was deep in thought.

'What should I call it, Mummy?' he said.

'Well, it depends if it's a boy or a girl,' she replied.

'I never thought of that.' He went deeper into thought.

'I want a girl, Mummy, and I'll call her Topsy.' It was not a problem for Pansy.

'Bullet if it's a boy, 'cause it will be fast, and… and Penny after Auntie Penny if it's a girl, 'cause she runs fast.' Lee gave a final nod of his head.

Catherine smiled and left it at that.

She kept her promise and played with the children. Of course it had to include horses. Catherine felt as tired as they did when she finally got them to bed. She checked the bedrooms once more for the musicians. Two in two of the bedrooms, one on his own. She was not bothered; that was for him to sort out. Catherine's thoughts now turned to an evening meal for nine o'clock for them. But what? She went back to the kitchen and looked around the cupboards and freezer.

Quorn mince for him, steak mince for them, done as a bolognese with spaghetti, wine, profiteroles, cheese and coffee. That'll do. She set about her task. She was finished by nine and was proud of her effort, as she was not known for her culinary prowess.

Things had worked out well; as the clock struck nine and echoed through the downstairs of the Hall, everything was set. She had just made up the table in the kitchen, as Leroy preferred that to a poncey dining room. When Leroy came through the door, she said, 'Everything's ready, just waiting for you and your friends to sit down.'

'Sorry, hun, we've decided to go for a pint instead.'

'You what?'

'I've ordered a taxi. We're going into Bodmin for a few jars. What have you done?'

'Spaghetti bolognese.'

'There you are then, see you later,' he said and was gone.

Catherine picked up the dishes of food and put everything, including the dishes, into the waste bin. She went into the drawing room, poured herself a stiff drink and picked up the telephone.

'Penny? Cath… Oh, I'm fine, just fine… I *do* phone… I know. OK. That pig has been at it again… It's just him and his work and since he got back in the charts there's no holding him. The locals… he's upsetting them right, left and centre… What? No, not yet. I bet it's not long, though, before someone does plant him one. I hope I'm there; you know the people we bought this place off, well he came storming around last night. I was listening outside the door, but these doors are so flaming thick it's difficult. What? Put a glass to the door? Never thought of that. Listen, I heard Antony Stuart-Palmer... No, that's his name... Penny, *please*. He said to Leroy something about his daughter, breasts bouncing up and down... Penny, will you please stop laughing, it's not funny. Penny, for heaven's sake, stop that on a public telephone. There was a policeman there as well. Penny, if you don't stop, I'm putting down this phone... Yes, we all know about the policeman's girlfriend... Penny, will you please listen. Penny, I'm putting this phone down... No, I am if you don't listen. Are you going to listen, 'cause the next time the phone just goes down... What do you mean, like knickers? Penny, that's it, I'll phone you when you are more sober... you've had more than that by the sound of you. Do you want to hear this or not? ...Good.'

Catherine stopped and poured another drink.

'Now listen, Penny, or down goes the phone. So what really happened I don't know, but as I say he's upset loads of people. Anthony wants to hold fox hunts, but you know he'll say no... I don't agree with fox hunting either, but what he fails to see is that these people have hundreds of years of breeding in this type of thing – to them it's a way of life. You know as well as me that his diplomatic skills on a scale of one to ten are about minus nine. You would think he would do his best to blend in, but not that big lug... No, he has never tried... Yes, still the same with me. Today, for example, he said to make supper for nine, for him and these musicians he has staying here because he is making a new album... What, oh, he's had the east wing converted into a recording studio... Penny, of course I told you, didn't I? I'm sure I did. Anyway, have supper ready for nine, so spot on nine I'm ready. In he walks, guess what he says... No, he didn't, Penny, Penny, don't start again. What he did say was, me and the lads are away for a few pints, what had I made? So I told him, so he says that's OK, it'll keep, and off his lordship goes. So I threw the lot, dishes and all, into the waste bin... What do you mean I didn't? I did – the lot.' Catherine paused; another drink. She was starting to feel a little light-headed.

'Penny, if I left him, you know what he would do... All mouth? You believe me, he isn't as far as the children are concerned.'

Catherine made herself more comfortable on the settee and brought her lower legs up until her heels touched the back of her thighs. She continued, 'And as for me, I get two broken arms and legs for my trouble... Police? What could they do? He hasn't touched me yet... We could stay with you, thanks, Penn. But no, it would only make more trouble for you. I had a good laugh tonight, anyway. Lee asked his dad if he and Pansy could have a pony each and he said yes. He loves them kids, you know, in his own tinpot way. What *about* me? Listen, Penny, Lee says if it's a boy pony he's calling it Bullet 'cause it will go fast, and if it's a girl, Penny after Auntie Penny because she runs fast... He did.' Catherine laughed. 'How's mother?' she asked. 'Oh good, give her my love, won't you. Listen Penn, when are you and Mum coming down for a holiday? It's really beautiful here, Penn. Of course I prefer London, but it is beautiful here... Sod him, Penn. This place is huge. We can soon lose that miserable git. Think about it anyway... She isn't? *My* God, when? *The* Gloria Stapleton, pregnant? Two months? That's her out for a few months. When did Clive call? He wants me back desperately? Good... Penny, how can I? If it was just me, I would come back tomorrow. Who knows better than you how much I love modelling... I know, we still have the flat... Mrs Mason? Yes she still lives there... Penny, you know what he has said for the last ten years. My days of being ogled at are over... Penn, I know it's stupid, but you try telling him that. No, Penny, no I can't, Penny. No... What contract? ...Gloria's? Whoever takes Gloria's place gets a jeans commercial? You're joking. Please say you're joking. Penny, say you're winding me up... You're not? Oh shit... Clive said what? ...He's phoning me Sunday afternoon for a reply? If I take the job, it'll be a one-horse race for the commercial... Oh, Penn.'

The drink was now having a real effect on Catherine. 'Yes, yes, I promise I'll ask him... No, I will, I promise... What if he says no? I'll kill the bastard... I will, Penn, one day. Penny, how is Ron? ...Oh good.' Catherine just had to change the subject or she would burst out crying again.

'Look, Penn, I'm going, it's after ten. I don't know what time he'll be back. Once he starts drinking, it could be anytime... Go to bed with a book... I know, in bed on a Saturday night with a book at ten o'clock... Penny, that was years ago... I know we would only now be getting ready to go out... Penny, please, I'm going. Take care, bye, Penny.' Cath sat for several minutes after she put the phone down. A jeans commercial, I'd give my right arm for a jeans commercial, she thought. But I know what that pig will say. It doesn't matter that it would be a dream job for me. Sod that. My place is with the kids. At that moment, Catherine felt so much hate for a person, she even frightened herself. If she had had a gun and he was there at that moment, she would have had no hesitation in pulling the trigger; no thought of what would happen to her, or what would happen to the children. Just seeing him dead was all she wanted.

She poured another drink, wandered into the hall and went to lock the main door. Has he got a key for the side door? They had agreed that they would always take a key for the side door if they went out at night. What they called the side door was actually French windows to the side of the main entrance.

If he hasn't, tough. She locked the door and went up the baronial staircase. Good job I'm not afraid of being alone. As she looked around, it seemed vast. If she was staying here, she would have to get a couple of dogs. Catherine went to bed, finished her drink, read her book until well after midnight, then fell into a deep sleep.

By his standards, Leroy Leonard had had a good evening. He and the musicians had gone into Bodmin and on a pub crawl. It made his evening when, after they had entered one public house, and while standing at the lounge bar, he felt a tap on his shoulder. 'Excuse me, please, but are you Leroy Leonard?'

'That's me.'

'I say, everybody, it's Leroy Leonard.'

Everybody looked, people came forward and, before he finished, he must have signed at least two dozen autographs.

'My name is Sidney Curnow. I live in Shawlworth. You've bought the estate, I believe. I'm a great fan of yours, Mr Leonard.'

'Call me Leroy, Sidney.' Leroy always had time for his fans.

Everyone was now standing round him and questions came thick and fast.

'How is your single doing, Mr Leonard?'

'About twenty, I think.'

'No, Mr Leonard, it's eleven,' said Sidney.

'You sure, Sidney?'

'I told you, I'm a big fan.'

'Hear that, Harv, number eleven.'

'Think you'll go back on the road again, Leroy?' asked Harv.

'Never thought about it. But hey, it's not a bad idea. You lads free?'

Everyone agreed they were.

'That's great, I'll phone Stu Iveson tomorrow, see what he says.'

'Sidney, did you say that you lived in Shawlworth?'

'Yes, Mr Leonard.'

'Tell you what, Sidney.' He handed him a card. 'Ring the Hall some time and if I'm free you can come to the Hall and see my new recording studio, OK.'

'Mr Leonard?'

'Leroy, Sidney.'

'Leroy,' Sidney stammered over his name. A big star like this and him calling him by his first name. 'That would be fabulous.'

'No problem, Sidney, a pleasure,' answered Leroy.

'You Leroy Leonard?'

Leroy looked up and before him stood a young girl in shorts and boob tube.

'None other.'

'Me and my friends are having a party. Fancy coming?'

'Your name is?'

'Sandra.'

'Well, Sandra, thanks for the offer, but how old are you?'

'How old do I have to be?'

'At least nineteen.'

'Then I'm nineteen.'

'No. Thanks, Sandra, but we have to make an early start in the morning. Thanks all the same.' Leroy would be polite for a record sale.

'Your loss,' she said and walked away.

They all smiled but said nothing.

'Right, lads, same again?'

'Please.'

'Same again, please.'

'Sure, Mr Leonard, on the house.'

'Many thanks,' he acknowledged.

'Robbie,' Satch began passing drinks. 'Nigel, Leroy, Sol, Harv.'

Sidney had gone to tell his friends about his offer to see Shawlworth Hall and to see the great Leroy Leonard's own private recording studio.

'Last orders please, ladies and gents.'

'Anybody fancy a chinkie, pizza or Indian?'

'I must admit I'm starvin',' said Robbie. The others agreed.

'Right, now we agree that we're starving, what is it to be?'

'Excuse me, Mr Leonard.' It was the landlord. 'There is a very good Indian restaurant just down the road. Go out the main door, turn right down the street for about a hundred yards and it's on the other side of the road.'

'Indian, lads?'

'Suits us,' they said in unison.

'Thanks, landlord, let's go then.' Leroy spoke and was in the lead.

'As the old north-east saying goes, I could eat a scabby hoss between two dustbin lids.' Outside it was still warm and, considering Bodmin was not a coastal resort, there seemed to be plenty of tourists about.

They soon found the Indian restaurant.

'Very original,' said Sol.

'What's that?' Nigel asked.

Leroy belched.

'The Taj Mahal for an Indian curry house.'

'Oh, is that all?' Sol looked disappointed – he didn't know why, but by this time they had all drunk about eight or nine pints of beer.

'Right, lads, in we go and may the best man win,' said Leroy.

'How do you mean?' Nigel looked worried.

'Middle of summer, but as hot as we can stand it. First one to stop eating pays.'

'You're on,' agreed everybody.

There was room in the restaurant, as it was only half full, so they had their choice of seats.

'There,' pointed Harv, 'table for six.'

'Great,' said Leroy. 'Right, lads, elbows in, starting blocks.'

'Good evening, sirs, what can I get you?' A waiter stood by.

'Right, Sabu.'

'Shush,' laughed the others.

People began to look and Leroy was not drunk enough to offend those who might buy his record if he was recognised.

'Sorry. Right, lad, the biggest plates of the hottest curries for these, and me of course, but please make theirs of meat and mine of prawns. Big plate of popadoms and are you licensed?'

'Yes, Sir.'

'Good, then keep six lagers coming thick and fast. Tomorrow we'll have bums like Japanese flags, but what the hell.'

By half twelve Nigel had lost and he had just given up before the others had thrown in the towel.

'God, I feel ill,' said Sol and looked it.

'Let me die,' groaned Robbie – at that moment he meant it.

'And me.' Satch was doubled over. Nigel could not speak. Harv groaned.

Leroy was feeling just as ill, but as he was Leroy Leonard, he said nothing.

'Your bill, sirs.' Again the waiter was by the table.

'You've done us proud, son.' Leroy heaped praise on him. How many times had he been with lagers to the table? Six? Seven?

'I'll pay,' said Leroy. He was drunk.

Nigel couldn't care less.

'What's the damage, son?' asked Leroy.

'Thirty-four pounds and seventy-five pence, please, Sir.'

Leroy counted out eleven ten pound notes.

'How many's there?' he asked.

The waiter counted it and said, 'Forty pounds, Sir.'

'Good. Pay the bill and keep what's left.'

'Thank you very much, Sir.'

'Can you get us a taxi to pick us up here and take us to Shawlworth?'

'Certainly, Sir.'

The waiter left, coming back almost immediately. 'Your taxi is on its way, Sir,' he informed him. 'Would you care to wait outside for him?'

'Yea, good idea. I think we could do with the fresh air,' said Leroy.

All staggered to the door and all felt decidedly ill. Outside, they all leaned against the side wall of the restaurant.

'I'm going to be—'

That's as far as Nigel got; he was sick by the time he had finished. Tears were streaming down his face and the inside of his nose stung where vomit had come down. The others had to look away; they weren't that brave.

'Glad I don't have to clean that lot up,' laughed Leroy. No one answered.

A car pulled alongside; the driver got out and walked around the car.

'Taxi for Shawlworth?' He looked at the floor. 'Mind, if that happens in my cab, you'll have to pay the cleaning bill.'

They nodded.

'If I shout stop, then hit them brakes as hard as you can.' Harv was now very unwell.

'Where to in Shawlworth?' the driver asked.

'The Hall. Know it?' Leroy staggered to the car.

'That's just been recently bought by a pop star, or so I've heard.'

'You've heard right, my friend. At your service.' Leroy raised his right arm, gave a flourish as if he was one of the musketeers, brought his arm down and across his body, bowed low and fell flat on his face. He stayed there.

'Oh great, just great,' said the taxi driver.

Leroy eventually tried to get to his feet. The taxi driver compared Leroy's efforts to that of a new-born foal trying to stand for the first time.

Eventually the driver had cajoled Leroy and his party into the taxi, after finding out who was paying.

Might have guessed, thought the driver, looking at Leroy.

'I want no form of carousel in the taxi, gents, OK?'

'I'll have you know I'm a married man,' Leroy said, thinking it hilarious.

'I don't know what it means,' said Sol.

'Has it anything to do with sex?' asked Satch. They were all laughing now.

The waiter must have told the taxi firm it was for six people, as they had sent a people carrier. It was brand new, so from Bodmin to Shawlworth Hall the driver not only kept a sharp eye on the road but on Leroy and his friends. The journey was uneventful apart from one snoring, someone else breaking wind and another moaning. As it happened, it was Robbie, Harv and Leroy, in that order.

The gates to Shawlworth Hall were still open, so the driver drove straight in up the long drive and pulled up at the main entrance.

'Fifteen pounds, please,' requested the taxi driver.

Leroy gave him twenty and they all fell out of the taxi. As the taxi drove away, Leroy searched for a key.

'Shit, no key.'

'How do we get in, then?' asked Harv.

'Follow me,' said Leroy and headed round the back.

'Hey, where are we going?' Robbie begged.

'Shut up and follow me,' said Leroy.

They did as they were told.

Chapter Sixteen

Sunday morning dawned, but compared with the last week or two it was far from the norm. The sky was overcast and rain was imminent. George Spring stood up, stretched, yawned and rubbed his cheek. He had been up all night, first in thought and then acting on his thoughts.

For George it began at ten o'clock the previous evening, when he resigned himself to the fact that he must take action over the shoots. After leaving the Pheasant on the Saturday lunchtime, he had returned home to find the light flashing on his answerphone. He pressed play.

'George, Blackwood here. Get your arse to the police station ASAP. Nasty case; old man badly beaten and robbed.'

'That was your only message.'

'Shit,' said George, but obeyed the call of Detective Chief Inspector Blackwood.

He eventually arrived home after giving his sergeant, Harris, strict instructions to contact him if there was any news from the hospital on the old man who was in intensive care. 'You stay at the hospital for as long as it takes,' Harris was told.

'Yes, Sir,' he replied.

It was well after eight o'clock at night, and by the time he did himself a meal, ate it and settled to his task, it was ten o'clock. George checked his list, cheque book, paper, bookings, names and addresses. Firstly, those for the opening shoot. Time was now of the essence. It took him a good half hour to sort those out, but now that he had started it, he did the rest of the list, which took him until past midnight. George then began to write explanatory letters to each and everyone concerned. He could have made up a suitable letter for all, but he thought that too distant and formal.

After three false starts, he managed to get into a 'flow' and only stopped for a coffee sometime later. Once he had drunk his coffee, he carried on. More letters; his hand ached.

God, I didn't think that there were that many bookings, he thought.

By the time he had finished them, the first cracks of dawn split the clouds. He looked at his watch: 4.45 a.m. 'Nearly five in the morning,' he moaned. 'What's left?' George sorted out the papers, which only left letters in envelopes to address.

George made more coffee. As he drank, he thought of Leonard. What would Blackwood call him? A caitiff. George had heard him use that term often enough, but did not know what it meant.

'Time to find out,' he said and walked over to a glass-fronted cupboard set in the wall. He opened the door and got out a dictionary.

Problem. How do you spell caitiff? Ky, no Ka, no C, try C. Cy, no Ci, no. Sod it, Ca. Got it. Caitiff: villain, contemptible person; Leroy to a T. I'll remember that, he promised himself. He put the dictionary away and returned to his task at hand.

Finished! He threw the pen down, satisfied with his work. 7.15 a.m. Oh God, I'm tired. Bed, shave, shit or shampoo? George could not make up his mind. Sod it, I'm going to bed. And he did just that.

Just as George was going to bed, Andrew Farmer was waking up. He lay for some time, undecided about what to do. He pulled the curtain to one side. Rain. That's it, stop here. Andrew cast his thoughts back to the previous afternoon, when Leroy was in his gaffer mood. Andrew go for this, Andrew do that.

After delivering the sandwiches and beer, Andrew went back to his cottage to plan the rest of the day. He switched on the television to see some sport. It was rugby, England versus Wales.

He left the television on, but did not take much notice of it. He was far too preoccupied by Leonard's new album. Andrew sat thinking.

His songs, or so he tells everyone, but if they only knew the truth. Oh yes, by law they are Leonard's songs but morally and in every other way they are someone else's and I know exactly whose songs they are: *mine*.

For the rest of that day and evening Andrew sank deeper and

deeper into self-pity, but he kept his promise to George and smoked indoors.

At Shawlworth Manor, Juliet woke and groaned. Her head was pounding. Oh God, never again. That is the last time I ever, ever get drunk. She looked at the clock: it was 8.30 a.m. She groaned again. Breakfast, she thought, but quickly dispatched that idea from her logical thinking. I'm going to be sick. She dived out of bed. No time for dressing gown, please let the loo be empty. At the Hall, Juliet had had her own bathroom; here it was different. She flew down the corridor into the bathroom and just reached the toilet bowl before a stream of bile shot from her mouth into the bowl.

'Oh God, I'm dying,' she said out loud.

'Juliet, is that you, dear?' Her mother came into the bathroom. She looked at her daughter sitting on the floor, tears running down her face – although she knew they were not from crying.

'Oh, darling, flush the chain quickly.' Seeing the bowl, Vanessa felt bile rising. She was not much better than her daughter was.

'Sorry, Mummy.' Juliet flushed the toilet.

'Darling, how many times must I tell you, wear a dressing gown.' Her mother looked at her daughter, who was only wearing a shirt and pair of pants.

'Mummy, I was in a hurry.'

'I know, dear, but you could have brought it with you.'

Once again Juliet apologised to her mother. 'How's Daddy?'

'The same as us.'

'He must be ill then. You look as bad as I feel, Mummy.'

'Cheek. You don't look very good yourself.'

'Pills please, Mummy.'

'That's what I have come for – pills for me and your father.' Vanessa held her left hand against her forehead.

Juliet had two aspirins and immediately felt sick again.

'I think I shall go and lie down again,' she said to her mother.

'Wait there,' commanded her mother. She returned a few minutes later with a dressing gown. 'Put that on first.'

Juliet did as she was told.

Vanessa went back into the bedroom with two pills for Antony, and handed them to him.

Antony's head was pounding, too, and it took all the energy he could muster to say, 'Thanks.'

'Darling, about Gladiator,' Vanessa said cautiously.

'Yes,' he replied. Antony felt like putting the pillow over his head, but didn't.

'The Edwards' place.' Antony did not expect to hear that.

'What *about* the Edwards' place?' he replied.

'Could we not stable Gladiator with the Edwards and then she could ride him to her heart's content.'

'Vanessa, that is brilliant.' He was now taking an interest. 'Stable the horse there, Juliet can go over whenever she wants; great.'

'Yes, but that does not solve the problem of the hunt.'

Antony groaned, wishing he had put his head under the pillow after all.

Catherine had slept soundly, but when she awoke she found that Leroy had not been to bed; his bed had not been slept in. Her mind tried to comprehend the possibilities. Accident: good, I hope it's serious, she thought, feeling no guilt. Lying drunk somewhere: it won't be the first time. Lying in someone else's bed: that's more like it, she thought.

She climbed out of bed and went to see to the children. They were both still asleep, so she tiptoed out of their room. They had wanted a bigger place and now they had it. But Lee and Pansy still shared a room; granted it was a lot bigger, but it was still sharing. In a place that big, Lee and Pansy had not wanted a room to themselves; they both had too vivid an imagination.

Catherine went back to her own room and asked those little men in her head hammering away to please stop. She had no idea that Leroy and his friends were sprawled out in a drunken stupor not far away.

It had seemed a good idea at the time to Leroy, when he had said, 'Follow me,' and had led the group to the hay barn. There they had collapsed in the hay, urinating and being sick as and when they wanted. Not one of them could have cared less. It was warm, it was soft – who could ask for more?

Leroy groaned and spat out some straw stalks. 'God, never again,' he said, having no idea where he was. The others began to stir; Harv looked at his watch: 10.30 a.m. He moaned.

'Help, help,' Satch was shouting.

'What's the matter with him?' Harv said.

'I'm stuck,' wailed Satch.

Robbie and Sol crawled on all fours to where the sound came from. Satch had fallen between bales of hay.

'Soppy sod,' said Nigel.

They pulled him onto the top of a bale.

'Where are we?' Again it was Nigel.

'Hay barn,' said Leroy.

'I've got a mouth like a Turkish wrestler's jock strap,' said Harv.

'Don't suppose anyone has anything to drink?' Satch was hopeful.

'I'm sure there's a tap on the wall somewhere,' Leroy said, looking around. 'There,' he pointed.

They all made a beeline for the tap, but Leroy was first. He turned it on and let the cool water run over the back of his head and neck. Next he cupped his hands and splashed his face.

They each took a turn; they felt a little better, but not much.

'Shit, it's nearly eleven,' said Leroy. 'We must get these songs done.'

They all groaned.

'Ha'way we'll go and have a shower, some breakfast and we'll be on top form.' Leroy was enthusiastic.

'My friggin' head won't,' said Harv.

They crawled out of the hay, and went outside. It was raining but it felt good. They trotted to the kitchen window and knocked hard on the glass.

Catherine had finished giving the children breakfast and answered the question, 'Where is Daddy?' as best she could.

It was nearly ten thirty before she managed to give the children their breakfast and clear away the dishes. By the time she had finished her chores it was eleven o'clock. She headed for the door, but just as she was about to open it, she screamed. There was a loud banging on the window. She spun round, shaking, and saw Leroy's face pressed at the window.

'You thick idiot! I could have had a heart attack.'

'Open the door, Cath, it's raining.'

'Where's your key?'

'Cath, it's soddin' raining, we're getting wet. Open the piggin' door.' Leroy was peeved.

Catherine went out of the kitchen and into the corridor. She turned right down the corridor, right again into another passage, and walked to a door at the end. She could see Leroy and his mates looking wet and miserable. 'Serves you right, pig,' she muttered.

Catherine pulled back bolts at the top and bottom of the door and turned the large key in an old, but very effective, mortise lock.

They all came trooping in like naughty schoolboys.

'Make us a coffee, Cath. Oh, by the way, this is Cath, the wife. This is Robbie, Harv, Sol, Nigel and Satch.' Everyone acknowledged each other but said nothing; they all returned to the kitchen. Once milk and sugar were sorted out and the kettle switched on, Cath turned to Leroy.

'You look a mess. Where the hell have you been? You're all covered in straw.'

'No key, came back last night – well, early hours of this morning – by taxi, no key.'

'So?'

'So, er, we slept in the barn.'

'You slept in the barn.'

'Cath, do you have to repeat everything I say? My head is poundin' – any pills?'

Cath went to a first-aid box, took out a bottle and placed it on the table. 'Help yourself, lads.'

Leroy was on the telephone.

'Stu, yea, it's Leroy. What's the chance of a tour with these lads?' He laughed. 'I read your mind, did I? Good… Already underway… Brilliant, you'll fill me in later on dates and venues… How much?' Leroy turned to the quintet around the table. 'Eight hundred a week plus expenses OK?' He got the thumbs up.

'Leroy.' It was Cath.

'Just a minute, Cath.'

'Leroy.'

'Cath, shush.'

'Leroy. I've something important.' Catherine once again realised, too late, that nothing was more important to Leroy than his music or forthcoming tour.

'Cath, shut it. Stu, yea, fine for the lads. Speak to you later.' He replaced the handset in the cradle. 'Right, lads, I'll show you the way upstairs, grab a shower, change of clothes and in the studio, say, for one thirty, OK?' He walked towards the door, let everyone pass, spun round and pointed to Cath, hissing, 'You, stay.' He slammed the door behind him.

Catherine sank slowly onto a chair, knowing now that she had no chance of doing a commercial. Not now, not ever.

Catherine waited for the inevitable outcome. She did not have to wait long; he came bursting back in.

'What is so important that you could not wait while I was on the phone, eh?'

'It doesn't matter anymore.'

'Oh, but it does, it does.'

'I was talking to Penny, that's all.'

'Oh, Penny is it? Go on, surprise me. Modelling.'

'No it wasn't, well, yes it was.'

'Either it was or it wasn't.'

'Gloria is pregnant.'

'And?'

'Well, they, er, want me to fill in for her and do some modelling and a jeans commercial.'

'Cath, when are you going to get it through your thick head that your modelling days are over. Finité, finished, done, never to return.'

'This is the twentieth century, Leroy.'

'I've got a head that's bouncing, I slept in a barn and I've got a full ten hours still to do.'

'Whose fault is that?'

'Don't get smart with me, lady.' Leroy was starting to get vicious.

Catherine left him and went to her room. Coming back out, she saw the children were playing happily in their room. When she went back to her room, this time she stayed. She summoned all her strength to stop herself crying, not wanting to give that louse any more satisfaction, when he came back any minute for a shower. Finally Leroy arrived.

'I could do it while you're on tour.'

'Who looks after the kids?'

'Your mother, my mother, we could move back to London and Mrs Mason would love to mind them.'

'You'd love that, back to London, wouldn't you. What about this place, pray tell.'

'We could close it up. Andrew could mind it.'

'The kids will stay and you will stay. Have you thought about school for them, eh? No. Why don't you do your modelling and let *me* look after them? I'm sure I could find time to book them into school one day in Glasgow, one day in Edinburgh, one day in Newcastle and so on. Now, why didn't I think of that before?'

Catherine didn't answer. It took all her powers not to cry, but she was so determined.

Leroy turned and went for a shower in the en-suite bathroom.

Catherine's eyes followed him. Please, please, please, God, let him fall and kill himself. She left the bedroom. She could not bear to be in the same room as him now.

Morning service had just finished and, to the pleasure of Reverend Peterson's faithful flock, the rain had stopped. It had been a regular enjoyable Sunday morning service for most people and none more so than for the Cawthorne sisters. Every Sunday morning, Ruby and Jane had breakfast, dressed in their best attire, left the cottage at nine forty-five for Reverend Peterson's ten o'clock service, were home for eleven fifteen and, having changed clothing, prepared Sunday lunch for two thirty. The routine never changed. Even now, when they had left home in the rain and the main topic of conversation had been that horrid man, Leonard. Even the rain could not dampen their ardour.

'Umbrella, dear.' Satisfied, Ruby locked the door. They now stood with Dr James, Albert and Patricia Bolitho, and the dear

Reverend Peterson in the church vestibule, the Reverend Peterson – in the eyes of the sisters – looking resplendent in his ecclesiastical vestment.

Only a few remained in church. Most had gone, but the sisters did love their after-service chat.

'Yes, that particular canticle is one of my favourites, too,' Reverend Peterson agreed with the sisters.

'How are you, dear?' said Jane, looking at Patricia.

'Well, thank you, Miss Cawthorne.'

'Good.'

'Albert?'

'Fine, fine.'

'You, dear Doctor?'

'You know me, Miss Cawthorne.'

'Well, the rain has stopped, thank goodness,' said Reverend Peterson, looking skyward.

'I hope it stays that way,' said Albert.

'Don't forget Wednesday.' Reverend Peterson spoke to Ruby and Jane.

'As if we would,' said Jane. Wednesday afternoon, the WI met in the church hall, with Ruby in the chair. 'We will most definitely be there.'

Turning to Dr James, he said, 'June hasn't forgotten, has she?'

Dr James assured the Reverend she had not. June Bright was Dr James's district nurse, and she was giving a talk on safety in the home on Wednesday afternoon.

'Excellent, excellent.' Reverend Peterson was pleased. 'Well, I think—'

'I tell you I *did*.' Sidney Curnow and Patrick Mann stood in the doorway.

Sidney and Patrick took the collections every Sunday for Reverend Peterson and then, when the service was over, they took it into the small anteroom, counted it, bagged it and gave it to the Reverend on their way out. They were always the last two out and, when they left, he could lock the door.

'Rubbish,' said Patrick.

'Gentlemen, please,' Reverend Peterson said. 'Remember you are in the Lord's house.'

'We're not arguing,' laughed Sidney.

'No, Reverend.' Patrick was laughing too. 'It's about last night.'

'Last night?' Everyone listened but only the Reverend spoke.

'Yes,' continued Patrick. 'Sidney was, er, out last night in Bodmin and he said he bumped into the new owner of the Hall and he invited Sidney up there to have a look at his new recording studio.'

'Oh, I see.'

'Big fan of his is our Sidney.' Patrick placed his hand on his shoulder. 'Danced many a night away in the sixties to Leroy Leonard and Rock Express.'

Reverend Peterson's eyes rolled back in his head and he crumbled to a heap on the floor.

'Oh, my good Lord.' The Cawthorne sisters placed their hands over their mouths.

'Merciful heaven!' gasped Trish.

Dr James dropped to the Reverend's side. 'Albert, here are my car keys. Open the boot and get my bag, there's a good chap.' Everyone was stunned.

'Is he OK, Doctor?' Sidney looked concerned.

'He has a strong pulse, Sidney, but I must check him over. Patrick, help me to place him on his side.' Patrick did as requested.

Albert came running back with Dr James's bag.

'Thanks, Albert.' He took a pencil light from his bag and shone it in the Reverend's eyes as he lifted each eyelid.

'OK there.'

Next he placed his stethoscope in his ears and, moving the vestment to one side, he opened the shirt and listened.

Everyone stayed silent and motionless, just staring at the drama before them.

'Hmmm,' said the doctor. 'OK there; roll up his sleeve, please.' He did not speak to anyone in particular as he reached for his blood pressure machine.

Trish reacted first. Rolling up the Reverend's sleeve she fell backwards when he suddenly jerked and moaned.

'OK, old friend, lie still. It's Dr James. Just be still.' Dr James wrapped the pressure bandage around the Reverend's arm and began to pump the bulbous end, placing the disc of his stethoscope into the inner joint at the elbow.

There was a hissing of air.

Reverend Peterson was coming round.

'Well, old friend, you seem to be OK, from what I can gather, but I want you to go to hospital tomorrow morning for tests.' Dr James looked at the Cawthorne sisters. 'He just fainted, he'll be fine.'

'Praise the Lord,' said Ruby.

'Gently, gently,' said Dr James. Reverend Peterson was trying to get up.

'I feel such a fool,' he said. 'Please, forgive me.'

'Don't you worry.' Albert looked concerned.

'Come on, let's get you home.' Dr James guided him along the path to the vicarage next door. Reverend Peterson turned.

'Thank you all, dear friends, for your concern.' He looked pale. 'Sidney, will you please do me one favour?'

'Of course, just name it.'

'Thank you, dear boy. On your way home you pass the home of Detective Inspector Spring. Would you be so kind as to ask him to call straight away.'

'Sure.'

Sidney and Patrick left.

'Dear ladies, please go home now,' said the Reverend. 'Have some tea. You both look shaken. I shall be fine. Trish and Albert, you please go and serve the public and many thanks for your concern.'

They all left.

'Now home, this is your doctor ordering you.'

'Dear friend.'

Once ensconced in the vicarage drawing room, the Reverend felt much better.

'A dry sherry, Doctor?'

'Sweet tea would be better for you.'

'You are right, but I think a dry sherry.'

'Very well. Thank you.'

'Reverend, may I ask a personal question? And if you answer, you know anything you say, if you wish, will be kept secret by me.'

'Please do.' The Reverend knew he could trust the doctor implicitly.

'Why have you asked for George?'

'Who better to bare your soul to than a policeman about murder.'

George Spring was awakened by a loud banging on the door. 'Oh, no,' he groaned.

Bang, bang, bang. The knocking got more urgent.

'If that's Harris, I'll kill him,' said George, climbing out of bed.

Bang, bang, bang.

'All right, all right, I'm coming.'

The letter box flap was lifted. 'Detective Inspector Spring? Are you there? It's Sidney, Sidney Curnow.'

'Where's the fire?' shouted George.

'Oh, you're there.'

'I'm here and this had better be good, Sidney.'

'Still in bed at eleven thirty, Mr Spring?'

'I've been up all night.'

'Oh,' said Sidney. 'Where's the fire?'

'What fire?'

'You asked me where the fire was. I don't know, so I'm asking you.' Sidney scratched his head.

'Sidney, what do you want?' George spoke slowly.

'Not me, Mr Spring, I don't want anything.'

'Then what are you doing breaking my door down?'

'No. Reverend Peterson, he wants you straight away.'

'This a joke, Sidney?'

'No joke, Mr Spring.'

'Sidney, take a deep breath and start at the beginning – right?'

'Right.' Sidney took a deep breath. 'Last night I was drinking in Bodmin when who should walk in but Leroy Leonard.'

'Get to the point, Sidney.'

'I am, Mr Spring. You said to start at the beginning. I got talking to him and he invited me up to the Hall to see his new studio. I'm telling Patrick, you know, Patrick Mann...'

'Yes, yes, please get on with it,' begged George.

'After the service we takes the collection and counts and bags it for the Reverend, so I'm tellin' him about last night. Well, he doesn't believe me, so by the time we gets to Reverend Peterson he thinks that we is arguing. Well, of course we explains we isn't and as he is stood there with Dr James, the Cawthorne sisters, and Albert and Trish Bolitho, we has a laugh.'

'Sidney...'

'Yes, Mr Spring?'

'Will you please get to the point.'

'Right away, Mr Spring.'

'Thank you.'

'A pleasure.'

George Spring sighed and gave up.

'Patrick starts tellin' Reverend Peterson about my meeting with Mr Leonard, how I am such a big fan of Mr Leonard's, got all his records. You know, Mr Spring, there's *Come back to me, Missing you, Broken love*—'

'Sidney.'

'Oh yes, sorry. Right, he says, Patrick that is, tells Reverend Peterson how I used to dance the night away to Leroy Leonard and Rock Express when the Rev's eyes roll back in his head and he goes down like a sack of hammers.'

'He what!'

'Lyin' on the floor, he be, Doc bendin' over him. The doc brings him round and helps him to the vicarage and the Rev says to me, can I get you to go as soon as possible. So here I am, told you I wanted nothin'.'

'Thank you, Sidney, goodbye, Sidney.' George closed the door.

Now there is a turn-up for sure. His policeman's hat was on again.

'Murder?' said Dr James. He knew Leroy was a murderer, but how did Reverend Peterson know about his sister?

'Dr James, what is murder?' Reverend Peterson seemed to be talking in riddles.

'Well, I suppose the killing of another person.'

'The law defines it as the *intentional* killing of another human being. That, that *man*, that animal killed my daughter.'

'Your daughter?' Dr James was dumbfounded.

'Beautiful, sixteen years of age, all to live for, now dead. All through that filth.'

'As I said, Reverend, if you want to explain.'

'I will, my dear friend. All in good time. If you can be patient, just until George Spring gets here. You will stay, won't you?'

For a second the Reverend looked worried. 'Of course I will,' he replied. *His* daughter? Dr James considered whether he should now divulge about his sister or wait and see what happened. I'll wait. He had to think quickly.

'Another sherry, Doctor?'

'Thank you, I will,' he said. He may not have wanted the first but he certainly wanted the second.

Reverend Peterson gave the doctor another sherry and went to the window, deep in thought. All this time he had been wondering why the name of Leroy Leonard had meant so much to him and now he knew: Rock Express. His only child, his own beautiful Allyson, dead. A solitary tear ran down his cheek and he muttered, 'Waste, a sheer and utter waste.'

'Sorry?' said Dr James.

'Oh, do forgive me. Thinking out loud, old friend.'

The doorbell rang.

'Should I go?' said Dr James.

'Thank you. It's probably George.' A grateful Reverend Peterson sat in his armchair. Again he felt weak.

'Come in, George.' Dr James stood to one side.

'Rev OK?'

'Yes, yes, he's fine now, but badly shaken.'

'Sidney said he fainted.'

'That's right.'

'Reverend Peterson wants to see me after he faints?' Detective Inspector Spring looked puzzled.

'Not because of fainting, George, but according to him, murder,' whispered Dr James.

'Murder? Oh come on,' George Spring laughed.

'I'm serious. That's what he says.' Dr James was emphatic.

They both entered the room where Reverend Peterson was sitting.

'George, thank you for coming,' he said, starting to rise out of the chair.

'Sit where you are, Reverend. Now what's this all about?' Reverend Peterson sat for a while before speaking.

'I want to tell you both about my past and that of Leroy Leonard. It may take some time.'

'I'm free, Reverend, so take all the time you need.'

'Me also,' the doctor agreed with the policeman.

'Thank you both. What I have to say is for you, George, and you, friend, alone – no one else.'

They both promised.

Reverend Peterson began. 'Many years ago I was the vicar of the church in Tuckingmill and Roskear in-between Redruth and Camborne. I was married and had a beautiful daughter, Allyson. I had everything: job I loved, wife and daughter who I loved more than anything. In the spring of 1963, along the road from us at Pool was the Flamingo Club, and Allyson asked if she could go to a pop concert there. Appearing was an up-and-coming band who had just made their first record and were called Rock Express. I asked what time she would be home; she said eleven thirty and she was going with some of her friends from the Technical College. One of her friends was her best friend, Janice, a lovely girl, so her mother and I said yes. When Allyson promised to be in at a certain time, I always knew she would keep her promise. She said she was going with Janice on the bus and would get the last bus home.' Reverend Peterson breathed long and deep and both Dr James and Detective Inspector Spring knew something horrible was to follow.

'You OK, Reverend?' said Dr James.

'Yes, dear friend. Oh George, how rude of me. A drink? Dry sherry? Please help yourself.' He pointed to the bottle.

'Thank you.'

'Please bring the good doctor another.'

'No, no more for me, thank you.'

George poured himself a drink and sat down. Reverend Peterson continued.

'Although the bus stop was just outside, I thought I would take in the night air and meet her and Janice off the bus. At eleven thirty the bus duly arrived, but instead of stopping it just drove straight past. I looked and could see, apart from the driver, and it being a single-decker bus, that no one else was aboard. I must admit that I was a little afraid that some mishap had occurred. I returned indoors and told my dear wife what had just transpired. She was of the opinion that they had missed the bus and were walking home. So I calculated that, if they came out at eleven thirty, just missed the bus and were walking, the distance being two and a half miles, it should take thirty to thirty-five minutes. When the hour of midnight struck and they had still not returned, I told my wife I would go and see if I could find them, as they should be now nearly home.'

Once again the Reverend stopped to gain his composure.

'But to no avail. I must have walked a good mile, but there was no sign of either one. I thought I had better return, as my dear wife had enough to worry about with one of us missing, never mind two. I returned home at approximately twenty-five minutes past the hour of midnight, hoping beyond hope that they were home. But I was just greeted by my wife, who by this time was extremely worried and requested me to phone the police. I said to her that, although Allyson was always strict about times and, if by some misfortune she could not keep her allotted time, she would do her very best to telephone. The police would view it differently. No disrespect to our police force, George; I mean that at that moment she was only an hour late and therefore could have gone to a friend's, stopped for a chat, or a number of other things.'

George Spring nodded in agreement.

'It was now one fifteen and both my wife and I were very worried. I was just about to telephone the police in Camborne for advice, when there was a knocking on the door. I went to the door with some trepidation and my fears were well-founded, for standing at the door was a uniformed officer. My dear wife was standing behind me and let out a little cry on seeing him. He asked us both if we were the parents of an Allyson Peterson, we confirmed that we were, and he said could we both accompany him to the hospital in Redruth. We immediately put our coats on and did just that. We waited with the questions until we were in the car on our way, to save time. I asked of the officer what he knew. He told us that our daughter had been brought from the Flamingo Club to the hospital, unconscious. She had not been involved in any physical skirmish and that was basically all he knew. After what seemed like a fifty-mile journey, instead of four miles, we arrived and were taken by the officer to the accident and emergency waiting room where there was also a reception desk. We gave our names and we were requested to wait. A moment later Janice came through the door in floods of tears. She came running over and hugged my dear wife. While this was happening, a doctor came and told us that our daughter was unconscious and in a critical condition due to drug abuse. We told him not to be stupid and that our daughter was only sixteen and had never taken drugs in her life. But, of course, he was right. Not knowing what they were, the drugs, and it being in the early days of drug abuse, they did their very best. They fought hard medically and my dear wife and I prayed for her safe return to us, but to no avail. Three days later she died.'

'Reverend, what about a police inquiry?' George said with compassion.

'Yes, a full and thorough investigation was carried out, but to no avail. Janice gave the best insight as to what occurred that night, but at the end of the day we had no proof or evidence as to the perpetrator of our daughter's death. We are convinced we know, but never have we been able to prove it. Janice said they arrived, met their friends at the door and entered the club. They went and ordered drinks – those who were eligible anyway. Janice was certain all Allyson had had to drink was orange and lemon juice – St Clements, I believe she called it – and they sat drinking and watching the musical gear being set up on stage. Later, approximately fifteen minutes, Janice noticed this one particular person staring at Allyson all the time and informed her of it. Allyson saw who it was and smiled, so he immediately came over and started chatting to her. He told her he was in the band, asked if he could see her after, as she was beautiful. But Allyson said no, but he would not take no for an answer. She refused his offer a few times and he said OK, could he buy her a drink? She agreed to that just to get rid of him, but told him in no uncertain terms that it had to be non-alcoholic and he agreed. He left them and went to the group of men working on stage and said something. Janice was sure he passed something to the person he spoke to, but thought it must be money, and this man went to the bar.

'While this was happening, the disc jockey started playing records, so they decided to go and dance. After two records, they thought they had better return to their table as the place was filling up. Returning to the table, there was a drink for Allyson in a pint glass and a note that said, "I bet I see you later; Leroy Leonard". She turned to her male companions, I believe three, and asked them all to take a sip for spirits or the like. They all said that there was definitely nothing in the glass of an alcoholic nature, so Allyson drank it. She said it had an unusual taste but was enjoyable. As the evening progressed, Allyson's mood changed. She was laughing hysterically, not just dancing but jumping about all over the place. She was soaked with sweat. This went on until about ten fifteen when she went very quiet and collapsed in a heap. The bouncers just wanted to kick her out for being drunk, but Janice said she hadn't been drinking, so they carried her to a first-aid room where she was looked at by someone from St John's Ambulance. He said she needed hospital treatment quickly, so they took her in their ambulance and I went with them.'

Reverend Peterson said that Janice told him he knew the rest.

'My dear, dear wife died six months later of a broken heart, and they are now buried side by side. I just had to leave and I came here. Now, I know, as I said, there is no proof that Leroy Leonard gave my daughter some form of drug or barbiturate, not knowing that it would turn out like it did. Allyson's friends said it was done probably to get her in the mood, but he killed her just as sure as he put a gun to her head.'

The doctor still decided to remain silent.

'Incredible,' was all that George Spring could say.

'The only time I heard the name of Leroy Leonard was at the hospital. And you can imagine the state I was in. When I found out who had taken over Shawlworth Hall, and found out the name, it troubled me. But to my shame, I did not associate the name with my daughter. Perhaps in the hospital I never heard Janice say his name, I don't know. Perhaps it went into my subconscious, and after thirty years… In answer to George, the police did hold a fine-detailed inquiry, but although it was proved at a post-mortem that it was drugs, Leonard and his friend denied any knowledge. They said there were five hundred other people in that room apart from them. When I heard Sidney and Patrick, again Leroy Leonard did not really click, but when the name Rock Express was spoken, it hit me like a thunderbolt, with the end result you know about.'

George was the first to speak. 'Well, Reverend, what can I say? As you have said, without proof no charges could be made. I would regard Leonard, knowing him the way I do, capable of anything, including that heinous act upon your daughter. But again, without evidence the hands of the law are tied.'

'How you must have suffered.' Dr James was full of sympathy for his friend. 'Before I go, I shall leave you something to help you sleep. Wait one hour after your sherry, take the medication and you will sleep until morning.'

'I shall do that,' Reverend Peterson agreed. 'Doctor, before you do go, may I ask a question of you?'

'By all means.'

'What you said to me about secrets applies to us also.'

'Yeess,' said Dr James.

'I personally could not help but notice – I don't know about the Inspector here – but over a period of time, every time Leroy Leonard's name has been mentioned *you* have acted rather strangely.'

'I have actually, especially about the shooting bit, and the names you called him,' George Spring agreed. It did not take a genius to work out his behaviour was far from normal.

Dr James sat, thought and said, 'Your ears only.'

'Our ears only; right, Reverend Peterson?'

'Of course, dear friend.' He looked at Dr James.

'You say he murdered your daughter, and I believe you. He also killed my sister.'

Chapter Seventeen

John arrived home to the smell of his pasty cooking.

'Hi, Linda, 'tis me,' he called.

'Hi, love, you've been a while.'

'Yea, I went by Miller's Pond and then to the old gamekeeper's cottage – you knows I go there – well, I'm just going to make a cup of tea and who should turn up but Sir Antony.'

'Sir Antony? What did he want?'

'If you listen, I'll tell ee. He was on his way over to Shawlworth Hall to see Leonard again, when he spots me and comes over.'

'To see Leonard again?' asked Linda.

'Linda, do you want to hear this or not?'

'Course I do. Pasty is ready.'

'Right, put it on a plate and let it cool down a bit.' Linda did as she was requested. 'I'm comin' to that,' said John. 'Yea, apparently George phoned him last night and says to'un, if he – Leonard – won't allow any shooting or killing, what about the Shawlworth Hunt? So that's how ee was going over to see that bastard again.'

'Language,' scolded Linda.

'Well, anyway, he tells me his news and I tells him what we know, has a cup of tea and that's that. He goes and I locks up and 'ere I am.'

'That pasty's OK for eating now,' said his wife.

John started on his pasty with relish and did not stop until his plate was empty.

''Ansome,' he said, sitting back and patting his stomach.

'What are we going to do now?' said Linda. 'Now that Carn Brea Castle is off.'

'Night in, watch the telly and then early night.'

'Trust you to think of that,' Linda smiled.

Next morning John awoke first, heard the rain and made himself more comfortable. As Linda was lying right up close to his side, arm over his chest, she stirred.

'Hmmm,' she murmured, 'love you.'

'Certainly did,' laughed John.

Linda smacked him.

'Hear the rain?' he said.

'Hmmm.'

'Let's have a lie in, then dinner time pop down to the Pheasant for a drink and tell them of the meeting with Sir Antony, 'cause don't suppose anything else exciting has happened.'

'Hmmm,' she replied.

Albert and Trish arrived back at the Pheasant, took off their coats and went straight into the lounge bar of the pub.

'Unbelievable.' Trish had said that at least three times from the church to the Pheasant.

They tried again to piece things together. 'He was fine until Sidney and Patrick came along, right?' said Albert.

'Right,' said Trish.

Albert was behind the bar, while Trish was putting beer mats on the table.

'Patrick was going on about Leroy Leonard and what a fan Sidney was, when bumf! Down goes Reverend Peterson. It just does not add up, it makes no sense.'

'I know,' said Trish, 'unbelievable.'

They heard the bar staff hard at work in the other room.

'Good,' said Albert, 'the girls are in.'

'How many times today?' asked Trish.

Albert cogitated. 'Twelve.'

'Bet it's more.'

'How much?'

'Pound.'

'You're on.'

Every Sunday, Albert and Trish had a bet on who could guess closest the number of times customers would ask, 'Do you serve Sunday lunch?'

The record was thirty-three. Today was raining, so Albert was happy with twelve. They didn't do Sunday lunches.

Once again the morning's events with Reverend Peterson became the main topic of conversation.

'I still can't work it out,' Albert confessed.

'I bet George will be in shortly and we will find out. Have you never thought that there might be some medical reason for it?' Trish remarked. That Sunday lunchtime neither George, Dr James nor Reverend Peterson came in.

When the hour of twelve struck, Albert opened the doors, looked out and saw John and Linda about ten yards away.

'Hello, you two. Not very often we see you both together on a Sunday lunchtime. Coming in?'

'Sure are,' said John.

'First one on the house,' Albert said quietly.

'Thanks, mate,' said John and they followed Albert into the lounge bar.

Once greetings were over and drinks served, John was ready to tell Albert about his meeting with Sir Antony – as John always called him – but the lounge bar began to fill up and both Albert and Trish were kept busy for some time. John and Linda were talking quietly when Andrew joined them.

'Hello, John.'

He turned. 'Andrew, nice to see you. Have you met Linda? Linda, Andrew.'

'Pleased to meet you,' he said. They shook hands.

'Albert, a pint for Andrew when you are ready, please.'

'Sure,' acknowledged Albert.

'How are you, Andy?'

'Oh, not too bad. He's on his high horse again. I told you about the musicians he was expecting; well, they arrived yesterday. Showed them to his studio and he had me running around for sandwiches and beer; oh, before that he got on to me about the state of the garden. We had a slight disagreement over that. I wanted to come down here to find out how Albert got on, but it was about half two before they arrived and after three before I got back home, so it was too late and then I had a, er, headache, so I didn't come out at all yesterday. I saw him and his mates going out last night, in a taxi about nine, but I don't know what time they came back.'

Albert brought John's pint.

'Sorry I've been so long. Initial rush over now by the looks of it.'

Trish joined them almost immediately.

'I've had three, how many have you had?' She looked at Albert.

'Four,' he said. He looked at the blank faces of Linda, John and Andrew.

'Private bet,' he laughed.

'Andrew's just been telling us that Leonard went out last night with them musicians he has stoppin' there,' said John.

'Yea, he went drinking in Bodmin,' said Trish.

'How do you know that?' said Linda.

'Found out this morning at church,' she replied.

'You tell 'em love, I'll serve,' said Albert.

Trish made herself comfortable and told them what had happened to Reverend Peterson at church that morning.

'So that's how you know,' said Andrew.

'Yes, Sidney and Patrick were discussing him; as soon as Leroy Leonard's name is mentioned, down he goes.'

'If you don't mind me saying, Trish, it was when the name Rock Express was mentioned,' Albert said on his return.

'Same thing,' she said.

'Well, not strictly true,' Albert once again was trying to formulate a connection.

'He thinks it's something to do with Leonard; I said it could be medical.'

'So what happened?' Linda was really interested.

'Dr James, the Cawthorne sisters, Albert and me were talking to Reverend Peterson when it happened, so Dr James examines him, says he's just fainted and heads the vicar toward the vicarage. Reverend Peterson turns and asks Sidney to get George Spring straight away. So that's why Albert thinks it's more than medical. Why should he want George?'

'Good point,' said John.

'Weird,' said Linda.

Andrew didn't speak.

'Another three,' said Albert.

'I'm going to win.' Trish was triumphant.

'Not yet,' Albert retorted.

'What is going on?' said Linda.

Trish explained.

'Well, I thought nothing else could happen, so I came to tell you my news.' John was disappointed. 'Don't think I'll bother now.' He didn't.

Albert and Trish had to serve, as another surge of requests for drinks came, so John, Linda and Andrew finished theirs and left. 'Bye,' they called.

'Bye,' came the reply, but Albert and Trish were too busy to look up.

It had been a busy lunchtime again and Trish won her pound.

'I don't feel like any lunch.'

'Neither do I.'

Both Cawthorne sisters bore a worried look on their faces for the poor dear Reverend Peterson.

'I hope he is well now,' said Jane.

'Jane, dear, Dr James is there. He's in good hands.'

'True,' agreed Jane. 'Why did it happen?'

'He *is* getting on a bit, dear.'

'Nonsense,' Jane cast scorn on her sister's remark. 'He's only middle-aged.'

'I know, dear, but anything can happen.'

'Such a lovely man.'

'I agree,' Ruby said.

'One minute talking away, next flat on the floor.'

'Frightening, dear.'

The sisters forgot about pop concerts out the back, rent increases and that horrid man for the rest of the day. Reverend Peterson was of far greater importance.

Reverend Peterson and George Spring looked at each other.

'This is too incredible for words,' said Reverend Peterson.

'This much doesn't even happen in one of Miss Marple's books,' said George, 'and that is fiction.'

'They say truth is stranger than fiction,' said Dr James.

'I know,' George still could not believe it, 'but the odds of this happening must be millions to one.'

'You asked me and I told you; now if you don't believe me…' Dr James was agitated.

'Please, dear friend,' said Reverend Peterson, 'don't get upset, but I think that you will agree the chances of this happening are phenomenal.'

'I know, but it's true,' said the doctor.

'Start at the beginning, Doctor,' said George Spring. 'We know that you are not lying, because of the way you have acted for some time now when Leroy Leonard has come up in conversation. And when you went into the corridor with Andrew.'

Dr James sat for some time to compose himself.

'You know I originally came from the North? Well, I moved for the same reason as the good Reverend here. My sister Michelle was very pretty and was a big fan of Rock Express. She formed his fan club and eventually met her pop hero. To cut a long story short, they married. It was not long after the wedding she came to me for help – help I could not give her. She wanted drugs. *My* sister, drugs. That scum always denied that he got her started on them, but I knew. I tried to help her; get her to a clinic. I told her, but no, travelling with him in high circles was all she wanted. From then on, it was all downhill: soft drugs to hard drugs, to degradation. After a period of time, he left her for someone younger, or just any pretty face. They divorced after three years. Once his money stopped, she had to get it from somewhere, because the drugs did not stop. Stealing, breaking and entering, handling of stolen goods, drug pushing, prostitution, blue movies, any way of getting money. Eighteen months later, after disappearing for ten months, she was found lying in a gutter in London, dead from a drug overdose. Ragged clothes, filthy dirty and dead, at twenty-two. He was to blame, but of course no one could prove anything. But the worst thing of all was when he was told – he just could not have cared less. And that, gentlemen, is the truth.'

Silence reigned.

'What can we say, Doctor?' said George Spring.

'I know, George. I came here, I had to leave the North. What would the law of averages be, me coming here to get away from that scum and Reverend Peterson for the same reason? I sometimes wonder if there is a God.'

'Please, dear friend. This could be some form of test of faith.'

'I'm sorry, Reverend. I want that man dead.'

'I must admit,' said Reverend Peterson, 'so do I, so do I. May God forgive me.'

'Gentlemen, I'm a policeman, remember,' said George. 'I have every sympathy with you but I have the law to uphold.'

'Of course, George, but what "the eye does not see",' said Dr James.

'Evidence is all I am worried about. I cannot act without evidence or witnesses.'

'I'll remember that, George,' said Dr James.

'So will I,' said Reverend Peterson, 'so will I.'

Catherine waited on tenterhooks on Sunday afternoon for Clive to call. Was Penny having me on? Surely not. She knew Penny was drunk, but even she wouldn't pull a cruel stunt like that. The waiting became a slow torture for her. She played with the children, she did odd jobs, but she always stayed near a phone.

Catherine sat in an armchair and was daydreaming: 'And… action.' She strutted in jeans, twirled, pranced, smiled and smoothed her bottom with both hands: 'Cut.'

Catherine jumped. The phone was ringing.

'Hello,' she squeaked. Her throat was dry with fear; she knew the answer she was going to give.

'Well?'

'Clive?'

'Course.'

'Well what?'

'You spoke to Penny?'

'Yes.'

'And?'

The conversation was going nowhere.

'Look, Cath,' said Clive, 'just say no and put me out of my agony. You've spoken to the lord and master and he said no. Am I right?'

'Yes,' said Cath.

'Cath, when are you… never mind.'

'Clive, he did say no. But tell me, is it a commercial for jeans?'

'Yes, it is. Top name for jeans, two weeks in the Australian outback, and the fee: twenty-five thousand.'

'How certain would I be of getting the contract, if I said I was interested? It's been ten years—'

'Cath, you know companies are falling over backwards to get you back. Cath, I mentioned your name when Gloria was out and they jumped at the chance. I told them it was very slim that you would do it, and I have been proved right. Look, darling, don't worry. I'll get someone at that price.'

'I bet you will,' agreed Catherine.

'That wasn't yours,' said Clive.

'What wasn't?'

'Price.'

'Sorry, I don't follow.'

'When I mentioned your name and told them the chances were slim, I said, "Look, you would not get her for double twenty-five thousand." They said, "How do you know until you try?"'

'Fifty thousand!' shouted Cath.

'Fifty thousand,' repeated Clive.

'You're joking,' said Cath, more calmly.

'I never joke about money,' said Clive.

'I'll do it,' said Cath.

'Cath, please don't piss me about.'

'I'm not. I'll do it.'

'Honest?'

'Honest.'

'Cath, what about Leroy?'

'What about that shit? I've been under his thumb long enough. Clive, you give me your word on fifty grand and a two-year exclusive contract to you and I'll do it.'

'No.'

'You won't? But I thought—'

'Cath, you give me exclusive rights and I'll give you fifty thousand and a five-year contract.'

'Then you have a deal, Clive, I promise. Leave Leroy to me.'

'Cath, I love you, could kiss you, die for you.'

'The contracts will do,' she laughed.

'Cath, please, you have never ever let me down. Are you sure?'

'Clive, I give you a one hundred per cent guarantee that I will do it.'

'Oh, Cath, this is great.'

'Clive, there's a but.'

'No, no, Cath.'

'Don't worry. When do I start the commercial?'

'Christmas, 'cause it's summer then.'

'Right, that's my first job and the contract starts after.'

'Phew, you got it. I'll start putting the word around now, though.'

'Clive, no press releases for twenty-one days. You know Leroy; he'll be off the scene by then, trust me. One word in the papers and the deal is off.'

'Cath, you have my word. I'm dreaming this. After ten years, the one and only Catherine Sullivan making a comeback exclusively to me.'

'I mean it, Clive, twenty-one days. So get the commercial contract drawn up, and your own, and as soon as they are ready, I'll sign them.'

'I still think I'm dreaming.'

'Bye, Clive.'

'Bye, Cath. I'll be in touch.'

'Careful what you say if he rings.'

'I will, I will.'

'Bye,' said Cath and put down the telephone. Had she really just done that? She felt calm and happy for the first time in ages. Two weeks over Christmas, her and the kids in Australia. She had three weeks to formulate a plan. All she knew was that, one way or another, he would be out of her life for good.

Chapter Eighteen

Monday morning dawned once again, with the sun shining and birdsong very much in evidence. Catherine had not slept much; she had too much on her mind.

Leroy groaned. 'I've got that pain back.'

'So what!' said Catherine.

'Thanks for the sympathy,' said Leroy.

'That's the last thing you get from me,' said Catherine, under her breath.

'No, it's bad this time.' Leroy sounded worried. He'd had this pain in his side on and off for weeks but had done nothing about it.

'Go to the doctor.'

'Have we got one?'

'No.'

'Then how can I go to the pissin' doctor if we don't have one?'

'Bound to be one in the village.'

'Who?'

'I don't know. Find out.'

Leroy climbed out of bed: seven thirty, Monday morning, album to do, lawyer to see at ten o'clock. 'God, I hate Mondays,' he said.

Catherine smiled. I hate you, Mondays, Tuesdays, Wednesdays, every day in fact.' She smiled again at the thought.

He showered, shaved and dressed. It was still only eight o'clock. He looked out of the window and saw Andrew. Opening it, he shouted, 'Andrew, wait there. I'm coming down.'

'Shit, what does this cretin want?' said Andrew, but he waited. Leroy came out the door.

'Andrew, have you got a doctor?'

'Not on me,' said Andrew, patting his pockets.

'Oh, ha bloody ha.' Leroy was not amused. 'Well?'

'Have I got a doctor?'

'Yes, pillock.'

'One in the village.'

'What's his name?'

'James, friend of yours.'

'What you on about? I don't know any James, especially a doctor; and no one in the village.'

'Knows you.'

'Me?'

'You.'

'James what?'

'No, Dr James, not James what.'

'No, you're wrong.'

'Not. Knows all about you; been asking about you. Described you and everything. Likes you so much he even wants to kill you.'

'Stop arsin' around. You sure?'

'Positive.'

'What's he like?'

'Two arms, two legs, two eyes…'

'Listen, you smart git, answer properly.'

'Doctor, about fifty-ish, very short, about five three.'

'You're joking.'

'Nope.'

'Well, well, well,' smirked Leroy.

'Know now?' said Andrew.

'Oh yes, I know now.' Leroy headed for the garage, turned back to Andrew, still laughing, and said, 'You are right. He will want to kill me. I'm now going to give him his chance.'

'Send in Mrs Treworthy,' said Dr James, his finger on the intercom. Every Monday morning Mrs Treworthy was and had been his first patient for years – blood pressure – so every Monday morning she had a check-up.

'Mrs Treworthy is here, Doctor, but there is a gentleman insisting on seeing you first.' His receptionist sounded agitated.

'Has he an appointment?'

'No, Doctor.'

'Is it serious?'

'He won't say, Doctor.'

'Tell him to make an appointment. Give him the first available one we have.'

'I… sorry, tell him what? Doctor, he says to tell you it's your old friend Leroy.'

Dr James shook.

'Doctor, you all right?'

'Yes, yes, I'm fine. You had better send him in.' There was a knock on the door and in stepped Leonard, the filth, the scum, who had ruined his life and the lives of his parents. But, above all, his sister's killer.

'Hello, Doc. I couldn't believe it could possibly be you when Andrew told me, but it is.'

'What do you want?'

'I've got a pain.'

'You have given many people much pain.'

'What's that supposed to mean?'

'Look, just go.'

'But I've got a pain.'

'Then find another doctor.'

'What is wrong with you?' said Leroy.

'You have the nerve to ask me that?'

'Look, if it's about Michelle, I had nothing to do with that.'

Dr James stood up. 'Please leave, Leonard, or whatever your name is.'

'I've told you—'

'And I've told *you*! You started her on drugs and you know it.'

'Couldn't prove it then, can't prove it now.'

'She never knew about drugs until she met you, you filth.'

'Don't know about drugs, but I was the first. Know what I mean, Doc?' Leroy winked.

'Just get out, you scum.'

'You have to treat me, I'm ill.'

'I don't, now get out and go to a doctor in Bodmin.'

'Listen, you little shit, I didn't kill her. I wasn't there I don't know anything about it, and if you say I did I'll have you in court so fast for slander your feet won't touch the ground. Now, are you going to treat this pain or not?'

Dr James lost it completely. He opened his door and screamed at Leroy to get out or he would kill him there and then. Everyone looked startled and his receptionist came to help.

'Get out. Get out, you filth, you animal, scum, vermin. Get out, get out!'

Leroy was smiling. 'Doc has Monday-morning blues,' he said, and left.

Dr James stood, calmed himself and said, 'Ladies and gentlemen, please excuse that outburst. It was unforgivable of me. Now, if any of you can wait until tomorrow, I would greatly appreciate it.' All left, apart from two.

'No more today, thank you,' he said to his receptionist.

'Very well, Doctor.'

One patient went in, which just left old Mr Dutton.

'Weren't that that Leonard bloke from up the 'all?' he asked.

'I do believe it was,' the receptionist replied.

'Doc don't like ee, do ee.'

'Apparently not,' she said.

Leroy went outside. Cheeky git, he said to himself. Blaming me for Michelle dying of a drug overdose. All I ever gave her was grass and then she didn't have to take it. She asked me what it was like.

'I hope the lads have made a start,' said Leroy. They had got two or three down on Saturday, had a late start yesterday but had still managed another four, although it was eleven o'clock at night before they finished. So Leroy let them get on with it; today he had business to see to.

Leroy drove out of the village and headed for Bodmin. He parked his car and went to the offices of 'J Fredricks, Lawyer', knocked on the door and walked in.

'Leroy Leonard, to see Fredricks.'

Uncouth man, thought the young lady at the reception desk.

'You deaf?'

'No, Mr Leonard.'

'Anyone with him?'

'I don't think so.'

'Good.' Leroy headed for the door marked private.

'Fredricks,' said Leroy and sat down.

'Do take a seat,' said Jonathan Fredricks.

'What do you mean? I have.'

'Precisely.'

'Get out of bed the wrong side this morning, did we?'

'What do you want, Mr Leonard?' he said impatiently. 'I have clients to see who have made appointments.'

'Heard of Spring? And don't say "Yes, comes before Summer".'

'Mr Leonard, I am a busy man. Please get to the point of your visit.'

'Detective Inspector Spring – have you heard of him?'

'Of course I have. First-class officer.'

'I want him charged.'

'You want him charged with what?'

'You tell me. You're the expert.'

'Please, Mr Leonard.'

'Well, he came to my house on Friday evening, uninvited, threatened me, swore at me, and told me he was going to throw me in jail.'

'Mr Leonard, these are serious charges. Please start at the beginning and this time the truth.'

'No calls until further notice, Anne,' he said on the intercom. 'And I am not to be disturbed. When Mr Casey arrives, tell him I am dealing with an emergency and I will be with him as soon as is humanly possible. Give him some coffee or something. Thank you.'

'Now, Mr Leonard, exactly as it happened. And I mean exactly.'

Leroy told his story and waited. Jonathan breathed heavily through his nose.

'Well, Mr Leonard, if that is the truth, then Detective Inspector Spring has some serious charges to answer.'

'Told you, didn't I.'

'Leave it with me and I will sort it out today.'

'Good, you'd better,' said Leroy and left. Jonathan picked up the telephone and dialled a number.

'Hello, Detective Chief Inspector Blackwood please. Donald, it's Jonathan. Bad news, I'm afraid. I have had some serious complaints made to me today about one of your officers... Who? Detective Inspector Spring.' There was a pause. 'I know, I know he would be the last one for me as well, but I have had these complaints made. When? Lunchtime? Fine, see you then.' Jonathan Fredricks placed the receiver back in its cradle.

'Thanks for seeing me so quickly, Donald.'

'Jonathan, what is this nonsense all about?'

'Look, Donald, I don't like this any more than you do. I happen to think that George Spring is a damn good cop. But when one of my clients lays these charges, what can I do?'

'I know that, Jonathan, but George Spring?'

'The man who is bringing these charges is adamant that he is telling the truth.'

'Well, I had better hear them,' said Detective Chief Inspector Blackwood.

'How about blackmail and wrongful arrest.'

'Oh, now come on, this has got to be a joke.'

'Afraid not.'

Jonathan continued to tell Blackwood about what had happened last Friday evening at Shawlworth Hall.

'Does look bad, doesn't it.' Detective Chief Inspector Blackwood had a worried frown on his face.

'It certainly does,' agreed Jonathan.

'This could finish him. He could even go to jail for this.'

'I know,' said Jonathan.

'He's such a good cop, unblemished record,' said Blackwood.

'Sorry, Donald.'

'Not your fault. Look, hold fast until I've spoken to George and then come and see me again.'

'I'll do my best,' said Jonathan, 'but—'

'Who has laid these charges anyway?'

'Leroy Leonard.'

'Never heard of him.'

'Bought Shawlworth Hall estate for ten million.'

'What is he, a pop singer?'

'Nail right on the head.'

'OK, leave it with me and I'll get back to you.'

'Seventy-two hours; that's all, I'm afraid.'

'OK, Jonathan. Thursday.'

Before Leroy went back to Shawlworth Hall, he once again pulled up in the surgery car park and went into the waiting room. It was empty apart from a gentleman standing at the reception desk.

'Thank you, dear lady,' he said.

'That's all right, Rev—' She got no further.

'Mr Leonard, please leave. Dr James is not here.'

'I'm not here to cause trouble. Just tell shorty to be at the Hall seven thirty Friday evening,'

'For what purpose?'

'Just tell him, darling. That's all.' Leroy turned to leave.

'Thank you, dear lady, for the letter for the hospital. I shall go this afternoon,' said the Reverend. He looked at Leroy. 'Are you Leroy Leonard of Shawlworth Hall?'

Leroy turned to see a distinguished gentleman wearing a dog collar.

'You are?' said Leroy. 'If it's to save my soul you are too late.'

'I hope I am, Sir. I hope you rot in hell.'

The receptionist gasped. Never in a hundred years did she expect that from Reverend Peterson.

'What is it with this place!' said Leroy. 'I've never met you before in my life, you wear a dog collar and stand there and say you hope I rot in hell. Is everyone mad here?'

'You are right, Sir, we have never met. But if you would care to come outside, or to the vicarage, I will explain how a man of God can hate another human being so much.'

'After you, Vicar. This place is mad, mad,' said Leroy, shaking his head.

Outside, Reverend Peterson said, 'Is it to be here then, or at the vicarage?'

'Get in the car,' said Leroy.

'Very well.' Reverend Peterson sat in the passenger's seat.

'Now, what's all this nonsense about?' said Leroy, getting behind the wheel.

'Sir, when you kill a man's wife and daughter, it's far from nonsense.'

'I don't believe I'm hearing this.' Leroy was dumbfounded.

'It's true, I assure you,' said Reverend Peterson.

'Well, I hope you can explain and it had better be good.' Leroy was now angry.

Reverend Peterson retold his story for the second time in less than twenty-four hours. When he had finished he was crying.

'Firstly,' said Leroy, 'I do not remember the incident, secondly, I was never charged with anything. How can I have killed your wife?'

'Because, Sir, if you had not killed my daughter, my wife would have not died of a broken heart.'

'Look, say one word of this to anyone, anywhere, and I'll have you for slander. I'm sick of being accused in this place. You're all raving mad.'

'Do you mean Dr James?'

'You know about him?'

'Yes.'

'Oh great, just great. One word, just one word from either of you and I'll do the pair of you. Now, get out of the car.'

'A pleasure to leave.'

'Sod off!'

'Because I am a man of the cloth, Sir, does not mean I am not a man. One day, one day.'

'You threatening me?'

'Oh yes, you had better believe I am.'

'Get out!'

'As I said, with pleasure.'

'Reverend, be at the Hall Friday night at seven thirty.'

'Why?'

'Two can play at this game. That house of yours – part of the village?'

'Yes, why?'

'Pay rent?'

'No.'

'You do now, bye.' Leroy drove away.

Reverend Peterson watched him drive away. 'One day,' he said, 'one day.'

Leroy flopped in a chair and just sat for a good five minutes.

'I don't believe it,' he said. 'I must be the only bloke that goes out the house with a pain in his side and, before lunchtime, gets accused of three murders.'

'Who's done that?' said Catherine, not that she was bothered. She had a lot more on her mind.

'Dr James and a vicar,' he said.

'Why does that ring a bell? Dr James?' asked Catherine.

'Michelle James's brother,' said Leroy. 'Says I killed his daughter and wife.'

'Well, you have been a busy boy.'

'Sod off,' said Leroy and went to his studio.

'I wish someone *would* kill you; solve all my problems,' she said.

'George Spring there?'

Sergeant Harris's hand shot over the mouthpiece.

'Sir, it's Detective Chief Inspector Blackwood for you.'

'Detective Inspector Spring here, Sir.'

'George, get to my office straight away.'

'Can it wait, Sir? This mugging case?'

'No, it can't… straight away.' Detective Chief Inspector Blackwood was in no mood for compromise.

'Why do I think this is not for a medal?' said George Spring.

He tapped on the door of Detective Chief Inspector Blackwood's office. 'Come in.' He went in.

'Sit down, George.'

George sat.

'George, I'm afraid some rather serious complaints have been made against you.'

'Me, Sir?'

'You, Sir.'

'By whom?'

'George, you know I've always thought of you as a first-class cop but you know I must go by the book. So, firstly, I want to hear your side and then I will have to go from there.'

'Very well, Sir.'

'This morning I had in my office the lawyer Jonathan Fredrıcks, who told me that one of his clients had charges to make against you.'

'What charges?'

'Well, if they are substantiated, you're looking at blackmail and wrongful arrest.'

'What!'

''Fraid so.'

George felt sick, 'Who is it, Sir?'

'Leonard, Leroy Leonard.'

'What, that bastard?'

'George, that's not going to help. I'm here to help you, so I never heard that. From now on, just answer questions, right? Just questions.'

'Sorry, Sir. Very well.'

'Do you know Leroy Leonard?'

'Yes, Sir.'

'Start again. I'm going to tape this.'

Detective Chief Inspector Blackwood set up a tape recorder, placed two tapes in, and asked if George was happy.

George nodded.

'This is Detective Chief Inspector Blackwood. Present is Detective Inspector Spring. Monday, 13th August 1992. The time is 2.15 p.m. Detective Inspector Spring, do you know Leroy Leonard of Shawlworth Hall, Shawlworth?'

'Yes, Sir.'

'Did you on the evening of Friday, 30th July, at approximately seven thirty in the evening, go to Shawlworth Hall?'

'Yes, Sir.'

'For what purpose did you go?'

'To see Mr Leonard about the Shawlworth shoots.'

'When Mr Leonard came to the door, what happened?'

'Nothing happened, Sir.'

'Please think, Detective Inspector. Did Mr Leonard come and answer the door?'

'Yes, Sir.'

'Did you say to him, "Detective Inspector Spring"? And did he say, "No, Leroy Leonard"?'

'Yes, Sir.'

'Did he show you into a room with old gear in? Musical gear?'

'Yes, Sir.'

'Did he then ask you what you wanted?'

'Yes, Sir.'

'What happened then?'

'I went on to explain about how I ran the shoots for the estate, and it had come to my attention via John Penrose, the game-keeper, that they were to cease.'

'Go on, Inspector.'

'He confirmed that they were to cease. I told him the first one was already organised and would he allow it to go ahead. He said no. I tried to explain that the Shawlworth shoots went back years and were famous.'

'What did he say to that?'

'He said it wasn't his problem, so I suggested that we paid him.'

'And?'

'He just laughed and said no. I then asked him why he was so against the sport.'

'What did he reply to that?'

'He started getting rather upset as to how I could call it a sport – "poor birds made to fly by beaters and then blasted by some git with a shotgun"? He then went on to tell me how he grew up in a north-east pit village; about his first job in an abattoir with his father; about the sight of blood and gore all over the place, the smell, and watching the men standing there with a knife and ripping open the animals after stringing them up. The animals' insides flopping out onto the floor, hides being ripped off and kids washing shit off tripe.'

'He has a point.'

'He then went on to ask me about by-laws for open-air pop concerts.'

'You then called him mad?'

'Well, yes, Sir.'

'Carry on.'

'I told him he couldn't do it; he said that his lawyer said he could.'

'Did you say you would fight him over this?'

'Yes, Sir, but not as a policeman using my influence. I meant as a Shawlworth resident.'

'Did you explain that to him?'

'No, Sir.'

'Carry on.'

'That was it, Sir.'

'You sure?'

'Sir.'

'Did you then say to him, and be very careful how you answer this, "One step out of line, Leonard, one step, I don't care how much money you have I'll get you; I'll have you in the nick in Bodmin so fast your feet won't touch the ground"? Did you say that?'

'Well…'

'Detective Inspector, please answer. Did you say that?'

'Yes, Sir, I did.'

'Interview ends 3 p.m.'

Detective Chief Inspector Blackwood switched off the recorder.

'George.'

'Sir.'

'Doesn't look good, does it.'

'No, Sir, but, but… blackmail and wrongful arrest?'

'Look, George, a good lawyer – and Jonathan is very good – stands up in court and says, "Did you say, I'll get you"? – threatening behaviour at the very least. And could it not be interpreted that, "If you go ahead with these concerts I'll have you", is blackmail? "I'll have you in the nick so fast"? "One foot out of line"? So, for some trivial reason, you're going to lock him up. Wrongful arrest, George. I'm no lawyer and even *I* make it sound bad.'

'So what happens now, Sir?'

'I don't know. Let me sleep on it.'

'Very well, Sir.'

'George, off the record, I'll do everything in my power to get you out of this mess. But no promises.'

'Thank you, Sir.'

'OK, George. That's all.'

George left the office in a daze.

'You OK, Guv?' It was Sergeant Harris.

'No, I'm bloody well not. If anybody wants me for the rest of the day, you don't know where I am. OK?'

'Sure, Guv, can I help?'

'Nope.' George left the police station.

As Sunday was a lost cause at the Manor House, it was Monday morning at breakfast before Juliet found out about the stabling of Gladiator at the Edwards' place.

'But, Daddy…' Juliet was none too pleased with the idea.

'Look, darling, I am trying to make the best of a bad job here. Look at things as they are, you must be realistic.'

'I know, Daddy, but Edwards' place, when we have good stable here for Gladiator?'

The door opened and the faithful servitor entered.

'Will that be all, Sir?'

'Thank you, Fielding.'

'Very good, Sir.'

Antony was despairing with his daughter. 'Look, can you ride your horse here?' he paused.

'Well…' Juliet was hesitant.

'Can you?'

'No, I suppose not.'

'So if not here, where?'

'Well, I don't know.'

'Oh, I give up.' Antony left the room.

'Your father is only trying to help, dear.'

'I know, Mummy.'

'Try and understand.'

'OK, Mummy.' Juliet stood up and walked toward the door. 'I'm going to brush Gladiator or something, seeing as I cannot ride him.'

'Very well, dear.'

'You all right, Mr Fielding?' Mrs Pengelly looked at him anxiously.

'Yes, I'm fine. Why do you ask?'

'You look a bit pale.'

'I must admit I do have a bit of a headache but no matter.'

Now that breakfast was over in the dining room, Fielding and

Mrs Pengelly cleared away the dishes and had a cup of tea themselves. This had become a regular thing now.

Mrs Pengelly looked at Mr Fielding and smiled. 'You're back at the Hall, you're miles away.'

'I must admit I was. How did you know?'

'When someone is miles away, you can tell by the look on their face if it's good or bad.'

'And mine?'

'Smiles. So I guessed you must be at the Hall, supervising breakfast for... how many? Ten, fifteen?'

'Once again you are right. It's now coming up to August 12th and I've seen as many as twenty for breakfast; both west and east wings full, laughing, merriment all day. I cannot remember the last time I saw Lady Vanessa smile. How times have changed, Mrs Pengelly.'

'Alice.'

'I'm sorry?'

'My name is Alice.'

He laughed. 'Very well, then. Mine is Vernon.'

'Vernon Fielding,' said Alice. 'Sounds like a surgeon's name.'

Again he laughed. 'Instead, a humble servant.'

'You don't put yourself down, Vernon. You are a proper gent.'

'You're a lady, Alice.' They both laughed.

'Mr Fiel— I mean Vernon, what was it like years ago at the big house?'

'Well, Alice, I started as a boot boy – that means I cleaned all the boots – and damned hard work it was at the height of the season. All day it would take me to clean them boots, because no matter how dirty they got, they had to shine.'

'How many staff, Vernon?'

'Oh, I don't really know. But let's see what I can remember. Outside: five gardeners, four in the stables, and two drivers – that's eleven. Inside: kitchen, about eight from cook down; upstairs four, no six; ground floor: another six. So that's twenty and eleven. I couldn't say for certain, but about thirty staff.'

'Mercy me.'

'They were good days though, Alice. Christmas was the best of all.'

'I can imagine.'

'Master Antony being the only child, you would have thought that he would have been possessive with his toys. But no, he would allow others to play with them. I was a young man myself when Master Antony was young. By then I was learning the trade; I was a junior footman. I got the job to play with him when he was alone; keep him amused. We would play cricket, rugby and, above all, he loved fishing – anything to do with sport. What is it they say, Alice? All good things must come to an end. And for the family they have.'

'Do you know what caused the sale of the estate, Vernon?'

'Officially no, but you hear things and Sir Richard, Master Antony's father, did not mind what he said in my presence because he knew that what I heard was kept a secret and never ever repeated.'

'So you won't tell me?' Alice looked disappointed.

'Alice, you live in the village.'

'Yes.'

'The village is part of the estate.'

'Yes.'

'How much rent do you pay? Although it may seem an impertinent question, I already know, because no one does.'

'That's true.'

'Sir Richard was too good. Please, I'm not saying he shouldn't have been, to his tenants, but the bottom line was he was no businessman. He employed an estate accountant and gave him financial autonomy over the estate's accounts. He robbed poor Sir Richard blind. He was caught and sent to jail, but by then it was too late. The estate never recovered. Staff were cut to the bone, until only two were left. People rallied round for all the kindness Sir Richard had shown – George Spring took over the shoots; Harry Spence came and did the gardens in his spare time; young Timmy, his son, used to help him.'

'Timmy Spence, that's the lad who drowned in Miller's Pond. Lovely boy, only fourteen.' Alice wiped an eye.

'That's him,' said Vernon.

'So apart from me in the house and John Penrose, the game-keeper – apart from us – nobody. For an estate that size. Now, when Sir Richard died, it came out that he hadn't done what he should have regarding the future of the estate – death duties or whatever – and so when it happened... I'll never forget the day Master Antony came back from the lawyers after seeing Mr Jonathan Fredricks and had to tell Lady Vanessa they were going to have to sell up. Poor Miss Juliet was hysterical, Alice; it was terrible, terrible.'

'My, my,' said Alice, 'I bet it was.'

'So, dear lady, here we are. One good thing came out of all this.'

'What's that?' said Alice.

'I met you, dear lady.'

Alice blushed and waved her hand at Vernon.

Chapter Nineteen

'Strange, very strange.' Albert looked deep in thought.

'How's that?' said Andrew.

'There's you, there's me.'

'So?'

'So where's everybody else?'

'Oh, I see.'

'No doc, no Reverend, no John and no George.'

'It is rather strange,' agreed Andrew.

'Even if it's just for a pint and a chat early on, at least two or three of them are normally here.'

It had been another fine day and so, after Andrew had mentioned about Dr James to Leroy, he pottered about the grounds all day. He only saw Leroy once more after that, when he returned with a face like thunder.

'There's still plenty of time,' continued Andrew.

'Suppose. I'm not bothered, it just seems strange.'

'Probably got things to do.' Conversation at this point was becoming boring for them both.

'I've got some news,' Andrew said.

'What's that?' Albert's face brightened.

'First, though, how's the Reverend?'

'Haven't seen anyone.' Albert once again looked glum.

'Listen.' Andrew was ready to start. 'This morning I got up early and wandered up to the Hall, when his master's voice comes bellowing down from an upstairs window, "Wait there".' So I waits. He comes out the front door and asks me, do I have a doctor? Not on me at the moment, I replied.'

Albert smiled.

'He didn't find it funny at all, so he asks again and I tell him there is one in the village. He asks what his name is and say James, a friend of yours. He looks at me blank like, and says he doesn't know any James, so I said *he* knows *you*.'

'What did he say to that?' Albert was now engrossed.

'It's all right, I'll serve,' Trish said sarcastically.

'Eh? Oh sorry, love. Go on, Andy.'

'James what he says. I say no, Dr James and tell him how Dr James loves him so much he wants to kill him. He asks me to describe him, so I do. Suddenly, a broad smile comes on his face, so I said you know now. Oh yes, I know, he says, and walks away, laughing. Then he turns and says, "You're right. He will want to kill me and now he's going to get his chance." Then he walks off for the car.'

Albert whistled.

'What's so interesting?' Trish joined them.

'Tell you later, love.' Albert once again was trying to put two and two together.

'So you have not seen anyone at all?'

'No, I wanted to see if I could find out what caused the Reverend to collapse.'

'I still say it's medical,' Trish was adamant.

'Well, I'm still not so sure.' Albert was just as adamant as his wife was.

'Good evening, Dr James.' It was George.

'Hello, George, nice to hear from you.'

'Doctor, I've spoken to Reverend Peterson and, if you are free, could you please join me and him tonight at seven at the vicarage.

'More bad news?'

'From my point of view, yes,' said Detective Inspector Spring.

'Mine also,' sighed Dr James.

'Not again.'

'Afraid so.'

'Reverend also?' said George.

'Do you know, George, if this was not so serious it would be funny.'

'Tell me about it.'

'Yes, I shall be there. See you later.'

'Goodbye, Doctor, and thanks.'

'Not at all, not at all,' said Dr James.

At 7 p.m. precisely, the three gentlemen sat in the same room as yesterday, each with a sherry.

'How did you get on at the hospital today?' Dr James looked at Reverend Peterson.

'I did not go,' replied the Reverend, sheepishly.

'May I ask why?'

'Circumstances, dear friend.'

'OK then,' said George. 'Who starts?'

'May as well be me,' said Reverend Peterson. 'This morning I called at your surgery for my letter for the hospital. Whilst I was there, in came this, this, gentleman. Your receptionist said for him to leave, as you had left. She called him Mr Leonard. He replied that he was not there to cause any trouble and asked her to tell shorty, I am sorry, Doctor, to be at the Hall at seven thirty on Friday evening. She asked of him for what purpose and he replied, "Just tell him", that's all. He turned to leave and, after I thanked your receptionist for the letter, I asked him if he was Leroy Leonard of Shawlworth Hall. Leonard asked me who I was and said that if it was to save his soul, I was too late. I replied, to my shame, that I hoped I was and that I also hoped he rotted in hell. Leonard then went on to accuse everyone here of being mad; that he and I had never met before and here I was wearing a dog collar and saying I hope he rots in hell. I told him if he wished to step outside, I would tell him why a man of God could hate another human being so much.

'Gentlemen, another sherry? No, then I shall continue. When outside, I asked him whether it was to be here, your car park, Doctor, or at the vicarage, but it turned out to be neither. He told me to get into his car, so I did. Leonard got into the driving seat and asked me what all this nonsense was about. I told him how he had killed my daughter and wife, and he said that he did not believe he was hearing this, and I had better explain, so I did. I told him the whole story. Firstly, he said that he did not remember the incident and secondly, he said that he was never charged with any offence, and how could he have killed my wife? So again I explained that if he had not killed my daughter, my wife would not have died of a broken heart. He then went on to say that if I made public any of this he would prosecute me for slander and again he accused us all of being mad. I asked him if that included you, dear friend, and he said, "You know about him?" I said yes I did and he said one word from either of us and he would do the pair of us. Then he ordered me out of the car. I said it would be a pleasure to leave and he told me to sod off. I said that just because I was a man of the cloth does not mean I am not a man and one day... He asked if I was threatening him and I said I believed I was. He then said be at the Hall at 7.30 p.m. on Friday. I asked why, but all he did was enquire if I paid rent. I said no, and he said, well two can play at this game, you do now. Then he drove off.'

'This is like some nightmare, but instead of stopping it's just picking up momentum,' said Dr James.

'Well, I suppose it's my turn now,' said George Spring and told Reverend Peterson and Dr James how he had been called into Detective Chief Inspector Blackwood's office and told that complaints had been made against him.

'I don't believe it.' Dr James was flabbergasted.

'No, neither do I. You are a fine policeman; honest as a day is long.' Reverend Peterson was equally as emphatic.

'Thank you, gentlemen.'

'What are these charges? Can you say, and who made them?' asked Dr James.

'No further, gentlemen.'

'What we three say to each other is in the strictest confidence from now on. Agreed?' said Reverend Peterson.

'Wholeheartedly,' confirmed the doctor.

'Firstly then, gentlemen, the charges are blackmail and wrongful arrest, and the perpetrator of the charges is, guess...'

'No, no, no.' Reverend Peterson thumped the arm of the chair.

'Not Leonard?'

'Yes, Leonard.'

'But how, when?' Dr James was dumbfounded.

'Last Friday night at the Hall,' he said. 'I tried to blackmail him and then, when that did not work, I threatened to throw him in jail for no reason.'

'The man is devoid of rationality,' said Reverend Peterson.

'George, what if he makes these charges stick?' Dr James now looked concerned.

'I don't really know,' said George. 'But, at the best, I'll be kicked off the force with no pension; nothing after all these years. And worst,' he paused, 'jail, gentlemen, jail.'

'Are, er, are you sure?' Reverend Peterson went pale again.

'No, I am not, about jail, but I am about being kicked off the force,' he replied.

'The man is evil. I wish by some form of *legerdemain* I could rid us of him,' said Dr James.

Neither Detective Inspector Spring nor Reverend Peterson disagreed with the doctor.

'Without further ado, gentlemen, I shall tell you my story and then we shall have to see how we can rid ourselves of this trash.' The doctor took the floor.

'I was ready in my surgery as usual this morning and rang for my first patient, who on a Monday always happens to be Mrs Treworthy. Well, this morning my receptionist informed me that someone was insisting on seeing me. It turns out to be that filth, that scum. He came into my consulting room grinning; came and sat down and, as calm as you please, said, "I've got a pain". I said, "You have given many people much pain". He was still insistent he had this pain. So I told him to find another doctor. "What's wrong with you?" he said calmly. "What's wrong with me? You have the nerve to ask me that." I could not believe what I was hearing. He said, "Look, if it's about Michelle, I had nothing to do with that". I stood up and asked him to leave. I told him that he was the one who had started her off on drugs. I was told that I could not prove it then and I could not prove it now. He then made a sick remark about how he didn't know about being the first with drugs, but how he was the first in another category. I again told him to get out, but he told me I had to treat him because he's ill. I said to him that I did not have to treat him; I told him to get out and find another doctor. He then called me a little shit, threatened me with court action and, after all that, said, "Now about this pain". Gentlemen, I just completely lost it, I opened the door and literally screamed at him to get out, or I would kill him there and then.'

'Not a smart move in front of so many witnesses.'

'I know, George, but that man had my blood boiling. I called him filth, scum, vermin and shouted at him to get out. He was still smiling as he left the waiting room; he turned to my patients and said I must have Monday morning blues.'

Once again doom cast its ugly head.

'Gentlemen, what can we do about this man?' Reverend Peterson looked very downcast.

No one spoke, because no one had an answer.

Leroy made a hasty exit from the bedroom, after shouting for Andrew to wait there. Catherine lay in bed, thinking that his pain could not be all that bad if he could make that quick an exit. Catherine knew she still had major problems with Leroy about her commitment to Clive. She was aware of the wrath of Leroy, but tried to lighten it by telling herself that she wasn't leaving him for good. She mused, If you believe that you're a bigger fool than even you thought of yourself.

Catherine lay for some time before coming to the conclusion that the sooner she told him the better. How and when still remained a problem. Suddenly Catherine dived out of bed, put on a dressing gown and left the bedroom. She looked in on the children, who were still fast asleep, and went down to the kitchen. She made herself a coffee and was now sure of her immediate plans. She picked up the telephone, dialled a three digit number and waited. 'Yes, could you please give me the name of a taxi firm in Bodmin and passenger information at Truro station?' Catherine wrote down the two numbers.

Firstly, she dialled Truro. 'Good morning, could you please tell me the times of the trains to Paddington from Truro this afternoon?' After a short wait, Catherine wrote down 3.30 pm. 'Thank you.' She flicked the cut-off switch on the phone base unit and dialled again. 'Good morning, could you please send a taxi to Shawlworth Hall for two thirty to go to Truro railway station. Yes, two thirty, thank you.' She replaced the receiver.

Catherine's plan was to take the children to London for a week's holiday to stay with Mrs Mason. Then she would return on Friday and tell Leroy over the weekend. That way, if he got nasty, the children would not be there to see it. Mrs Mason. Catherine again picked up the phone and dialled.

'Hello, Mrs Mason? Catherine here... Oh fine, just fine. I was wondering if I brought the children up to London and stayed with them until Friday, could they please stay with you then until next week sometime? ...They can? Oh that's lovely. I, er, don't really know when next week, because of circumstances. I will give you the full story when I see you tonight. I should think about seven thirty or eight. Bye for now, and Mrs Mason, thanks.'

Good, thought Catherine, now the children. She went up to their room and woke them up.

'Lee, Pansy, listen to Mummy.'

'Yes, Mummy?' Lee yawned and rubbed his eyes.

'How would you like to go on a secret trip? So secret only you, Pansy and Mummy know about it?'

'Not Daddy?' Lee was now wide awake.

'Especially not Daddy, because the surprise *is* for Daddy.'

'What is it, Mummy and where are we going?' Lee was asking all the questions, Pansy was falling back off to sleep.

'Well, I want to get Daddy a surprise present from you and Pansy for getting the ponies for you both. But I cannot get it here so we are going to have to go to London, stay in the flat – just the three of us – and see Mrs Mason. That is why it must be a big, big secret from Daddy.'

Lee nodded. Pansy was asleep.

'Lee, will you do Mummy a favour?'

'Course, Mummy.'

'Pansy has gone off to sleep. When she wakes up, tell her you have a secret and must hide from Daddy in case she tells him.'

'I will, Mummy.' Lee was enjoying the cloak and dagger intrigue.

'Good boy; now Mummy is going to get ready and then I shall get you some breakfast. OK?'

'Yes, Mummy.'

'Good boy.'

'Mummy, when are we going on our secret trip?'

'This afternoon by train.'

'Oh great, Mummy, train.'

'Remember, not a word.'

'Not a word.' Lee looked around and placed his finger to his lips.

Catherine felt like crying again and hurriedly left the room. That morning she showered and dressed in double-quick time, and then proceeded to pack a suitcase; just enough of her clothes for four days and enough for Lee and Pansy for a week. Catherine felt pleased; everything was falling into place nicely. Money, God, what about money? Use plastic, phew. Her heart was pumping fast, but it calmed down.

She heard bedroom doors closing. God, who's that? He's back. Then she remembered the musicians. They must be going to the studio; better act as normal and take some coffee and toast for them.

Having finished the packing, Catherine returned to the kitchen and duly made coffee and toast for the musicians. By the time she had walked along the corridor, into the main hall, up the stairs, along the upstairs corridor, through the door and finally into the studio, her arms were dropping off. They thanked her; she replied, 'Pleasure,' left and once again returned to the kitchen.

That tight-fisted git has millions in the bank and won't even allow someone to help in the kitchen, she thought. That's a wife's job. I wonder if he would say the same if his mother was made to do it? She imagined her in the kitchen of his old house, described by him as two up two down and an outside netty – it was ages before Catherine found out that netty was a colonial term for toilet – and bathing him on a Friday night in a tin bath in front of the fire.

Catherine gave the children their breakfasts in the bedroom just in case. She waited, washed and dressed them, then said, 'Remember, not a word.'

'What about, Mummy?' asked Pansy.

'Shh,' said Lee, 'it's a secret. I'll tell you about it.'

'Good boy,' said Catherine and went downstairs. This time she went into the drawing room, picked up the phone, dialled a number and waited. Finally she spoke.

'Penny, listen, I haven't got much time. I'm coming to London with Lee and Pansy... Yes, today. Can you be at the flat for nine tonight? Good. Penny, listen, I did… yes. Listen… No, I'll tell you all about it tonight… Right, good.'

Catherine heard the front door slam.

'Penny, I've got to go,' she said and slammed down the phone.

Catherine tried to look innocent. Leroy came in, flopped in a chair and sat for five minutes before he even spoke. He started talking about murders, not that she was bothered, as she had other things on her mind.

'Dr James and a vicar,' Leroy continued.

'Why does that ring a bell: Dr James?' she said.

'Michelle James's brother,' he replied. 'Says I killed his wife and daughter.'

Catherine was miles away, but remembered saying something about him being a busy boy.

'Sod off,' he replied and went up to his studio.

'I wish someone would kill you; solve all my problems,' Catherine said.

She ran through the morning's events. Train time confirmed, taxi booked, Mrs Mason sorted, Penny sorted, check handbag for money and credit cards. Handbag, where have I put the flaming bag? Kitchen, I'm sure it's in the kitchen. Catherine found her bag in the kitchen. Credit cards there and forty pounds in cash. That's enough for the taxi fare and odds and ends. If I can't get any money, I'll just pay the rail fares with the card.

She looked at the clock: it was nearly noon. Lunch for that lot. She set a tray with a good-sized quiche, crisps and sausage rolls – veggie, of course, for the lord and master – bananas and a dozen cans of Coke. I'll never make it with this lot, she thought, but London and the chance to be away from that pig gave her determination. She set the tray down and told Leroy that she was taking the children out and had ordered a taxi to go to Bodmin.

'Why not take a car?' he said.

Think girl, think: 'I have a bad headache and don't feel like driving.'

'OK, as long as you are back by teatime for us.'

You'll have a long wait, mate, she said to herself. Catherine returned to the children's bedroom, having first stopped off to collect the suitcase.

'Now remember, a big surprise for Daddy, OK? No sound. Right, downstairs.'

Lee and Pansy crept down, looking all about them for their daddy.

Catherine had another flash of inspiration. 'If Daddy comes down, just say we are going to Bodmin to do some shopping, OK.'

'OK,' they agreed.

The next two hours dragged for Catherine, but Leroy never showed and she breathed a sigh of relief when the taxi finally arrived at two thirty. 'Come on, children, quickly,' she said and they ran to the door. Catherine opened the door, told the children to get in and looked towards the east wing. She could see no face at the window. She threw the suitcase into the back and climbed into the front.

'Let's go please,' she said.

'Seat belts, madam, for the children,' said the taxi driver.

'Please just drive and I will see to them once we are away from here.'

'We're on a secret mission,' said Lee.

The taxi driver thought in a hurry. Truro station? She's doing a moonlight from the old man.

'OK,' he said and drove away.

Once clear of the estate, Catherine said, 'You can stop now.'

'Very well, madam.'

He pulled over. Catherine went to the back of the car, fastened Lee and Pansy in their seat belts, returned to the front passenger's seat and said, 'Thank you, let's go.'

Catherine wondered what Leroy would say when he found the note she had left on the kitchen table, knowing he would not follow her as his music was far too important.

Leroy was not a happy man. It was four thirty and that silly cow had not brought any coffee yet, or asked what he wanted for his evening meal. He waved his hands as a signal for them to stop playing, so they became silent. 'Lads, we have done well. We have nine backing tracks down, so take five and I'll go and rustle up some coffee.'

They did not need telling twice. They put down their instruments and joined Harv and Leroy at the mixing desk.

'Won't be long,' said Leroy and he went in search of his wife.

I told the silly moo to be back from Bodmin in time for tea and evening meal, he thought to himself. She'd better have a good reason for being late with the coffee. Leroy made straight for the kitchen and was more than surprised to find it empty. He then headed for the drawing room, which again was empty. He went into the main hall and shouted, 'Cath, Cath, where are you, Catherine.' He got no response.

She's in for it when she comes in. Leroy was adamant about that. He stormed back to the kitchen, put the kettle on to boil. Mugs. He found mugs. Milk, in the fridge. Spoon. He headed for the drawer. Coffee, now where the hell is the coffee? He saw a container marked coffee and opened it. It was empty. What's the pissin' use of having a tin marked and then being empty? At his third try with the cupboards, he found a jar of coffee. Yes, she had a lot to answer for. Six times he spooned coffee into cups, poured milk and spooned in sugar.

Shit, what if they don't take sugar? Sod it, they do now. Water. Right. Once again he switched the kettle on. Tray, oh God, tray. He had left it in the studio. He began to look round for another tray. That's when he found the note:

I have taken Lee and Pansy to London to stay at the flat. I shall be back on Friday, the children will not. I had to get away from you for a few days. I will be back, as I said, on Friday.

Leroy crumpled up the note and flung it across the kitchen. 'The bitch, the bitch!' he shouted. 'Just goes, not even a word. The cow.'

He could not find another tray, so he went back to the studio empty-handed.

'If you want coffee, we are going to have to go to the kitchen. I left the tray here and that silly cow has gone to London. Forget about making my tea.' Leroy felt a fool and Catherine had to pay.

'Don't worry about tea,' said Harv. 'Must be stuff we can rustle up for ourselves.'

Leroy was not a person who cooked his own meals; that's what he had a wife for. He also did not like to admit that he couldn't boil an egg.

It was eight fifteen in the evening when the taxi pulled up outside the flat. Catherine and the children alighted. Catherine paid the fare and then went to the door – Mrs Mason was waiting for them.

'Thank God you're here,' she said.

'What's wrong, Mrs Mason?'

Mrs Mason flicked her eyes to the children.

'Go into the bathroom, darlings, and wash your hands.'

The children ran off and did as they were told.

'Sorry about that, dear, but he's been on the phone and he insists you phone him at nine tonight. He made it clear, in no uncertain terms, that you had better comply.'

'I'm sorry, Mrs Mason. Did he swear at you?'

'No, dear. If he had I would have put the phone down on him and he knows that as well. No, but I must admit, my dear, he had a few choice words for you.'

'I can imagine,' Catherine exclaimed.

'I've made you and those dear children a shepherd's pie, as I did not know exactly what time you were arriving, and some coffee is hot.'

'Mrs Mason, you are an angel.' Catherine gave her a hug.

'Come up when you are ready.'

'Thank you.' Catherine went to look for the children.

'Lee, Pansy, come on. Mrs Mason has made your favourite, shepherd's pie.'

'Coming, Mummy.'

They all climbed the stairs to Mrs Mason's and sat down to a very enjoyable and welcome meal.

'That was excellent, thank you,' said Catherine.

'Thank you, Mrs Mason.' Lee gave her a kiss.

'Bless you, dear,' she said and gave him a hug.

'Thank you, Mrs Mason,' said Pansy and also kissed Mrs Mason; in return she got a hug.

Catherine finished her coffee. 'Mrs Mason, may the children stay here while I make a phone call?'

'Of course, dear.'

'You be good for Mrs Mason. I'll be straight back as Pansy is nearly asleep now, and Penny is coming over in a few minutes.'

'Do you need to talk to Penny?' said Mrs Mason.

'Yes, I really do.' Catherine had picked up on Mrs Mason's meaning.

'Then why don't you let them stay here tonight? They can sleep in my spare bed, I can tell them stories and we can play games.'

'Oh please, Mummy, please,' said Pansy. 'Can we, please?'

'Please, Mummy,' said Lee.

'Mrs Mason, are you sure?'

'I would love it, my dear. Now off you go.'

'Mrs Mason…' Tears began to well up in Catherine's eyes.

'You go, my dear, and do what you have to. You can tell me all about it in the morning, and don't worry. Lee, you go with Mummy and get your night clothes and then come back here.'

'Yes, Mrs Mason.'

'Good boy.'

Catherine and Lee left. Downstairs, Catherine gave Lee night clothes for himself and Pansy and he went back upstairs. She picked up the phone and dialled the Hall.

'Leroy, you wanted me to phone.'

'What are you doing there?'

'I had to get away for a few days.'

'What for, woman?'

'I have a lot to think about and I can't take any more of the arguments and your hurtful remarks.'

'So when are you back?'

'Friday.'

'Kids with you?'

'No, they'll be staying here.'

'Why?'

'Because, Leroy, we cannot go on like this. You are killing me slowly.'

'Well, I've already killed three today. One more won't hurt.'

'Leroy, you just don't understand, do you?'

'It was only a joke.'

'Every hurtful thing you say is just a joke.'

'Did you leave anything for us to eat?'

'If you look in the fridge, you'll see a load of stuff. Also in the freezer.'

'Is it cooked?'

'No.'

'Then what am I supposed to do?'

'Leroy, is this necessary?'

'Friday.'

'Yes, Leroy, Friday.'

The phone went dead. Catherine replaced the receiver and sighed. The buzzer sounded, so she went to let Penny in.

'Sorry I'm late.' They kissed. 'Traffic.'

'Penn, it's great to see you. Come on in.'

'Bottle opener?'

'Good,' said Cath, 'I could do with a good drink.'

'I thought you'd need it,' Penny said.

'How are you, Penn?'

'Fine. Where are Lee and Pansy? I thought they were coming with you?'

'They're upstairs, spending the night with Mrs Mason.'

'So we can talk for hours and get smashed.'

'We can,' laughed Catherine, 'just like old times.'

Two drinks were poured and both settled in chairs.

'Firstly, about Clive,' said Penny.

'I'm doing it.'

'You're not?'

'I am.'

Penny screamed.

'What about shithead?' Penny looked at Catherine with concern.

'He doesn't know.'

'He doesn't know? When are you going to tell him?' Penny questioned.

'When I get back on Friday. I'm going back alone and the kids are staying here with Mrs Mason.'

'What for?'

'Why do you think, Penn? What do you think he is going to be like when he finds out. I don't want them there for that.'

'Cath, I'm worried.'

'*You're* worried,' laughed Catherine.

'Do you want me to come with you?'

'No, I'll go alone. If I get broken bones it will be worth it to get him off my back once and for all.'

'Why don't you talk to a lawyer before then?'

'That's a good idea, Penny. I'll phone Clive first thing in the morning. He'll know someone.'

'Promise?'

'I promise. Now Penny, let's forget all about it and have a real old girl's chinwag.'

They knocked their glasses together, said 'cheers' and did just that.

Chapter Twenty

Detective Inspector Spring, Reverend Peterson and Dr James sat for some time before the answer to Reverend Peterson's question was acknowledged. 'I cannot go within ten miles of him now,' said George.

'I don't want to,' said Dr James.

'But we must. We cannot go on like this because of him. Am I going to run, again? Are *you*, Doctor? And are you going to join us, George? Are we going to run for the rest of our lives because of that animal?'

'For the first time in my life,' said George, 'I don't know what to do.'

'Nor I,' said Dr James.

'I do. If I get kicked off the force I will go on the run. I'll have no choice, because I'll have ripped Leonard's head off first.'

'This is a nightmare,' said Reverend Peterson.

They had another sherry, but no matter how hard they tried, no solution was forthcoming.

'We shall have to kill him,' Reverend Peterson said.

'Reverend, what are you saying?' responded Dr James, aghast.

'I'll pretend I never heard that,' said George.

'Then I'll do it myself.'

'I think we should stop,' said George.

'Me too.' Dr James felt the same as Reverend Peterson, but to actually carry it out…

'I'm sorry, gentlemen,' Reverend Peterson said.

The clock struck nine, so George asked if anyone fancied a pint in the Pheasant.

'No thank you, dear friend,' said Reverend Peterson. 'You and the good doctor go.'

'I have to call in and see a patient,' said Dr James. 'Nothing important, just dropping off a prescription and then I will join you, George. Thank you.'

'You sure you won't come, Reverend?' said George. 'Reverend, a drink?' repeated George.

'No thank you, George. No more drink, no more of anything.' Reverend Peterson looked serene.

George and the doctor said goodnight to the Reverend, left and went their separate ways, ready to meet up later for a drink.

Queer thing to say, George thought, as he made his way to the lounge bar. But then everyone is under stress.

Dr James drove to deliver his prescription with a feeling everything was far from right.

Reverend Peterson closed the door after the two men left, and sat down at his bureau. He wrote two letters – one to the doctor and one to the Cawthorne sisters – and placed them on the table. He then went to the garage, found a rope, and returned to the passage.

Slowly and deliberately he climbed the stairs, tears rolling down his face. He placed a chair by the landing rail, slowly tied one end of the rope to the thick heavy rail, and dropped the other end over. He looked over, pulled it back and made a hangman's noose. He placed it over his head and pulled it tight. Reverend Peterson climbed onto the chair, placed one foot on the rail, and said a little prayer. Then, before him, he saw the face of his beloved Allyson smiling at him. He stepped forward to greet her, smiling too.

'Damn,' said Dr James. He had been longer than he hoped, as was usually the case. He was just going to deliver the prescription and meet George in the Pheasant, but when he arrived he got waylaid in idle chat from a lonely person. So it was nine forty-five before he finally left to join George in the Pheasant, but he was still puzzled by the remark of Reverend Peterson, so he decided to call there first to make sure he was OK.

He arrived at the vicarage door, knocked, waited and knocked again. Getting no reply, he looked in the window, saw nothing out of the ordinary and so returned to the door. He tried the door handle – the door gave, so Dr James stepped into the passage.

It was just after 9 p.m. in the lounge bar when George Spring entered. Albert and Andrew were still making heavy weather at conversing.

'Hello, George.'

'Albert, Andrew.'

'Hello, Mr Spring,' said Andrew.

'We thought you had got lost. No doctor?'

'He's coming in later, shouldn't be long.' George was worried.

'Pint is it, George?'

'No, Albert, make it a whiskey – a double please.'

Albert raised his eyebrows, but did as commanded.

'Everything OK?' asked Andrew.

'Afraid not,' George said and drank the double in one go.

'Can you tell us, George?' Albert had never seen George like this before.

'I'm sorry, I cannot,' said George, 'Another please.'

Albert gave George another. That one went the same way.

'Steady on, old friend,' said Albert.

'I've got news,' said Andrew.

'Andrew, I am very sorry. Please have a drink with me. But if it's about him up there, I don't want to know.'

'I'll shut up then,' Andrew said.

George held out his glass. Albert took it and felt very uneasy.

'George, please, slow down a bit for me. Please.' Albert was now worried.

'I will, I promise. I've just had a very bad day; very bad.'

'I thought the Reverend might have been in earlier.' Albert again was trying to make conversation.

'No, he was with me and the doctor from seven until now,' said George.

Both Albert and Andrew waited, but no information was forthcoming.

'Dr James coming in, you said?' said Albert.

'Er yea, yea, he should be here anytime now,' said George.

'Well, I think I shall go home,' said Andrew.

'Yes, OK.' Albert looked at him. 'See you some more.'

'Night, Mr Spring.'

'Yea, goodnight, Andrew. Look, I'm sorry, a very bad day.'

'Sure, Mr Spring, I understand.'

Andrew left and Albert busied himself at the bar. George took his time with this drink; after two sherries and two doubles he was starting to feel it.

'What time is it, Albert?'

'Five to ten.'

'I thought he would be in by now,' said Albert.

'Must be held up somewhere,' replied George.

The door burst open and Dr James staggered in. 'George, George, for God's sake, quick...'

'What is it, Doctor?'

'Reverend Peterson. For God's sake, will you come?'

George followed the doctor outside.

'Get in,' the doctor said.

'What the hell is wrong?' asked George. 'Tell me.'

'You'll see soon enough,' he said and sped to the vicarage. He jumped out of the car and ran inside, closely followed by George.

'Oh no, God no,' said George.

Reverend Peterson was swinging from the rope. His face was blue, his eyes wide open.

Detective Inspector Spring sat on the stairs. He had seen suicides before, but the vicar? Not the vicar. He had only been talking to him an hour ago. Come on, he thought, you're the cop.

'You haven't touched anything, have you?' he said. Dr James shook his head.

'Good, right, come with me.' They went into the drawing room and George picked up the phone.

'Hello, Detective Inspector Spring here, whose that? Right, Sergeant, I want a photographer, duty officer, police doctor and ambulance to the vicarage at Shawlworth... A suicide... Yes, as soon as possible. It's the vicar. Get them here now.' He slammed down the phone.

'There's a letter here for me,' said Dr James, reaching for it.

'Leave it,' said George. 'Everything as it was until the team gets here.'

'We should never have left him,' said Dr James. 'I had a feeling something was wrong.'

'Me too, Doctor, but this? No, not this.' George stood with his head in his hands.

They sat in stony silence until they saw the flashing blue lights through the window.

Detective Inspector Spring went to the front door. He tried not to look at Reverend Peterson but failed. His eyes were drawn to him as if by a magnet.

'Right, Guv.' It was Detective Constable Roberts. 'What have we got?'

'What we have, Detective Constable, is a very dear friend of mine who could see no other way out but to hang himself.'

'Oh, sorry, Sir.'

'You will be if you don't change your attitude,' said Detective Inspector Spring. 'Look, I'm sorry, it's not your fault.'

'No sweat, Guv.' Roberts understood.

Detective Inspector Spring turned to the doctor. 'It's just a formality, Doc. Phil, photos of the table in there and, of course, here. Then get him down, Roberts.'

They went about their allotted tasks.

Detective Inspector Spring was with Dr James, explaining that there would have to be a post-mortem and an inquest in case of foul play. But once he and Dr James gave evidence, he added, there would be no problem.

'Finished, Guv.' Roberts poked his head around the door.

'Thanks. I'll make a statement in the morning and get Dr James to do the same.'

'OK, Guv. I'll get away then.'

'Roberts.'

'Sir?'

'Thanks.'

'You're welcome, Guv.' He meant it.

When alone, the doctor and Detective Inspector Spring still could not believe what had happened.

Dr James exploded out of the chair. 'This is all down to that evil bastard, Leonard.'

'You know that and I know that, but how do we prove it?' asked George.

'So he's going to get away with it again.'

'Doctor, what can I do? He's committed no crime in the eyes of the law. Do you think I wouldn't be up there now, dragging him out of bed, if I thought for one second he had something to answer to. I went once before, remember, and now I have charges hanging over my head. Me! Don't you think I'm sick?' George was mad, angry and shouting.

'I'm sorry, George. What a mess. Oh. Can I, can I open my letter now?'

George waved his hand at the table.

Dr James picked up the envelope, opened the flap, took out a sheet of writing paper, unfolded it and read. He never said a word; he just handed it to George, turned his back and wept.

George read the following:

My dear friend,
　　By the time you have read this I shall no longer be with you. Please don't be angry, I am not taking the easy way out. This will be the hardest thing I have ever had to do. Tell dear George I am sorry. I have asked for the Lord's forgiveness and, if granted, I shall be with my darling wife and daughter. Goodbye, my dear, dear friend, and think only good of me.
　　Your everlasting friend,
　　Lewis Peterson

George placed the paper on the table, clenched his fists and just said, 'Shit.'

'Something is very wrong,' said Albert to Trish. 'Did you see that?'

'Course I did,' she replied.

'Do you think I should follow them?' he said.

'Oh, come on, love, we're busy. You know we'll find out soon enough.'

'Yes, but—'

'Albert, no.'

Albert didn't mention it again until he saw the flashing blue lights go past the window.

'There you are,' he said. 'I told you something was up.'

'Albert, please.'

Albert looked at the clock: 10.20 p.m. Damn, another half an hour at least before I can get everybody out, he thought.

At exactly ten thirty Albert rang the bell and shouted, 'Time, ladies and gents. Let's have your glasses, please.'

'You're quick,' said Trish.

'Come along please, time. Could I please have your glasses.'

'Albert,' whispered Trish, 'ease off.'

Albert ushered the last one through the door; it was just after ten forty-five when a police car and ambulance drove slowly past.

'There, there!' Albert was excited. 'I told you something was up.'

'What now?' Trish looked at him.

'Ambulance and police car coming from the vicarage.'

'You're joking.'

'I'm not.'

'Something must be up,' Trish agreed.

'I'm going up.'

'Oh no you're not, you're helping with these glasses first,' said Trish.

'But—'

'Glasses.'

Albert transferred the dirty glasses from the tables to the bar in double-quick time and shot out the door before Trish could stop him.

What about the Cawthorne sisters?' said George.

'I'll tell them in the morning and give them their letter,' answered Dr James, who by now was a lot calmer.

There was a knock at the door.

'This had better be a genuine reason,' said George, 'or else.' He was in no mood for nosy parkers. He opened the front door.

'George, this is genuine concern, I promise.' It was Albert.

'Come in,' said George. He noticed one or two people watching at the gate.

'Is the Reverend OK?' Albert looked around for him.

'Come into the drawing room.' George did not wait for a reply; he just wanted to get out of that damned passage.

'Hello, Dr James.' Albert still could not see Reverend Peterson.

'Sit down, Albert.' George pointed to a chair. Albert sat.

'Albert, everyone will find out soon enough, so you may as well be the first.'

'First for what?'

'Reverend Peterson took his own life about an hour and a half ago.'

'Oh no, George. Doctor, he's not serious?'

'He is,' Dr James said quietly.

'But how?'

'He hung himself.'

'Hung himself?' Albert was in a state of shock. 'But why? Does anyone know? You two were with him, couldn't you have done anything to stop him?'

'Albert, don't be a fool. Do you honestly believe we would have let him do that without trying to stop him? Talk sense.' George was angry.

'I'm sorry.' Albert felt ashamed. 'So do you know why?'

'We do,' said Dr James, 'but are sworn to secrecy.'

'Tell me one thing,' said Albert. 'Is Leonard involved?'

No one spoke.

'He is, isn't he. That bastard is at the bottom of this. I'll kill him I will, I swear to God I'll kill him.'

'Albert, go home. There's nothing anyone can do anymore for Reverend Peterson. We are going now, so please go,' George requested, and the three headed for the door.

'Don't forget in the morning, Doctor... statement,' George said, locking the front door.

'I won't. What time?'

'Oh, any time that suits you.'

'Lunchtime. By the time I've done morning surgery, seen the Cawthorne sisters, and got to Bodmin...'

'That's fine.' George Spring felt very tired, what with sherry and all the whiskey.

'Detective Inspector Spring?' George turned; it was Alice Pengelly. 'Is the Reverend OK?'

He explained for the last time that evening, knowing that, by ten o'clock in the morning, everyone would know.

'Doctor, you had better get to the Cawthorne sisters early in the morning before surgery,' said George.

'I think I had better do it now,' he agreed.

George, the doctor and Albert went home.

'Where've you been? You've been gone nearly half an hour. Bet you've been having a good chinwag. When you, the doctor, George and Reverend Peterson get together, you're like a bunch of old women,' Trish laughed.

Albert just went to the optic and placed three measures of whiskey in a glass. He drank it down.

'Albert, what's wrong? Has Reverend Peterson been took to hospital?'

Albert shook his head.

'Albert, will you please tell me what's wrong.'

'He's dead.'

'Who's dead?'

'Reverend Peterson.'

'Albert, that is not funny.'

'Am I laughing?'

'How?' Trish sat down.

'He killed himself.'

'Oh my God, no. How?'

'Hung himself.'

Trish placed her hand to her mouth and began to weep.

'All through that bastard Leonard.'

'How do you know?'

'I asked Doc and George if they knew; they said they did. So I asked if it was down to Leonard and they never answered, so I knew it was.'

'Why him?'

'I don't know. They said they were sworn to secrecy.'

'Poor Reverend Peterson.' Trish was now sobbing.

Next morning, Alice Pengelly called into the village shop early, on her way to the Manor House with the morning papers.

When she arrived at the Manor House, Vernon was already setting out the breakfast dishes.

'Morning, Alice,' he said.

'Oh, Vernon, something terrible has happened.'

She began to weep, and not for the first time since hearing the news.

'Sit down, Alice, and tell me all about it.' Vernon was unflappable.

'It's the Reverend Peterson. He's dead, killed himself last night.'

'How?' Vernon Fielding could not believe his ears.

'Hung himself, he did.'

'Dear God, are you sure, or is this what you have heard?'

'No, Vernon, it's true. Last night I took Pixie out for a walk – 'twas a lovely evening. About eleven it were, when I sees these blue lights outside the vicarage. So I goes over, just as they were pulling away. So I admit I stopped at the gate, chatting to old Mr Granger, but he knew nothing. Albert from the Pheasant came runnin' up; he goes straight to the door and is let in. After a while, he, Dr James and George Spring comes out and George tells me himself.'

'Good heavens!' Fielding was shocked. 'That poor, poor man.'

The service bell rang.

'Better get on with breakfast,' said Alice.

'Take your time, Alice. I'll explain to Master Antony and Lady Vanessa, don't worry.' He headed for the dining room.

Fielding tapped on the door and entered.

'Good morning, Sir, Lady Vanessa, Miss Juliet.'

'Good morning, Fielding.'

'Sir.'

'You all right, you look pale?'

'Well, Sir, I do not feel a hundred per cent today.'

'Summer cold, Fielding?' Lady Vanessa asked.

'No, my lady, nothing like that.'

'Do you need a doctor then?' said Antony.

'Sir, if I may explain.' He swayed back and forth.

'Chair, quick,' said Antony.

Juliet grabbed a chair.

'Thank you, Sir,' said Fielding. 'I shall be fine now I am seated.'

'You sure?' Lady Vanessa was concerned.

'Yes, my lady.'

'Now explain please, Fielding. No lies. If you're not well, you tell us.'

'Thank you, Sir. May I start by apologising for the breakfast being late this morning.'

'Don't need to faint just because the breakfast is late,' Juliet tried to make light of the situation.

'Juliet dear, don't be silly.'

'Sorry, Mummy.'

'No, Sir. Mrs Pengelly has arrived this morning with some very sad and disturbing news. She is very upset, hence the late breakfast.'

'Has something happened to her?' enquired Lady Vanessa.

'No, my lady. Reverend Peterson.'

'Lewis?' she said. 'Has he been taken ill?'

'No, my lady, he's dead.'

'Fielding, are you serious?' Antony Stuart-Palmer sat down.

'How, when?' Lady Vanessa went pale.

'Poor man,' said Juliet.

'Last night, my lady. He, he took his own life – he hung himself.'

'Dear God, no,' cried Lady Vanessa.

'You sure, Fielding?' Antony spoke quietly.

Fielding told them the story Alice had told him of her meeting with George Spring.

'But why?' said Juliet. 'Why should he want to hang himself?'

'I don't know, Miss. Neither does Alice, I mean Mrs Pengelly.'

'No, it can't be true,' said Antony. 'Fielding, take the rest of the day off, tell Mrs Pengelly to do the same. Forget breakfast.'

'She will have it ready by now, Sir.'

'Right. We will see to it ourselves. Thank you, Fielding. Now go and rest.'

'Thank you, Sir.' Fielding left.

'Darling, I'm going to see Dr James, he'll know what's going on. What time is it?'

'Five past nine.'

Antony Stuart-Palmer dialled the surgery.

Dr James had risen early that morning, still unable to comprehend the previous evening's events. God, what do I say to them? How do I tell them? Come on, you've had to do it before. But this? He sighed, felt for the letter and left the house at seven forty-five; he got into his car and drove to the Cawthorne sisters.

'We *are* late this morning,' Jane said.

'We have nothing spoiling,' replied Ruby, 'especially on a Tuesday.'

'I know, dear, I just thought a few cakes for dear Reverend Peterson at teatime.'

'Good idea.'

The sisters were always up and ready to greet each day by seven thirty but this morning they were a little late. It was now seven fifty and they were just clearing away the dishes from breakfast. They placed them in the hot soapy water.

'You wash, dear, I'll dry,' said Jane.

'Very well,' her sister replied.

There was a knock at the door.

'Now, who can that be at this time of the morning? I'll go, dear, your hands are wet,' said Jane.

'If you wish, dear.' Ruby began washing the dishes. 'It's probably the post.'

Jane Cawthorne opened the door and was more than surprised to see Dr James.

'Dr James, it's unusual for you to call at this hour. Is something amiss?'

'I'm afraid so, Miss Cawthorne. May I come in?'

'Of course, nothing too serious I hope. Please.' She stood to one side.

'Who is it, dear?' called Ruby.

'Dr James,' Jane replied.

Ruby came through, drying her hands.

'Doctor,' she said, 'is anything wrong?'

'I'm afraid so, ladies. May we sit down?' he said as they entered the living room.

'Oh dear, it sounds as if it's really bad,' said Jane.

'The worst,' said Dr James.

'But how can it concern us?' Ruby was now also anxious.

Dr James sighed and began. 'Ladies, I want you to prepare yourselves for some tragic news that I must tell you and, dear God, wish I didn't.' The sisters held hands. 'Last evening, at around nine forty-five, Reverend Peterson died.'

'Oh God, no,' they screamed together.

Dr James sat quietly until the sisters regained their composure.

'Was it a heart attack?' said Ruby. 'I always said he did too much.'

'No.'

'Brain haemorrhage then, it must be.' Jane was weeping.

Ruby placed her arm around her sister's shoulder.

'No, Miss Cawthorne. He, he took his own life.'

'Oh, dear God, no.' Jane swayed backwards and forwards on the chair. She was now in floods of tears. 'Why, oh why?'

'Do you know why and how?' Ruby was remarkably calm.

'I do know why and he hung himself.'

Ruby clasped her hand to her face; Jane was still swaying, sobbing. 'Why?'

'I do know, but the Reverend swore me to secrecy. I'm sorry.'

'Just answer one question, yes or no, just yes or no,' Ruby said. 'Was that man Leonard involved?'

'Yes.'

'Right,' said Ruby. Her eyes became slits and her lips no wider than two pencil lines. 'That's all I need to know.'

'I've brought a mild sedative,' said Dr James.

'No, I'm perfectly calm, thank you, Doctor,' said Ruby. 'But Jane needs one.'

'A glass of water, please.'

Ruby left Jane to her swaying and questioning why, to fetch the water.

'Thank you,' said Dr James. When she returned, he took two yellow pills from a small bottle. 'Take these, please,' he said to Jane and gave her the water.

She took the pills and swallowed them with water.

'He left this for you,' he said and handed the letter to Ruby.

'Will you read it please, Doctor,' Ruby said.

'Are you sure?'

'Perfectly sure.'

Jane was now calmer.

Dr James opened the envelope, unfolded the paper and prayed that he kept his composure. He cleared his throat and began.

My dearest of friends,

When you read this I shall no longer be with you both. When in the past I have asked a favour of you both, you said I only had to ask. Well for the last time...

Dr James again cleared his throat and continued,

Please remember me as a good man and forgive my final act. I have prayed for Him to forgive me for this act, and I await His decision. If granted, I shall be happy again, so please be happy for me. Think of the happy times we had, the laughs, the afternoon teas and the Sunday mornings together. I must go now to get our Lord's decision. Please take care of yourselves and I shall be looking forward to seeing you both in years to come. I know there is a place for you both.

All my fondest love,

Lewis Peterson

Ruby Cawthorne sat, back straight, as if she had a rod of steel as support.

'Thank you, Doctor.' No emotion showed, unlike her sister, who was again swaying and sobbing.

Dr James gave Ruby the letter and said, 'I'm very sorry but I must go, morning surgery.'

'I understand. Don't worry, I'll see to her.' Her voice was ice cold and flat.

'You sure you are all right?'

'Perfectly, Doctor. My mind has not been as clear for many a long year. Please, your surgery.'

She showed Dr James to the door.

Chapter Twenty-One

John Penrose had thought long and hard about his situation and, although he hated doing it – and Leonard even more – on Monday he started dismantling the pens and letting the birds go. By Tuesday morning, he had completed the job and was going to check the estate for traps and nets. He knew the location of some that he had laid himself.

Never even got a pint last night, he said to himself. Call in for one lunchtime. Just one, don't want that pig on my back any more than necessary. John continued the rest of the morning disarming traps and pulling up nets. He was looking forward to his pint, as again it was a lovely summer's day.

'Sorry I'm late,' Dr James entered his surgery waiting room; it was fuller than usual. Oh God, yesterday, and Leonard, he thought. Everyone stopped talking; George was right.

'Give me two minutes and send in the first patient.' He looked at his receptionist and went into his consulting room.

He had seen three patients when his receptionist interrupted him.

'Doctor, sorry, but Sir Antony Stuart-Palmer is on the line.'

'Put him through.'

'Sorry about this,' he said to his patient. He picked up the receiver and listened.

'Yes it's true… ten forty-five? Very well,' he said and replaced the receiver.

'Sorry about that.' Dr James apologised again.

For the next hour that he saw patients, it followed a regular pattern. Yes, he had heard about Reverend Peterson. Next. Ingrown toenail; yes, he had heard about Reverend Peterson. Next. And so on and so on.

Finally he got the message he wanted: 'That was your last patient, Doctor.'

'Thank God for that.' He pressed the intercom button. 'When Sir Antony arrives, will you bring in two coffees please.'

Dr James busied himself for the next twenty minutes or so and did not stop until there was a knock on his door.

'Come in.'

Antony Stuart-Palmer came in and sat down.

'Peter, what's all this rubbish about?'

'It's true I'm afraid, Sir Antony.'

'Don't be so formal, I'm not a sir. Call me Tony or Antony, for God's sake.'

'Very well, Antony, it's true.' He then went on to explain how he and George had had a meeting last evening with Reverend Peterson, but how each had sworn the others to secrecy; how they had left him about nine, how he had had a horrible feeling something was wrong, gone back and found him, then gone for George.

'You being a doctor and George a policeman, I can understand that. Just tell me, was Leonard at the bottom of it?'

Peter James nodded.

'I knew it, I knew it. Why did I have to sell him the estate? Why not someone else?'

'Don't be silly, Antony. You were not to know things would turn out as they have.'

'I know, I know. I just feel so helpless.'

'We all do,' replied Dr James.

'So, Leonard again,' repeated Antony.

'I know, but can we really blame *him*? Oh, I know he is guilty, but when you cannot prove anything.'

'Sometimes when the law's hands are tied, you have to help untie them.'

'That's all people are talking though, Tony – threats.'

'Don't be too sure, dear boy.'

'Look, I'm sorry, I have to go and see George to make a statement. I'm sorry.'

'Don't be. I have to go, people to see.' Tony shook hands with Peter and left.

John was whistling as he breezed through the door of the lounge bar.

'Pint please, Albert,' he said.

'Can't see what there is to whistle about.'

Albert was not a happy man, thought John.

'Well, I know, what with Leonard and that, but it is a lovely day.' John was puzzled.

'Is it?' Albert pulled John a pint.

'Have I done something to offend?' said John.

'You mean you haven't heard?' Albert looked astonished.

'Heard what?' John was puzzled.

'About Reverend Peterson.'

'You got me there, boy,' John said.

'John, I'm sorry. Have that on the house. Reverend Peterson is dead.'

'Albert, that is not funny.'

'I'm not laughing.'

'When, how?'

'Last night.'

'Heart attack?'

'No, he committed suicide.'

The questions and answers were thick and fast. 'Oh God, no.' John sat on a bar stool. 'I honestly did not know. With me and Linda living on the estate.'

'I'm sorry, mate.' Albert felt guilty.

'How, er, how, you know?' John gestured.

'Hung himself.'

'Dear God.'

John finished his pint. 'Look, I must go and tell Linda,' he said.

'In tonight?'

'Yea, I'll pop down.'

'See you then.'

John hurried out the door.

Linda saw John hurrying up the village path.

'Forget your sandwiches?' she said, opening the door.

'Linda, Reverend Peterson has killed himself.'

'John, if this is your idea of a joke…'

'No, I'm serious. Last night, hung himself.'

'Dear God,' said Linda. 'How do you know that?'

'Called in for a pint. Albert told me.'

'What made him do that?'

'Dunno,' said John, 'never asked.'

'You wouldn't. Half a story again, that's you all over,' she said.

'I'll find out tonight,' John promised.

'We both will, 'cause I'm coming too,' Linda said.

'Look, I gotta go. See you teatime, OK? Bye.' John was gone.

Andrew spent the morning by the lake, clearing weeds from the edges and wheeling them to the back of his cottage, wondering on several occasions what the blue lights were for that he saw last night on his way home. As it got to lunchtime, he thought, I'll make this trip the last and have some lunch. He came from around the back of the cottage, left the wheelbarrow by the door and went and made himself some lunch. I know one was a police car and the other an ambulance, but where were they going? he pondered.

Leroy was not a happy person. After what that bitch had done to him and the farce of trying to cook something the previous evening. But he had got his own back. Leave the kitchen in a mess and make it worse by Friday. The others didn't seem to mind, but he did. She should have been there to cook and clean; that was a woman's job.

By lunchtime Tuesday, the twelve backing tracks were on a master tape. All that was left now was his vocal. The lads had packed their gear away, left their names, addresses and telephone numbers, and Leroy assured them that as soon as the tour was arranged he would tell them.

Once they had gone, Leroy turned to Harv and said, 'We'll go and get something to eat and make a start later.'

'Fine by me,' said Harv.

They went through the hall to the kitchen. Leroy picked up the phone and dialled a number. While he waited for an answer, he said, 'Grab some bread, butter and anything else you can find,

Harv. Hello, that you Fredricks? Good. Listen, about that pillock, Spring. Forget it.' He listened. Course I'm playing games. Make the git sweat a bit. Look, you're getting paid, right? So forget it. OK, next time he might not be so keen on coming up here, shooting his mouth off.' Again he listened. After a while he snapped. 'Charge what you like. Doesn't bother me, just do it. I pay the piper, I call the tune, so when I say do something, you do it.' Leroy slammed down the phone.

'That's fine, Dr James,' said George, after reading through his statement.

'Call me Peter, will you,' he replied. He felt closer to George now, like some form of bond had developed between them.

'After all this, I feel numb,' he said.

'Me too. I woke this morning thinking I'd had a nightmare,' said George.

'You coming in for a pint tonight, George?'

'Yes, why not? My fate will be sealed by then.'

'How's that?'

'These charges of Leonard's. I get to know today.'

'Oh God, I forgot about that, what with Reverend Peterson.'

'I know, I nearly forgot myself,' said George.

'Sorry, Guv. Blackwood wants to see you.' It was Sergeant Harris.

'Right, I'll go. George, see you tonight and good luck.'

'Thanks, Peter.' George stood up and headed off to discover his fate.

'George, sit down.' Detective Inspector Blackwood pointed to a chair. George Spring sat down.

'George, there's no easy way round this. I'm afraid I have made enquiries and laid the facts as they stand before the powers that be, and I must tell you that—' His phone began to ring.

'Damn.' He picked up the receiver. 'I thought I said no calls for the next twenty minutes.'

'Who? Fredricks? OK, then put him through. Sorry about this, George.'

'OK, Sir.' George did not care anymore.

'Jonathan, how can I help?'

Pause.

'He's with me now… I'm just about to tell him… He's what? Is he mad? I've a good mind to do him for wasting police time… Thanks, bye.' Blackwood replaced his receiver. 'George, that was Fredricks. As you have gathered, he's had this Leonard bloke on the phone, dropping all charges against you. Apparently he only wanted you to sweat a bit.'

George Spring laughed.

'It's not funny, George.' Detective Chief Inspector Blackwood was not amused.

'I know, Sir, I'm sorry. If I don't laugh I'll cry,' said George.

'Off the hook, eh? Relieved?' said Blackwood.

'No, Sir.'

'No?' Detective Chief Inspector Blackwood looked puzzled.

'That bastard Leonard caused a very good friend of mine to top himself last night.' George was full of hate.

'I think that you had better explain.' Detective Chief Inspector Blackwood was suddenly very interested in Leroy Leonard.

George explained everything from the very beginning: about Leonard, the doctor, Reverend Peterson and himself, and also about the other village members.

When he had finished, Detective Chief Inspector Blackwood said, 'This sounds like something from a Dorothy L Sayers' novel.'

'I know, Sir, I know. But it is the truth.'

'This bloke sounds a right caitiff,' said Blackwood.

'OK, George, you're off the hook as far as this Leonard bloke is concerned, but stay clear of him, right.'

'Yes, Sir.'

'I mean it, George. Stay clear.' George left the office.

That bastard! He makes me sweat and causes the death of poor Reverend Peterson. I'll have his guts for garters, thought George, as he made his way back to his office.

'OK, Guv?' said Sergeant Harris.

'Great, just great,' he said. 'Mr Leonard has very kindly dropped all charges. He's only been responsible for the death of a good friend – I'm very grateful to him.'

Sergeant Harris made himself scarce for the next hour.

That evening, Albert, as at lunchtime, did not feel like opening the doors of the Pheasant; but his many tourist customers did not know and had never heard of Reverend Peterson. They talked about it, but only as though they were talking about the weather. Albert still had to smile and say he was fine and, yes, it was a nice day.

The first to enter that evening was Andrew.

'Evening, Albert. Pint please.'

'Andrew, I've blown it once today, so before we go any further, have you heard about Reverend Peterson?' asked Albert.

'No, should I?' Andrew was not following Albert.

'He's dead. Last night he committed suicide, and it's all down to that boss of yours.'

Andrew looked long and hard at Albert before he spoke. 'How?'

'Hung himself.'

'Jesus, what's Leonard done now.'

'I don't know,' said Albert. 'George and the doctor know, but are sworn to secrecy.'

'Who found him?'

'Doc. He and George were with him until nine, then Doc went back later – about ten to ten – and found him.'

'This is awful.' Andrew still found it hard to believe. Albert and Andrew discussed the merits of Reverend Peterson and the failings of 'that man Leonard' for some time, interspersed with patrons' requests for more drinks from Albert. It was around 8 p.m. when John and Linda walked in the door, closely followed by Dr James.

Cordial greetings were exchanged, drinks ordered and supplied; then the doctor found himself centre stage regarding the tragic happenings of the last twenty-four hours.

Dr James began with the call from George and the meeting with Reverend Peterson, George and himself that followed.

'I believe what took place was confidential?' Albert was the first to interject.

'That is correct, so I'm afraid it must now remain only between me and George. If anyone finds that unfair, then I am sorry, but that is how it must be.'

George Spring entered the room and joined the group; again greetings were exchanged and drinks ordered.

'I was just explaining to everyone that what took place last evening must remain between us.' Dr James looked at George.

'He is correct, I'm afraid,' said George.

'Look everyone, may I say something else? This terrible happening I feel has brought us all closer together. All of us here have been affected by Leonard. What I am getting at is that, when I am on duty or in the surgery, Dr James is fine. But when we are socialising, like now, please call me Peter.'

'The same for me; the name is George.'

'Go on, Doc... I mean Peter.' John felt awkward.

'When George and I left, we apparently had misgivings about Reverend Peterson and agreed later that if we had only voiced those opinions, things might have turned out differently. George asked if I would care to join him for a drink. I said I would, but first I had to see a patient and I would meet him later. I got held up longer than I expected, but when I did finally leave, I had this feeling I had to call in on Reverend Peterson. So that is what I did. I knocked on the door, but received no response, so I looked in the window. Again, nothing out of the ordinary so I returned to the door. I found the door to be unlocked, so I went in. You know the rest.'

'That must have been awful for you, Peter,' said Linda.

'It was. I shall not forget that in a hurry. I know I have seen plenty of bodies, but in those circumstances, and a dear friend to boot – horrible.'

Once again George agreed with the doctor.

'All down again to our boss, John,' Andrew said.

'I wish to God he weren't.' John spat it out.

'What happens now, George?' Linda spoke again.

'How do you mean, Linda?'

'Well, poor Reverend Peterson, when will the funeral be?'

'Under the present law there has to be a post-mortem, so as to rule out foul play, and then an inquest. That is set for a week come Friday, by the way. You'll have to be there, Peter.'

'Of course; I understand,' replied Peter.

'So once that has been cleared, the funeral can go ahead.'

'Who will organise that, George? You?' John spoke.

George felt a tap on his leg; it was the doctor. 'As George and I have been taken into the confidence of Reverend Peterson. I thought *we* might arrange it. I do not think Reverend Peterson will be buried here in Shawlworth.'

George caught on straight away.

'Not in Shawlworth?' Albert said, but he spoke for everyone. 'That's insane, he has to be buried here.'

'I don't think so,' said Peter. 'Again, I'm afraid you will have to be patient.'

'Well, I'm sorry,' said Linda. 'I agree with Albert. He should be buried here, where we can tend him, put flowers on his grave. I know what the Cawthorne sisters will say when they find out, if he's not buried here.'

'Please give us twenty-four hours to make enquiries about something and then things will hopefully become clear. Please, I beg you, don't let us fall out over this. We must stick together. Remember, the name's Peter.'

'You're right, of course,' said Albert. 'Of course we trust you both and know whatever the reason is, it's for the best for Reverend Peterson.'

'Thank you, Albert,' George felt humble, 'but I assure you the doctor is right and, of course, it goes without saying you'll all be at the funeral.'

'If you will excuse us both now, we are going up to the Manor House to see the Stuart-Palmers. I think that it is only right to keep them fully informed about what is happening. Leonard may own the Hall, but the Stuart-Palmers are still our figureheads.' Peter spoke and George nodded in agreement.

Outside George and Peter both breathed a sigh of relief.

'I hate doing that – keeping information from friends in the same boat as us, George,' said Peter.

'I know, but will it solve their problems to know about the Reverend's past?'

'Very true. Come on, let's go.'

Antony Stuart-Palmer had arrived back home to an anxious wife and daughter eager to learn any more information about the poor Reverend Peterson.

'Darling, where have you been? You have been gone ages.' Vanessa looked worried.

'I've been to see Peter, and then I had something else to do.'

'Daddy, please. Reverend Peterson?' pleaded Juliet.

'It is true, he committed suicide last evening, sometime between nine fifteen and ten o'clock.'

'How?' said Vanessa.

'How what, dear?'

'Antony, how did he kill himself?'

'Oh, er, I er, I don't know.'

He looked sheepish.

'You don't know? Sometimes I wonder about you, dear, I really do.'

'I was too busy finding out why he did it to think about how.'

'*Why* did he do it then?' Juliet asked again.

'Because of Leonard.'

'Leonard!' his wife said. 'What's *he* got to do with the Reverend's death?'

Once again Antony was lost for words, except to say, 'All Peter would tell me was that Leonard was at the bottom of it. But he would not say why.'

'So where else have you been?' Vanessa enquired.

'Just, er, out,' he replied.

'Daddy, you never were a very good liar,' said Juliet.

'Antony, I want to know where you have been and for what reason.' Vanessa was adamant.

'You don't,' he said sulkily.

'Antony, what have you done?'

'Daddy, please I'm getting worried.'

Antony Stuart-Palmer sat down; he looked ghastly. 'I've done a very stupid thing,' he said, 'very stupid.'

'Well what, for God's sake.'

He sat for a while then said, 'After I came out from seeing Peter, I was so angry with Leonard I could have killed him there and then.'

'So?'

'I, er, went for a bit of a walk to cool off and, er, bumped into someone.'

'Who, Antony?' Vanessa was getting impatient.

'Jerry, Jerry Tonkin.'

'Jerry Tonkin!' Vanessa couldn't believe she was hearing this.

'Who's he?' said Juliet.

'I'll tell you – he's an animal. He makes Leonard look like a saint; he would mug his own granny for fifty pence.'

'How does Daddy know him?'

'Your father caught him once, poaching on the estate with his young son. Of course, your father was no match for him – no man around this area is – but his son ran away. They ran after him and nearly caught him, but the boy jumped into Miller's Pond and got into difficulties. Tonkin could not swim, so your father saved him; Tonkin could not thank your father enough. He promised never to poach again and said that if ever he wanted any favours doing, all he had to do was ask. The poaching on the estate dropped dramatically, because if anyone did it and Tonkin found out about it, they never came back and everyone finished up in hospital. Not with a black eye either.'

'Daddy, what have you done?' Juliet was now really worried.

'Well, as I said, I was angry and Tonkin could see this and asked me what the trouble was. So I told him about—'

'Daddy, you never told him about *me*, did you?'

'No, dear, of course not. I just said how Leonard had been upsetting people and that just because he was a pop star he thought he was lord high and mighty.'

'So what happened then?'

'So Tonkin asked, "Do you want him taken down a peg or two?" and, er, I said yes.'

'I don't believe I'm hearing this.' Vanessa spun round.

'Mummy, what will he do?' Juliet was now frightened.

'Put it this way, darling, if Tonkin gets hold of him, Leonard will not be walking for a good while.'

'You mean—' said Juliet. Her voice quavered.

'Yes, at least two broken legs and that's if he is in a good mood. Tonkin, I mean. But for your father it could be arms, legs and back.'

'Daddy, what have you done?' Juliet was now crying.

'I know, darling, I know. I was a fool but I was so angry with Leonard, I just never thought.'

'You'll have to go back and see Tonkin and tell him you didn't mean it,' said Vanessa.

'I know, but will he listen? You know what he is like.'

'Then you'll have to tell Leonard to get out for a while.'

'Oh sure, I'm going to say to Leonard, "Get out for a while, as some bloke I've hired is going to put you in hospital for a couple of months".'

'God, this is a mess,' said Vanessa. 'Juliet, will you please stop crying.'

'But Mummy, what if Daddy goes to jail?' she pleaded.

'Don't be silly, it hasn't got to that yet. Now, dry your eyes and stop snuffling.'

'Nothing will happen for the next few days and I will see him before then, I promise, darling.'

'Promise, Daddy?'

'I promise.' Antony kissed his daughter on the head. For the rest of the day, the matter of Tonkin and Leonard was not mentioned.

'What are we having for dinner?' said Antony. 'No Mrs Pengelly.'

'What do you want?' said Vanessa.

'What can you manage?' he said diplomatically.

'Just leave it to me and Juliet,' said Vanessa.

Antony busied himself until dinner, angry with himself over Tonkin and the agreement he had made.

While Vanessa, Juliet and himself were having an after-dinner drink, the doorbell rang.

'Who can this be?' said Antony. He put down his drink and went through to the door. He opened it.

'Peter, George, come in. Nice to see you both,' he said, ushering them towards the lounge and Vanessa and Juliet.

'Come in, please,' Antony said as he opened the lounge door.

'Peter, George, how nice to see you.'

'Lady Vanessa.' Peter James was the first to greet her.

'Lady Vanessa,' George said.

'Call me Vanessa, please.' It seemed it was time for friendships to progress.

'Mr Spring, Dr James,' said Juliet.

'Please sit down and can I get you both a drink?'

'No thank you, I'm driving,' said George.

'I must decline as well,' said James. 'I have to pop out later.'

James acted as spokesperson. 'We have come to fill in the details of the tragic death of Reverend Peterson.'

'How did he die?' Vanessa asked.

'He hung himself from the stairhead banister rail.'

'Oh, the poor, poor man.' Vanessa shook her head.

'Why did he do it, Doctor?' Juliet enquired.

'I'm sorry, Juliet, but I cannot tell you. George and I know, but we were sworn to secrecy by Reverend Peterson.'

'I see.' Vanessa understood, or at least tried to, and continued, 'I believe that animal, Leonard, is the instigator of this.'

'Yes, Vanessa, he is.' James could tell her that much.

'When is the funeral?' Antony asked.

George answered that question. 'First there has to be a post-mortem, to rule out foul play, and then an inquest. That is a week come Friday and then the funeral.'

'It will be here, of course.' Vanessa took it for granted.

'Possibly not,' said James.

'But it must be.' Vanessa looked at her husband.

'When the facts are known, perhaps you can understand.'

'Just what are those facts? Can you say?' Antony was interested.

Peter and George looked at each other. George Spring answered but knew exactly how far to go.

'All I can do,' he said, 'is to tell you part of the past life of Reverend Peterson. But please, it must remain confidential.'

'Of course,' said Vanessa. 'Would you like Juliet to leave?'

Juliet looked daggers at her mother.

'No, because all we can tell you is part, not all, of his past. If it was disclosed, it would cause minimum damage.'

'You know it all, though?' said Antony.

'We do,' acknowledged George.

'Very well, it's more than good of you to go this far,' continued Antony.

'Reverend Peterson was married, and had a daughter.' George got no further.

'Married with a daughter?' Vanessa could not believe it.

'It was many years ago. His daughter died through tragic circumstances at the age of sixteen, and his wife died of a broken heart. They are buried side by side. So Peter and I agree that, if there is room next to them, or permission is given to lay him above his wife, then that's where it should be.'

'Well, I never,' said Antony. 'All these years and we never knew.'

'I see why now,' said Vanessa, 'and understand. Where are they buried, do you know?'

'At the churchyard on the old A30 between Redruth and Camborne, on the left as you go through Tuckingmill and before you get to Roskear.'

'I've heard of the places, but never been,' said Vanessa.

'I have,' said Antony. 'Tin mine near there – South Crafty.'

'That's it,' said George.

'Look, I'm sorry but I must go. Patient, you know.' Peter stood up.

'Me also,' said George.

'Well, goodbye to both of you,' said Vanessa, 'and thanks for coming.'

'Daddy,' Juliet caught her father's attention. 'Ask Mr Spring,' she whispered.

'About what, darling?'

'You know, about earlier today. He'll tell you, go on.'

'Look, darling, you might as well say out loud now what you mean, as we are all interested.'

'Daddy about…' she said and mouthed, 'Tonkin.'

'Juliet, please.'

'Oh God, Daddy, Tonkin, Tonkin.' She was no longer whispering.

'We talking about Jerry Tonkin here?' George Spring was interested.

'Juliet, I would have sorted that myself.'

Her father was silently angry.

'Come on, Antony. If it concerns that lowlife, I want to know. Once you get mixed up with him, he won't let go.'

'I saw him today. After leaving Peter and going for a walk to cool off, I bumped into Tonkin. One thing led to another and I told him how Leonard was upsetting people. You know about Miller's Pond, me and Tonkin?' George nodded. 'So he told me to leave it to him and that we would have no more trouble with Leonard.'

'Do you know what will happen to Leonard?'

'I have a good idea.'

'You don't. Now, you don't do anything else. You leave Tonkin to me, I'll sort him out. And Antony, don't ever, ever do anything like this again – especially not with the likes of Tonkin.'

'I'm sorry, George, I was angry.' Antony answered like a chastised schoolboy.

'I hope so, because you don't do deals with people like him. I mean it.'

Dr James broke in. 'Look, I'm sorry but I must go.'

'Yes, so must I. Now remember, Antony, leave him to me.'

'Goodnight, Peter, goodnight, George, and thanks.'

On the short drive back to the village, George said, 'I can't believe Antony would get mixed up with Tonkin.'

'Is he that bad?' said Peter.

'You'd better believe he is. When he gets brought in, it's four coppers and a dog job, and then we are only using minimum force to justify an arrest.'

'I've been thinking, they are going to have to know; I mean Albert, John, Linda and the others, about the burial. We just tell them the same as we told the Stuart-Palmers.'

'You're right, of course,' agreed George. 'There's still plenty of time, though. As I said earlier, it won't solve their problems.'

'How do we go about it?' said Dr James.

'How do you mean?' George looked puzzled.

'Well, are we going to have to go to Roskear and see the vicar there?'

'I suppose so. It's as good a place as any to start.'

'When?'

'Sunday. We're bound to catch him then,' said George.

'Sunday morning it is,' said Dr James.

They pulled up in the village; it seemed unusually quiet, even for Shawlworth, but then not every village has the vicar commit suicide.

Unbeknown to Detective Inspector Spring and Dr James, things had been a lot more lively in the Pheasant. After they left, Albert had continued to fraternise with Linda, John and Andrew, and conversation had continued about Reverend Peterson and his final resting place, when Albert all of a sudden spun away and headed for two youths drinking and laughing further along the bar.

'What did you say just then?' he accused.

'What about?' one replied.

'You know very well what about,' Albert said. 'I picked up some of your conversation.'

Linda, John and Andrew had never seen Albert so mad before. Trish came through from the bar when she heard his voice.

'Calm down, boss,' one youth replied. Both had stopped laughing.

'I won't ask again.' Albert was now threatening.

'Albert, I'll sort this, you go,' said Trish.

'You won't, I will.'

'Look, all he said was we've come to see the most swinging vicar in town, but all we are doing is hanging about here.'

'He did, did he?' said Albert and before anyone could move Albert had swung his right fist straight into the youth's face. He fell back, blood pouring from his nose.

'Albert, have you gone mad!' said Trish.

John and Andrew ran to them; Albert was struggling with Trish.

'Get that scum out of here,' Albert was shouting.

'I think you had better leave, lads,' said John, helping to pick the lad up.

'That bastard's bust me nose,' the boy said, tilting his head back.

'Get out or it'll be your neck!' Albert was still shouting and struggling.

The two youths left.

'What the hell was all that about?' queried John.

'Nothing,' said Albert. He was now a lot calmer.

'You bust a bloke's nose and say *nothing*,' said Andrew.

'Did you hear what that sick git said? Did you?' Albert was getting angry again.

'No,' said Andrew.

'Can we see the swinging vicar instead of hanging around here.'

'Oh God,' said Linda.

'They were drunk,' said Trish.

'I don't give a shit,' said Albert.

'They're sick.'

'Albert, please,' Trish tried to calm him. 'Everybody is looking.'

'I don't care,' Albert said. 'Nobody – nobody – says that about Reverend Peterson and if they come back they are barred, right.'

'Right,' Trish agreed. 'Now go and have a drink with John and Andrew and I'll keep Linda company.'

'Sorry, folks,' said Albert.

'Don't be sorry,' said John. 'I would have done the same thing if I had heard him. Don't you worry.'

'And me,' said Andrew.

Chapter Twenty-Two

'Clive, it's Catherine.'

Catherine had been up early that Tuesday morning, checked on the children and been told that they were fine. Mrs Mason told her not to worry and said that she would see to their breakfasts for her. Once again Mrs Mason had grown wings in the eyes of Catherine.

'Catherine, love, where are you phoning from? It's early.' Clive had just arrived at his office.

'The flat,' she replied.

'What flat?' Clive said. 'Cath, you're not in town?'

'I am.'

'When did you get here?' he quizzed.

'Last night,' Catherine replied.

'Come straight over,' Clive said.

'I need to talk,' Catherine said.

'Fine, fine, get here as quick as you can.'

'An hour?'

'Great, see you then.'

'Thanks, Clive.'

Catherine replaced the telephone receiver and proceeded upstairs. Mrs Mason was an angel, but Catherine dare not ask again. As she mounted the stairs, squeals of laughter greeted her. Catherine walked in, as the door was already open.

'Mrs Mason, thank you ever so much for looking after the children for me. I must dash, as I have to see my agent. Lee, Pansy, come along. Thank Mrs Mason.'

Mrs Mason smiled winked at the children and said to Catherine, 'I'm sorry, there is no Lee or Pansy here. All I have is a Freddie the Frog and Princess Alicia.'

'Oh,' said Catherine.

Lee and Pansy were laughing.

'Please don't think I am poking my nose in, my dear, but you do have a lot of work to do. So if you wish, you can leave them with me.'

'I couldn't ask again,' said Catherine.

'You haven't, I'm offering,' laughed Mrs Mason. 'Tell you what, let Pansy and Lee decide. Right children, go with Mummy to see boring things, or come with me, spaghetti on toast for dinner and then a visit to London Zoo?'

They both jumped up and down. 'Mrs Mason, Mrs Mason,' they cried in unison.

'I know, I'm an angel. Now off you go, shoo.' Mrs Mason escorted Catherine to the door.

'Susie, as soon as Catherine arrives, show her in please.'

'Not Catherine Sullivan?' said Susie.

'None other,' he beamed.

'Is she back, Mr Barratt?'

'She is, exclusively to us,' Clive said proudly.

'Mr Barratt, how did you pull that off?' Susie could not believe it.

'Pure skill,' he said, looking at his fingernails and then rubbing them on the lapel of his jacket.

Clive went back into his office, whistling.

'Well, well,' Susie was pleased.

Susie worked away for nearly an hour, until the opening of the door caused her to look up. 'Miss Sullivan,' she jumped up, 'how lovely to see you again. It's been too long.'

'Susie, it's lovely to see you again.'

'Mr Barratt is waiting for you.' Susie ushered her to his office door.

'Susie, go in and tell him I phoned and said I've gone to Top Style instead.'

'You haven't changed your mind, Miss Catherine, have you?'

Susie tried to keep a straight face and entered the office.

'Catherine… oh, Susie, what is it?'

'I'm afraid Miss Catherine has just phoned and said could I tell you she has gone to Top Style instead.'

'Susie, you're joking – she wouldn't, she couldn't? I'm ruined. Susie, I'm finished.'

Clive began pacing up and down. As he turned his back, Catherine and Susie quickly changed places.

'Susie, get straight—' he said. 'Catherine!' His face beamed. 'You sod, you so and so.' They hugged for ages.

Catherine laughed. 'Got you again.' It was just like the clock had been turned back ten years.

'I'll get you back,' he said. 'Catherine, have you told him yet?'

'Not yet.'

'Are you still going to do it?'

'Give me the contracts and I'll show you.'

'I've got ours ready, but the commercial one is being drawn up. They couldn't believe it when they found out.' He passed her the contract.

'Pen please.'

'You're not going to read it?'

'Do I need to?'

'No.'

'Then give me a pen.'

Catherine signed the contract and handed it and the pen back to Clive.

'I honestly thought I would never see the day again – a contract with Catherine Sullivan's name on it.' He kissed the contract.

'Fool,' said Catherine. 'Clive, I need help.'

'Name it, anything and you've got it.'

'I need a good lawyer, fast.'

'Can I ask what for?' he looked worried.

'I'm divorcing that pig. I've had enough and also, when I tell him about this, he's promised me two broken legs.'

'You don't need a lawyer, because if he lays one finger on you I'll kill him myself.'

'Clive, leave it to the law – I've got a police inspector down there I can rely on – I'm sure of that – but I need a lawyer to get things started.'

Clive picked up the phone. 'Susie, give me a line please.' He dialled a number.

'Everett, Clive Barratt here. I have a dear friend who needs to see you quickly... Tomorrow, eleven thirty? Good... No, I'll bring her myself.' Clive put down the telephone. 'Sorted,' he said. Could you be here for ten forty-five?'

'Yes,' said Catherine. 'Clive, I have something else to say. I'm back working for you, I'm divorcing Leroy, but please, I know we once had something going, but that was twelve years ago. I love you dearly, but like a brother.'

'I know, Cath, I realised that years ago. It's just great to have you back and things as they were. I won't lie, Cath, I still carry a torch for you. But I promise, brotherly love only.'

'Thanks Clive. Now tomorrow, ten forty-five.'

Catherine left the office and headed for the flat. She had to have time for herself; she had to work out tomorrow. I'll also phone George Spring, she thought.

Catherine got George Spring's number from directory enquiries and tried several times to phone him during the rest of the day, but she only got his answering machine.

'I'll try later tonight,' she said.

The children had had a great day with Mrs Mason. Catherine sat and told her all the news, as well as what she intended: divorcing Leroy.

'Best day's work you ever did,' Mrs Mason said.

Detective Inspector Spring had said goodnight to Dr James and was just settling down when the phone rang. 'Oh no, I don't believe this,' he said, picking up the phone.

'Harris, this had better be good,' he said.

'I'm sorry, is that Inspector Spring?' It was a woman's voice.

'Yes, it is Detective Inspector Spring. I am sorry, I thought it was my sergeant. How can I help you, Mrs, Miss...' He waited for a reply.

'It's Mrs, Detective Inspector, Mrs Leonard.'

'Leroy Leonard's wife?'

'Yes.'

'Well, how can I help you, Mrs Leonard?'

'Please, call me Catherine.'

'Then how can I help, Catherine?'

'Detective – Mr Spring – I never know what to call someone with a title,' she laughed.

'Then call me George.'

'Thank you, George.'

'Now fire away.'

'George, can I see you please.'

'Well, of course. When?'

'It must be strictly confidential.'

'Before I can give any promises, I must know what it is about first.'

'I'm in London. I'm coming back on Friday; can I see you then?'

'Of course. He has summoned several of us to be there on Friday night.'

'Oh yes, I forgot about that. I'll see you then.'

'Look forward to that, Catherine.'

'So shall I,' said Catherine.

Now I wonder what she wants, he thought again. He pondered, not for the first time, what such a beautiful woman saw in a pillock like Leonard. She seems complaisant to like him. He was brought back closer to home when the name of Jerry Tonkin once again flashed in his mind. What the hell had Stuart-Palmer been up to, mixing with the likes of Jerry Tonkin? He knew he could sort him out without any bother, but he still wished he didn't have to.

Catherine replaced the telephone, glad that she had managed to get in touch with George Spring. She found to her surprise that she had only met him the once, but remembered that he was about six foot tall, with iron grey hair and deep blue eyes.

The children were in bed asleep, tired out after a great day. Catherine herself was tired, so she decided to have an early night to be fresh for her meeting tomorrow with Everett Kinsley.

Next morning dawned, bright and sunny. Catherine was just about to shower when there was a tap on the door. She knew it could only be Mrs Mason.

'Come in,' she called.

'Catherine, dear, good morning. How are you this morning?'

'Fine.'

'Look, dear, last night you said about Mr Kinsley. Well, how about I take care of the children again for you.' She put her hand up. 'I'm offering.'

'Look, just till lunchtime. Then the four of us will go out and you will let me buy you a thank you tea.'

'That would be lovely, my dear. About an hour?'

'Yes, please.' Catherine had run out of ways to express her thanks.

Catherine was glad that was over. She had kept her word to Clive and they had gone across London to the chambers of Everett Kinsley. Catherine explained she wanted a divorce on the grounds of mental cruelty and was told she would have to be separated for two years first. She enlightened him as to what Leroy had threatened to do if she left him, but he told her that nothing could be done until the offence was committed. The best news was that the flat in London was in her name, so she could live there and have him barred from the place. She told Mr Kinsley that she wanted him to represent her, but asked him to wait until she gave him the go ahead. He gave her his card. They had both left and now she was back, looking forward to an afternoon out with Mrs Mason and the children.

'It's Wednesday morning,' said Trish.

'I know that. So?' Albert didn't have a clue what she was on about.

'What were you going to do Monday?'

'Look, Trish, I'm not in the mood for games, right.' Albert was still mad over the incident of last evening.

'Tilling. You were going to phone Tilling.'

'Shit, so I was. I'll do it this morning,' he said.

'Don't forget,' Trish said.

'Look, I said I'll phone him so I will, right.'

'Oh, who got up the wrong side this morning?'

'Who got out,' said Albert, 'not up.'

'Pardon me for breathing,' said Trish and went into the public end of the Pheasant.

Albert followed her in. 'I'm sorry, love,' he said, 'but those two last night really got to me.'

'It's ages since I saw you like that, my macho man.' She kissed Albert.

'Behave yourself,' he said.

At Shawlworth Hall, Leroy Leonard was thinking it was not such a good idea to let things pile up in the kitchen; it was now a major operation to find a clean cup or plate. He had achieved his objective, but the smell was a bit iffy. The fact that it was the height of summer did not help, but dirty pans and dishes also attracted many flies. Of course, it was all Catherine's fault; she was the one to blame, going away like that. Just wait till she gets home.

'Harv,' shouted Leroy. 'Give us a hand, will you?'

Harv was lounging in the drawing room. He sighed, got up and found his way to the kitchen.

'This place is like a pigsty,' he said.

'I know, I know.' Leroy was not amused. 'Want any breakfast?'

'Not off that lot, I don't,' he said.

''Tis bad.' Even Leroy had to agree.

'Come on, let's get stuck in to this lot or we'll get AIDS or something just as nasty.'

Once again, Leroy, under his breath, blamed that woman.

It was a good two hours before the kitchen bore any actual resemblance to a kitchen. Harv stood back and admired his handiwork.

'There you go,' he said proudly.

'It's friggin' dinnertime now,' moaned Leroy.

'Right,' said Harv. 'Coffee, sarnie and then back to these vocals. They're great, the ones we've done, but still another nine to do. I must admit, you're still excellent for a wrinkly.'

'Cheeky sod.' Leroy was secretly proud of his work.

'OK then. Sarnie or what?'

'Yea, yea a sarnie,' said Leroy, after which they returned to the studio. By the end of the day another four tracks were down on the master tape.

Detective Inspector Spring walked up the lane to the cottage that was only just visible. It was early Wednesday evening and he was off duty, but he was steeling himself for trouble. He arrived at the cottage door and knocked. After a short wait, the door was opened by a young lad.

'Your dad in?' Detective Inspector Spring said to the boy.

'Who's asking?' he replied.

'Look, son, yes or no.'

'Da, filth,' he shouted and walked away.

Again Detective Inspector Spring waited and then Jerry came to the door.

'Whatever it was, nothing to do with me.'

'Very glad to hear it, Jerry.'

'What's it about then?'

'Just a word, Jerry, that's all.'

'Shoot.' Jerry yawned and scratched his bare stomach.

'Yesterday, Jerry, you never saw Antony Stuart-Palmer. You never spoke to him either, right.'

'Now, why should I do that, Mr Spring?'

'Because, Jerry, I'm telling you, that's why. Last night I spoke to him and he said he did something he now regrets. Look, Jerry, you and I know what he's like – salt of the earth, really. But come on, Jerry, this over nothing? His wife and daughter are worried sick.'

'I owe that man my son's life, Mr Spring. So if it comes from him, I haven't seen him for ages, right.'

'Right, Jerry, thanks.'

'What for, Mr Spring? Just for making a social call? No need.'

George left to phone Antony, pondering whether perhaps there really was honour among thieves.

Chapter Twenty-Three

Some form of normality was slowly coming back to Shawlworth Village. By Thursday, people were still talking about poor Reverend Peterson and asking about the funeral, but progress was being made. Except, that is, for one place – the residence of the Cawthorne sisters. Jane could not or would not believe that Reverend Peterson was dead.

'Jane, dear, you must pull yourself together.' Ruby was really concerned for her sister's well-being.

'Ruby, that poor man.' Jane's eyes were red from crying. No more tears would come, but not for want of trying on Jane's behalf.

'Jane, he's dead and no matter what you do it will not bring him back. Do you want me to get Dr James to call?'

'No. I would never have believed you could be so, so *callous*.'

'Jane, will you please stop this. I miss him as much as you do, but we cannot bring him back. If there were any way, do you not think I would do it? Truthfully speaking, Jane dear, now I am getting more worried about tomorrow evening.'

'Tomorrow evening? What are you talking about, tomorrow evening?'

'Shawlworth Hall.'

'Ruby, I am in no mood for silly games. Now either you stop or I am going out.' Jane was at last forgetting about Reverend Peterson.

'I am not playing games. Listen, dear, tomorrow is Friday. Friday evening, seven thirty, Shawlworth Hall, this Leonard creature. Remember?'

'Ruby, we cannot go there tomorrow.' Jane was shocked that Ruby could think of such a thing.

'We can, Jane, and we will.' Ruby's eyes glinted. 'I want to see that man face to face and when I do, God help him.'

'You go on your own.'

'I will not. You are coming if I have to drag you there by your hair.'

'Ruby, what are you saying? I've never see you like this before. You're frightening me.'

'You are going and that is the end of it,' Ruby said. 'I want to hear no more about it; the subject is closed.'

'It's for you, Guv.' Sergeant Harris passed the phone to Detective Inspector Spring.

'Who is it?' he mouthed.

Harris shrugged his shoulders.

'Detective Inspector Spring.'

'George, it's Peter.'

'Peter, how can I help?'

'Not a bad time to call, is it?'

'No, go ahead, Peter.'

'Well, you know when we called at the Stuart-Palmers, you told me about certain charges that had been dropped by a mutual person who we know.'

'Yeess?'

'Well, you were told to stay clear.'

'Yeess?'

'Friday, seven thirty in the evening, we both have to be some-where.'

'Damn.'

'Exactly.'

'I'm still going.'

'Is that wise?'

'What can happen? Room full of people, I'll be OK. No, I'm still going.'

'If you're sure,' said Dr James. He was concerned. 'What if it turns nasty?'

'Then I'll run. I mean it, no way am I going to get involved in anything.'

'Look, are we going to the Pheasant? We did promise some information.'

'Yes, you're right, we did. But it will have to be quick. I'm being pressured for a result on this mugging case I've got.'

'About eight?'

'Fine.'

'See you then, bye.'

George Spring sat for a while. What could possibly go wrong? he mused. No, I am definitely going. I want to see his face when I mention Reverend Peterson.

Andrew heard the sound of someone whistling and turned. Leroy was leaning from a window in the east wing. Andrew had decided to go for a walk down to the stables, to look in on the horses for Catherine. He had just passed the east wing when he heard the whistle.

'Andrew, tomorrow night, half six, I want you to take Harv to Truro station for the seven thirty train to Paddington.'

'Yea, OK.' Andrew walked away. That would have normally bothered Leroy, but today he was in an especially good mood. When the morning post had arrived, a large brown envelope, one which Leroy had been waiting for, finally came. It contained the information on the rent rises for the villagers. He had perused the figures and was more than happy with the outcome.

If that git in the pub doesn't agree, see how he fancies three-hundred-a-month rent. That silly duffer, the vicar, thirty-five a week; the smart-arsed copper, twenty-five; and as for those two old biddies, another twenty-five. For the villagers who were just getting letters, the rents ranged from fifteen to forty-five pounds a week – except the shop, which was fifty but the one which pleased him the most was the surgery: one hundred a week.

Leroy rubbed his hands. This will wipe the smiles off their smug faces. Leroy loved it.

The master tape was coming along very well. Harv had done a great job of the mixing and his vocals sounded really good. For Leroy, everything was coming up roses. He felt in such a good mood that he might even forgive Catherine when she arrived home tomorrow.

'How many tracks are down now?' Leroy asked Harv.

'Ten finished, two to go.'

Leroy looked at his watch. 'It's half seven. Let's knock off now, go down and get a good drink.'

'I'm with you, boss.' Harv never refused a drink.

'Tell you what, you have a breath of fresh air first, seeing as we have been cooped up here all day.' Leroy switched everything electric off and they headed through the upper floor of the Hall, descended the master staircase and went out for a walk by the lake. The slight breeze felt good.

Down in the village at the Pheasant it was a busy evening for Albert and Trish.

Linda and John were already present as Andrew walked into the lounge bar and bid everyone a good evening.

'We are definitely going.' Linda was talking to Trish. 'Are you going?'

'You bet, as support for Albert.'

'Trish?'

'Yes?'

'Can I ask what he is doing about the concerts in the pub?' Linda enquired.

'He phoned Mr Tilley yesterday and Tilley said he thought we had a good chance of stopping Leonard from doing them. But the rent! We told him about the agreement and reminded him that he was there. He agreed he was, but said how could he foresee what would happen, with things turning out the way they have? He told us to fight him – ombudsman, tribunal, so that's what we are going to tell him tomorrow night.'

'We have no choice.' Linda looked forlorn. 'If John doesn't do what that pig says, not only does he lose his job but we lose our home as well. All through that pig.'

'I never told him.' Andrew answered Albert's question as to what Leroy's response was when told of Reverend Peterson.

'So he still does not know?'

'Not unless someone else told him, and if they did he has never said nothing to me,' said Andrew. 'All he's said to me today is he wants me to take the sound bloke to Truro station tomorrow night to catch the seven thirty train for Paddington, and his wife Catherine's away.'

'She been away, then?' Albert stated the obvious.

'She went with the children on Monday and haven't seen her

since, so what's wrong now I don't know. Probably that shit on his high horse again.'

George Spring and Dr James walked in. Greetings were exchanged again and drinks served at the expense of Dr James, who ordered his usual malt and whatever the others fancied.

'Well, everyone,' George spoke for himself and the doctor. 'Reverend Peterson.' Five people gave him their undivided attention. 'We told you that he may not be buried here, so we owe you some form of explanation. We can tell you the same as what we told the Stuart-Palmers last evening and only that. The fact of the matter is, Reverend Peterson was married.'

'You're joking,' said Linda. 'Where's his wife then?'

'His wife is dead,' George continued. 'Years ago he had a daughter who, at sixteen, died under tragic circumstances, and his wife died of a broken heart. They are buried side by side and we thought that Reverend Peterson should either be laid to rest, next to them if possible, or dispensation be sought for him to be buried with his wife.'

'We see now,' Trish said sadly. 'Of course he should be buried with his wife and daughter.'

'Where's that?' said Albert.

'Near where you are originally from,' said George.

'Me?' Albert looked surprised.

'Tuckingmill,' George said.

'You mean the church between Tuckingmill and Roskear.'

'That's the one.'

'How come?' Albert was really interested.

'In the spring of 1963 his daughter went to a pop concert at the Flamingo Club and died because of a spiked drink.'

'I remember that,' Albert was excited. 'I was at college at the time. I wasn't there at the concert but it was the talk of the place. Wait a minute. Allyson, that's it, Allyson. Oh my God...'

'What?' said Trish.

'Allyson Peterson was her name. Well, bugger me,' he said.

'Peter and I are going to see the vicar of the church on Sunday, so we'll inform you of the outcome.'

'Changing the subject, are we all looking forward to tomorrow night?' said Peter James.

'Can't wait,' John said mockingly.

'Andrew has to go to Truro for half seven tomorrow, haven't you?' Albert said.

'Eh? Oh, Truro, yea.' Andrew was miles away.

'How is everyone going?' asked Linda.

'Well, how about you and John coming with me and Albert?' Trish offered.

'OK, thanks.' Linda looked at John.

'OK by me,' he said.

'George, you come with me and we'll pick up the Cawthorne sisters.' Peter looked at George.

'Fine,' he replied.

'That's all settled then,' Albert said. 'Tell you what, drinks on the house in memory of Reverend Peterson.' They all drank to the memory.

'You sure about tomorrow?'

'Look Penn, I've told you I'll be OK. Thanks for the concern, but I will be, I promise.' Catherine and Penny were sitting in the flat with another bottle of half-consumed wine. The children were safely in bed and a taxi ordered for nine thirty in the morning. The children were more than happy to stay with Mrs Mason, so everything was set. Catherine would arrive home at teatime, get Friday night over, tell him on Saturday or Sunday about the commercial and five-year contract, and take it from there. As far as Catherine was concerned, it was now up to Leroy.

'Cath, you know what a pig he can be.' Penny was still not convinced.

'I know, but if he starts, all I have to do is pick up the phone.'

'If you can,' interrupted Penny.

'Pick up the phone, call Everett Kinsley and tomorrow night I'm seeing George, I mean Detective Inspector Spring.'

'George, eh?' Penny mocked.

Cath blushed; she felt foolish.

'Have another drink and shut up.' Catherine reached for the bottle.

'Is he, you know?' Penny was now teasing.

'Penny, don't start.'

'Come on, Cath, you can tell me.' Penny was really going to town.

'There's nothing to tell.'

'Have you seen it?'

'Penny, have I seen what?'

'Has he showed you his truncheon yet?'

'Penny, now that's enough. You're just as bad as when we spoke on the phone.'

Penny was hysterical.

'Just once, that's all.' Before Catherine could explain any further, after realising what she had said, Penny screamed and rolled onto the floor in convulsions of laughter.

'I mean I've seen him, just once, at the Hall last Friday. When he came to see Leroy.'

Penny had tears rolling down her cheeks; she wiped her eyes with a finger and sniffed. 'I believe you, Cath. Thousands wouldn't.'

'Fool,' Cath said quietly, but couldn't help smiling herself.

Chapter Twenty-Four

'There's no way I am going in an obsequious manner to that pig,' Vanessa said through a mouthful of toast.

'Mummy, not with your mouth full,' Juliet reprimanded.

'Sorry, darling.'

Breakfast on Friday morning was rather lively in the Manor House.

'No one is asking you to go tonight with that attitude but don't forget the sort of person you are dealing with, that's all I am saying,' said Antony.

'What have we got to lose?' Vanessa asked. 'There are no shoots, and now it looks more and more likely that there will be no hunts so that also means no Hunt Ball, so what have we got to lose?' she repeated.

Antony remained silent.

'Do I have to come tonight, Mummy?' Juliet looked concerned.

'No, darling, of course not.'

'Oh good,' she smiled. 'Daddy.'

'Yes, darling.'

'When are we moving Gladiator?'

'I thought Sunday.'

'Very well.' Juliet was resigned to the fact that her beloved horse was going.

'Have you exercised him lately?' her mother enquired.

'Mummy, really, where can I take him?'

'Sorry, darling, I forgot.'

'I'm going now to groom him and exercise him along the lane.'

'Be careful, Juliet,' her father warned.

'I will Daddy. Bye.' Juliet left the room.

'I could kill that man,' said Antony.

'Come on, come on,' Dr James tapped his fingers on his desk and waited for the phone to be answered.

'Hello?' At last someone spoke.

'Miss Cawthorne, Dr James here, it's about this evening.'

'Yes, Doctor.'

'Would you like a lift to the Hall with myself and George Spring?'

'That would be very kind; a lift to and from the Hall would be greatly appreciated.'

'I take it that is Ruby?' he said cautiously.

'You are correct, Doctor, but how did you know over the telephone?'

'Elementary, my dear Miss Cawthorne,' he laughed. 'No, to be serious, when I told you about Reverend Peterson you seemed the much calmer of the two. I apologise for laughing; I did not mean to cause offence.'

'Not at all. You are perfectly right. I am afraid that Jane has taken it rather badly.'

'Yes, I could see that. Should I call round? I'm free at the moment.'

'Would you, please. It would ease my mind,' she said gratefully.

'I shall be there in fifteen minutes,' he said.

Ruby replaced the receiver and went to her sister.

'Jane, dear, that was Dr James. He phoned to ask if we would wish to go to the Hall tonight with him and Detective Inspector Spring. I said that we would be most grateful.'

'Oh dear.' Jane dabbed her eyes.

'He is coming round to see you, dear.'

'Why?' Jane enquired of her sister.

'Just as a favour to me. I am worried about you.'

'There is no need.'

'Better to be safe than sorry.'

'What can he do?'

'I don't know, dear. I am no doctor.'

'Can he bring dear Reverend Peterson back?'

'Jane, please.'

'I'm sorry, Ruby.'

'Shall I make some tea?' Ruby suggested.

'That will be nice. Yes please, a nice cup of tea.'

'I'll get it for you, dear.' Ruby went into the kitchen.

Ruby had just scalded the pot when Dr James arrived.

'I'll get it, dear,' Ruby called and went to the door, not waiting for an answer.

'Hello, Dr James. Thank you for calling; she's in there. Would you like a cup of tea?

Dr James deduced that 'she's in there' referred to Jane.

'Thank you, Ruby, I would love one.'

Dr James walked as directed and greeted Jane Cawthorne.

'How are you, Jane?' he said.

'Hello, Doctor. Oh, this terrible news has hit me hard.'

'I know, but you must think of yourself.' Dr James tried to comfort her. 'I could give you pills, but that would not solve the problem. You must find the cure within yourself.'

'That's what I keep telling her, Doctor.' Ruby had returned carrying the ceremonial tray.

This time questions had to be asked.

'Milk and sugar, Doctor?'

'Yes please, one sugar,' he replied.

Duly served, he waited until the sisters had their tea and then said, 'The funeral of Reverend Peterson and burial may not be here.'

'Not here?' The sisters looked horrified.

'No; please let me explain,' he quickly said. 'Reverend Peterson had been married.' He waited for the expected response.

'Married?' said Ruby.

'No, not Reverend Peterson,' said Jane.

'I'm afraid it's true.'

'When?' Ruby again spoke.

'Let me explain,' said Dr James, placing his cup on the table. 'In the spring of 1963, Reverend Peterson was married with a daughter – a girl of sixteen – named Allyson. Due to tragic circumstances, she died, and six months later Reverend Peterson's wife died of a broken heart. They are buried side by side.'

'Oh that poor, poor man.' Once again Jane began to weep.

'Doctor, I am having a strange premonition,' said Ruby slowly, 'but does this have anything to do with Leonard and the Reverend taking his own life?'

'I don't know what made you think that?' Dr James looked incredulously at Ruby. 'But yes, you are right.'

'This is an incubus,' said Jane.

'So George Spring and I thought that he should be buried with his wife and daughter if possible.'

'Quite rightly so,' agreed Ruby.

'George and I are going to se the local vicar at Roskear on Sunday to clarify the situation.'

'When can the burial take place?' Ruby asked.

'I am led to believe by George that there has to be a post-mortem and then an inquest – in this case a mere formality – and then he can be released for burial.'

'I see,' acknowledged Ruby.

'So…' Dr James clapped his hands. 'This evening, seven fifteen. And Jane, are you sure you will try for me?'

'I promise, Doctor, and thank you.'

'Good, good, then I shall see you this evening. Goodbye, ladies.'

'I'll see you to the door,' said Ruby.

'No, please, I'll find my own way,' insisted Dr James. 'Until this evening then.'

'Goodbye, Doctor,' Jane and Ruby spoke as one again.

After an uneventful train journey and taxi ride, Catherine once more found herself back at Shawlworth Hall. It was about four thirty when she picked up her suitcase, watched the taxi go down the drive and walked into the Hall. Catherine dropped her suitcase in the main hall and went to the kitchen. She was surprised to find it tidy, apart from a few dirty cups and plates. She put the kettle down after filling it, plugged it in, sat down and waited. She began to wonder if it would have been better for Penny to come with her after all.

'Well, well.' Catherine jumped; Leroy was leaning against the door.

'Don't start, I'm too tired,' Catherine begged.

'Me, start? Now, would I? My wife goes off for four days,

takes the bairns, comes back without them. Me, start? Never.'

'Leroy, do you want a coffee?'

'No, pet, I want an explanation.'

'I've told you. We have to talk.'

'About what?'

'Us.'

'What about us? All I've ever asked is you be there for me and the kids.'

'Leroy, I want a life of my own.'

'Like what?'

'Like earning a living for myself.'

'There's about eight million in the bank and you want to work? Every other woman I know would give her right arm for a place like this and just laze about.'

'Laze about in a place this size? You must be joking. It would take three people full time just to keep it clean. What about when you go on tour? What am I supposed to do, sit here every night on my own, kids in bed about half a mile away?'

'Don't exaggerate,' he sneered.

'No, but look at the size of this place – huge. One woman and two children.'

'Yea, well, get—'

'Get what, Leroy?'

'I don't know.'

'No, you never do.'

'Look, I cannot stand here arguing with you. Andrew is coming at half six to pick up Harv, OK? I'll be upstairs; when he comes send him up.'

'Yes, Leroy, certainly, Leroy.'

'There's no talking to you when you are in this mood,' he said and left.

Catherine murmured, 'Yes, the children are fine.' She made a coffee, carried it through to the main hall, picked up her suitcase and went to the bedroom.

After Catherine had showered and changed her clothing, she felt better. She had forgotten about her coffee – it was cold. 'Damn,' she said. After unpacking the case, she took the dirty laundry from herself and the children downstairs, put it in the washing machine, programmed it, and went and made herself another cup of coffee. She sat and actually drank this cup, vowing to herself that she would tell him tomorrow. That's if she didn't kill him first.

Catherine picked up the phone and dialled Mrs Mason's number.

'Mrs Mason... Catherine... Yes, I'm fine, safely home. How are the children? Good... Hello, darling, how are you? Good... No, Lee, I'm sure Daddy has not forgotten about your pony... Hello Pansy, you miss me? Mummy misses you too, darling... Bye... Mrs Mason, thanks... No, I haven't told him yet... tomorrow... I probably will need luck... Goodbye, phone you tomorrow.'

Catherine walked into the laundry room and checked on the washing machine. OK. Catherine was bored already and she had only been back about an hour and a half. I cannot take much more of this, she thought. She was adamant about that.

Catherine had gone to the drawing room and was flicking idly through the pages of some fashion magazines she had bought at Paddington station when she heard someone at the front entrance. It was Andrew.

'Hello, Mrs Leonard. Nice to see you back.'

'Nice to see you, Andrew.'

'I've called to take the sound engineer to Truro for the seven thirty train.'

'So I believe.' Catherine ushered him in. 'You are to go up to the studio.'

'Thanks. I don't suppose you will have heard about the local vicar.'

'No, what happened?'

'Hung himself Monday evening.'

'No. What made him do that?'

'Guess.'

'Oh, dear God. No, not Leroy.'

'Right first time.'

'You, er, you go up, Andrew. Does he know?'

'Not yet.'

'Leave that to me.'

'OK, Mrs Leonard. If that's what you want.'

'Please, Andrew.'

Andrew went up to the studio. All was quiet even though the door was open, but he could hear voices.

'Sure you are climbing, Leroy, but there are some good numbers there.'

'Name one,' Leroy challenged.

'Fame, Irene Cara, Fantastic Day, Haircut 100, ABC are still there, and so are Dexy's Midnight Runners.'

'I said one, not four,' laughed Leroy.

Andrew walked in; Leroy turned.

'Andy, my old son. All ready?'

'Yes, Mr Leonard.'

'We are formal this evening,' said Leroy. 'Mr Leonard indeed.'

'Right, I'm ready. I'll see Iveson on Monday and as soon as things are sorted, you will let me know. You sure you want me as your sound man for the tour?' Harv enquired.

'You bet I want you.' Leroy put his arm around Harv's shoulder. 'Best I've heard in a long time.'

'What with the single in the charts, tour and new album, you cannot fall off. Another fortune in the offing,' Harv commented.

'Lolly, lovely lolly,' sang Leroy.

'You ready?' said Andrew.

'Be right there.' Harv picked up his bag.

'Andy, watch that car and bring the keys straight back to me here. I'll leave the east wing door open for you. Should be finished by then; you should be back by eight.'

Harv and Andrew left.

Leroy smiled; he had just had an idea. Wait till everyone arrives, say I've got work to do that could not wait. Oh of course, I am sorry. Have a good look around the Hall, do whatever you like. I'll mention figures and then let the idiots sweat for an hour. Brilliant.

Catherine busied herself in the drawing room: drinks ready, everything tidy. Should I make something for them to nibble on? Then she realised that she had not done any shopping and so quickly discounted that idea.

'There you are,' it was Leroy.

'What are you smirking about?' Catherine asked.

'Me?' Leroy put his hand on his chest. 'Nothing.'

'I know you.'

'Well, if you must know, I've got the figures for rents through.'

'Stuart-Palmer won't be paying rent.'

'I know, I know, but when they hear what I have to say it'll be just as good.'

'You are sick.'

'Don't get smart, Cath,' Leroy threatened. 'Wait till you see the look on their faces. It will be great, the doc, the vicar.'

'You'll have a job.'

'Why, may I ask?'

'Because, husband dear, after your little set to with the vicar on Monday in the evening, he hung himself.'

'Don't be funny, Cath. How do you know that? You have just come back from London.'

'Andrew just told me.'

Leroy had suddenly gone pale and sat down. 'You have to be joking.'

'Can you see me laughing?'

'That... er... that doesn't change anything.'

'Does it not? When these people come tonight, what are you going to say? Sorry I caused the vicar to kill himself?'

'No! No! I'll, er, I'll just say...'

'Well, what will you say?'

'I don't know.'

'Leroy, go look in a mirror.'

'Why?'

'Your face.' Catherine paused. 'It's a treat.'

Tommy Curnow had arrived at the Pheasant. Trish, Linda, John and Albert were having a drink to calm their nerves.

'I am not looking forward to this one little bit,' Albert said nervously.

'Ditto,' agreed John.

'Come on, it might not be as bad as we think,' Linda tried to make light of things.

'You don't really believe that, do you, Linda?' said Trish.

'Not really,' Linda admitted.

John was the first to move. 'Come on, it's quarter past. I suppose we had better go.'

'Shouldn't be all that long, Tommy,' Albert said. 'We should be back for nine.'

'No problem, Albert. We'll manage OK.' Tommy smiled. 'Good luck.'

'Yea, I have a feeling I'm going to need it.' Albert was not looking forward to the encounter.

'Come on, slowcoach,' Trish called from the door.

They all got into the car and drove towards the Hall. As they passed the cottage occupied by the Cawthorne sisters, they saw them being escorted down the path by Dr James; George Spring was behind the wheel of the car. Albert blew the car horn; an acknowledgement wave came from George.

Both cars virtually arrived together at the main entrance to the Hall. As Albert's car was the first to arrive, they only had to wait a short time before George pulled up. They stood in a group just long enough to cordially greet one another and make a short reference to poor Reverend Peterson before they walked together to the main door.

Catherine felt extremely embarrassed. She had just opened the door to the Stuart-Palmers and she was inviting them in. 'Hello, er, Sir, the Right…'

'Catherine, I said it's Antony,' he smiled. 'This is my wife Vanessa.'

'How do you do, Catherine.' Vanessa looked – she had to agree Catherine was a very beautiful woman – she took Catherine's hand and shook it warmly.

'Lady Vanessa…' Catherine knew she was bright red and shaking.

'Please, it's Vanessa. Are you ill, Catherine?' Vanessa enquired.

'No, just very, very nervous. You would think after parading in front of thousands of people, I would have my nerves under control now,' Catherine answered.

'Why are you nervous? Not of us I hope,' said Antony.

'Well, yes, really. You will think it silly, but I am nervous because I am showing you into Shawlworth. Your home, now mine.'

'Don't be silly,' Vanessa laughed. She had taken to Catherine straight away.

'Please, this way.' Catherine had just shown them into a room they knew better than her. She was just about to ask if they would like a drink, when the crunch of tyres on the gravel caused her to break off.

'That must be the others,' she said. 'Please excuse me.' She headed for the door, turned and said, 'Please help yourself to a drink.'

As soon as the door closed, Vanessa turned to Antony and whispered, 'She is utterly charming. What does she see in a pig like him?'

'They say love is blind,' Antony whispered back. 'I wonder where he is?'

Catherine opened the door. First to greet her was George Spring. 'Catherine, lovely to see you again,' he smiled. He took her hand and held it for an embarrassingly long time.

Catherine smiled back at him. 'You too,' she replied.

'Yes, let me introduce everyone to you,' George offered.

'Please come in first,' she said. They all assembled in the hall.

'Firstly, these are the Cawthorne sisters. Next we have Linda Penrose; Trish Bolitho; John Penrose, your gamekeeper; Albert Bolitho, licensee of the Pheasant; and finally, but by no means least, our good doctor, Dr James.

Catherine greeted them all in turn and led them to the Stuart-Palmers; no introductions were needed there, as everyone present knew the them.

'May I get you all a drink?' Catherine asked. She had just poured herself a sherry and pulled George Spring to one side to request he stay after the others had gone, when the door opened and Leroy Leonard walked in.

No one spoke; he received hostile ice-cold stares. 'Sorry about this,' he said, 'but I have some work to finish in my studio. Be about an hour. Have a look around the Hall, go anywhere you want.' He turned to the Cawthorne sisters. 'You two fancy coming with me to the east wing?'

'My dear young man, I have no wish to go anywhere with you. Not now, or ever.' Ruby's voice was ice cold.

'Please yourself. I just thought that you might want to hear the music that is going to be blasting out in the amphitheatre.'

'Let me correct you.' Ruby was now venomous. 'Firstly, it is not music, and the only way you will play that rubbish there is over my dead body, or preferably yours.'

George Spring was doing his best to restrain himself, but he was fully aware of the consequences. Leroy's mood changed. 'Just you lot be here when I get back, that's all.' He stormed off.

'I most humbly apologise to you, my dear, in your home, for what has just occurred. But I do not regret one word I have just said,' Ruby said to Catherine.

'No need to apologise.' Catherine was again bright red. 'I am most sorry about this and my husband's manner.' Catherine was struggling; George came to her rescue.

'Why don't we do what he said and have a good look around the Hall and meet back here in about forty-five minutes?'

To ease the embarrassment for Catherine, everyone agreed and placed their glasses on the table. Jane spoke. 'You sure, my dear, you have no objection to all of us wandering through the Hall at will?'

'Not at all, feel free to go anywhere you wish.' Catherine was only too pleased to get away. As she walked past George, she gave a very secretive tug on his jacket sleeve.

Everyone went out into the great hall, split up and went their separate ways.

George just followed Catherine. She headed for a small room used as a store room, knowing George was following her. They entered, but left the door open just in case.

'George, thanks for coming. I am going to need your help, desperately, or I'll kill that pig.'

'Calm down, Catherine. Just tell me.'

'Not here. Can you meet me tomorrow morning?'

'Course I can. Where?'

'Can I come to your place?'

'Sure, what time?'

'Ten.'

'Do you know where I live?'

'I'll find it.'

'Village square, well, pond.'

She nodded.

'With the pond in front of you, bottom left-hand corner.'

'Thanks, George.' She squeezed his hand and left.

Everyone had gone their separate ways and had been wandering for the last twenty minutes.

Outside, John was alone when he heard the car coming. It came into view and he recognised Andrew behind the wheel. He watched Andrew park the car by the east wing and disappear, only to return a minute later. He walked towards John.

'John, do me a favour, please,' Andrew asked. 'Come with me.'

John followed Andrew around the corner to the east wing door.

'Try that door for me, please.'

John tried the door. 'It's locked,' he said.

'Thanks,' Andrew nodded.

'Andrew, what's this all about?'

'John, you know what a bastard he can be? Well, he told me when I came back from the station to bring the car keys to him in the east wing and he would leave the door open.'

'But it's locked.'

'Exactly, so I am going to have to go through the front. When he finds out, probably he'll go mad. I just wanted you to witness the door was locked. He must have forgot.'

'I see,' said John. 'Course I will.'

'Thanks, I'd better go,' he said. 'I had to be back by eight, but what with traffic and one thing and another... now this... he'll probably dock me half an hour's pay.'

'Yea, you be off.' John nudged Andrew away.

Andrew went to the main entrance and rang the bell; Catherine soon came and answered the call. 'Andrew, something wrong?'

''Fraid so, Mrs Leonard. Leroy asked me to bring the car keys back to him in the east wing. He said he would leave the door open. Well, it's locked; John verified that for me because you know what Leroy is like. He said I had to be back by eight; it's nearly twenty-five past now.'

'Come on, I'll come with you.' Catherine headed for the stairs. 'I'll explain for you.'

'Thanks,' said Andrew.

Dr James was on the stairs looking at paintings; the two Cawthorne sisters were on the upper level, not together but not far apart; there was no sign of the others.

Catherine and Andrew went through the communicating door to the east wing. The studio door was open, with music blasting out. Catherine and Andrew entered and stopped suddenly. Leroy Leonard lay on his stomach on the floor, a trickle of blood running down the back of his neck. Next to Leroy on the floor was an old miner's lamp.

Catherine screamed as Andrew knelt down by the prone Leroy.

'Go and get Dr James and George. Hurry.'

Catherine ran out through the communicating door, along the upper corridor and down the stairs, frantically searching for Dr James and George Spring. Dr James was at the bottom, talking to George and John.

'For God's sake, hurry,' she cried.

'What's wrong?' George enquired.

'It's Leroy, I think he's dead!' shouted Catherine.

'Stay there,' he said to John. 'Doctor, come with me.' They ran up the stairs back to the studio.

Andrew was still kneeling by Leroy, but moved to allow Dr James there. Dr James held Leroy's wrist, felt his neck and shone a pencil light in Leroy's eyes, then stood up.

'He's dead, I'm afraid,' Dr James said quietly.

'Catherine, wait outside please.' George ushered her out. 'Andrew,' he called, 'you as well.' George closed the door.

'How long, Peter?'

'Very difficult to say, but by the state of the body, no more than half an hour,' he said. 'But that's up to the police doctor.'

'Shit! Shit!' remarked George.

'What will you do now, George?' Dr James looked concerned.

'Seal this place off and phone my boss.' God, Blackwood is going to love this, George thought.

'Come on,' he said to Dr James. 'You sure he's dead?'

'Perfectly sure,' reiterated Dr James.

'Come on then.' George went to the door.

Outside, Catherine and Andrew waited; George Spring and Dr James came out.

'Apart from through the house, any other way in here?' George said to Catherine.

'Yes, there is a door at the end of the passage at the foot of these stairs. But it's locked,' she said.

'You all wait here until I return,' George commanded, as he descended the stairs.

They did as they were told. When Detective Inspector Spring returned, he said, 'That door is locked and double bolted, with the key in the lock.' He turned to Catherine. 'How did you know it was locked?'

'Andrew was supposed to come in that way, but found the door bolted. John verified it for Andrew, so Andrew came in the main entrance and that's when we found Leroy.'

'Right, we'll have to go below and round everybody up. I shall have to phone my boss.'

'There's a phone in the drawing room and we'll get everybody in there,' Catherine said.

'OK,' said George.

They walked through into the main hall. Trish and Linda were just coming out of a bedroom.

'Trish, Linda, downstairs please,' George ordered. They all walked down the stairs, Trish and Linda looking at each other.

'In the drawing room, please,' George had now taken command.

He took a head count: Trish, Linda, Catherine, Dr James, Andrew; already there were Antony and Vanessa Stuart-Palmer.

'The Cawthorne sisters,' he said. 'John and Albert. Will everyone please wait here.'

George left and went looking for Ruby, Jane, John and Albert.

John and Albert were outside; George requested them to go to the drawing room, which just left the Cawthorne sisters.

'Anything wrong?' Albert enquired.

'Leroy Leonard has been killed,' said Detective Inspector Spring.

'Never,' said John.

'Who? How?' asked Albert.

'Have you seen the Cawthorne sisters?' George was looking around.

'No,' they both answered.

They went back inside. Ruby and Jane were coming down the stairs.

'This way please, ladies,' said George.

They all went into the drawing room.

'As you all know by now – apart from Ruby and Jane – Leroy Leonard is dead.'

Jane gasped.

'I must ask you all to wait here,' George commanded. 'Catherine, a phone please.'

'Here,' she pointed.

'No, another please.'

'Kitchen OK?'

'That's fine.'

'I'll show you.' Catherine headed for the door.

'You OK?' George was by the side of Catherine Leonard as she walked to the kitchen.

'I'm fine, George. I'm going to tell you something.'

'Don't,' said George, 'not now. Wait.'

'Why?'

'Please, Catherine.'

In the kitchen Catherine pointed to the phone.

Chapter Twenty-Five

Detective Chief Inspector Blackwood sat with his wife and friends. It was his wedding anniversary and he was having a convivial evening and enjoying it. He was just about to pour more drinks when the telephone rang.

'I'll go, dear,' his wife volunteered.

'If it's for me, I'm not in,' he said.

His wife quickly returned. 'It's Detective Inspector Spring, says it's very urgent.'

'This had better be good,' he warned.

Detective Chief Inspector Blackwood picked up the telephone.

'George, this had better be good.'

'Oh, it's good, Sir,' Blackwood heard.

'Go on then.'

'There's been a murder, Sir.'

'Where?'

'Shawlworth Hall.'

'Who?'

'Leroy Leonard.'

'You there now?'

'Yes, Sir.'

'Who phoned you?'

'I was already here.'

'George, a bloke is murdered and you are already there. A bloke I gave you strict instructions to stay away from.'

'Yes, Sir.'

'You and anyone else who's there stay put, I'll get those necessary straight over and I'll be there myself. George, you have some very serious explaining to do.'

'Sir.'

Detective Chief Inspector Blackwood slammed down the phone.

George returned to the drawing room. When he entered the room, he was greeted by a flood of questions.

George held up his hands. 'Please, one at a time.'

Once again a cacophony of voices burst forth.

'Look, we are going to get nowhere like this,' he pleaded. 'Antony, you first.'

'Leroy Leonard is dead. Was it suspicious?'

George gave an affirmative nod.

'What happens now?' Antony said.

'Everyone has to remain here until my boss arrives with a squad.'

'For how long?' Albert questioned.

'I'm sorry, I don't know. There is the crime scene to see and then he will want statements from everyone before we are allowed to go.'

'You included?' Catherine looked at him.

'Me included,' he said.

'How did it happen?' Linda asked.

'I'm sorry, no questions of that nature until all statements have been taken.'

'So all we do now is wait?' Trish deduced.

'What about me?' said Andrew.

'Everybody.' George was firm on that point.

'Mrs Leonard, may I phone the Pheasant,' requested Albert, 'just to let my stand-in know?'

'Albert, not a word about this, mind. Just say you and Trish have been delayed.'

'OK, George.'

Albert did as requested, after getting Catherine's permission.

'May I phone Juliet?' Lady Vanessa asked of Catherine. Again, consent was given.

'Juliet, darling, listen Daddy and I will be late.'

There was a pause.

'I'm sorry, darling, I cannot tell you. Please just expect us when we arrive.'

Another pause.

'Darling, no you cannot come over. Just wait until we return.'

More silence.

'Juliet, I must go. Just wait. Bye bye, darling.' Vanessa put down the phone.

Everyone sat in silence, apart from Jane Cawthorne, who was again weeping.

Catherine broke the silence. 'I'm sorry. Would anyone like another drink? Is that all right, George?'

'As long as everyone keeps a clear head for his or her statement,' he said.

It was nine thirty when the police cars and an ambulance arrived.

'I'll go,' George said to Catherine.

George went to the door with some trepidation. The first in line was Detective Chief Inspector Blackwood.

'Crime scene,' he said. He turned to a uniformed officer. 'You stay here.'

Inside he turned to George. 'Where is everybody?'

'In there, Sir. No one has left or been near the crime scene.'

'Except the killer.' Blackwood was in a bad mood. To another uniformed officer he said, 'In there. Right, crime scene,' he continued. George led the way, followed by Detective Chief Inspector Blackwood, Sergeant Harris, a doctor, a photographer, a fingerprint expert, one more uniformed officer and two ambulance personnel.

'You are a pillock, George,' Detective Chief Inspector Blackwood said. George Spring just carried on walking.

'Here we are, Sir,' George said.

'You stop there,' he said to the uniformed officer, pointing to the top of the stairs. Turning to the ambulance men he told them to wait outside as well.

Detective Chief Inspector Blackwood, Detective Inspector Spring, Sergeant Harris, the police doctor and the fingerprint expert went in.

'What's that noise?' said Detective Chief Inspector Blackwood.

'It's the tape recorder, Sir,' said Sergeant Harris. 'It's run off.'

'Stop it then,' ordered Detective Chief Inspector Blackwood. 'At the mains, Sergeant – fingerprints.'

'Sorry, Sir.' Sergeant Harris went red.

'OK, Doctor, what can you tell us?' enquired Blackwood.

'Single blow to base of skull, heavy object, dead about one and a half hours, deep indentation. I would say swinging action.'

'That?' Blackwood pointed to the lamp.

'Yes, very possibly.'

'OK, thanks, Doc. For the time being, report as soon as possible.'

'Certainly, I'll do a PM tomorrow; answers Sunday.'

'Fine.'

Blackwood turned to the photographer. 'OK, do your stuff.'

Once he was finished, it was the turn of fingerprints.

'All smudges mainly, Sir,' he said.

'The lamp?'

'No Sir, sorry.'

'Bag that, Sergeant.' Blackwood pointed to the lamp. 'Then mark the outline and let's get him out of here.'

'George, any other entrance to here?' Blackwood questioned.

'Yes, Sir. Down the stairs, along the passage and a door to the outside. But I checked it straight after we found the body – it was double bolted and locked, key still in lock.'

'OK,' Blackwood acknowledged.

'You ready, Sergeant?'

'Yes, Sir.'

Blackwood shouted to the ambulance crew, 'Right, you can get him to the morgue.'

They laid down a stretcher and rolled Leroy onto it before covering him over.

'Off you go,' Blackwood ordered.

The ambulance crew carried Leroy Leonard down to the ambulance.

The fingerprints expert and doctor left.

'Close the door, run a tape across and leave it for now. Got that lamp, Sergeant?'

'Yes, Sir.'

George felt helpless. Ordinarily, he would be doing all this. While waiting, he recalled saying to Dr James, 'Course I'm going, what could possibly go wrong?'

'What's that?' said Blackwood. He pointed down the stairs.

'Sir?' George looked.

'*That*, man. What is it?'

George went down two steps and picked up a pearl-coloured button. 'Bag it, Sergeant. Evidence possibly.'

Once again Detective Chief Inspector Blackwood took over. 'Right, let's go and see that lot.'

Detective Chief Inspector Blackwood led the way downstairs, this time followed by Detective Inspector Spring, Sergeant Harris and the uniformed officer.

Detective Chief Inspector Blackwood turned to Sergeant Harris and the uniformed officer. 'I want you to search every room, just in case. *Every* room.'

'Sir, this place is massive,' protested Sergeant Harris.

'Then you had better get started, hadn't you, Sergeant.' Blackwood didn't wait for a reply. He turned and headed for the drawing room, which was lucky for Sergeant Harris, as he stood pulling faces and mouthing, 'I had better get started.'

'George... with me,' Blackwood ordered.

George didn't protest about any of this, because he knew he was in it up to his neck.

'Wait outside, Constable. I am Detective Chief Inspector Blackwood,' he addressed the gathering. 'At this moment, what has happened to Mr Leonard is being treated as murder.'

Gasps were heard.

Detective Chief Inspector Blackwood continued. 'So before anyone can leave, I need statements from everyone. George, outside.'

George left the room, as commanded.

Detective Chief Inspector Blackwood led him down the main hall, opened a door and went in. It was the store room George had been in with Catherine.

This is it, thought George.

'George, in all my years as a copper I have never, never had my best officer in charge of a murder who was also the chief suspect. I warned you to stay away, but no.

'You report everything, and I mean everything, to me and hope that this mess has a satisfactory ending. Now, I want statements from everyone tonight and you in my office tomorrow morning with copies for me. And I want a statement from you and, George, if you try to hide anything, I'll throw the book at you myself.'

'What do you mean by that, Sir?' George was angry.

'I'll tell you exactly what I mean. If it was you who topped him, or one of *them*, and you hide or cover anything up, I'll arrest and bust you myself. Now go and do your job and get out of my sight.'

Back in the main hall, Detective Chief Inspector Blackwood said to the constable at the drawing room door, 'Constable, go to the main door. I'm taking him to drive me home. You stay there and come back with the other officer and Sergeant Harris. George, where's that button?'

'Here, Sir.'

'Find out where it came from; that should not be too difficult, even for you.'

Detective Chief Inspector Blackwood left. The constable followed him to the main entrance and stood on duty as the officer drove Blackwood home.

George stood for a minute, collected himself, said, 'Shit,' and went back into the drawing room.

'George, it's half past ten,' Antony said. 'How much longer?'

'I'm sorry, but this is a murder inquiry. Statements first.'

'That could take hours,' protested Albert.

'Yea, can we not do it tomorrow?' agreed John.

'Sorry, they must be done now,' said George.

'Andrew, you first. Catherine, do you have another room we could use?'

'Kitchen OK?' Catherine said.

George took Andrew's statement first, because he had found the body. That completed, he told Andrew that he could go and asked him to send in one of the Cawthorne sisters.

Jane was first. She explained that she had spent all evening with Ruby, apart from when Ruby went to the toilet while they were upstairs.

George thanked her for her statement. There was a knock on the door.

'Come in,' Detective Inspector Spring called. It was Sergeant Harris.

'Nothing, Guv.'

'Sergeant, that police officer with you, when I have got Miss Ruby Cawthorne's statement, get him to give them a lift home.'

'Sure, Guv,' he replied.

Ruby gave her statement, saying that she was with her sister all evening. George thanked her. She left.

'Sergeant,' George shouted.

'Guv.'

'Left in the drawing room should be eight people. You take four and send four down here, or we are going to be here all night.'

Sergeant Harris left. Soon after, Detective Inspector Spring heard voices. Antony Stewart-Palmer, Vanessa, Dr James and Catherine came in.

'George, please. Juliet will be going frantic.'

'Give her a quick call.' George looked at Catherine; she nodded.

Antony picked up the phone.

'Vanessa, you first, then Antony, then Peter and you last, Catherine, because you live here. OK?'

Catherine smiled. She and Dr James went into the passage.

Vanessa explained that she had stayed with Antony. Why should they want to look around? They knew the place inside out.

Antony gave virtually the same statement. As he and Vanessa left, the clock struck midnight.

'Peter, you next,' said George.

Peter gave a full statement, explaining that he had wandered around looking at paintings, etc. He said he was alone. Finally it was Catherine's turn. She said that she had been alone all the time.

She went to the kitchen and made coffee. By one o'clock in the morning the statements had been completed and collected by Detective Inspector Spring. Sergeant Harris had departed with the lamp, giving Dr James a lift home. That only left George and Catherine.

'You OK?' he said.

'Yes, yes, I'm fine. Very tired after the train journey and then this.' Catherine looked shattered.

'I've just had a thought. You will be alone in this enormous place once I leave,' George said.

'Oh God, I had never thought of that.' Catherine looked concerned.

George picked up the phone and dialled the Pheasant. 'Albert, it's George. Were you in bed?' he asked.

'No, just about to, though,' Albert replied.

'Look, I have finished at the Hall and just realised that Catherine... Mrs Leonard... is going to be here by herself. This place is massive and, with what has happened... well, could you put her up for the night?'

'Course we can. We will have a room ready for when she arrives.' Albert was only too happy to agree.

'Thanks, Albert.' George put the phone down.

George turned to Catherine to tell her about the Pheasant, when he saw that she was sobbing quietly to herself.

George felt embarrassed, but did not know what to do. Catherine came to him, placed her arms around him and laid her head on his shoulder. She sobbed uncontrollably. He had seen this many times before. Delayed shock. George just stood and let Catherine get it out of her system.

'I'm sorry, George,' Catherine said eventually. 'I now feel embarrassed.'

'No, please, it's only natural,' he tried to reassure her.

'The Pheasant, you stay there this evening and tomorrow. Is there anyone to phone?'

'Oh my God, the children. They are in London at our flat; well, upstairs with Mrs Mason.' Catherine looked horrified.

'Look, you must get some sleep. I'll come over to the Pheasant in the morning, first thing, right? Now, do you want some clothes for tonight and in the morning.'

'Yes, but they are upstairs. Will you come with me, please?' Catherine asked.

'Course I will.' George was only too happy to help.

Catherine locked the front door. George was waiting in the car, engine running. Catherine sat in the front passenger seat, placed an overnight bag on her lap and they set off for the Pheasant. Outside the Pheasant, George got out of the car, walked round and opened the door for Catherine. She stood next to him. 'Thank you for all you have done,' she said and squeezed his hand.

When Catherine had gone into the Pheasant, George drove the short distance home, left the car at the front and went indoors. But he had no thought of going to bed.

It was two o'clock in the morning when Detective Inspector Spring finished the coffee he had made. He looked at the pile of statements – he had taken seven, Sergeant Harris four. Sergeant Harris's looked fine at first viewing, so why of the seven he took were three lying? Detective Inspector George Spring sighed. Three lying; *why*?

Next morning in the Pheasant, Trish and Albert were up early. They still had the lounge and bar to see to.

'Let her sleep,' Trish answered to Albert's question of what they should do about Catherine Leonard.

'Fair enough,' Albert answered.

'You go make a start in the bar and I'll hang on here a bit,' Trish told Albert. 'In case she comes down and fancies some breakfast.'

'OK, love.' Albert did as he was bid.

Catherine woke after managing just a few hours sleep, remembered where she was and then remembered the events of last evening. The first things that came into her mind were the children. Mrs Mason, must phone her and Penny. The newspapers. Oh God, the newspapers. She jumped out of bed, put on a dressing gown, found the bathroom, showered, came back to the bedroom, threw on a pair of jeans and a jumper and went downstairs. She found Trish in the kitchen.

'Good morning,' she said. 'Oh please forgive me, I cannot remember your name. It's unforgivable after you kindly gave me a bed for the night.'

Trish laughed, 'It's OK, Mrs Leonard. It's Trish and my husband is Albert.'

'I am Catherine, and thank you very much. Please, do you have a public phone?'

'Certainly not. You use this one here, as much as you like. I am going to help Albert in the lounge. There's the phone, coffee, milk, sugar and kettle just boiled. Just help yourself; I'll come back later and do you some breakfast.'

'Please, I couldn't eat, but this is very good of you. I'll pay for the calls and of course the room,' Catherine promised.

'You will not pay a penny for anything,' Trish vowed. 'Now, I mean it and you stay for as long as you want.'

'Thank you, you are both very kind.'

Trish left Catherine to her own devices.

'Mrs Mason, where are the children?' Catherine asked.

'Still in bed dear, why?'

'Last night Leroy was killed. It looks like murder, so can you do your best to keep them away from the television, wireless and press. Once this gets out, the press will be there probably, so could you please do your best until I get there.'

'My dear, how dreadful. Of course, I'll do my best, don't worry about things this end. Are you all right?'

'Very tired, still shocked, but OK. Look, I must phone Penny.'

'OK dear, bye.'

'Penny, it's Catherine.'

'Hello, Cath. You OK?'

'No. Last night Leroy was killed; looks like murder.'

'Cath, you serious?'

'Course I am, Penny.'

'Cath, I'm on my way down there. I'll get Clive to come.'

'No, Penny, just you please, Penny. Just you and Mum.'

'Right, we will be there some time this afternoon.'

'Penny, listen, get the train to Truro, then get a taxi to Shawlworth Village and ask for the Pheasant pub. I'll be here. I couldn't stay there last night.'

'Truro, Shawlworth Village, Pheasant. Catherine, stay there till we arrive. Bye.'

'Penny, if the taxi driver asks where Shawlworth is, tell him just west of Bodmin, bordering the moor.'

'Cath, don't worry.'

During the rest of the morning, Catherine met George Spring and told him that the original reason why she wanted to see him no longer mattered, but thanked him for being there. He then left for an appointment with his boss. Catherine tried to formulate a plan for the immediate future and looked forward to the arrival of Penny and her mother. By lunchtime in the Pheasant, the first of the media began to arrive.

Catherine kept well out of the way, but Albert and Trish were having a hard time of it.

John came in at lunchtime. He just managed a quick word with Albert, but conversation was a waste of time, so he gave up and went home.

Of all the times Albert had tried to clear the Pheasant at closing time, this was the hardest. He even thought of getting the local policeman to come and help, but eventually managed. People went their separate ways apart from the television cameras, radio announcers, press reporters and photographers. Those outside stood idly about, smoking. No one knew that peeping at them through a curtain upstairs was the once-famous model and wife of murdered pop star, Leroy Leonard.

Chapter Twenty-Six

Detective Chief Inspector Blackwood sat in his office and stared at Detective Inspector Spring. He finally spoke. 'George, I just cannot believe that you have been so stupid. I told you to stay clear of Leonard but no. Under any other circumstances I would have said, George, murder, take charge, and known that a good, thorough job would be done. So now tell me how I can put you in charge of a murder, when you are one of the prime suspects.'

'I didn't kill him, Sir.'

'Prove it to me now, George.'

'Well, that might be difficult.'

'Try me.'

'Because I'm telling you I didn't. But I was alone.'

'George, good enough for me, but not a jury. These statements first.'

'I've read them all, Sir. Do you want mine?'

'Go on, go on.'

'They're all OK, apart from three.'

'Those are?'

'Antony Stuart-Palmer, his wife and Ruby Cawthorne.'

'Why those?'

'Because they lied, Sir.'

'Can you prove it?'

'Yes, Sir.'

'Well, one of the people there last night, we can almost say with certainty once we get the pathology and forensic reports back, is a killer, so start with them. George, once again I'm putting my neck on the block for you. Clear this mess up, quick.'

'Yes, Sir.'

'Keep me fully informed.'

George left and went back to his own office.

In the Manor House, it was approaching lunchtime. Antony, Vanessa and Juliet were in the drawing room discussing last night's events, when Fielding entered and announced that two police officers were here to see them.

'Show them in please, Fielding.'

'Very good, Sir.'

Detective Inspector Spring and Sergeant Harris entered.

'George, come in. Nothing wrong is there?' Antony asked.

'This is Sergeant Harris. Can I please see you and Lady Vanessa alone?'

'Why, George?' Antony again questioned.

'Please, this is an official visit.'

'Juliet, please leave,' her father said.

'Oh, Daddy,' Juliet protested.

'Let her stay. We have nothing to hide,' Lady Vanessa said.

'Very well. Last evening in your statements you said you both stayed in the drawing room until everyone returned.'

'That's correct.'

'That's a lie.'

Lady Vanessa jumped up. 'George, I know you are only doing your job, but please do not call us liars.'

'I'm sorry, but it's true.'

'George, I hope you can prove what you say.' Antony was getting angry.

'I can. When we all left the room last night, I went first to the end of the Hall to a kind of store room with Catherine. She had something important to tell me, I was gone about five minutes. When I returned, I came back to the drawing room. It was empty.'

Antony and Vanessa Stuart-Palmer sat down.

'Of course, you are right, George,' Antony said. 'We know Shawlworth Hall inside out, so we quickly went down past the kitchen, up the back stairs, across to the east wing, saw Leonard and begged him to change his mind. He just laughed, so we made our way back the way we had come. But I swear, when we left him he was still alive. We crept past the kitchen when we heard someone in there moving about. Then we did go straight back to the drawing room, that is the truth.'

'It is, George, I swear,' said Lady Vanessa.

'Why didn't you say this last night?'

'Because when we found out he was dead, if we had said that, we would be number one suspects straight away and we did not kill him.'

'It still would have been better,' said George.

'We know that now,' Antony said. 'Sorry, George.'

'Right then, two new statements please.' George Spring looked at Sergeant Harris.

Once the statements were given, Detective Inspector Spring and Sergeant Harris left to see Ruby Cawthorne.

As the two police officers pulled up outside of the Cawthorne sisters' cottage, Sergeant Harris turned and asked, 'Do you believe them, Sir?'

'This time I do, funnily enough. But now it doesn't look good for this lady, does it?' Detective Inspector Spring was concerned.

They climbed out of the car, walked down the path and knocked on the door.

The door opened. 'Good morning, Inspector, and you, young man.'

'Good morning, Miss Cawthorne.'

'Ruby, please.'

George gave a sigh of relief. All through the interview he kept Ruby in his sight, just so he could tell the difference between her and sister Jane. They were ushered into the living room; Jane was seated at the table.

'I'm sorry,' said Detective Inspector Spring, 'if we are interrupting your lunch.'

'Certainly not, dear man. Please sit down, both of you.' Jane pointed to the chairs.

'Thank you,' they both sat.

'Now how can we help you? I suppose it's about this dreadful business last night,' Ruby enquired.

'Yes, I'm afraid it is,' George Spring's mind was racing. How to be diplomatic.

'Last night in your statement, you said you never left Jane.' He was looking at Ruby.

'That is true, Mr Spring.'

'Jane said you left her to go to the toilet.'

'That's right, of course I did, whilst in one of the bedrooms. I noticed an en-suite bathroom and used that,' Ruby said.

'So let's be clear, you were with Jane, where?'

'At the stairhead.'

'You left Jane there, went to the bathroom and came straight back to Jane.'

'I told Jane to wait there until I returned. Yes, that is how it happened exactly.'

'May I see the cardigan you wore last evening, please.'

'Of course, but how will that help?'

'Please, Ruby.'

'Very well,' Ruby agreed, brought the cardigan and handed it to Detective Inspector Spring. He examined the cardigan.

'I'm very sorry, Ruby, but I have done my best to allow you to vindicate yourself. But I must tell you that I know you have lied not once, but twice, to me since the death of Leroy Leonard.'

'How dare you!' Jane sprang to her sister's defence.

'I'm sorry, but it's true,' he said.

'Please explain,' Jane replied.

'When Ruby gave her statement, she said she had spent the evening with you, but you said she left you to go to the toilet.'

'She did, but she was confused. I don't know.'

'I can accept that, but just now I asked if after the toilet you came straight back to your sister. She said she did.'

'She did,' interrupted Jane.

'I'm sorry, she did not.'

'You had better prove this, Inspector.'

George took the cardigan, laid it out and, turning to the sisters, said, 'See, here a button is missing.' George put his hand in his pocket, pulled out the button from the stairs and placed it on the cardigan. It matched exactly.

'Where did you find that?' Jane looked pale; Ruby was looking horrified.

'Quite close to the body of Leroy Leonard.'

'Ruby?' Jane was speechless.

Ruby sighed. 'I'm sorry, dear, I did go and see Leonard. But, Inspector, he was already dead.'

'Ruby, what are you saying?' Jane could not believe what she was hearing.

'I only wanted to tell him what I thought of him for the death of dear Reverend Peterson, and how he did not frighten me with threats.'

'You did threaten to kill him; we all heard you.'

'Yes I did and I have been a stupid woman, but on oath, I didn't kill him.'

'Could I have a new statement please, Sergeant? You know I could arrest you now for wasting police time.'

'No, Inspector!' cried Jane.

'No, of course I won't,' said George hurriedly. 'But honesty is always the best policy.'

When the statement was taken, Detective Inspector Spring asked Ruby, 'When you were there, was any music playing loudly?'

'To start with, then it stopped.'

'Thank you, that's all I need to know. That will be all for now.'

Outside, Sergeant Harris made a comment about the awards on the wall.

'Top rifle and handgun shots in their heyday,' George Spring informed him.

'Never.'

'Best in the country,' he said.

'What about that one then, Guv? The statement,' Sergeant Harris said.

'Don't know, but I think I believe her,' said Detective Inspector Spring. Sergeant Harris started laughing.

'What's funny, Sergeant?'

'Well, Guv, if you believe all them that only leaves you.'

'It's not funny, not funny at all.'

Detective Inspector Spring drove back to Bodmin a worried man.

Late that afternoon in Shawlworth Village, the frontage of the Pheasant was crammed with reporters and media people. By now, news reports were being broadcast on the television and wireless and evening papers were already being printed, carrying the story of the suspicious death of Leroy Leonard.

How the media had got hold of the news that Catherine was at the Pheasant, no one knew – perhaps a lucky guess – but they were there in great numbers. Inside, Albert, Trish and Catherine felt under siege. 'I'm not opening up tonight,' Albert said.

'Look, I'll go. You shouldn't have to put up with this.'

'You will not,' said Trish. 'I've told you, you can stay for as long as you want.'

Catherine looked at her watch; hopefully Penny and her mother would not be much longer.

'I cannot thank you enough,' Catherine said gratefully.

There was a knocking on the back door.

'If that's the press, get rid,' said Trish.

Albert was soon back with George Spring and two ladies.

'Penny, Mum.' Catherine ran to her mother and hugged her.

George explained that he had pulled up behind a taxi and two ladies had got out and told him who they were so he had brought them round the back.

'Do they know Catherine's here?' George enquired.

'I cannot see how; we never said nothing.' Albert shook his head.

'They have their ways and means of finding out,' said George.

'Do you remember yesterday's date?' said Albert.

'No, why?'

'The glorious twelfth,' he said.

'So it was,' said George.

'Albert, thank you very much for allowing me to stay, but I think we should return to the Hall.'

'How are you going to get through that lot?' Albert asked.

'I don't know,' replied Catherine. 'I don't fancy running the gauntlet of that lot.'

'No problem,' said George. 'This is what we will do – your car, Albert, round the back, yea?'

Albert nodded.

'Let me make one phone call first,' George said. He picked up the phone and dialled. 'Right, I want three PCs at Shawlworth Hall in the next twenty minutes. Report to me at the Hall gates… Of course it's Detective Inspector Spring.' He turned. 'Right, in ten minutes, Albert, if the coast is clear, I want you to take the ladies to Shawlworth Hall. I will create a diversion out the front.'

Albert loved the cloak and dagger stuff.

'Right, out the back.' George led the way; it was all quiet and the three ladies got in as quickly as possible.

'Albert, count to thirty and off you go.'

George went through to the front of the Pheasant and opened the door; everyone surged forward. 'I am Detective Inspector Spring, Catherine Leonard has been staying here—' He stopped talking and played for time.

'Where is she now?' someone shouted.

'That I cannot say,' said George.

Albert shot out of the car park, careered up the road, had turned left and was gone, but someone still shouted, 'There she goes.'

Everyone ran for cars or vans.

George sprinted for his car, but was not the first away; Albert by now had reached the T-junction, had turned right and was coming to a stop. The gates were locked; Albert and the ladies ran through the side gate – locking it behind them – and into Andrew's cottage.

Andrew had been smoking again and was waving his arms about. 'Get them gates open quick,' Albert shouted.

By the time Albert and Andrew got outside, they were already arriving.

'Too late,' Albert said.

'Albert, it's me.' Albert spotted George in the mêlée.

'Clear a way, I am a police officer,' George was shouting but to no avail.

Reinforcements arrived in the shape of three uniformed officers and a driver.

'Thank God for that,' George said. 'You four clear an opening for my car.'

The policemen, with great difficulty, did as commanded.

George drove his car to the gates, got out and again shouted to Albert to open the gates. He turned to the crowd and shouted, 'One, just one, of you set foot through that gate and I'll do you for trespass.' George drove through.

'Shut the gates, Andrew,' George called. Albert and Andrew closed them quickly. As soon as they were shut, George Spring came back, called the four policemen to come through the side gate, then departed to the cottage. 'You OK, Catherine, ladies?' he said.

'Yes, OK, thanks to you,' Catherine said. 'George, this is my sister Penny and Mother.'

Detective Inspector Spring shook hands and said he was pleased to meet them.

'Right, this is what we will do. I'll go open the car door, get the constables to stand in a line from the cottage to the car, you bend down, into the car, then up to the Hall.'

Once everyone was in place, George thanked Albert and told him he would probably be collared by all the media outside the gates when he went. He thanked Andrew for the use of his cottage, took the ladies to the door and requested them to wait. Detective Inspector Spring opened the door and said to the line of officers, 'When the ladies are in the car, driver, you get back, you three up to the Hall, ASAP.' He turned to the ladies. 'I'll open the rear door; once you see me, get in the driving seat and start the engine. Down low and into the car. Don't worry.' He smiled at Catherine. 'It will be OK. Right, let's go.'

George ran to the car; flashes start to go off immediately. He opened the rear door of his car, jumped in the driving seat and started the engine. Catherine, Penny and their mother, bent double, came out of the cottage as quickly as possible and got into Detective Inspector Spring's car. As soon as the door closed, George gunned the car up the long sweeping drive. Back at the gate, Albert was running the gauntlet of the media and secretly loving every moment of it.

Chapter Twenty-Seven

When George pulled up outside the Hall's main entrance, Catherine said, 'The car has been there all night.'

'It will be OK; it will come to no harm. You go into the Hall just in case – these press boys will try anything – I'll just wait here for the constables to arrive.'

'Fancy a coffee, George?' Catherine asked.

'Yes, lovely,' he thanked her.

'I'll make four – three for your men. We will be in the kitchen when you're ready.'

'OK, I should not be long.'

The three officers came into view.

'I want one at the front, one at the back and the other continuously walking around. Got that?' George instructed.

'Yes, Sir.' One must have been elected spokesman on the way up because he said, 'How long are we here till, Sir?'

'Till dark, then you walk to the main gate. Someone should be there to pick you up and drop one off – he spends the night in the main hall.'

'Very good, Sir.'

'Have a look round, then come back here. Mrs Leonard is sending coffee out for you, but be on guard,' George warned.

'Yes, Sir.' Again the spokesman spoke.

Detective Inspector Spring went into the hall and through to the kitchen.

'There you are.' Catherine looked at him. 'Your coffee is ready.'

'Thanks.'

'Penny, take these outside please,' Catherine requested.

'Catherine, may I use your phone please?' Detective Inspector Spring requested.

'Of course, help yourself. Do you want me and Mother to leave?'

'No, of course not.'

'Sure?'

George picked up the phone and dialled Police Headquarters in Bodmin.

'Detective Inspector Spring here. Send a car to Shawlworth Hall at dusk to pick up three constables at the main gate. Send one to spend the night in the main hall. Got that? Good.'

'George, that is more than good of you.'

'I need to go out for an hour, but when I return could you please come to the studio with me. I wouldn't ask, only it's very important. Your mother and sister can come too, please.'

'OK, George.'

'I don't know – in the room where he died,' said her mother.

'The dead cannot hurt you, Mother.'

'Catherine, dear, don't be gruesome.'

'We'll go with you, George.'

'Thanks,' said Detective Inspector Spring. 'I've got one officer at the front, one at the back and one walking around the hall, so if you see or hear anyone, don't worry. See you in an hour.' George Spring left.

'Seems a nice man,' said Catherine's mother.

'He *is*, Mummy, very nice,' Catherine agreed.

The phone rang.

'I'll answer it, dear, in case it's the press.'

Penny came in.

'Hello,' said Catherine's mother.

'Who is it?' mouthed Penny.

Catherine shrugged her shoulders.

Catherine's mother placed her hand over the mouthpiece. 'It's a Dr James for Detective Inspector Spring.' Catherine held out her hand; her mother passed over the telephone.

'Hello, Dr James, Catherine Leonard.'

'I'm sorry to trouble you, my dear, but is George there?'

'No, I'm sorry, he isn't. He has just left, but he is coming back in an hour.'

'Would you please ask him to phone me at the Pheasant?'

'Of course, Doctor.'

'Thank you, goodbye.'

'Goodbye.' Catherine replaced the receiver.

Dr James returned to the lounge bar, but it was a tight squeeze – not only locals and tourists, but now media people. By this time John Penrose, Andrew and Dr James were uncomfortably close.

'I came here to get away from this lot,' Andrew said. 'It's like a football match up there.'

'So what was George doing?' asked John.

'I came out of the cottage just as he walked up. Came to check on the gates, so he said.'

'Funny,' said Dr James. 'That should not take an hour.'

'Sorry?' Andrew said.

'Oh nothing. Just me, dear boy.'

Albert came over. 'I'll have to close early at this rate; they are drinking me dry.'

'Someone always profits from someone else's misfortune,' a man standing next to John with a camera said.

'What?' Albert was again riled.

'Not again,' said John. 'Albert, leave it, we don't need another broken nose.'

'Well,' said Albert.

'I would keep quiet if I was you, pal,' Andrew warned.

The gentleman with the camera thought discretion the better part of valour, for he never spoke.

Detective Inspector Spring rang the bell at Shawlworth Hall. He had been true to his word; it was almost an hour since he had departed.

Penny came and opened the door.

'Come in, Inspector,' she said.

Catherine and her mother were waiting at the foot of the main staircase.

'You sure about this?' George Spring asked again of Catherine.

'Of course. Come on, let's go.' Catherine led the way up the broad staircase.

George opened the door to the studio and switched on a light. Immediately the chalk outline of Leroy's body sprang into view.

'Horrible,' said Catherine's mother.

'Let's get this over with. This machine, are you familiar with it?' he asked Catherine.

'Not really,' Catherine admitted. 'I know it's for what is called a master tape. He runs copies off from there to a cassette.' Catherine looked. 'There, there's a cassette recorder with a tape in.'

'So what's on there should now be on *there*?' he deduced.

'That's a demo tape,' Penny said. 'I know that you make loads of them and send them to who you want.'

'So that should play on any cassette recorder,' George said.

'It should,' Catherine agreed.

'If this music on here is Leroy's, will it be new or old?'

'Well, he's had it for years but it has been put away for ages. His record is in the charts so they want songs for a new album.'

'If he was taping at the time of his murder, would it come out on the tape?'

'If he had a microphone switched on I suppose it would, but I really don't know.' Catherine shook her head.

'I'll take this cassette tape for evidence; it just may have speech on it.'

'If you think it will help,' Catherine said.

'That's it then. Once again, thanks. I must be going now, nice to have met you,' he said to her mother. 'Penny, nice to meet you. One final thing, Catherine. That lamp: where and why did Leroy keep it in here?'

'It was his grandfather's, I believe. His grandfather gave it to him years ago; he keeps it there.' Catherine pointed to a shelf by the left of the entrance.

'Catherine, anything you want, please get in touch straight away.'

'I will. Thanks, George.'

George turned to leave, smiled and put his hand in the air, for he heard Penny say, 'He can arrest and touch me anytime.'

Catherine answered, 'Shush, he'll hear you.'

'George,' Catherine came running after him. 'I almost forgot, Dr James wants you to call him at the Pheasant.'

'May I use your phone? No, it's OK, I'll call in. Catherine, you sure you are OK?'

'Look, I promise I am fine,' she smiled.

'Anytime.'

'I will, promise.'

George pulled up in his car. No way, he thought. The front was jam-packed with cars, vans and people. PC Trevithick just stood scratching his head.

George drove his car home, parked up and walked over to the Pheasant. PC Trevithick was still pondering the best course of action to take concerning his traffic problem – normally a snarl-up would have involved a herd of cows, tractor and a push bike.

'Problems?' Detective Inspector Spring said.

''Ello, Sur.'

'I would just give it up as a bad job,' George advised.

'I think ee be right, Sur,' he agreed.

'Hey, I forgot. Want a night's overtime?'

''Ow be that, Sur?'

'Spending the night at Shawlworth Hall.'

'What if anythin' be a going wrong 'ere?' PC Trevithick said.

'Never thought of that,' George smiled. 'OK, just a thought.'

'Thank ee, Sur.' PC Trevithick saluted as George walked away.

George laughed as he thought of PC Trevithick putting on cycle clips and dashing off to a farm about a missing cow.

'Good God,' he said as he opened the door of the Pheasant. It was solid with people.

After about a dozen 'excuse me's, George fought his way to the corner.

'What a struggle,' he said. It was red hot in the lounge.

'George, there you are. About tomorrow, what time?' Peter James had caught him off guard.

'Tomorrow?'

'Roskear; the burial of Reverend Peterson.'

'Oh hell, I forgot about that.'

'We still going?'

'Yes, of course.'

'What time?'

'Let's see, nine thirty, my place?'

'Fine.'

Albert signalled an offer of a drink, but George shook his head.

'Look, I cannot stick this. I'm going for a bath and a quiet drink at home. Anyway, I have work to do.' George once again fought his way to the door. Outside the evening air felt good.

'I'm sorry, Sur, you can't park 'ere.' PC Trevithick was using his authority. George once again laughed. I can sleep safe in my bed tonight now, he mused.

Having bathed, George just put on a pair of boxer shorts, his slippers and his yellow dressing gown. Downstairs he poured a cool beer from the fridge, went into the living room and looked at the pile of statements. Cassette tape still in my jacket pocket, he thought to himself. Right, once again statements first. He settled down for a long evening. First, Andrew pulls up in car; door locked. John tries door, locked, goes in front. Catherine and him find body. NOT PRESENT. George read Andrew's full statement and made notes. Catherine sees me in store room, goes to kitchen, has coffee, hears door bell; it's Andrew. ALIBI FOR 20 MINS, NO ONE.

Antony and Vanessa slip up back stairs, beg Leroy, come back down, hear Catherine in kitchen, go back to drawing room. ALIBI EACH OTHER. Change statements.

Albert parts from others, goes to lake, comes back, meets John outside. ALIBI NONE.

Linda and Trish in each other's company at all times, never saw anyone else until told to go downstairs. ALIBI EACH OTHER.

John just wandered about, talked to PJ and me outside, later met Albert coming from lake area. ALIBI PARTIAL PJ, ME, AB.

Doctor Peter James seen on stairs, talked to me and John ALIBI MOST OF THE TIME – BUT...

Detective Inspector Spring, first five minutes Catherine wandered about around back, came back and found PJ and JP on stairs, talked. ALIBI PARTIAL ONLY.

Cawthorne sisters, already lied twice, now said Jane on stairs but not seen by anyone. Ruby admits to seeing Leonard, not on stairs or landing when we came, but came downstairs. ALIBI VERY POOR. LYING YET AGAIN.

After three hours it looked bad for the Cawthorne sisters and if Antony and Vanessa had lied once, could they not be lying again? Are any of them telling the truth? He was no further forward. He got up from his chair, retrieved the cassette tape, loaded it into his machine, pressed the start button and waited. Nothing. George took it out and looked at it. Right way up? 'It needs rewinding, you fool,' he said. He put it back in the machine, rewound it again and pressed the start button. This time rock music blasted out. George quickly turned down the volume. He listened to the tape until the end; there was no speech, just singing. To George it was a cacophony of rubbish. Sorry, Catherine, he thought.

George sighed. Over three hours and no further forward, back to the start. He was certain he had missed something, but what? He also had spent nearly an hour looking for anything in the grounds, but had turned up nothing there either. 'Come on, George, your career depends on the outcome of this. Get your finger out, son. He was now getting angry with himself. Bed. Tomorrow, Roskear and another interview with the Cawthorne sisters.

Next morning George was ready when Dr James called.

'Still like a madhouse out there.' Dr James pointed to the Pheasant.

'I don't know why. They know by now that Catherine is up at the Hall.'

Better check the Hall, George thought. He picked up the phone and rang there.

'Hello, Catherine.'

'No, Penny. Cath is still in bed.'

'It's George Spring. Listen, Penny, did that policeman arrive last night?'

'Yes thanks. He left this morning. Those three from yesterday came back, we have had no bother. I took a walk to the gates; there are still masses there.'

'That's good. Bye, Penny.'

'Bye gorgeous,' Penny laughed.

George smiled and replaced the receiver.

'Ready,' said Peter.

Outside, some reporters came running over.

'Any further forward? Has an arrest been made? How did he die? Is it right that he was killed with a blow to the back of the head?'

George answered. 'To the first, progress is being made; the second, no one has been arrested yet; as to how did he die, you will have to wait for the official coroner's report.'

'When will that be?'

'About Wednesday of this week,' he replied. 'Peter, get me out of here.' Peter drove off.

Two hours later they returned to Shawlworth Village. All the media had been and gone, and someone said that Catherine had been spotted at the Hall. Peter and George had seen the present vicar of the church, and had even seen the grave of Reverend Peterson's wife and daughter. They were buried in a corner spot with one space left between Mrs Peterson and the wall. Reverend Peterson must have planned it. That's it. That's where he will be buried. Reverend Rothwell had no objections and said he would arrange everything at his end. He asked if they could give him a day, and George had said Friday, but that he would confirm it as soon as possible.

'You coming for a pint?' Dr James asked.

'No thanks, I have to see the Cawthorne sisters again. You tell them in the Pheasant. As I pass John's on my way to the Manor House, I'll call and tell them as well. If they're in the pub, obviously you tell them?'

'Fine, see you later.' Dr James went off.

Detective Inspector Spring found himself again on the doorstep of the Cawthorne sisters. He knocked and almost immediately the door opened.

'Oh dear, are we in trouble again, Inspector?'

'May I come in?'

'Certainly.'

George did not know who he followed in.

'Ruby dear, it's Inspector Spring again.'

Right, keep your eyes on Jane, he thought.

'Ladies, I am very annoyed. This is the third time I have had to see you about statements. The first time you lied, and now I find the second time you also lied. So here I am again for the third time. Now I must tell you that if it was anyone other than you two you would have been in jail by now, locked up and the key thrown away.' Detective Inspector Spring was not adopting a rodomontade attitude to the sisters. He continued, 'I have a murder case to solve. Because of the delicate position I find myself in, I have to solve this as soon as possible, but if you keep lying to me how am I going to make any progress?'

The sisters did not speak.

'Ladies?'

'Inspector, we have nothing further to say. When we tell you we did not kill him, we did not kill him, that is the truth, but if you do not believe us then so be it. If you must arrest us for concealing evidence, we have nothing further to say.' Ruby set her jaw.

'Ruby dear.' Jane looked at her sister.

'You both or one of you saw something, didn't you?'

'How long have you known us, Inspector? Have we ever lied to you before this?'

'No, never,' he agreed.

'Then believe us when we say we never killed him and that is all we are prepared to say; nothing further. You must do whatever you must do. Now, shall we get our coats?' Ruby was adamant.

'You know you are putting me in a very difficult position, don't you.'

'Yes, we do, and believe me when I say we are very, very sorry, but the matter as far as we are concerned is very definitely closed.'

'Very well, ladies, I shall go. But please reconsider.'

'I'm sorry, but no.' Ruby was definite.

'Very well, I shall say goodbye for now.' George left Ruby and Jane. He had not arrested them because deep down he knew they had not done it, but recognised they knew something. At the Hall that night they had definitely seen something. George called at John and Linda's, but no one was at home so he went on to the Manor House. Damn, he thought, I forgot to tell Jane and Ruby about the funeral.

Antony Stuart-Palmer, his wife Vanessa and daughter Juliet had finished breakfast on Sunday morning, but the atmosphere was far from cordial. Juliet had really gone to town on her parents for lying to the police. You, pillars of the community, acting like common criminals. Her father took so much, then said that that was enough; Juliet was now going too far. For the rest of Saturday and Sunday morning a stalemate had been reached.

'What about Gladiator?' Juliet snapped.

'What about him?' Antony was not in the best of moods.

'I thought we were moving him today.'

'Juliet, a lot has happened, you know.'

'I know.'

'Well then,' said her father, 'you will have to be patient. Your mother and I have a lot to think and worry about.'

'Especially when you lied to the police?' said Juliet quietly.

'That's it, Juliet. Until you can be more civil, please find somewhere else to stay.'

'Antony, you're not asking her to leave?' Vanessa was horrified.

'No, no, of course not. I mean go to her room, go and see Gladiator until she can be more civil. Anywhere from here, that's what I mean.'

'Be glad to,' said Juliet.

'She's right, you know. I feel like a common criminal. Will George ever trust us again?' Vanessa was really worried.

The door opened. It was Fielding.

'What time is lunch, Sir?'

'Why do you ask, Fielding?'

He coughed politely. 'Well, Sir, Miss Juliet has just stormed off to the stable. I asked would she be in for lunch, but she did not reply.'

'Just do it for the normal time.'

'Thank you, Sir.' Fielding backed out of the door.

'Do you think he heard?' Vanessa was mortified.

'I don't know, but you know Fielding – soul of discretion.'

The next time Fielding entered was much later, to inform them that Detective Inspector Spring wished to see them.

'Show him in please, Fielding.'

'This way, Sir,' he said and stood to one side.

'George, come in, sit down. Drink?' Antony offered. George sat, but refused the drink. 'No thanks, I'm driving.'

'Not more bad news,' said Vanessa.

'Firstly, Peter and I have sorted out the funeral arrangements for Reverend Peterson. It's to be next Friday, time to be arranged, at Roskear.

'Thanks for letting us know, George. Appreciated,' said Antony.

'What about this Leonard affair?' Vanessa asked.

'Well, all I can say at the moment is that I have almost eliminated you from the inquiry.'

'We didn't kill him, honestly,' Antony said.

'I am almost convinced of that,' George said.

'Thanks.' Vanessa looked relieved.

George took his leave, returned home, made a light lunch, once again went over the statements and listened to the cassette tape, fully convinced that he was missing something and the answer was there in front of him.

Chapter Twenty-Eight

The bar in the lounge was virtually empty compared to earlier. Dr James, Andrew, John and Linda were having a drink with Albert and Trish on the other side of the bar.

Dr James had told them of the smooth organisation of the funeral. Now Andrew wondered how they would choose another vicar.

'Don't really know,' said Dr James. 'Church council make a request to the Bishop of Truro and advertise, I suppose.'

'Sounds good to me,' said Albert.

'Seems quiet in here now, but up there, God,' Andrew complained. 'They must never sleep.'

'Come on, wife, lunch,' said John.

'Yes, master,' laughed Linda.

'What happens now to you?' said Trish. 'And you, Andrew?'

'How do you mean?' said John.

'Well, he's dead right. So is Catherine staying or going?' Trish reasoned.

'Yea, see what ee means.' John looked worried.

'I'll give it a day or two and ask,' said Andrew.

'Will ee? That's great.' John brightened up considerably.

George Spring sat quietly in his chair for ages. He had read the statements twice, and pictured in his mind where everybody was on the night. He had a lot of checking to do, but a plan was formulating. He had the policeman's gut feeling that he had found the something that he had overlooked. Evidence. That is what he had said to Reverend Peterson and Dr James. Now he felt the evidence was falling into place and the finger of suspicion was pointing at one person. If the final pieces fell into place, he knew who the murderer was.

He took the cassette from the unit. It was too early to tell Blackwood, but yes he knew; he knew.

Monday morning found Detective Inspector Spring back in Detective Chief Inspector Blackwood's office.

'Update please, George.'

'Well, Sir, I have made good progress.'

'How good?'

'I think I know who killed Leroy Leonard.'

'Good, is he or she banged up?'

'Not yet, Sir. I have one or two loose ends to sort yet.'

'What if they do a runner?'

'No chance, Sir.'

'George, I've covered for you twice. I won't a third time.'

'Sir, by Friday you'll have your collar.'

'Friday.'

'Friday, promise.'

'Right. Inquest tomorrow 2 p.m. on the vicar. No problems foreseen. You and that doc to be there, OK?'

'So can we arrange the funeral for Friday?'

'Don't see why not.'

'That all, Sir?'

'Yes, but George, remember what I have said.'

'Will do, Sir.'

George Spring under any other circumstances would have been overjoyed by such a quick result, but knowing who he may have to arrest for Leroy's murder made him feel sick. It was at times like this he hated being a policeman.

George sat in his office, working out a plan of action. By tea-time he had worked out a format and was ready to put his theory to the test.

'No, Mother, I have made up my mind, I am not staying here.' Catherine, her mother and Penny had spent all of Monday morning discussing Catherine's future plans. They had started with when Leroy's funeral would take place and where. Catherine had said back in the north-east, but that she would have to ask George about when. Then the phone rang.

'Hello, Catherine Leonard speaking.'

'Hello, dear, it's me, Mrs Mason.'

'Hello, is everything OK?'

'Fine, just fine, but outside for two days now, press and television reporters have never left us alone.'

'Oh dear,' said Catherine. 'I thought that might happen.'

'It's just the children; they have started asking questions.'

'Should I come and get them, do you think?'

'Well, dear, what I had in mind was – if it's all right with you – I have a relative who owns a small family hotel in Rhyl. I have phoned and luckily they have two spare rooms, so I thought I would take the children to the coast for a few days, say till Saturday.'

'Could I speak to them, please?'

'Hello, Mummy.' It was Lee.

'Would you and Pansy like to go to the beach for a few days with Mrs Mason?'

'Yes please, Mummy,' Lee said excitedly.

'Very well then. Have a nice time, I'll see you on Saturday. Bye bye. Put Mrs Mason on,' Catherine said quickly.

'Hello, dear.'

'Thank you, Mrs Mason. I was frightened then he was going to ask about Leroy.'

'I must go then, dear – phone Rhyl, packing, you know. See you Saturday… I overhead you telling Lee.'

'Bye.' Catherine replaced the receiver.

'Those children should have been with me,' her mother said.

'Mother, please. We have had all this before. Not now, please.'

'I'm just saying, dear,' her mother was persistent.

'Where were we?' Penny changed the subject quickly.

'Staying here,' answered Catherine.

'Well?' queried Penny.

'I'm not staying,' Catherine reiterated. 'I'm moving back to London.'

'This place?' said her mother.

'I'm going to offer it back to the Stuart-Palmers.'

'Don't be silly, Catherine. They had to sell it in the first place,' her mother said.

'I know, but if they just kept the Hall, sold the farms, village and Manor House, that should bring them in, what, 1.8 million? It's still a long way short of what we paid, I know, but—'

Catherine faltered.

'Catherine, you are mad.' Her mother was dismayed.

'Mother, I am not silly. I know what I am doing.'

'I sincerely hope so, because I don't.'

'I'll phone Jonathan Fredricks. He'll know.'

'Whose he?' Penny asked.

'Leroy's lawyer; very good with figures.'

Catherine phoned him and explained the situation. After offering his condolences, he told her to leave it to him and said he would phone her Thursday.

'Mother, you are going on about money, but what good did it do Leroy?'

'Very well, dear.'

The phone rang again.

'Hello, Catherine Leonard.'

'Catherine, it's Clive.'

'Yes, Clive.'

'Look, Catherine, as you know there is not one person in the country who does not know about you and Leroy's death. This phone has never stopped ringing; TV commercials, lost count of the modelling jobs. What do I do?' Clive sounded embarrassed.

'That's your job, Clive, to sort out. We have a five-year contract, yes?'

'Yes.'

'Then do your job, Clive. I'm sorry, you can imagine what it's like.'

'I know. I feel awful for you.'

'Thanks. Just do whatever you think is best. If them ghouls want Catherine Sullivan, make the bastards pay through the nose.'

'You've got it. Bye.'

'Bye, Clive.'

'Where will you live?' Penny asked.

'The flat, where else? I love that flat, I'll convert the master bedroom into two and I'll move into the kids' room.'

'Cath, you're worth millions now and you're still going to live in that flat?' Penny could not work it out.

'Penny, I love that flat.'

'OK, OK, keep your shirt on.' Penny admitted defeat.

George Spring sat in his living room. After having put his theory to the test, he had found everything that he suspected was now proven.

He picked up the telephone, dialled Shawlworth Hall and spoke to Catherine. She gave him the information he required and he then phoned Dr James and told him of the inquest tomorrow at 2 p.m.

God, I hate this part of the job. He was angry. Harris will have to do it, that's all. How can I? he thought. George decided to get drunk.

Chapter Twenty-Nine

Tuesday morning dawned on another bright day. Shawlworth Village was back to its quiet self once again, with local people going about their everyday jobs. Even the gates of Shawlworth Hall were deserted.

Things picked up as the morning came to a close. Tourists again were the main attraction and most people who could get to Reverend Peterson's funeral on Friday had made arrangements. Two coaches had been laid on, and a notice in the village store for people to put their names down for a place on the buses was soon filled.

The organisation had now been taken over by the church council. The Bishop of Truro was going to officiate and adverts had been placed for a new vicar for Shawlworth.

In the afternoon Detective Inspector Spring and Dr James attended the inquest. A verdict of 'suicide whilst the balance of the mind was disturbed' was brought in.

That evening in the Pheasant, the lounge bar was again full. Only John was in the corner. George Spring was expected, along with the doctor, to tell them about the inquest.

George Spring was at that moment knocking on the door of the Cawthorne sisters for the third time in as many days. Once again he was invited in and found himself in the living room.

'Have you come to arrest us this time, Mr Spring?' Jane looked very concerned.

'No, Miss Cawthorne, I haven't.'

'Praise the Lord for that.' She clasped her hands together.

'What I am going to do is tell you a story.' He smiled, hoping to put them at ease. 'But you must promise me faithfully that you will never ever repeat it to anyone.'

'We give our solemn word that it will never be repeated by us,' Ruby swore to Detective Inspector Spring. George began.

'Once upon a time, there were two sisters who saw something, or maybe one saw and told the other, about a very serious situation that had just occurred. These two sisters agreed to say nothing, because, in their eyes and possibly in the eyes of many other people, what this person had done was to the benefit of all and was a form of poetic justice. In the eyes of the law, that person had committed a serious offence and must be punished, but these sisters vowed never to speak of it to anyone – even to the policeman who assured them that, although he had to arrest that person, he was going to move heaven and earth for that person on their behalf.

'The policeman admired these two sisters who were willing even to sacrifice their own freedom to protect the guilty person, so he told them to be patient as he was going to get more than their evidence. But these sisters must help him by keeping quiet for the next few days.'

George stood up. 'So, ladies, please don't say anything, because if people found out that I had been round here telling you fairy stories, well… it wouldn't do my reputation as a policeman any good now, would it?' He winked. 'The real reason for me coming is to tell you the funeral for Reverend Peterson is Friday, 11 a.m.'

'Thank you for telling us about the funeral, dear Mr Spring.' Jane's eyes twinkled with tears.

'I'll show you to the door,' said Ruby.

'Thank you,' said George. 'Don't worry. Mind, I don't want anyone finding out about my fairy stories.'

At the door, Ruby took George Spring's hand, looked him straight in the eyes, held his gaze like a magnet and said, 'The good Lord never blessed me with marriage and therefore no children, but if he had blessed me with both, if in answer to my prayer he had given me a son, would that he were just like you. Thank you.'

George kissed Ruby on the cheek, turned and quickly strode away. He did not want anyone to find out about his fairy stories – that was bad enough – but crying… By the time George reached the Pheasant he had regained his composure, but he still surprised everyone by asking for a large scotch instead of his normal pint.

Dr James still had not arrived, so George explained to them the funeral arrangements for Reverend Peterson. However, they already knew from the notice in the shop, so he gave them the findings of the inquest.

'Couldunt spekt non uther,' said John.

Dr James came bursting through the door. 'Sorry I'm late,' he said. 'Early labour for young Ruth Chandler.'

'Malt please, Albert,' Dr James requested.

'How's things going, George?' Dr James looked at George Spring.

'Come on, Doc, you know better than that,' George said.

'Sorry,' he replied.

'This is a very funny position for everyone,' Albert remarked.

'How?' said John.

'Oh, come on,' said Albert. 'We all drink, all live together, for all we know, John, our wives could be mixed up in this mess, and it's George's job to find out who killed Leonard. I'm sorry, George, but *he* could be the guilty one for all we know. If he isn't, he is going to have to arrest one of us. Just great, isn't it.'

'You have only said what everyone else must be thinking and you're right, Albert. My boss has already told me that he has to put a copper in charge of a murder investigation who is also a prime suspect. It's weird; it must be a first,' George said.

'Come on,' said John. 'We all know it wasn't us.'

A cloud of doom fell on the corner of the lounge bar.

Andrew came in, ordered a pint and turned to John.

'Not good, I'm afraid, for both of us,' he said.

'Come on, tell me,' John requested.

'Catherine Leonard is selling up, and moving back to London.'

'Cannot blame her really; living on in a place that size, just her and two children. Not to mention the fact that your husband was killed there,' Dr James said.

'S'pose better start lookin' for tother place to live.' John was really downcast.

'Come on, you don't know that.' George Spring tried to improve things for John. 'Someone might buy it who wants a first-class gamekeeper.'

'Pigs might fly,' moaned John. He was not for cheering up.

Chapter Thirty

In police headquarters at Bodmin, Sergeant Harris was busy with reports when the telephone began to ring.

'Sergeant Harris... No, I'm sorry he isn't... hang on till I get some paper... Right, fire away... Stu Iveson.' He wrote this down, followed by five names and telephone numbers. 'Yes... I will as soon as he comes in... Right... Many thanks, bye.' Sergeant Harris replaced the receiver, walked over to Detective Inspector Spring's desk, dropped a piece of paper on his blotter and returned to his own desk. Once again the phone rang.

God, thought Sergeant Harris, we are popular today. 'Hello, Sergeant Harris... Sir... No, Sir... Yes, Sir, as soon as he comes in... I know, Sir... Yes, Sir, ten to eleven... I don't know, Sir.' Sergeant Harris again replaced the receiver.

It was another thirty minutes before George Spring walked in through the door.

'Morning, Sergeant,' he said.

'Guv, Detective Chief Inspector Blackwood wants to see you as soon as you come in, and there's a message on your desk from some person called Iveson.' Sergeant Harris nodded towards the blotter.

'Good, I've been waiting for that.' George Spring looked pleased. Finally the original question he had asked Catherine had come to fruition.

'Better cut along and see Blackwood, Guv.' Sergeant Harris tried to be helpful.

'On my way,' Detective Inspector Spring answered.

Once inside Detective Chief Inspector Blackwood's office, he was told to sit.

'Reports are back on Leonard.' Detective Chief Inspector Blackwood had a sheaf of paper before him.

'That was quick,' George commented.

'Listen. I've told you I want a result on this.' Once again Detective Chief Inspector Blackwood went off on a tangent. 'I've put you in charge of this when really I should be suspending you and putting someone else in charge. If you were not my most experienced officer, and I believed you might be guilty... George, get a result.'

Was that a compliment? thought George.

'Layman's or technical?'

'Sorry, Sir?'

'These reports. Want them in plain English?'

'Please, Sir.'

'Right, firstly the lamp. It was, in the opinion of the pathologist, the murder weapon. Forensics found hair and tissue matching that of Leonard on its base. According to them, he died of a single heavy blow to the base of the skull and brain stem, causing a massive haemorrhage of the brain surface. It was a swinging action.'

'I wonder, could a woman have caused such an injury?' enquired George.

'You will have to ask *them* that,' said Detective Chief Inspector Blackwood. 'Anyway, I thought you had a suspect?'

'I have,' agreed George, 'but I must be sure.'

'George, pull your finger out,' Detective Chief Inspector Blackwood warned.

George Spring returned to his office.

'Sergeant, get me Pathology,' he said.

Sergeant Harris did as he was told.

'Leroy Leonard,' said Detective Inspector Spring. 'Could a woman have delivered that blow?'

He received his reply and replaced the receiver.

Detective Inspector Spring picked up the piece of paper Sergeant Harris had left and began dialling.

After his fourth dialling, Detective Spring sat back, put his hands behind his head and said, 'Bingo.'

'Result, Guv?' Sergeant Harris enquired.

'Yes. One more thing to check,' he said. 'You are with me all day Friday, Sergeant.'

'Me Guv? Why?'

'Firstly, funeral at Roskear near Camborne, then you make an arrest.'

'Augh, come on, Guv. I didn't even know that vicar.'

'Sergeant, what title is before my name?'

'Detective Inspector.'

'Yours?'

'Sergeant.'

'Guess where you are all day Friday.' Detective Inspector Spring was pleased.

Sergeant Harris was far from pleased.

'Daddy?'

'Yes.'

'About Gladiator.' Juliet and her father had had from Sunday until now, Wednesday afternoon, to cool off.

'What about him?' her father enquired.

'Well, he hasn't had much exercise, you know.'

'I know, darling, just give me time.'

'But Daddy…'

'Not again please, Juliet.'

'He will be missing it, you know.'

'Juliet.'

'God.'

'Look, have you thought that Catherine Leonard may now not be staying and the new owner may allow you to exercise Gladiator here once again?'

'But, Daddy, that could be ages away,' pleaded Juliet.

'You don't know that,' Antony argued.

'You don't know it will be soon either,' countered Juliet.

The telephone rang.

'Hello, Antony Stuart-Palmer here,' he said. 'Hello, Catherine, how can I help… Yes… Yes… I see… Very well. Goodbye.'

He replaced the receiver and scratched his head.

'That's was funny.'

'How, Daddy?'

'Catherine Leonard just asked if I, your mother and you could be at the Hall for eight tomorrow night.'

'Me?' Juliet looked puzzled.

'That's what she said.'

'Why me?' Before Antony Stuart-Palmer could answer, Vanessa came in.

'Who was that?' she said.

Antony told her of the conversation he had just had with Catherine Leonard.

'Juliet as well?' Vanessa enquired.

'So she said.' Antony was adamant.

'Strange,' Vanessa mused.

'Very strange,' agreed Antony.

Over a period of four and a half days the press had been having a field day with Leroy Leonard and his death.

'Pop Star Murdered' headlines in bold print sprang from every newspaper in the country. Some articles were true but most a figment of the imagination according to many people. Television and radio had given a great deal of time also to the Leonard affair.

One station took a different angle: 'Pop star husband of famous model', but basically they were all the same.

The gates were now deserted, the three police officers withdrawn and a form of normality returned.

'When is Leroy's body released for burial, did you say?' Penny asked.

'I don't know, I'm waiting for George to phone.'

The main entrance bell rang.

'Who's that, I wonder,' Catherine said. The three of them were in the drawing room. Once again it was a balmy evening, so none were feeling very energetic.

'You go.' Catherine looked at Penny.

'Augh, Cath, it's your house,' said Penny.

'I don't know,' said their mother. 'You're like a couple of children. I'll go.'

Catherine's mother saw that it was Detective Inspector Spring. She opened the door and invited him in. He followed her into the drawing room.

'It's Detective Inspector Spring, Catherine,' her mother said.

'George, come in, can I get you a drink?' Catherine asked.

'No, thank you, I'm still on duty,' George replied.

'That sounds ominous,' Catherine said nervously.

'Two things. Nothing to worry about. One, Leroy was killed with that miner's lamp. Two, Friday night may I bring everyone here again who was here last Friday, to give a full explanation?'

'You know who killed Leroy?' Catherine looked at George wide-eyed.

'Explanations on Friday, if you agree.'

'Of course I agree.'

'Thanks, I will let everyone know.' George was grateful. 'Catherine, not a word to anyone, OK?'

'I have Antony, Lady Vanessa and Juliet coming over tomorrow night,' Catherine said.

'Please, say nothing. I will see everyone concerned on Friday at the funeral of Reverend Peterson.'

'Very well. When will Leroy be available for burial? I'm taking him back to the north-east?'

'I'll find out for you,' said George. 'Must be going.'

'I'll see you out.' Catherine took his arm.

In the great hall she stopped. 'George, I'm leaving Shawlworth.' Catherine looked at him.

'I thought you might,' he said.

'I'll miss you,' Catherine admitted.

'I shall miss you too,' he replied.

'Invite me back,' Catherine smiled, 'for a holiday.'

'I'm inviting you now.' George looked into Catherine's eyes.

'George, please.'

'I think I had better go.'

'I want to see you before I go. Can you meet me Saturday? That's if you haven't arrested me for Leroy's murder, on Friday,' Catherine joked.

'If it keeps you here, I might just do that,' he smiled.

'George, please go,' Catherine begged.

George went home an unhappy man. When he arrived he picked up the phone.

Chapter Thirty-One

Thursday morning in the Pheasant, Albert and Trish were going about the routine that had taken over their lives: cleaning the public bar and lounge bars, ready for lunchtime opening.

'Why is Tommy in all day tomorrow?' asked Trish.

'Well, lunchtime we won't be here and tomorrow night I won't feel like it one little bit,' Albert said. 'Everything happens on a Friday.'

'How do you mean?' Trish enquired.

'Well, Friday we find out about the future when George goes to the Hall, the next Friday Leonard is killed, tomorrow is the funeral of Reverend Peterson.'

'Just a coincidence.' Trish looked up as she was busily polishing a table.

'Yea, you're right. Just me being morbid.'

'Come on, slowcoach. Get them pumps sorted out, chop, chop,' Trish ordered.

Albert did exactly that, but his heart was not in it. He was a worried man.

In his office, Detective Inspector George Spring had spent all morning going through the evidence. Once more he had checked the new evidence and was satisfied that all the pieces were in place; apart from one. The killer would have to supply that information.

'Harris.'

'Guv.'

'Tomorrow afternoon we make an arrest.'

'In connection with the killing of Leroy Leonard?' Sergeant Harris looked surprised. 'You know who killed him, Guv?'

'Yes.'

'Who, Guv?'

'Just meet me in Shawlworth Village, let's see,' George did a quick mental calculation of time, 'at one thirty in the afternoon.'

'OK, Guv. Expecting bother?'

'No, none at all. Harris.'

'Guv?'

'I want you to make the arrest.'

'Me, Guv?'

'You, yes – all right? Just do it. I'll be there, don't worry.'

'OK by me,' Harris shrugged.

God, I hate this job. Again Detective Inspector Spring was not looking forward to Friday.

'Now, I don't want you breaking down tomorrow.' Ruby was being stern.

'I shall try not to, dear,' promised Jane.

'There are two buses going, are there not?' Ruby asked.

'I believe so.'

'I wonder which we are on?'

'Does it matter?'

'Not really.'

'I still wish he had been buried here,' remarked Jane.

'Look, dear, we have been through all this. He is being buried next to his wife and daughter.'

'I know it's the best place, but we cannot go there every week with flowers.'

'He will never be from our thoughts,' Ruby said.

'Never, dear,' agreed Jane.

'Come along, dear, we shall never be finished at this rate.' Ruby and Jane were dusting.

'Ruby dear, what will happen to you know who?'

'That is up to Detective Inspector Spring, dear.'

'Yes I know but, but—'

'Jane, dear, we promised that lovely man we would not speak of it.'

'We don't hang them anymore, do we?' Jane looked worried.

'Don't be silly, dear. We haven't done that for years. It depends,' replied Ruby.

'On what?'

'I don't really know, perhaps they might bring a charge of manslaughter.'

'Could they?'

'I don't know. It all depends on, oh dear, what do they call it? Public prosecution, department of public prosecution? Anyway, they will weigh up all the evidence and charge accordingly.'

'But what if we were allowed to give a character reference in court?'

'They may allow it. We will ask George Spring tomorrow.'

'Well, if we can, I am definitely going.' Jane was adamant.

'After me, dear, after me.' Ruby was equally adamant.

'How are we going, darling?' Vanessa looked at her husband.

Antony Stuart-Palmer put down his morning paper and said, 'Vanessa, at times you do talk in riddles.'

'The funeral, dear, the funeral tomorrow.'

'By car, how else?'

'Well, Fielding said that Mrs Pengelly had told him that buses were laid on from the village. He calls her Alice now.' Vanessa smiled.

'Vanessa, what are you talking about? One minute funerals, next minute buses and finally Fielding calling her Alice.'

'I know what I mean,' Vanessa pouted.

'I'm pleased you do, because I don't.'

'Buses tomorrow from the village for Reverend Peterson's funeral, right?'

'Right.'

'How are we going, by car or bus?'

'Car.'

'Fielding calls Mrs Pengelly Alice.'

'That must be her name. So?'

'So rather friendly.'

'Vanessa, please.'

The telephone rang.

'Hello Antony Stuart-Palmer... Hello, George... yes, eleven... We were just talking about that... Car... Tomorrow, eight o'clock... We are going tonight... You know, is it important? ...Very well, bye.'

'What was all that about?' Vanessa enquired.

'George asking about the funeral, but mainly could we be at the Hall at eight o'clock tomorrow night.'

'What for?'

'He did not say.'

'We will ask tomorrow.'

'Better not.'

'Why?'

'Just leave it, Vanessa.'

Vanessa looked puzzled.

'You sure about this, dear?' Catherine's mother said.

'Look, Mum, I know what I am doing.' Catherine was determined. 'Please, he will be here shortly so could you and Penny please leave us alone.'

'I still think that you are foolish.'

'Mother, please go for a walk around the estate – anything – but I wish to be alone with Jonathan and then the Stuart-Palmers.'

Penny and her mother left. Catherine poured herself a drink, sat down and waited for Jonathan Fredricks to arrive.

She did not have to wait long.

'Mrs Leonard, nice to see you. I mean under the circumstances.'

'My name is Catherine, yours Jonathan, OK.'

'Fine,' he smiled.

'Jonathan, would you like a drink?'

'No, no thanks. Driving.'

'Of course, sorry I forgot. Right, down to business.'

'Well, let me say I think you are foolish,' he said.

'Look, just details please.'

'Bottom line, you stand to lose a million at least,' Jonathan told her.

'That's a lot,' Catherine said. 'I didn't expect that much.'

'I told Leroy at the beginning he was paying over the odds, but Leroy being Leroy, what's a million or two.'

'So what do you recommend?' Catherine asked.

'Well, we can put it on the market, hope to get what he paid for it, you keep it or sell at a loss.'

'Damn, I thought things could work out,' Catherine said. 'I've got the Stuart-Palmers coming over at eight.'

'There is a way; a loss for you, but a way,' Jonathan said.

'What's that?' Catherine looked hopeful.

'Sell off the farms and village.'

'I said that.'

'I have made enquiries and you should have no bother getting 1.75 million for them, that leaves the Hall grounds and moors, say 3.5 million, making a total of 5.25 million.'

'Go on,' said Catherine.

'You get 1.75 million for the village and farms. The Stuart-Palmers give you 2.5 million, that makes 4.25 million. Then you do a deal with the National Trust, they give you another million, say twelve months later. The family are allowed to remain, you get 5.25 million, they can then open up to the public. "Pop star murdered here." The crowds will flood in, but only if you could handle that.'

'I won't be here, will I, although I don't like the idea.'

'They won't have to play on it, or advertise it. I don't think one household in the country has not heard of Shawlworth Hall or where it is situated, but it's up to you.'

'So I'll lose seven hundred and fifty thousand. Jonathan, how do you know they have 2.5 million left?'

'Trust me. I never said this, but I am their lawyer as well. You may well get it all back, it depends on what the Trust says; on how much they will agree to.'

'How do you know they will buy it?'

'I have already spoken to a friend of mine. He said Shawlworth is steeped in history and is a listed house, so he said that the committee and directors would look at the application very favourably.'

'If they say no?'

'Then you will have to sell privately.'

'But you think it will work?'

'Yes, I do.'

The bell rang at the main entrance.

'That will be them now,' Catherine said. 'I'll let them in.'

Catherine showed Antony Stuart-Palmer, Lady Vanessa and daughter Juliet into the drawing room.

'Jonathan, what are you doing here?' Antony went across to shake his hand. 'It is good to see you.'

'You too, Lady Vanessa, Juliet,' Jonathan reciprocated.

'Can I get you all a drink?' Catherine asked.

'Catherine, may I introduce Juliet our daughter.'

'Hello, Juliet, very pleased to meet you.' Catherine smiled and shook her hand.

'You are right, Daddy, she is very beautiful,' Juliet said.

'Thank you.' Catherine blushed deeply.

'Juliet, dear, you are embarrassing her,' Lady Vanessa admonished.

'It's OK, Lady Vanessa,' Catherine laughed.

'Catherine, please, it's Vanessa.'

'Sorry – drinks,' repeated Catherine.

Catherine sorted out a scotch and two white wines, then turned to Jonathan. 'You take the chair please, will you?'

Jonathan waited until everyone was settled, then put the plan before the Stuart-Palmers.

'Mrs Leonard, sorry, Catherine, is selling up at Shawlworth,' began Jonathan, 'but she has—'

'*You* have,' Catherine corrected him. 'It was your idea.'

'*I* have – that the village and farms be sold off to sitting tenants, Catherine getting the proceeds from that sale. That leaves the Hall, Manor House, gamekeeper cottage and gatehouse. You then give 2.5 million to Catherine, that makes a total of 4.25 million. Then, when you are settled, you sell to the National Trust a year later and give Catherine another million. Catherine has already agreed to the deal. It is now up to you.'

'If it can be done, that would be fantastic.' Antony Stuart-Palmer was beaming.

'Oh, Daddy, can we?' Juliet was nearly in tears.

'There is a condition first.' Catherine winked at Juliet's mother. 'In the stables are two top thoroughbred jumpers. You must promise to look after them and ride them out every day.'

'They would be company for Gladiator.' Juliet was ecstatic.

'Juliet. Please, it might not work out.'

'Oh, it will. I know it will.'

Lady Vanessa looked at Catherine.

'Thank you very much, Catherine. Are you sure? If it works out, promise you will come for a holiday.'

Before Catherine could answer, Jonathan broke in. 'I forgot to say that you open to the public; due to what has happened here the customers will flood in.'

'Oh, my dear, not at your expense.' Vanessa looked concerned.

'I already have good reason for coming back. I will be only too happy to come back to see you all and make sure Juliet is looking after those horses.'

Juliet ran over and flung her arms around Catherine's neck.

'Juliet, please show some manners.' Lady Vanessa was horrified.

'So I can get, or try to get, this sorted out?' Jonathan asked.

Catherine, Antony, Vanessa and Juliet all looked at him. No answer was necessary.

Chapter Thirty-Two

Friday morning and the buses duly arrived on time for the funeral of Reverend Peterson. Some were already waiting, others pulled back lace curtains, waiting for this very moment before venturing out of the door.

'Time to go,' Trish called to Albert.

'Coming,' he replied. Albert joined Trish by the door.

'Albert, for goodness sake.' Trish straightened his tie.

'Come on, it's OK, we want a good seat,' he said, pushing Trish's hand away. Albert locked the door. The Pheasant was staying closed at lunchtime as a sign of respect for Reverend Peterson.

'Hi, you two.' They turned to see Linda and John coming towards them.

'Hi, Linda, John.' Trish and Albert greeted their friends.

Together the four walked to where the buses were parked.

'Mornin' all.' Mrs Blake stood with a clipboard. 'You are on number one bus, me dears,' she authorised. Mrs Blake also directed the Cawthorne sisters, Dr James and Detective Inspector Spring onto the same bus.

Everyone gave subdued greetings to one another.

'Right, driver.' Mrs Blake mounted the steps of the bus. 'Everyone on board 'ere, you can go now please.' The bus left for the funeral. Detective Inspector Spring sat next to Dr James; everyone thought he looked rather concerned.

'Poor man.' Ruby nodded towards Detective Inspector Spring, but her exclamation was directed to sister Jane. They knew that the funeral was not the only thing on the mind of Detective Inspector Spring.

'Ashes to ashes, dust to dust.' The final act was conducted over Reverend Peterson; tears were shed, verbal accolades given, ceremonial flowers and earth thrown on the coffin. Once this was done, people made their way back to their allotted bus, dabbing tear-filled eyes and none more than Jane Cawthorne.

During the drive back to Shawlworth Detective Inspector Spring had a quiet word with Dr James, Trish and Albert, the Cawthorne sisters, and finally Linda and John. He had already made the same request at the funeral to be at the Hall for 8 p.m. to Antony and Vanessa Stuart-Palmer.

'Great,' whispered Albert.

'What?' Trish was equally as quiet.

'The pub.'

'What about it?'

'If we go, who will run it?'

'He wouldn't want us all there if it was not important.'

'I know that. Well?'

'Well, what?'

'Who's going to run it?'

'Oh, for heaven's sake, Albert. Shut it!'

'But—'

'Albert, people are looking,' Trish said, embarrassed. Albert kept quiet, but he was not pleased.

Soon the buses were pulling back into the village square, some people alighting and heading home, others standing in little groups talking.

Detective Inspector Spring saw Sergeant Harris parked outside his house, smoking a cigarette.

'Damn,' he said. What was about to take place was inevitable but he was not looking forward to it at all.

'Mornin', Guv. How did things go?' Sergeant Harris enquired.

'OK for a funeral,' he replied.

'We going now, Guv?'

'No. Change this lot first, then a cup of coffee. After that we go.'

Indoors, Detective Inspector Spring removed his black tie, told Sergeant Harris where everything was to make a cup of coffee, then retired upstairs to change his clothing.

During coffee, Sergeant Harris had noticed the concern showing on the face of Detective Inspector Spring.

'I don't mind making the collar, Guv.' Sergeant Harris tried to ease the tension.

'Thanks, but it does not make it any easier,' he said and drank the remaining coffee. 'Come on, let's get this over with.'

Detective Inspector Spring and Sergeant Harris soon found themselves knocking on a door.

'No, Mother, you cannot.'

'Catherine.'

'Mother, you and Penny were not here last Friday, so how can you say you wish to be there later this evening.'

'What is so important?'

'I don't know for the hundredth time.'

'There you are then.'

'Mother, NO, NO, NO.'

'She is right, Mother,' Penny agreed.

'Well, I don't see why not,' Catherine's mother said stubbornly.

'Oh, Mother, you can be so, so infuriating at times.' Catherine was losing her cool.

'It's OK, Cath, we'll go for another walk or some thing don't worry.'

'Thanks, Penn.'

As 8 p.m. rang through the main hall, the same people gathered as before at Shawlworth. Detective Inspector Spring took the chair.

'Ladies and gentlemen, thank you for coming. The reason I have asked you here this evening is to tell you that the murder of Leroy Leonard has been solved.'

Everyone looked at each other, but no one spoke.

'Let me say this has been the hardest case I have ever worked on, and probably ever will, from the point of view that the person arrested for this murder is someone I know and like.'

'Can you just tell us who it is and get it over with?' Dr James broke the silence.

'Firstly, I knew it was not me. Then I found out it was not the Cawthorne sisters. Then I excluded Antony and Lady Vanessa – they gave an alibi of sorts to Catherine. Albert said he went straight to the lake and I believe him, because the murder weapon was kept on a shelf to the left of the door. If Albert had gone in, and whoever did would have had to be quick, Albert would have not seen it. He only has one eye, his right, so if you cover your left eye, the field of vision is greatly reduced.

'So that leaves Linda, Trish, Dr James and John. I did not think it was Trish and Linda; they were too calm when we saw them. I know that is no reason to exclude them, but at the time I accepted their story.

'That leaves John and Dr James. With them it's the time factor; they gave each other partial alibis, then I was with them, so time played a big part in me excluding them.'

Dr James jumped up. 'George, you have got us all here, you tell us one of us is a murderer, then tell each and every one that they did not do it. Now, what the hell are you playing at?'

'I'm sorry, but one is missing and is now under arrest.'

'Well, I would be pleased to know who?' Dr James was very sarcastic.

'When I excluded all of you, even on flimsy evidence, because we all hated Leonard and you are all dear friends,' George looked at Catherine, 'that only left one. Once I started putting two and two together and getting my suspicions verified,' George struggled, 'the rest was easy.'

'For God's sake, who then?' Dr James was now getting angry with frustration.

'Andrew Farmer,' George divulged.

Everyone except the Cawthorne sisters looked surprised.

'Andrew! But he wasn't even here. I saw him drive up,' said John. 'You are wrong, Detective Inspector.'

'He *was* here.'

'Well, I wish you would explain it to me.' Dr James sat crossed-legged, arm on the back of the chair supporting his head.

'Please bear with me,' pleaded George. 'When I excluded all of you for whatever reason, I concentrated on Andrew. What did I know about Andrew? How did he get the job of gardener? Advertised maybe, but the impression I got of Leroy Leonard was of everything done at the last minute. Probably when the grass was six inches high, he would have told Catherine to cut it. Next, what boss have you ever heard of who goes off smoking cannabis with his gardener? What gardener smokes it? I know it happens, but they just seemed as if they knew each other before. The night I came to Shawlworth Hall to see Leroy about the shoots, Andrew was sitting out front playing a guitar and, of course, smoking. I warned him about it, then went and saw Leroy. Now the night of the murder, Andrew pulled up, tried the door – it was locked and John was called to verify it, because Andrew said he knew what Leroy was like – went in through the front with Catherine and they both found the body. Catherine came for me and Dr James. It only took two minutes.'

'Exactly, George, so please tell me how Andrew did it. You even checked the door yourself,' said Dr James.

'That's true, I did. It was locked and double bolted.'

'I give up.' Dr James flung his arms in the air.

'Please, Doctor, give him a chance,' begged Catherine.

'Thanks, Catherine. When Catherine and Andrew found the body of Leroy, Andrew said to Catherine, go and get Dr James and me.

'If Leroy had, in fact, left the east wing door open as promised, Andrew could have made his entrance that way, killed Leroy and left that way too, locking the door behind him and putting the key in his pocket. As soon as Catherine left, he dashed down the stairs, put the key back in the mortise lock, shot the two bolts across and ran back upstairs.

'So when John checked the door, it was locked. When I checked the door, it was locked, double bolted and the key in position for me.

'Catherine explained about a master tape machine and cassette tape, so I took the tape home and played it, hoping for speech. But there was nothing, just music. The songs on the tape were ones that had never been heard before according to Catherine and had just been recorded. I was hoping I had missed something and could hear the voice of a murderer, but nothing. Then it suddenly hit me: one of the songs on the tape Andrew had been playing that Friday night. How did Andrew know about that song? I phoned Leroy's manager and asked him if he had ever heard of an Andrew Farmer. He said he had, and Leroy had been paying him every week for the last twenty years. Ten pounds this week, twenty that; Andrew would phone him every week and tell him where he was. Iveson, Leroy's manager, would post it off to that address, so once Leroy settled down, where better to keep an eye on him but employ him at Shawlworth Hall? Andrew was not blackmailing him; Leroy was blackmailing Andrew. Why send Andrew money and blackmail him at the same time? Andrew cleared up that when he was arrested.

'How did he murder Leroy? I checked my theory and it worked. Andrew pulled up in the car earlier than John saw him and parked at the back of the cottage. He ran up along the boundary fence, cut across to the east wing – the door was open – went in, came out, locked the door, ran across back to the boundary fence, down to the car, drove up and met John. If asked why he was late, Andrew had plenty of excuses ready: punctures, traffic jams, accident, ran out of petrol.

'I checked for tyre marks at the back of the cottage and found them. In the tyre treads were plants from the borders that Andrew had taken out and dumped in a heap around the back. And finally, up by the boundary fence were footprints that matched Andrew's shoes. Due to the trees, not much light gets through, so there is no grass and the earth is soft. Finally, when I told him he had been seen leaving the studio he admitted it, exactly as I said.'

'So why was Leroy blackmailing him?' Catherine asked.

'Because all the songs that Leroy had made a fortune from in the past and was going to make another from in the future were Andrew's.

'So he just handed them over to Leroy? There you are, you can have these…' Dr James was again being sarcastic.

'Dr James, you and I know why Reverend Peterson killed himself. People present know he was married with a daughter and that she died in tragic circumstances. Then his wife died of a broken heart. This will have to come out later, so, the reason Reverend Peterson committed suicide was that his daughter, in the spring of 1963, went to a pop concert at the Flamingo ballroom. She was approached by the singer of the group, but rejected him. He sent a drink for her that was spiked with drugs and she died. It was not meant to happen, but it did. That was why he fainted when he heard the name Rock Express on Sunday morning. That was the name of the group connected with his daughter; ergo Leroy Leonard killed his daughter. He approached Leroy in the doctor's car park, but Leonard just threatened him.'

'Yes, George, but what has this to do with Andrew?' Dr James could not see the connection.

'You know Leroy went on stage, told one of the group to get her a drink, passed something over to put in it. Remember Allyson's best friend thought it could be money for the drinks? It was the cocktail of whatever it was, to make her more receptive. So he got the drink and put in the cocktail as he was told.'

'Not Andrew!' gasped Dr James.

'Andrew,' George continued. 'So Leroy put the blame on Andrew. He knew nothing about drugs, so it must have been Andrew. Leroy said give him the songs, he would see him right; no one need ever know. Andrew was young, and people had seen him carrying the drink.'

'So Leroy made a fortune out of Andrew and was going to make another,' Catherine said. 'That is despicable. Not only that, he brought him to Shawlworth just to rub his nose in it.'

'Fraid so,' agreed George. 'The final straw for Andrew was in the Pheasant.'

'In the Pheasant?' Albert looked at George.

'Yes, you know we mentioned about Flamingo and you said Allyson Peterson. Well, Andrew was there.'

'Yea.'

'Well, when he found out it was Reverend Peterson's daughter, that was it for Andrew,' he said.

Ruby Cawthorne stood up, looked across to Catherine and said, 'I apologise for what I am about to say in your home again, but having said that, once again I do not regret it.

'Having heard what Mr Spring has had to say, I can now speak freely. My sister and I knew who had killed that, that, man, but vowed never to divulge it because as far as we are concerned he did us a favour. A terrible, terrible thing to admit to as a Christian, but knowing now what that poor man must have suffered over the last twenty years – also poor Reverend Peterson – that is how we feel. I publicly apologise to you for lying and causing confusion. I went to find him that night to tell him what I thought of him again after his outburst in here. He said the east wing, so it was not hard to find. I opened the door, heard loud music and saw this person disappearing down the stairs. I did not see who it was, but recognised his clothes later on. He didn't hear me. I went into the room, and found the body and panicked. We are sorry, Inspector, but not repentant. Can we help in any way?'

'May *I* say something, please.' Catherine came to the front. 'In the beginning I loved my husband, but as time passed I got to know what a pig he was, which has only been confirmed by events today. Dr James, I know why you hated him and I don't blame you. I am leaving Shawlworth Hall. I signed two new contracts before Leroy's death, one for television commercials and one for modelling, so I would not have much time here. But I promise I shall be back as and when I can. George, if there is any way I can help Andrew, he just has to ask. I shall also give him back all the rights to the songs.'

'They are worth a fortune,' Dr James said.

'I know, but I am not poor due to what has happened. Work is flooding in for me. Don't get me wrong, I did not want it this way. Anyway, I have sold Shawlworth Hall, so I am financially sound.'

'May we ask who has bought the estate, my dear?' asked Jane Cawthorne.

'I can do better than that. I can introduce you to the new own-ers,' Catherine smiled.

Everyone looked, including George Spring.

Antony and Lady Vanessa stood up.

Catherine continued. 'I have instructed my lawyer to write to every householder in the village, offering them first refusal on buying their own property. But those that don't shall remain part of the estate. George, I want Jonathan Fredricks to represent Andrew. If my help as a character witness for him will be of use…'

'But he murdered your husband,' George said.

'I know, but look what he put Andrew through for twenty years. He has suffered enough.'

'Very well,' said George.

Once Catherine had done that, everyone offered to go to court on Andrew's behalf.

'Well, that is it then, ladies and gentlemen.'

George Spring was interrupted by Dr James.

'One final thing. Mrs Leonard mentioned she knew about me – I suspected she did – I told George, so now I will write the final chapter on Leroy Leonard. They say, folks, nothing is stranger than the truth. Leroy Leonard's case has proved a classic example. Agatha Christie couldn't have invented such a story – Andrew, Reverend Peterson, and now me, all personally involved. We all had reason to dislike him, hate him even, and although I have no proof, I believe Mrs Leonard hated him as much as us. You know I came here years ago and do not regret it for one moment. But why should I hate him? My sister was a young beautiful girl who met and married a pop singer. He gave her drugs – oh, he denied it – but I know he did. Once hooked, he left her. She was found eighteen months later: dirty, ragged in a gutter, dead from a drugs overdose. You can guess the rest.'

After he had finished speaking, everyone went home in stunned silence.

Next day Catherine, Penny and their mother had packed, and by the afternoon they were ready for the taxi.

Antony Stuart-Palmer had arrived and was waiting for the key.

'What time is the train?' Penny asked.

'Four thirty on a Saturday,' Catherine answered. 'Antony, move in whenever you wish.'

'Thank you, Catherine,' he answered.

'Here's the taxi,' Penny informed them.

'Put the cases in the car. I have one final call to make.'

Antony had picked up two cases, Penny and her mother some of the others, and they went to the car while Catherine dialled a number.

'Mrs Mason, you're back from Rhyl? Tell the children I'm coming home... Yes, tonight.'

Printed in the United Kingdom
by Lightning Source UK Ltd.
136201UK00001B/48/A